THE PERIL OF DREAMS

"Shoot them," WaterStone ordered.

Aesop blew on the fire within his hand. It mushroomed into a wall of bright blue flame, rushed forward over my head, and filled the tunnel with a roar, a flash of sapphire brilliance, and a sudden heat.

The conflagration washed over the monks. They became human-sized torches.

A portion of the fire rebounded off the wall, returning back the way it came. I stood there fascinated and watched the flames cool from blue to yellow to a smoky orange. It smelled of sulfur and burnt flesh. Too late I realized that the backwash would engulf me too.

In desperation, I threw my hands before my face. My hair singed, the skin on my arms blistered, and I fell backward . . .

PAWN'S DREAM

ERIC S. NYLUND

AVON BOOKS • NEW YORK

PAWN'S DREAM is an original publication of Avon Books. This work
has never before appeared in book form. This work is a novel. Any similarity to actual persons or events is purely coincidental.

AVON BOOKS
A division of
The Hearst Corporation
1350 Avenue of the Americas
New York, New York 10019

Copyright © 1995 by Eric S. Nylund
Cover art by Eric Peterson
Published by arrangement with the author
Library of Congress Catalog Card Number: 94-96573
ISBN: 0-380-77887-4

First AvoNova Printing: May 1995

Printed in the U.S.A.

RA   10 9 8 7 6 5 4 3 2 1

To my parents, Bjarne and Stella, for teaching me to be brave and bold.

To Diane for her patience and understanding.

To Robert for that tedious first draft edit.

To Pam. Without your help I would have never made it.

To my brothers scattered throughout the world for years of adventure: Fred, Steve, Jason, Carl, Illmord, and Scott.

To the late Joseph Campbell for pairs of opposites.

To my agent, Lynn Seligman, who had faith in me when no one else did.

To John Douglas, whose kind words and enthusiasm were legion.

To Syne for assistance with the copy-editing . . . and for the last mile.

Sweetest Dreams to all.

1

was a sound sleeper, for good reasons, but the smell of smoke always woke me. All someone had to do was light a cigarette in the next room, and I'd wake from a coma. That's how I stopped her. I slept through her rampage, content to dream, but when she started to burn the place up, my internal smoke detector went off. I caught her with a can of hair spray in one hand, a lit match in the other, poised over a pile of magazines, a couple of books, and a torn curtain.

Now, I had to sift through her aborted bonfire and find the bills before I went to work. The electric company wouldn't accept arson as an excuse for nonpayment. I know, because I've tried it before.

Debussy's *Clair de Lune* serenaded me as I poured more water on the still steaming pile. She must have turned the radio on before she started. A vision of Nero with violin flashed through my mind as I examined what survived her burnt offering.

Hestor, of course, was long gone. I made all the arrangements for her visit to the hospital. It wasn't her first stay there.

I always called her Hestor when she did crazy things

like this. I could handle it when she talked to the picture of Dad, or put the plants in the dishwasher, but this was the third time she had crossed the line from mere annoyance to insanity.

A deep sigh escaped me, and I wished for another hour's sleep. I was so close to escaping the Abbey. I could almost taste the famous spiced fish of the merchant city, Sestos. It could wait, though. An extra day added to twenty years of solitude would make no difference now.

Returning to my search, I found my first edition copy of *Through the Looking Glass, and What Alice Found There*. It was charred along the edges, warped from water, and stuck to the back cover was the electric bill. I set my prized book aside and laughed. It was either laugh or cry, and I couldn't afford the latter. What else had she thrown into the fire? I dug deeper into the pile, smearing my hands with water and warm ash.

Near the bottom, I uncovered a circle of gold, shining among things blackened and scorched. I brushed aside more char to find an envelope. The circle of gold was a foil seal on the back, and etched onto it was the symbol for yin and yang. I think it meant balance, or recycling, or something like that. I picked it up, smudged the gold with my sooty fingers, and turned it over. It was addressed to Roland Pritchard, me. Written over our address in shaky capital letters was: RETURN TO SENDER, ADDRESS UNKNOWN. There was another line scribbled there, but Hestor's penmanship disintegrated into gibberish.

I righted our dusty sofa and sat down to examine the strange letter. It was soaked, so I sponged it as best I could on the nearby curtain. Outside the sun had set and the color drained from the sky. I had better hurry or I'd be late for work again.

Along the envelope's edge was a smooth incision sealed with tape. I ran my finger across it, and wondered why she had read it, taped the thing, then tried to burn it. Peeling back the moist flap, I found a wet letter folded twice inside, and something else a muddy green that

showed through the paper. As I delicately opened the
letter, trying not to smear the ink, I discovered the dull
green was money, a hundred dollar bill, and under that,
a business card. I removed the cash from the letter. It
was real.

I don't like to look a gift horse in the mouth, especially when I needed it, but it was odd that Hestor didn't
take this hundred and run down to the liquor store. I set
it aside to dry, then tore the envelope open searching for
more. Empty.

The business card had the same yin-yang symbol
etched in gold as was on the envelope. The name Eugene
Rhodes, Rhodes Industries International, and a toll free
number were printed also in gold. It meant nothing to
me.

I read the blurry note:

Mister Pritchard:

*The purpose of this letter is to locate any rela-
tives of Clay Pritchard. I have financial and personal matters of a delicate nature to discuss with
his blood relatives. My investigative team recently
discovered his grave in this portion of the state.
For that reason, I am calling on all "Pritchards"
in the hopes of reestablishing contact with this
long lost branch of our family. Please feel free to
call my office if you have any knowledge of Clay
Pritchard, or of his relatives. I hope to hear from
you, and in any event, please keep the money for
your inconvenience.*

Maybe this was less of a mystery than I originally
thought. Any mention of Dad sent Hestor into fits, particularly discussion of his death. I looked at the money
again; Benjamin Franklin smiled back at me. I couldn't
believe she'd forget the money though.

I got up and washed my hands, taking the letter with
me. As I reread it, my eyes kept landing on the word
relative. It disturbed me because Hestor never mentioned

any of her in-laws. There were no cards or phone calls at Christmas, nor any photographs of either of their relations. We had only one picture of her and Dad, and that comprised the entire Pritchard family album.

Still, a hundred bucks was a small fortune to me, and I didn't want to lose a chance to make more. No one sent real money through the mail these days. Whoever was looking for us had money, and money to waste.

I knew Hestor thought she had good reason to hide the letter, but it was addressed to me, and I'd make the final decision. Besides, she was always seeing demons and dreaming up conspiracies.

I picked up the phone and dialed before I changed my mind.

It rang twice, then, "Rhodes Industries International," answered a crisp female voice.

"Hello, my name is Roland Pritchard. I got this letter about Clay Pritchard."

"Hold one moment, please." The phone went silent.

A new operator answered, so I repeated my name and purpose. I heard others talking in the background, my family name echoing in their conversations.

"Thank you for calling, Mister Pritchard. Do you have any information pertaining to Clay Pritchard?"

"He was my father," I said.

She was silent for a moment, then the phone clicked. "Could you please describe your late father for me, sir?" Her voice had a slight nervous tremble to it.

I had the feeling something was wrong here, and I considered hanging up, forgetting the whole thing, and just going to work. I might have too, but my curiosity was stimulated.

"Hang on a moment." I reached over and gingerly unhooked the picture of Dad and Hestor from its place on the wall. They were sailing on a thirty-foot yacht over sun sparkling waters. It was the only time I had ever seen her laughing. Hestor had left it untouched in her reign of terror through the apartment. She always did.

"His hair was all salt and peppered," I told the operator, "part black, some white, but mostly silver. He stood a shade over six feet, had a sturdy build, and large hands."

"Anything else sir?"

"Oh, he smoked, black European cigarettes, and wore a Cartaga watch."

The watch was only a blur in the picture, but I knew it was a Cartaga because I wore the same one. Hestor had it in a box with some old bills. I found it when I was thirteen and had worn it ever since. It had an odd design: a five-sided asymmetrical lozenge of gold, set with a heavy beveled crystal. The face was black and reflective, a solid piece of jet. The numbers, even the individual second marks, were inlaid with silver. It kept good time too.

The only thing missing was the original gold band. Somehow it picked up the surrounding light and re-flected it, appearing more like the water about the boat than metal or leather. I had to settle for a plain black leather strap to replace it.

"Mister Pritchard, are you certain about the watch? A Cartaga?"

"Yeah, I'm wearing it." Ten minutes after six, it read. I had to get ready for work soon.

"Please hold one moment, sir." This time she didn't even try to hide her excitement.

Before I could answer her, a pleasant lifeless music filtered through the receiver. I replaced the picture on the wall and straightened it while I waited.

"Roland?" A new voice cut off the watered-down melody. He spoke my name as if he knew me, and in a way, I recognized him also. It was the voice of a general, a rich, perfectly smooth baritone, capable of command-ing men, armies, even countries. Although I was familiar with the voice, I could not place the man behind it.

"Yes, this is Roland Pritchard." I tried to sound con-fident, but was only partially successful. It would be easy to be lulled by that voice, to trust it. I maintained my guard, however. Hestor tried to burn his letter and the rest of the apartment along with it. Why? Even the insane have reasons for their actions.

"I am Eugene," he explained. "I believe I am related to your late father, his cousin."

"Cousin?" Was it possible I had a family I didn't know about? Hestor never mentioned him.

"Based on the description of your father, I suspect you to be the person I have searched for. If possible, I wish to see you this evening, face-to-face, so we may discuss this further, and in private."

When he said, "if possible," I got the feeling he meant it was absolutely necessary. Before I said yes, though, I considered speaking to Hestor. It might be useful to drop a few hints, see what she knew about this Eugene, or any of Dad's relatives. Bringing up Dad as a topic of conversation, however, had its own risks. Who knew how she'd react? No, I couldn't ask her. Not yet anyway.

"All right," I replied, "I could see you tonight. Why don't you give me directions?"

"I shall send a car to pick you up."

"No, thanks. I can get there on my own." I wanted to have some control over the situation. Getting into a car that was sent by a man I didn't know was out of the question. He could be anyone.

He paused, and I sensed his annoyance at my refusal. Rapidly, he gave me an address downtown, on B Street, the business district. "I look forward to seeing you," he said, then there were several clicks and a dial tone.

I looked again at the hundred on the table. The edges were curling slightly as it dried. There were plenty of other hundred-dollar bills out there, one for every Pritchard in the city. That implied there was money to be made from this, but there was more to it than that. Hestor knew something, and she went to great lengths to isolate me from it. What was I, a long-lost prince and heir to the throne of Luxembourg? No, I didn't believe in fairy tales.

Before I left, I called work to clear my absence with Sam. He was accustomed to my *family emergencies* that popped up on a regular basis. He didn't like it, but I had worked the graveyard shift for over a year now, and he owed me time off. He give me half the night off, which gave me enough time to meet this relative of mine, but I'd have to go in later to finish my shift.

I had one more call to make: the hospital. Hestor got checked in, and was about to be sedated again. No, I did not want to speak with her, thank you. No use getting her upset again by bringing up this letter, or her fiery habits.

I caught the bus downtown and got off on B Street. Two bums approached me and asked for money. They were professional drunks, dirty and pathetic. I explained to them that I was as broke as they were. The only cash I had was the hundred deep in my pocket, and that was mine, wet or not. I reminded myself to break it later at work.

The building that matched the address was a high-rise office tower, ugly in its generic construction. Rows of smoked glass, marble, and concrete climbed into the evening sky. There were only the street numbers and the curious yin-yang, head eating tail logo, etched in gold over the entrance.

I walked up to dark glass doors and they automatically opened for me. The cool interior air blasted me as it rushed out. Inside, the lobby was full of people, dressed in expensive business attire, waiting for elevators. I was the only person wearing jeans, and this prompted a pair of suspicious glances from the two security men by the doors. I thought it odd that all these people were here, wide-awake, and working at seven in the evening. Trying to look inconspicuous, I walked over the black and white marble floor to the receptionist who sat at a desk labeled INFORMATION.

"Can I help you, young man?" She glanced over the counter at my dirty sneakers with obvious distaste.

"Please," I said, and ignored her sneer. "I am looking for Eugene Rhodes. Can you tell me which office he's in?"

Her features warmed when I said his name, and she even managed to smile at me, then reexamined me through her thick glasses. "You must be Mister Pritchard. Mister Rhodes is expecting you. If you'd please, take the last elevator, sir,'' she said and pointed to the back wall.

I thanked her, then circled behind her desk, and walked to the mirrored doors on the far wall of the lobby.

A frowning security guard stood by the elevator. He nodded to me and said, ''Good evening, sir.''

I gave him a nervous smile, then looked around for the call button. There was none. I started to ask him how to work the elevator, when the twin doors opened silently for me. Hesitating for only a second, I entered, and the doors sealed behind me. It was true I had no idea what I was getting myself into, but my curiosity pushed me on. Three white buttons without numbers formed a triangle to the right of the door. I reached to push the top one, but it lit up before I touched it. There was a slight acceleration, a silent wait, then the mirrors parted again.

Stepping out, I found myself in an office larger than the Gas n' Mart I worked in. Most of the lights were dimmed, but a circle of harsh illumination bathed a man sitting at his desk at the far end of the room. Behind him was a wall of windows that held a panoramic view of the dark San Diego Harbor. Murky globs of red and blue light rippled and shimmered on the black water below. The man spoke softly in German into the phone. I recognized his voice.

He noticed my arrival, then waved me forward, still talking. Advancing, I saw on the left wall a map of the Caribbean, which revealed the secret routes of pirates. Opposite that, was an oil painting of British Redcoats battling American Revolutionaries; it looked like the good guys were taking a beating.

He put the phone down, stood, and greeted me. ''Roland,'' he said, using the voice of a general again, commanding, but softened now. ''You look much as Clay did when he was your age.'' He offered me his hand.

I shook it with my firmest grip and he matched me.

I knew him. I didn't know from where, but I was

certain I recognized this man. Perhaps it was his similarity to Clay. He had the same black and silver hair,
the same muscular build. The feeling I had went beyond
mere awareness, however. It was an instinct long dor-
mant, a suggestion that I should be wary or fearful of
him. I was.

"Please sit down and make yourself comfortable."

"Mister Rhodes," I began.

"Call me Eugene." The lights from his computer
screen flashed underneath the glass top of his desk, and
cast strange reflections upon his face.

"OK . . . Eugene, I'm confused why you went to so
much effort to find me. Am I in some sort of trouble?"

A quick smile appeared, then vanished from his face.
"With any situation there are dualities involved, good
and bad things. But the truth is your father and I were
very close at one time. When he died, I lost touch with
your family. I only wish to make amends for my poor
social habits." He pushed a button on his keyboard.
"There is also the matter of a small trust which belongs
to you."

"Trust?"

"Money," he explained. "Your father and I owned
two small businesses together. I owe you a share of the
profits from those companies." He paused to gauge my
reaction. "Naturally, you must prove you are his son."

"I brought his watch," I said, and pulled my sleeve
back to show him. The five sides of gold warmly reflected the harsh quartz light.

Eugene's eyes widened and relaxed again. "Yes, that
is a Cartaga watch, but there are several of those scattered throughout the world. How do I know this particular watch belonged to Clay?"

"There's an inscription on the back." I removed it
and handed it to him.

He donned a set of glasses, then squinted at the tiny
characters engraved in gold. "This appears to be written
in Greek. Would you mind if I kept it for a day or two
and have it translated?"

"I can read it. It says,

'I arise from dreams of thee
In the first sweet sleep of night.
When the winds are breathing low,
And the stars are shining bright.' "

"You read Greek?"

"Just a few words," I lied. "The quote is Shelley, though, not Greek."

He closed his eyes, and concentrated a moment while he held the watch. Then he said, "Yes, this is Clay's. I am sorry I doubted your word." He handed my father's heirloom back. "It is a pity, though, the original band is missing."

I slipped it on, grateful for its return. "Now about these companies my father owned."

"Before we discuss your trust further, I must absolutely confirm your lineage, for legal reasons. There is a test that will prove beyond a doubt if you are Clay's son."

"A test? Like a blood test?"

"No, but something similar to that."

This wasn't quite right. Why should Eugene want to give any of his money to me? Friendship with my father was a fine reason, but he didn't get this fancy office and a private elevator by throwing his wealth away. And if Clay was so rich, why had he left Hestor and me destitute? There was also her reaction to Eugene's letter. I couldn't forget that.

"Is there a problem, Roland?" His voice was a touch firmer.

"It's just my mother. She had a very unusual reaction to your letter."

"Your mother!" His face flushed and he rose halfway from his chair. "She lives?"

The wary feeling I had before intensified. "Hestor? Sure she's alive."

"Hestor?" he whispered to himself, confused. "Yes, Clay would have remarried. I should have anticipated that." He then said to me, "My apologies. I believed . . .

well, never mind. Your father was married long ago, and I thought you meant his first wife.''

"Dad was married to someone before?'' I wonder if Hestor knew.

"You did not know? It is of little importance now. You must understand it was a very long time ago.'' He ran his hand through his hair, which I noticed was drawn into a tight ponytail and neatly tucked in behind his jacket. ''I honestly do not know why your mother, what did you say her name was, Hestor? I do not know why she would react adversely to our meeting. If you wish, you may discuss the matter with her first. When you are ready, call me, and we shall speak again. It is, after all, your money.''

"Thanks, I hope it doesn't bother you.''

"No, no, I can appreciate your caution.'' He chuckled. ''You are very much like Clay in that respect.'' He stood, and again offered his hand. ''I shall wait for your call, Roland. Do not worry, the tests are a mere formality. I feel certain you are part of the family.''

He shook my hand, then returned to his computer and ignored me.

I had more questions, yet I found myself walking back to the waiting elevator. I had been dismissed.

Once downstairs, I quickly crossed the lobby and exited, my every step closely watched by the security men. I was relieved to be free of that building. Eugene was in complete control there, and for some reason I found that disturbing. What I didn't understand was why he couldn't look up my birth certificate to verify my relationship to him. There must be a tidy sum of money involved if he wanted additional tests. That uneasy feeling, the instinctive fear, returned. I glanced behind me, but no one was there.

Briskly, I walked to the trolley station and I waited for one of the red cars. It dropped me off a block from work. No one got on or off there but me. Still, I felt like I was being watched, so I took a good look around but saw nothing. I marched down the street.

Above me, there were no stars in the sky. The marine

layer clouds covered every square inch of the night, and glowed ghostly yellow over the city, reflecting a phantom kingdom above the skyscrapers.

I had to visit Hestor tomorrow, see how she was settling in, and if she had any clues about Eugene. It could be difficult to communicate with her, especially when she was in such a psychotic state. Eugene claimed he didn't know her, which was unusual considering *her* reaction to *his* letter. I wonder what caused Clay and him to lose touch with one another? He seemed to care very much about Clay's first wife, judging from his explosive reaction. You would think he'd know that his own cousin had remarried.

My speculations died when I spotted the flashing blue and red lights at the Gas n' Mart. Four police cars and an ambulance blocked the entrance to the parking lot. Had the place been held up again? If so, Sam would find a way to blame it on me, he always did. Normally only one or two cops followed up a robbery at our store. It happened all the time. In this part of town it was almost routine. So why all the excitement?

Yellow police ribbon circled the area, and already there were gawkers who hoped to see blood and gore. I saw a flash of light inside the store, behind the counter. Pushing my way through the people there, I got to the police line. A cop, not much older than myself, stopped me. He looked slightly bored, and slightly annoyed at the local gang members who tried to discover if one of their own got shot.

"Let me through," I demanded, "I work here." Behind him, two paramedics carried a black zippered bag out of our store. Sam kept a gun with him when he worked. I hoped he wasn't dumb enough to use it.

The cop noticed me. "You said you worked here?" He took out a notepad and leafed though the first few pages. "Are you Roland Pritchard?"

I nodded.

"You better come with me then," he said and lifted the boundary tape. "The detective wants to talk to you."

He led me to a plainclothes cop who was questioning

the girl that dealt drugs on the pay phone outside our store. While I waited for him to finish with her, I saw through the front window, men taking pictures and collecting stuff in little plastic bags.

The detective then turned to me, "Mister Pritchard, could you spare a couple of minutes to identify someone for us?" He was unshaven and the odor of stale coffee lingered about him.

"Was Sam shot? Is he alive?"

"He was shot about twenty minutes ago, killed instantly."

Damn, I'd give odds he pulled his gun and got nailed for his heroics. Stupid. There couldn't have been more than eighty bucks in the register.

"We need you to look at the videotape," he explained, "see if you recognize the man who did this."

"Yes, of course." Whatever happened would have been recorded on the store's security camera. I had to see what was on that tape, my curiosity at work again.

"Good," he said, then placed a fatherly hand on my shoulder and guided me to his Buick parked on the street. "Let's go downtown where we can take a careful look at it."

I didn't like the way he touched me, and I didn't like being this close to him. He needed a bath. The younger cop I saw before joined us and took the front seat for himself. I got into the back and we drove off.

Instead of returning downtown, however, the detective got on the southbound freeway and headed for the Mexican border.

"Aren't we going to the station?" I asked him.

The younger cop turned to me, "We're going to a safe place, don't worry."

I was worried. There were no door handles in the back of this car. And were those bloodstains on the floor? It was too dark for me to be certain.

Just before the San Ysidro border crossing, we took a side lane marked, "For Emergency Vehicles Only," and passed the long lines of cars crossing for the Tijuana night life. The detective waved to the border patrol officer there, and we passed through. He skirted the center of Tijuana, avoiding the traffic of Revolucion, where the clubs were, and kept to the darker side streets of the residential part of town.

We then stopped in front of a small stucco house with a dirt lawn. Above me in the sky, the moon was only a faint blur behind the thick clouds. The younger cop got out and opened the car door for me. I followed them inside, apprehensive, but still curious to see that tape.

The detective went in first, turned on the lights, then closed the curtains. The place looked as if someone threw a party, and forgot to clean up. Fast-food wrappers, beer bottles, and dining insects were scattered on the floor. A moldy scent, like old bread, welcomed us. I stood in what might be considered the living room. One sofa and matching chair, their stuffing coming out, and an entertainment center were clustered in the corner, away from the windows.

"It's a safe house," he told me. "Pardon the mess, but the maid hasn't been in this year."

"So why are we here?" I took an involuntary step back toward the door.

"Take a look at this," he said, pushing the tape into the VCR, "and you'll see why."

I had to see what happened, so despite my better judgment, I inched closer.

The monitor warmed up, and there was Sam tending the register. The time stamp on the bottom of the screen read 19:20:17. He was doing his usual exemplary job, and stealing beef jerky at the same time. Three or four people passed in and out of the store, then a man in his forties walked up to the register. He could have been a professional wrestler because he completely filled out a sports jacket with his bulk and was shiny-smooth bald. He was no taller than Sam, but easily twice his width. Again I sensed something familiar, an instinctive reaction of distrust, when I saw him, just as I had with Eugene.

"Cigarettes," he said to Sam. The bald man had

smoked his entire life, and his voice was full of gravel and spit to prove it.

When Sam turned to reach for the smokes, the man pulled a pistol free from his jacket. "Pritchard," he hissed, "you're a dead man," then pointed the gun to the back of Sam's head. He shot him.

Hardly any noise escaped the gun, yet Sam was knocked to the wall from the impact. His body slid from the camera's view, behind the counter. The back wall was spattered with blood and brains and pieces of powdered doughnuts. The man then moved behind the counter and fired until his gun was empty. I saw the expression on his face change from anger, to resolve, and finally amusement.

He snorted a laugh and walked out of sight, leaving Sam there, but taking his cigarettes. The tape continued to run, and showed nothing but the deserted counter dotted with blood. A girl outside screamed, then ran in to find what was left of Sam.

The detective leaned forward and paused the tape. "We were hoping you could tell us who that man is. It seems he had a little grudge against you."

"I've never seen him before," I said, ignoring the feeling of familiarity.

"Where were you when this happened?"

"I had a meeting with my cousin. I have his phone number if you want me to prove it." If I had been at work instead of with Eugene, I'd be as dead as Sam. That bald guy was after *me*.

The detective lit a cigarette. "We had a chat this evening with your neighbors. I understand your mother is in the hospital. What did you do to her?"

"I didn't do anything to her. She had a nervous breakdown all by herself. You can check with the hospital. This has happened to her before . . . she has problems."

"Problems enough for someone to come after you?"

"No, her problems are personal. She drinks too much, and is a little nervous." I shifted in my seat away from the detective. Not only was I growing to dislike him, but his stench was getting worse.

"Then how about you? What did you do that someone would want to kill you like that?" He pointed at the screen with his cigarette. "That was a professional job. The guy wasn't even worried about having his picture taken." The video was frozen: parts of Sam and powdered sugar and money still on the counter.

"Nothing." I swallowed, my throat suddenly dry. "I just work for a living, like you. No one would want to kill me." His eyes narrowed, and I could see he didn't believe me. After seeing the tape, I didn't really believe it either.

"What do you know about the Bishop family?"

"Bishop? Nothing." That name did mean something to me, just as the face of the bald killer, and the voice of Eugene had. It was a sleeping memory, barely a dream, ghostly and insubstantial.

"What about the De Marco or the Chandler families?"

I shook my head. "Should I know them?"

"I'm asking the questions here. You just answer them." The tone of his voice hardened, and he smashed his cigarette into the floor. "OK, let's start over from the beginning."

He repeated his questions, carefully watched my response, and occasionally scribbled a note or two while I talked. I suspected he knew I withheld something, but what could I tell him? That I had a vague feeling I recognized the killer? That would get me nowhere.

He finished a pack of cigarettes and called his wife once. By the fifth round of interrogation, the same answers began to visibly irritate him. His voice rose, and I wanted very badly to be back in my apartment asleep.

The other cop entered from the kitchen and brought with him the scent of insecticide. He held a portable phone in one hand, a nervous look on his face. The detective took the phone, then went into the hallway to whisper into it.

I noticed the younger cop had changed into jeans and a sweatshirt. He smiled at me, but there was no friendship in it, more like a shark grinning at its next meal.

The detective returned and announced, "We've finished for tonight."

I exhaled, relieved to be done. Now I could go home and get some much-needed rest. "Great," I said, "when can we head back?"

"I'm sorry," he said, smiling for the first time. "You're going to be staying with us for a while."

"You're keeping me here against my will? On what charges?"

"We don't have to have charges," he whispered, and walked over to me.

I guess I wasn't expecting it, not from a cop anyway—he grabbed my arm and pulled me up, then twisted it around my back. He shoved it up as far as it would go, until I heard my joints crackle and pop. I struggled, tried to kick him, but he was too well positioned behind me.

The younger cop came to help—him, not me—and punched me in the gut. I doubled over from the dirty blow, then the detective released me. My arm was too far bent out of shape, so I couldn't get it free to break my fall. I landed wrong and the wind was knocked out of me. The detective helped me up by placing his foot into my stomach at high velocity, then my head.

I decided to lie there.

After a few more ugly moments of this, which I don't recall too well, the two dragged me downstairs. It smelled of urine and something rotting. There was a solid metal door on the far side of the basement. When they opened it, the door squealed as if it hadn't been used in a long time. I got a quick look at the place, cinder block and green paint, no bigger than a large closet.

The detective pushed me in, then slammed the door shut.

"Hey," his younger partner said, "you forgot to read him his rights."

They both laughed.

The detective then yelled through the door, "Sweet dreams, young prince."

I lay on the floor, held my stomach, listened to the blood pound through my head, and watched the purple dots grow in front of my eyes.

At least I'd get some sleep. I had important things to do tonight. My awareness faded, and I entered the world of my dreams.

2

I walked the murky hallway for what I hoped would be the last time. Each black tile on the floor had been polished by the thousands of footfalls, from countless acolytes. These stones held an aura of dread that chilled my spirit and doused my hopes. I never knew if the winds from the lake sucked the warmth from the corridor, or if it was the proximity to the Oracle's tower.

It was just up ahead, deserted as usual. There was no need to post guards here. Who would want to face the wrath of a captive and insane god? Still, I recalled the rumors of men having tried. I always wondered about the two who had survived. One was insane; we never quite understood what happened to him. The other was stone silent, or so the story went.

Despite what the tower contained, its entrance fascinated me. Set apart from the normal construction of the Abbey stood an archway built to mammoth proportions. Carved along its edges, in a grey-green stone unlike any other on the island, were the legends and warnings of the dark secrets that lay beyond. Some of them I could read, but others were as obscure as the Oracle itself. The Elders whispered that the arch was made this large to let the gods who imprisoned the Oracle pass freely. My theory: it was built this huge to intimidate people. It did.

Thirteen months of sanitation duty was bestowed upon me when I made a charcoal rubbing of the characters in this arch. If I had only known it had been done and catalogued in the central library. It was worth it, however, for in my possession I still had that rubbing. I studied it late at night, and pondered what forbidden things slept within the Oracle's tower.

Climbing onto the ramparts, I took in the view, appreciating my lake for the last time. Over the mirror of dark blue, lay the distant shore, and the city of Sestos, kingdom of merchant princes. When the wind blew at night, I could smell the perfumes and spices, the animals, and the curious smoke from the port. I often dreamt I was there amid those lusty scents, wandering the crowded streets, tossing a gold coin to those performers who caught my fancy, and sampling cuisine from lands whose names I could not pronounce. I would be there soon or die trying.

Of Sestos I knew much, although my information was somewhat old. The last mention of it in our libraries dated from before the collapse. Since then, the bridge that had once spanned the lake had shattered, and a policy of isolationism erected iron walls about our island. There were wars, but certainly the merchant princes had no part in those. Sestos was a center of trade, a city of economics, and had little to do with political matters. I was certain.

Wonders from every corner of Meredin poured onto the blue stones of the city's marketplace. Portals in the lake, held open by the mightiest of magics, led to every country and every sea. Some texts even hinted that they transported ships to other worlds.

The princes of Sestos live in enormous palaces, surrounded by strange and private gardens that are full of exotic and rare flora, and equally exotic and rare women for their eyes to rest upon. No farmers or peasants inhabit the city, for they import every scrap of food, and export every trace of waste. It is a place of art and decadence, where the rare and unusual are as common as the books in our library.

Encircling the city are the Forests of Anac, cultivated in sections as a potted flower, left wild and dangerous in others. The merchant princes acquire beasts, both fair and foul, from distant lands to populate their forests and pleasure their hunts.

Indeed, Sestos was likely to be even more splendid now, having had decades to refine itself like a cool port wine. Men only rarely came to the Abbey, so I had no news of the recent curiosities there, just beyond my reach. Then again, who would want to come here? Only those insane enough to petition the Oracle or those who would beg the council for the ancient information moldering in our libraries.

Barring any ill fortune, I would be there tomorrow. Speed was essential, because once the sun set, the mountain winds swept over the lake and made sailing impossible. So what was I doing here daydreaming? WaterStone would be looking for me, and I had to avoid him at all costs.

Hastily, I descended the stairway back to the perpetually cold hallways. I hoped none spotted me as I returned to the dormitories to gather the pouch that contained my scant possessions. I entered my cubicle and overturned my pallet. Good, the sack was still where I had hidden it. Within were a few things I had borrowed from the Abbey. After twenty years of service, I felt no remorse over the petty theft. Three jars of ink, several scraps of parchment, four quills, and a loaf of hard bread were all I should need to ply my linguistic skills in Sestos. Tucked in the bottom, was the fragment of the rubbing taken from the archway, my prize. It was in a scroll tube, sealed with the wax of two candles.

Suddenly sensing a presence behind me, I turned. Adrenaline burned through my blood when I saw WaterStone in the doorway, blocking my only escape. Damn, I had been too slow.

His slight build only accentuated the fact that he required no physical strength to bully, even though he had it. WaterStone had political power on the island, power enough to sway the council, power enough to do whatever he pleased.

"What are you doing?" he whispered. "I understood you were on commissary duty this morning."

"No sir," I said, trying to appear nonchalant. "I traded with Booklight and properly recorded it in the duty manifest. You can check if you want."

"Do not be coy, Roland. It is an insult to your intellect as well as mine. You know I am not here to talk of commissary duties." He stepped into my cubicle, and immediately I wished for a larger space to be in.

"Sir?"

"I would caution you in this hasty decision to depart." He sat on my pallet, then glanced at the sack next to me.

"How did you find out?" I sighed.

"You know as well as I that knowledge is hard to come by, but rumors flow from the tongue with a practiced ease." His hand clenched into a fist as he said this.

It must have been Booklight who had revealed my plans, as he alone knew. I could not blame him for telling WaterStone, who could be extremely persuasive. I only hoped my friend was undamaged.

"Very well." I rechecked what I had packed, as if it still mattered. "So you know I want to talk to the strangers. That is not against regulations, or is it?" In theory, I had the choice to leave or stay. In practice, however, no one ever left the Abbey.

"It is not against regulations," he replied, "but to refuse your commission is almost a criminal act. Such an occurrence has only been recorded twice in our history. Both times such a loss . . . You know we are unearthing certain provocative items from the secondary library. We need your talents, Roland. You are the best linguist here, in spite of your youth."

"But I am still a free man," I said, inadvertently glancing below his white belt.

He noticed and said, "*That* is the smallest sacrifice we must make, and it is for the good of all." He stroked his short black beard. I had seen this gesture of his before when he outwitted a member of the council, or when he punished some junior acolyte for an infraction of the rules. It worried me.

"I merely want to see the things we study here, the outside world." I said *merely* as if leaving was such a small thing to ask. Five years ago, two acolytes, brothers, desired to leave. WaterStone protested, but at the time could not persuade the council to make them stay. The following morning, their bodies were found off the south shore, and their deaths labeled accidental. I always wondered how those weights became *accidentally* tied about their necks.

"I cannot permit you to throw away such a promising career. I had hoped you would sit by my side on the council. If you stay, I shall make certain this becomes a reality. Such honors do not come every day."

"The honor of the council? The honor to stay here and never walk in wondrous cities, among normal men?" I stopped, realizing I had gone too far.

His jaw clenched, then his lips tightened to a white line. I feared he would beat me, or worse. It was within his power to do so and get away with it. He relaxed though, and said, "The loss of your linguistic talents is doubly unwelcome now, for we have discovered the Beltane Codices in the ruins of the old library."

It was an obvious ploy to get me to stay, but I had to ask. "The Codices? What condition are they in?"

"Most of the passages are discernible. And as you are the ranking scholar in Elder languages, I considered you first to transcribe all thirteen volumes."

"They will surely be magically protected," I said, failing to control my anticipation over the texts. Legends claimed they were written by the gods who had created Meredin.

"They are," he replied, and leaned forward. His voice dropped to a whisper, "But arrangements have been made with an accomplished sorcerer to circumvent those unpleasantries."

I considered. I honestly considered staying for a few

moments, then, "No. I cannot. I am truly sorry, WaterStone, but I never felt like I belonged here. I did not volunteer for this way of life. Left here as a child, unable to care for myself, I had no choice in the matter." There was also no guarantee he would allow me to translate the Codices. He knew exactly what to offer me, and I almost fell for it.

"Because you did not choose to be here does not mean you are unwanted or unappreciated by us."

"I realize that, sir, but I am compelled to see the outside world—if only for a brief time, to taste, to sample what all here have experienced. Perhaps then I shall return."

"The experiences you seek are what drove us to the Abbey and this life of isolation." He shook his head. "I can see I am wasting my words. You know the rules. None may refuse their commission and return. The risk of becoming involved with outside politics is too great. Our knowledge must not be corrupted by those elements."

I nodded.

"Furthermore, it is highly unlikely that you, a scholar untrained in the ways of war and magic, could survive the hostilities out there."

"That would be true under normal circumstances, but I hope to leave with the strangers." I said it without thinking; without realizing I had just told him the method of my escape. Stupid!

WaterStone was silent a moment and glared at me. The cords on his neck stood out and his face flushed. He stood from my pallet, exhaled, then put a fatherly hand on my shoulder and announced, "I shall go with you then. These strangers may try to take advantage of you. They would think twice before doing so with a full White Robe in attendance."

"Thank you," I lied. "Your concern is appreciated."

Now my task was twice as difficult—outwit WaterStone, *and* persuade the strangers to help me escape. I had no choice in the matter. I was trapped.

Reluctantly, I followed him to the waiting library. His

voluminous robes of white expanded behind him, in front of me. He appeared divine, surrounded by the flowing cloth, seemingly gliding upon the clouds. The white robes were symbols of enlightenment, and only bestowed upon special council members. In reality, they were symbols of power alone, devoid of any spirituality.

It struck me then why I hated him. It was WaterStone who confirmed the policy of isolation. He alone held the Abbey's knowledge for his personal gain. Our histories and stories needed to be shared with the rest of Meredin, not locked away. We deluded ourselves. The Abbey was built during the collapse of the Golden Age to protect the world's knowledge from loss. I feared the outer world never missed that lore and continued on just fine without it. We were likely as much a relic as the histories within our libraries.

We arrived at the chamber where the strangers were sequestered. I expected them to be aggravated. The room was designed with comfort in mind, the lack of it that is. The Abbey did not treat its visitors well. The fireplace had no fuel, and the flue was left ajar so the winds could howl through at night. Hard splintered stools, an uninteresting collection of books, poor light, and a cold stone floor comprised the remainder of the amenities. The strangers had been here for two days.

WaterStone stopped before the entrance and, without turning to face me, said, "I shall do all the talking. Remain silent. I may allow you to speak with them, but only after I have finished." He entered then, and I followed obediently.

I saw the strangers at last, a man and a woman. A fire blazed in the hearth where none should be. There was no wood burning, just flames flickering atop bare stone. Curious.

"Finally," the woman said, and jumped off the stool. Her short hair bounced once as she stood, a wave of sable. She wore thick leather fighting skins, which revealed nothing of her feminine nature. Her armor served only to intimidate, bristling with worn spikes and numerous scars as testament to past combats. My eyes fell upon her empty scabbard. The Abbey still insisted that visitors carry no weapons onto the island. Good. This woman appeared capable of extreme behavior. Her eyes darted to WaterStone, then landed on me and narrowed as if she recognized me.

The man remained seated and gave us the briefest of glances. He wore the light silks of a Kubonian merchant. His eyes were keen and piercing, dark, not drugged and pleasure filled as all Kubonians I had ever read of. Along both arms, from his wrists as far back as I could see, were tattoos of dark red and blackened flames that consumed his flesh.

The man turned to her and whispered, "Please remain calm. These fine monks are in all likelihood another delegation sent to try our patience." He returned to reading his book, *The Properties of Mythic Amphibians*, confiscated from the nearby shelf.

"Most honored guest," WaterStone said, "we plan to delay you no further. I am WaterStone, White Robe of the council. We have reviewed your petition and have decided to grant your request."

The man rose, surprised, and obviously relieved by our positive response.

In normal circumstances, any with the impudence to come to the Abbey of Glossimere and barter for knowledge were denied outright. I therefore concluded these two had something of value, or something WaterStone wanted. Also, according to the rumors, the strangers possessed a scroll case inscribed with a Sarteshan character. This was unusual, as the Sarteshans never committed their flowery prose to mere paper or leather, but preferred stone, so their words would last forever.

The man bowed low. "WaterStone, we are pleased the council chooses to honor our unprecedented request. I am Aesop of the De Marco clan, and my traveling companion is known as Smoking Bear."

De Marco? The name had a familiar ring to it. I glanced at the woman called Smoking Bear. I believe I had seen her likeness in a history text, but was uncertain.

I had not seen many women, mostly I only dreamt of them, but she seemed beautiful to me. Her sharp unyielding features were joined flawlessly, and I found myself wondering what she might look like if she smiled. She returned my gaze, also curious, but without any obvious signs of friendship.

Aesop stepped closer and blocked my view. "What is it that the council would ask of us in return for their services?"

"We shall be honored to translate your document," WaterStone replied, "provided we may make a copy for our archives."

"And what else?" Smoking Bear demanded.

"Nothing else."

"We are flattered by your offer," Aesop said with a slight bow. "If there is anything . . ."

"Unbelievable," she interrupted. "Two days you kept us waiting? For an even swap?"

"My companion only wishes to express her surprise at the generosity of the council. On behalf of the entire De Marco clan, I extend our appreciation."

She did not appear grateful at all, but contained her fury, clenching and unclenching her fists.

"Roland, see to the translation," WaterStone ordered. "I wish to have a conversation, in private, with our guests."

A private conversation? WaterStone had not given me a chance to speak. If I blindly translated the document, I would have nothing to barter with.

"Wait," I said, surprising myself. I could not afford the luxury of playing verbal chess with WaterStone. He was too good at it. I had to be blunt. "*I*, however, do require a favor in exchange for my services."

"I knew it," Smoking Bear said, and strode toward me. "I knew there'd be a catch to this. Two days we waste, delayed by these robed fools, and still we play games."

The intimidation I felt from her was overwhelming. It was nothing compared to the slight discomfort I experienced before with WaterStone. His was a subtle threat, like swallowing poison, slow, smooth, and certain. This woman was violent in the most basic of terms. She could kill me with her bare hands, and maybe even enjoy it.

"I only desire to leave the Abbey," I told her quickly.

Aesop stepped between Smoking Bear and me, then asked, "Why would any such as yourself wish to leave this scholar's paradise?"

I took a moment to process his question, shocked by his politeness after facing the temper of Smoking Bear. Good, at least I had his curiosity. He looked like a man of intellect, one who would not deny my meager request. Perhaps this Aesop was even a merchant prince of Sestos.

"Ignore this youth," WaterStone said. "Poor Roland is a competent linguist, but in other respects his wits are dulled. He fell as a child, and, aside from his talents with words, he makes little sense now."

"I am no idiot savant," I replied, outraged at his lie.

"My apologies, allow me to fetch another who is more qualified to . . ."

Aesop held his hand up, commanding silence. "I would hear the boy out."

WaterStone held his tongue. I had never seen him so easily quieted before.

Aesop looked at me, studied my face as if he saw something that intrigued him. "Is this true?" he inquired with a slight smile. "Are you mad?"

"No sir. I am sane, and an expert in many languages. I could be of great value to you and your associate if you would only take me with you. Possessing a Sarteshan poem and understanding its meaning are two entirely different things."

"And how did you know it is a *Sarteshan* poem without looking at it?" Smoking Bear asked, and took a step closer. This time Aesop did nothing to stop her. He crossed his arms and waited for an answer. His kindly face soured and turned suspicious.

"I am an expert in Elder languages," I explained without delay, "so I assumed the document was in Eldrich or a variant language, perhaps Sartesh. Additionally, you wear the traditional garments of the Northern provinces. I concluded from these observations that you were interested in one of the three city-states there. The other two, Vimina and Oeta, use an oral tradition and paintings respectively as their prominent forms of communication. While it is rare for the Sarteshans to commit their words to anything but stone, it is not unheard of. I can cite several examples of . . ."

Aesop smiled to his companion. She did not smile back, but at least stopped scowling. "I like someone with a fast mind," he told me, "but do you have any idea of the dangers involved in such a journey? We can use your knowledge, yet I fear you would not survive to be of use to us."

"He's a little scrawny," she interjected.

"Please," insisted WaterStone, "the boy is an embarrassment to the Abbey. Let me find you a replacement." While he spoke, although his voice betrayed nothing, I noticed a bead of sweat snake down his temple. "Had I known he would trouble you, I would never have considered him for the task. There are better acolytes that can assist you, free of charge."

"A moment please, while we consider." Aesop then placed his hand over his chin and thought. When he did this, the white silk of his shirt fell away, and his arm was again aflame with tattoos. He motioned to Smoking Bear, and they walked to the far corner of the room to talk.

WaterStone took a step closer to me. I heard his teeth grind together while we waited.

I knew if I failed to escape today, I would die. Perhaps he would have me drowned in the lake, make it appear as if I had tried to swim to the distant shore. I edged closer to the fireplace to keep my distance, and to keep the chill of fear from freezing my blood.

The De Marcos exchanged several wild hand gestures and sharp words, then returned to our corner of the library. The fire that burned nothing popped once.

Aesop gave me a hard look and said, "You are now in our employ," then handed me the scroll.

Silently elated, I moved to the wooden table to examine their document. While I wanted to shout, or dance, or throw my arms about Aesop and thank him, first I had to prove my worth. They might decide to leave me if I failed in the translation.

The case was thick leather. It cracked slightly when I handled it. Engraved upon the seal was the Sarteshan character for earth, two swirls, one black, the other white, each consuming the other. It was old, maybe twenty years if exposed to the elements, possibly much older if it had been properly cared for.

I gently pulled the scroll free and noticed it was soft to the touch. It was the highest quality vellum, perfectly tanned, but discolored. I upped my estimation of its age by several decades. The vellum unrolled easily, still supple. Burned onto one side with great skill were the geometric characters of the Sarteshan language (as I expected). In many areas, however, the words were indecipherable, at odd angles, or broken into segments. It made no sense to me. I turned the piece over. Perhaps there was another passage I could start with. No. The reverse side was blank ... almost. Numerous stains, lightened by the years, marred the back side. Why would the tanner who made this do such an outstanding job on one side, yet ruin the other?

"Can you tell me how you acquired this?"

"Is it necessary for your translation?" Aesop asked.

"Although I can read most of the words, they appear to be arranged in a senseless manner."

He frowned. "My family obtained this from an enemy clan at great personal cost. I understand that it was originally in the hands of a priest of some sorts."

"Good, very good," I muttered, then returned my attention to the scroll. That was the clue I needed to understand this mess. "Here, this mark, and this one. Now where are the rest?"

"What are you doing?" Smoking Bear asked, and peered over my shoulder.

She made me uncomfortable. Not because of her ferocity or her attractiveness, though there was that, but because I never could work well with another pair of eyes hovering over my shoulder. "The priests of the Sartesh Empire are notorious for hiding their sacred writings," I explained. "They employ unusual encoding schemes to protect their documents from falling into the hands of infidels. With this particular piece, they used a primitive, yet effective mechanism: folding.

"Observe as these false marks align." I carefully wrinkled the document until the two seemingly random stains on the back joined. Separate they appeared to be nothing at all. When brought together however, they formed the right hand side of a butterfly. Even the mottling within the stain seemed to be part of an intricate design upon the insect's wing. I marveled at the hidden craftsmanship.

Turning the piece over, still creased, my suspicions were confirmed. "See," I showed her. "Here, and here, the words come together. When I discover the remaining parts of the butterfly, then all the words will make sense."

She nodded and raised an eyebrow. "Good."

The last parts of the insect, masquerading as stains, were more difficult to find. My candle burned low while I searched for the other pieces of the puzzle.

Aesop continued to read patiently while I worked. Smoking Bear lost interest in my efforts, paced for several minutes, then fell asleep on the floor next to the fireplace. WaterStone left and reappeared several times, each time more anxious, and each time more curt with the De Marcos. He apparently wanted this translation as badly as they did.

Finally I had it, the completed butterfly, and the translation. It was not the real passage, but it would do for my purposes.

"I am done," I announced.

"Then I shall fetch a copyist," WaterStone said, as if the characters would evaporate from the leather if he delayed.

When he left, I turned to my new allies and whispered, "With luck we will be gone before the winds are too strong to cross the lake. We must be careful. Many who come to the Abbey disappear under suspicious circumstances.''

Aesop nodded, yet appeared indifferent.

Smoking Bear hissed to him, ''I told you this would be harder than you thought.''

WaterStone returned then with the copyist. He was Libred, a small pitiful excuse for a man. He had done many distasteful things to gain WaterStone's favor. I did not like him. When he saw the contorted vellum, he asked how he could copy such a manuscript. I explained to him that the document must be creased for the words to make sense.

''But there could be dozens of variations on this theme,'' he protested.

''Just make the copy,'' WaterStone snapped.

He smiled nervously and began transcribing the poem onto clean parchment.

For once I was glad of WaterStone's temper and impatience. Had he listened to the copyist, he might have discovered my deception.

When Libred finished, I unfolded the vellum, rolled it, and returned it to the original container. In my haste, I nearly knocked over the copyist's ink onto the irreplaceable document.

''You are not translating it?'' Aesop asked me.

''No, I shall have ample time once we are abroad.''

''What about the Abbey's copy?'' WaterStone demanded with a hint of annoyance.

''Binder is more than adequate for the job,'' I answered. ''Besides, he will appreciate the work.''

WaterStone paused to look over the two strangers, then his gaze rested on me. ''Again, honored guests, I urge you to leave this boy with us. Roland is skilled, yes, but he is also reckless and deceitful.''

Smoking Bear snorted. ''That's what I like about him.''

''As you wish, Lady De Marco,'' he replied, and smiled unsincerely. ''Allow me to call an escort to see you to your boat. If you could wait here, I shall return momentarily.'' He and the copyist then left, their footsteps echoing behind them in the corridor.

"Let us go now, quickly," I urged, "before he can warn the others of our departure.''

"Are you sure you can translate it?" Smoking Bear asked.

"Yes, but not if I am dead.''

"Dead?''

"We can continue this conversation on the boat,'' suggested Aesop. "We have what we came for, or at least as much help as we are likely to get.''

"Agreed,'' she said, then turned to me. "Do you know of a quick way to the docks?''

"There is a tunnel through the cellar. It is faster, and there is less of a chance of being spotted.''

I went to the doorway and glanced both ways. Empty. We walked, then jogged through the cool hallways. Was I paranoid? Slightly, but then I knew the lengths WaterStone might go to keep any knowledge from leaving the Abbey, let alone me.

I stopped at the entrance of the tunnel and tried to light the torch that hung there. I was never very good with the flint and tinder, and failed thrice to produce a flame.

"No time for that nonsense,'' Aesop said. He held his hand out, palm side up. His tattoos glowed, then they spilled onto his hand as if alive. A white flame shot forth, sputtered, and stabilized within his cupped palm.

How did he manage that? He even held the fire without burning his hand. Smoking Bear had apparently seen this sorcery before, as she said nothing. I had heard tales of magic, but to actually witness such a feat . . .

Down the stairs, into the predictably frigid passage, we marched single file. The underground route was built so supplies might be taken directly to the cellars. Perishables were never brought through the halls near the libraries. Vermin and other undesirable creatures could infest the collections.

The odor of mold and rotting food was thick in the air, and water fell from the ceiling in large drops. We were doubtless well below the surface of the lake. Twice, the falling water threatened to douse Aesop's palm-sized fire. He cursed as one hit his flame and sizzled into steam. Monstrous shadows surrounded us and danced about the magical light while we wound our way though the tunnel.

The slope then gently turned upward. Four more turns and we would be at the exit, the docks, and the freedom I so desired.

Smoking Bear raised her hand suddenly, a signal to halt. She reached for her empty scabbard.

WaterStone, accompanied by six acolytes, stepped around the corner ahead. They held enormous crossbows, cocked and loaded. I had seen this type of weapon before. They were from a time when the Abbey warred with the outer world. The bolts could pass clean through a man, and then some.

"You are more of a fool than I gave you credit for, Roland," WaterStone said grinning. "I knew you would be foolish enough to try this route." Fiendish shadows caressed his face. In the smoky light, his robe was the color of blood.

There was nothing I could do against six crossbows. I had gambled and lost. "Very well," I sighed, "I shall surrender peacefully, but let the others go. These two have done nothing to you." I stepped forward, shielding the De Marcos from the crossbows. I was as good as dead already. There was no point in taking my new friends along with me.

WaterStone chuckled. "You have it backwards, Roland. You are the one who shall be spared, for the moment. We have special plans for you. Since you tried to escape once, we must assume you will attempt it again. An example must be made of you, so others do not act on similar absurd thoughts. As for the De Marcos, I shall be happy to kill them here." He said to Aesop, "Your opponent in the Bishop family has paid us handsomely, both for the translation, and for your bodies."

Smoking Bear responded with a subvocal growl.

Bishop? An instinctive hatred welled within me. I should know that name. But from where?

"I shall give you the opportunity to remove yourself from this tunnel," Aesop replied. His stare remained fixed on the fire in his palm. "Normally, I am not this generous, but I do not wish our new companion to think me impulsive."

"Shoot them," WaterStone ordered.

Aesop blew on the fire within his hand. It mushroomed into a wall of bright blue flame, rushed forward, over my head, and filled the tunnel with a roar, a flash of sapphire brilliance, and a sudden heat.

The acolytes fired their crossbows at him. The bolts whistled through the air, into the fire storm that thundered toward them. The shafts turned to ash, and the steel heads melted, then boiled to nothing, before they touched Aesop.

The conflagration washed over the monks. They became human-sized torches.

A portion of the fire rebounded off the wall. It lost much of its momentum, but returned back the way it came. I stood there fascinated and watched the flames cool from blue to yellow to a smoky orange. It smelled of sulfur and burnt flesh. The temperature jumped, and too late, I realized that the backwash would engulf me too.

In desperation, I threw my hands before my face. My hair singed and the skin on my arms blistered. I fell backwards, landed wrong, and the wind was knocked from my body.

In the distance, over the ringing in my head, I heard Aesop say in a distorted voice, "Quickly, before the water comes."

"Why magic?" Smoking Bear shouted. "And why underground? I could have taken them."

Someone pulled me to my feet, but I could not see who. My body was numb, my vision clouded.

"Are you injured?" someone inquired.

I formed a response, said something, but all I heard was static. My eyes adjusted to the faint illumination, then I spied the light at the end of the tunnel.

"Hurry!" Aesop said next to me.

"Too late," Smoking Bear said. "Hold your breath!"

I did not.

From behind, came the sound of rushing air and water. Odd, it almost sounded like a toilet flushing, except it got louder instead of dying away. Someone pulled me toward the light. One step, then another, then the water crashed about me. It engulfed me and tossed me to the floor.

The water felt remarkably cold and wonderful on my burns. I decided to lie there, immersed in it, content to let the frigid liquid surround me. I drifted into a light sleep, buoyant and relaxed. I let the current pull me this way, then that.

An unwelcomed force clamped onto my leg, then tugged me through the water. With a swift heave, I left my weightless state and returned to the world of gravity. I lay on an unyielding wooden surface that rose up and down. I coughed up fluid.

From the unpleasantness of the experience, I concluded I was still conscious, and still alive.

"I told you our journey promised to be dangerous," Aesop said.

"No thanks to you," Smoking Bear told him. "He's in shock, but I think he'll survive."

"Excellent. Raise the sail, and get us away from this place."

My sentiments exactly.

3

~~~~~~~~~~~~~~~~

Waking up was never one of my strong points, especially waking up in pain. Was I burned? No, that was only a dream. My aches were from the beating last night, courtesy of the detective and his young friend.

The stench in this closet was intolerable—urine and the odor of decay. I blocked out any speculation of the source of those smells. Upon opening my eyes, one of them slightly swollen, I saw a thin line of honeysuckle light filtering beneath the door. I held my hand in front of my face. In the darkness all I made out was its outline.

Question one: where was the toilet in here? I thought I heard one flushing a second ago. I needed to use it.

Question two: why was I here? My two captors were no ordinary police, and I was in no ordinary trouble. Who would take such drastic action against me, and why? Whoever it was had plenty of resources, enough to buy off those two cops, and enough to then stash me down in Mexico. Could it be Eugene? He was the only one I knew with that kind of money. I didn't get the impression he wanted to harm me; however, he had mentioned there was money involved—those two companies Dad and he owned. But why go to all the trouble to find me, only to get rid of me again?

My ribs throbbed from the kicks they had received last night. Fortunately, it only hurt when I breathed, and I was doing as little of that as possible in here. I took stock of my injuries: a busted lip, my nose was bloody but not broken, a lump on the head, and a few bruised ribs. I tried to stand, became dizzy, and sat back down again. That kick to the head worried me. I could live with the other aches and pains, but a concussion was another matter. I sighed and inadvertently took a breath of the foul air.

My third question: why did the bald man shoot Sam? By all rights I should have been the one working last night, and the one who was killed. Whoever sent the assassin had his wires seriously crossed. That tended to eliminate Eugene from my list of suspects. If he wanted to kidnap or kill me, he had the opportunity when I saw him yesterday. None of it made sense. Something stank here, and it wasn't just this cell.

I stood again. Bells rang in my ears, but the dizziness eventually faded. Good. At least I could stand and try to defend myself if they came down here. I probably didn't have a chance against the two of them. I rubbed the lump on my head and a dull pain spread through my skull.

When I touched my head, a fragment of last night's dream came back to me—the fire in the tunnel, my hands brought up to protect my face, and the flood after that. Did I survive? In a rush, back to front, the sequence of events flowed from my memory. Yes, I was alive. I was also on my way to Sestos, city of pleasure. That was one bit of good news in all this. WaterStone got caught in that blast, turned into a human flare, and that was good too. If ever a shifty character haunted my dreams, it was him. I never liked WaterStone, especially after he made a pass at me in the observatory.

I only vaguely remembered the events that led up to my escape. I had translated something for the two strangers, Aesop and the warrior woman, Smoking Bear.

Yes, some bit of trickery on my part, but I forgot exactly what. The rest of the dream was misty and obscure, too distant, then gone.

I'd almost miss the Abbey of Glossimere. Over twenty years of my dreams invested in researching the histories and languages, but it was time to explore the rest of that world. The only thing I would miss out on was the excavation of the secondary library. It had been destroyed, buried under the great bridge when it collapsed. I'd like to see what was in there. Still, I was on my way to Sestos, and I could live with that.

Why was I so concerned with my dreams? I ought to be worried about the jam I was in here, in the real world. They were, after all, only dreams. A few more beatings like the last, and I'd be dreaming forever.

Above me, I heard footfalls across the living room, the door opening to the basement, more steps down stairs, then a jingling of keys and a click. The door swung outward.

I blinked and held a hand up to shield my eyes from the painful light. Fresh air flowed in and cooled my skin, gave my sense of smell a vacation. Through my fingers, I saw the detective make a face at the stench. He dug into his pocket, fished out his cigarettes, and lit up.

He took a puff, then said, "Glad to see you're up."

"Could I get some water?" I croaked past my cracked lips.

"Sure." He withdrew from the room and left the door wide open. Across the basement, I noticed the younger cop watching me, smiling his predatory smile. In his right hand he held a black nightstick. He looked ready to use it.

Were they here to beat me up again? Probably not if the detective was civil enough to get me some water. Still, I prepared myself for another round.

The detective returned with a tiny paper cup you'd find beside any water cooler.

I took it and drank slowly, trying not to let the cup touch my split lip. I almost said thanks to him, but caught myself. "So, what's on the agenda today? More beatings, maybe a little torture?" I applauded myself for the sarcasm.

"For you, nothing, if you just be quiet and sit tight."

"Then how about showing me where the bathroom is around here?"

He shook his head. "Sorry, Pritchard, but I have strict orders you're not to leave this cell."

"Orders from whom?"

He ignored my question. "I'll get you some food, and if you have to go, just go on the floor. No one here will mind."

If the detective was trying to provoke me, he was doing a good job. "What's going on here? Why are you keeping me?"

He took a step closer. "You don't get it do you? You really don't know what's going on?"

"Should I?"

He considered a moment. "I don't know. Maybe, maybe not. My job is to keep you alive and quiet, one day, two at the most. That's all I'm getting paid for."

Paid? This was beginning to sound like a conspiracy Hestor might imagine. She once claimed the mailman left a bomb in our mail slot. And another time, she thought the landlord entered our apartment to strangle us while we slept. In retrospect, I wonder if any of her ravings were true.

"All you have to do is be a good little citizen and make my life easy."

"And if I don't?"

He stuck his face an inch away from mine. I could smell the stale coffee and smoke on his breath and gagged. "I'll tell you what you're going to get if you're not quiet," he spat out through clenched teeth. "I'll leave my buddy in here with you for a few hours. He'd like that, you wouldn't. So don't push your luck, kid, unless you want your stay with us to turn into a real nightmare."

He might do it, so I kept my comments to myself. Besides, I had the feeling he didn't know much either. I upped the amount of trouble I was in by another notch.

"I'll be back to check on you later," he said, then slammed the door shut behind him. Again I heard him jingling the keys and their footfalls up the stairs.

I examined the door. There was no handle on this side, only smooth metal and the heads of a few steel bolts. I recalled a padlock on the other side when they tossed me in here last night. By touch, I made my way around the cell, four by three paces of solid cinder block. Escaping this place was impossible, from the inside anyway. Who was I kidding? What could I do, bust down a solid metal door, or rush those two cops? Not likely.

It was possible someone might notice my absence and look for me. Hestor was busy. I chuckled, and realized the hospital would try to track me down for not paying her bills. There was no one at work who really cared, other than Sam, and he wouldn't be looking for anyone. What about Eugene? He was waiting for me to take those tests. Would he come searching for me when I didn't show? Assuming he even knew where I worked, he might find out about the shooting. Then he'd have to trace the movements of the two cops to Mexico—an unlikely chain of events. I could rot in this place forever with no one being the wiser.

Time passed. My only clock was the light streaming through the bottom of the door. There were probably small windows in the basement, so the light was representative of the position of the sun outside.

The detective never returned with the food he promised. I successfully resisted the urge to foul my own cell. Upstairs I heard them laughing, watching cartoons on the television.

Unable to really see in the dim light, I traced imaginary scenes upon the black walls of my cell for a diversion. First, I sketched the face of the bald killer, outlined his wrinkled forehead, his crow's feet, and downright mean stare. I erased that and started on something more pleasant, a massive butterfly with silky wings, slender body, and feathery antenna. Upon its wings were designs and swirls that appeared like drops of water, stains on leather. It alighted on the imaginary branch of a dead tree and flapped its wings twice. Then it changed. The body fattened and the wings sharpened into those of a bat, then another head sprouted, a long, snaky appendage. I closed my eyes and squeezed the distorted image from my mind. Maybe that kick to my head had done more damage than I thought.

When the light beneath the door faded from a golden line to a dim gray thread, I heard a knock upstairs at the front door.

The television went mute, and my captors said something to one another, muffled by the floor between us. Silence. A few creaking footsteps over the floor, then the door opened. More voices, the two I knew, and a deeper one.

The three talked for a few moments, and the younger cop, I think, laughed. The voices then raised above a normal speaking volume. I made out a few expletives. One of them shouted. A gun fired.

What was going on up there?

Without warning, I was violently thrown to the floor. The earth pitched, and an explosion rocked the house over my head. It was no explosion, however, because it continued, even grew in intensity. There was a rumbling as something massive moved past my cell, grinding against the cinder block walls through the earth. Above me, I heard the foundation crack. There was the sound of wood snapping, glass shattering. Dirt rained upon me. I crawled to the frame of the door and stood in it.

The noise stopped abruptly, except for the house popping and cracking, settling back onto a broken foundation.

An earthquake? If it was, the fault lay directly under the house. No light came from under the door, and all there was to breathe was dust. Had I been buried alive? I yelled for help, then coughed from the lungful of dirt I inhaled.

"Roland?" someone shouted back. I recognized the resonant voice, no longer muffled through distance and barriers. It was Eugene's.

"Here," I shouted into the metal door and choked again.

Footsteps over creaking wood, then the same jingling of keys, and the door swung open.

He stood over me, smiled briefly, and helped me up.

His friendly face was a sight for my swollen eye. I couldn't help grinning like a fool. I had been rescued from whatever those two had planned for me, saved from whoever had paid them to abduct me. I silently chastised myself for suspecting Eugene was behind this.

He dropped his smile when he noticed my beaten face. "You are injured. Can you make it up the stairs?"

"Yes, I think so," I said, holding my ribs with one hand. "How did you find me?"

"I had you followed after you left my office."

"Followed? Why? Did you suspect this would happen?"

He frowned, then admitted, "Yes, but we can discuss this later—when we are far from this place."

His arm about me for support, I hobbled up the first steps. "What happened up there? It sounded like an explosion or an earthquake?"

"You will see for yourself," he said quietly.

We made our way up the stairs, which tilted to one side, and back into the living room of the safe house. Now, however, it was no longer a living room, nor a safe house. The entire foundation had torn its way through the bottom of the place, as if a bomb had been planted directly under the house. Concrete, earth, rocks, and jagged lumber lay haphazardly on the floor. In the center was a gaping hole and the source of this mess. At the bottom, I saw the cinder block of my cell, virtually untouched by whatever force caused the destruction. Water sprayed into the room from a broken pipe, and I almost lost my footing on the mud about the rim.

I backed away from the hole and looked about for my two captors. Every window was shattered, and a section of the far wall had been blown out. The supporting beams in the corner were snapped by a mass of stone, and nearby the ceiling sagged. Beyond that, in the dirt yard next door, was the sofa, thrown thirty feet, and the detective's younger friend, bloody, his limbs at odd angles.

Questions formed in my mind, but Eugene shook his head when I looked to him for answers and headed for the front door.

There, under a section of concrete, lay the detective, lifeless and crushed. I didn't know how. It was as if the earth had been given a life of its own to avenge me. The rock formed what appeared to be a giant hand, and its fingers were wrapped about him. It had squeezed him almost in half. This was no explosion.

"Come, Roland. All will become clear in time. However, I believe it prudent to leave here immediately."

I could only nod to Eugene, stunned by the sight. More questions came, and with them speculations of how this had occurred. All my answers were equally unbelievable. The only *reasonable* explanation was that blow I had taken to my head, that I was imagining all this. When I stepped over the hand of stone, I glanced again at the detective and shuddered. It all looked real enough to me though.

Outside, people gathered in the street and stared at the house, wondering like me what was going on. I saw it lean drastically to one side, shift on a crippled foundation, then collapse.

Eugene pointed me toward a black Mercedes on the street. My motions were still limited, so he opened the door and helped me in. He was stronger than he looked. A few people approached him and asked questions in Spanish. Eugene ignored them. He started the car and sped away.

"OK, what's going on, Eugene?" I asked after we were well away from the house. "Why was I kidnapped? And why was my boss shot? You know, or you wouldn't have had me followed."

He sighed, "These people work for the enemies of our family."

"Enemies? We didn't even know if I belong to your family yet."

"I am sorry to introduce you to the methods of family politics in this fashion, but it is unavoidable. Even though it has yet to be proven that you are a member of our family, there are those who would exterminate you solely based on rumor and suspicion."

"I hate to ask, but why?"

"I cannot tell you, yet. Only after we discover if you truly belong to our bloodline, then I shall answer all your questions. Until then, it might be dangerous for you to know more."

That was ridiculous. How could things get any more dangerous? "What about my mom? If these enemies of yours want to get rid of me, they might be after her too."

"I took the liberty of moving her to a very private hospital. I do not believe anyone is interested in her, only you."

"How did you manage that? There are release forms to sign, bills to be paid. You're not even related to her."

"There are ways."

Just like there are ways to buy police, or arrange for people to be shot? I carefully examined Eugene. I liked him, and was thankful for his timely rescue, but that feeling of caution remained. There were also a few things about his story that didn't ring true. If he had me followed, then why did he wait until this afternoon to get me? He'd have known since last night about my capture. He also just walked into the safe house, knocked on the door, if I remembered correctly. I couldn't hear them clearly, but it sounded as if their conversation began friendly enough. Maybe they knew each other. Then, the explosion that was not an explosion. How could I explain that? Despite all this, I decided to trust him, for now, and only because I had to.

"How did these people find out about me? You must have sent letters to a hundred different Pritchards. Why suddenly do these guys come out of the woodwork?"

"I suspect a person in my employ secretly works for another family."

"You mean like a spy?"

"Yes, they are exactly like spies. This conflict between the families is an ongoing war, and rarely they take hostages, like you, but often they do not.'' He glanced in his rearview mirror.

I swallowed. ''So this was how my father was killed, in some feud?''

Eugene frowned as if I had triggered some unpleasant recollection. ''We never knew specifically who killed Clay, but rest assured he was murdered.''

I pondered that for a moment, then asked him to pull into the first gas station he saw. I explained my need to find a bathroom, being deprived of one all day. He did, and it gave me a chance to review some memories I had of my parents. The accommodations inside were not what I'd call sparkling, but still vastly superior to where I had just been.

There was not really much to remember of Dad, just a feeling of love and of bonding. I was only a kid, what was I supposed to remember? I always thought he had died in a boating accident; that's what Hestor claimed. Then again, how much could I trust someone who wet her bed and saw things living in the refrigerator? Eugene at least seemed to have his facts straight. I made a mental note to ask him more about Clay later. Make *him* prove he was *my* cousin.

My most vivid memories were really of Hestor. She wasn't always unbalanced as she was now. If I didn't know better, I'd think she had started out as an entirely different person, then slowly lost her mind.

I reviewed the day of her first breakdown. Weird. It was my junior year of high school. She had been nervous for a while, but nothing beyond the limits of normal behavior, whatever that is. When I came home that afternoon, she had cut out the one-eyed pyramids from several dollar bills. She had taken the little triangles of money and pasted them all over the house, every corner, every wall, every door and window. I counted them later—147 bucks ruined. She had lost all control when I tried to remove them, claimed the ''demons'' would get her. It took three paramedics to sedate her. Our relationship went downhill from there.

I finished doing what I came to do, then washed up as best I could. Outside, Eugene waited with the engine running.

I climbed back into the sedan, grateful for the air conditioning running full blast. "What can you tell me of the family that captured me?"

"I can tell you nothing specifically," he said, "as I am uncertain who exactly kidnapped you."

"I don't understand. Didn't you say there's another family responsible for this?"

"No. I said there were other families, plural. It could be any one of three groups, perhaps more. In the past we have aligned with some clans, declared war with others, and changed sides as we felt convenient."

"I see," I said, not fully understanding. "Where are you taking me now?"

"Anywhere you wish. I would not blame you if you were even suspicious of my intentions after your ordeal." He paused, waiting for me to say something. "But if you have no objections, I would like to take you to my desert estate. You should be safe there."

What if I got out right here? Could I return to my apartment and pretend this never happened? No. If I went back, then my mysterious enemies could pick me up again. I had little choice but to go along for the ride. Eugene knew that.

"All right," I agreed, "let's get out of here."

He drove east and crossed the border at Otay Mesa. From there we left San Diego, and sped into Arizona. The sun disappeared behind a set of low clouds, washing the desert in reds and shadow. The fiery colors deepened and darkened, then the desert melted into blackness.

We drove for a while without saying anything to one another. Eugene was unwilling to tell me any more until I proved I belonged to his family. And what if I couldn't? Did I know too much already? A man with his power and wealth could make me disappear if he needed to. I thought of that stone hand, reaching from the earth to crush the detective.

His car phone beeped once. He picked it up, spoke

briefly in French, then hung up. "Try to get some sleep," he told me. "We have a long drive ahead."

I closed my eyes and tried to relax. The butterfly returned as I dozed, dancing across the inside of my eyelid. I drifted into sleep, crossed the black void, and entered my dreams. My inner ear detected the pitching and rolling motion of a boat. Feeling seasick, I sat up, wide-awake.

"Difficulties sleeping?"

I nodded and massaged the lump on my head.

"I was wondering if you might tell me more of yourself, Roland. Perhaps we could determine if you are of my bloodline before any testing."

"OK, what would you like to know?"

"Just talk," he said, "about anything." He didn't look at me. His eyes were fixed past his headlights, on the splotched asphalt racing toward us.

"I suppose you found out all about my mother when you moved her from the hospital."

"No, I have yet to make her acquaintance. I had others take care of that for us. She sounds intriguing, tragic actually, but tell me about you, Roland. What makes you different? I see so much of your father in you, you must belong to our clan. Tell me of your adventures. Were you in college?"

"Yes, I had a scholarship to UCLA. I went there for a while."

"For a while? What happened?"

"My sophomore year, Hestor was in an accident." Was this what he wanted to hear, all the sordid details and failures of my life? "She felt uneasy with me being away all the time. She wanted me to come home. We argued about it, then she got drunk, and plowed into a parked car—killed two kids. She was laid up in the hospital for a while, then got sued, and, naturally, she had no insurance. I quit school and got a job. Someone had to pay the bills."

"How did you manage that? The expenses must have been monumental."

"They were. About a year ago, I gave up and filed for bankruptcy."

"Another in your situation might not even have tried. You were courageous to do so."

"Do you mind if we talk about something else?" Dredging up these memories always burned me. How could one person screw up my life so completely? It wasn't really Hestor's fault. She was crazy at the time. Still, I hated her when I really thought about it.

"Of course," he said. "You seem to have a talent for languages. Very few Americans can read Greek."

"Oh, the inscription on the watch. I've picked up a few languages."

"Like French, or German?"

"No, I know very few modern languages, just English and Greek. *'Prin d an telenthsh episcein mhde kaleein kw olbion all entncea,'* " I quoted. " 'Call no man happy till he dies, he is at best but fortunate.' "

"Impressive."

"I also know a little Latin. *'Entia non sunt multiplicanada praeter necessitatem.* No more things should be presumed to exist than are absolutely necessary.' "

"An unusual phrase. I am confused, however. Was the focus of your studies in college classical languages?"

"No, I was a biology major. Why?"

"Then I assume you took the usual courses, biology, chemistry, mathematics, perhaps even some literature. How did you ever manage to learn Greek and Latin?"

I shifted in the leather seat. "The languages are hard to explain." That's all I needed was for him to think I was as crazy as Hestor.

"Try," he suggested, using that commanding tone I found so hard to resist.

"Dreams," I confessed. "Sometimes my dreams are normal: fragments of strange scenes, like walking naked through a grocery store. Most of the time they're not like that at all."

He sat there waiting for more. "Go on," he prompted after a moment of silence.

"My usual dreams are a series, one following the other. Ever since I can remember they've been that way" (ever since Dad disappeared, and Hestor checked out of *Hotel Reality*).

"There is nothing especially unusual about that. Many people experience serial dreams as you have described."

"That may be true, but for the last twenty years, I've learned things in my dreams: languages, history, even geography."

"How?" he calmly asked. The leather on the steering wheel strained as he gripped it tighter.

Strange. Any normal person would be questioning my sanity just now, or asking if I had recently sustained a blow to the head (I had, but that was beside the point). "In my dreams, I am an acolyte at an Abbey. This Abbey is the last depository of knowledge in the land of my dreams."

"The land of your dreams? You mean you are not in a normal place when you dream?"

"No, not even in the same world, I think. But it's just a dream. I don't believe it's real or anything crazy like that."

The car slowed, and he flicked the lights off. Outside, the desert stretched to either horizon. It was a sterile landscape, full of reflected moonlight. He pulled over, then killed the engine. The winds blew in earnest, sand-blasting the paint of the car.

"It is no small wonder we never found you," he whispered. "Clay must have left you at the Abbey of Glossimere when you were a child."

"Glossimere? I didn't tell you the name of the Abbey! How do you know?" I stammered.

"The dreams, they are what make us special, what give our family its unique abilities. Every time we sleep, we dream of that realm. It is as real as another country or planet. We have searched for you a long time, Roland."

"How can this be?" Even Hestor wouldn't believe something this farfetched.

"That I cannot answer, but I know it *is* real. You live

there, interact with its people, and may even die there. Some of the other families claim to originate from the land of dreams. When they sleep, they come here. I do not know which interpretation of reality is more accurate."

If this was true, then last night my life really had been in danger. It wasn't just a somatic fantasy. I had almost surrendered willingly to WaterStone. "Impossible, it can't be true."

"Then how do I know of the Abbey? The Abbey of Glossimere where a council of White-Robed monks carefully guard the secrets of that world's past? Does SilentSpeaker still sit on the council, or WaterStone, or perhaps Everus?"

"I still can't believe . . ."

"How do you explain the languages? What others do you know? Eldrich? Sartesh? Cusdialiac?"

"Yes," I whispered, "those and more."

"They have no earthly counterparts, do they?"

"No, although Latin does have some Eldrich roots . . ." It *was* true. I couldn't explain why or how, but the evidence was plain. I had always found some justification, an excuse for the languages and my other dream-learned skills, but in reality there was only one: my dreams were real.

Eugene again spoke, not in English, but in Eldrich. "I will send some of my men to the Abbey for you at once. Gods, you have not accepted your commission yet, have you?"

I answered him in Eldrich, forming the words slowly, my mouth unaccustomed to speaking it for real. "No, I escaped with all my parts intact. I do not know where I am right now."

"You must recall. There are dangers, other family members who know of your existence. They will also be searching for you."

It was difficult. I strained to recall how I left the Abbey. Only the basic outline of last night's dream remained: a flash of fire, the rush of water, then collapsing on a wooden deck. "I'm on a boat," I said, finally remembering. "I am on a boat, and sailing to Sestos. I am certain, well, fairly certain."

"Excellent, I shall look there. Whatever happens do not, under any circumstances, leave that village."

"How will I remember that? When I dream, I all but forget my life here. I only barely recall the events of my escape, and that was the most exciting thing to happen in twenty years."

"Your memory shall improve now that you realize the truth. It may take a while, but you will learn to accept the reality of your situation . . . that or it will drive you mad."

I still wasn't completely convinced, yet the whole thing did make sense in a distorted sort of way. How could he speak in Eldrich? It was not a language native to Earth.

"Eventually," he explained, "both worlds shall become clear in your mind. Until then, however, you must be extremely careful."

"How do you know about the Abbey? Are you a monk there?"

He laughed, then it died in his throat. "I have been there once before, to visit the Oracle. An unpleasant experience." He paused, then said, "But that is a tale for another time. First we must go home. I must get some sleep and arrange an escort for you. Also, you can meet some of our family. My two sons are abroad presently, but your cousin Sabrina is home. You will like her.

"You must be well rested," he continued in a serious voice. "Tomorrow we put your blood to the acid test. We see if you are a sorcerer like the rest of us."

4

*T*he bald assassin, my captors, my rendezvous with Eugene in Sestos—I remembered everything; but one by one those memories faded as I crossed the void of sleep.

I awoke and inhaled a sweet scent and moist air. Beneath my body, I felt the firm wooden deck as it rose and fell on the waters of the lake. Through the fog of my half sleep, I heard someone say, "Get up, we're almost there."

I rolled over and found myself on a sailboat, the De Marcos' sailboat. I had escaped the Abbey and was on my way to Sestos, city of delights. My hands were wrapped in a thick gauze and they itched. Scratching them on the deck proved fruitless, so I let them irritate me.

Smoking Bear sat close by with her legs crossed in a lotus position. She had her sword balanced in her lap and a whetstone in one hand. The corners of her mouth flickered into a smile, then she said, "If you don't mess with that dressing, your burns will heal quicker. You're lucky. Aesop could have overdone that piece of magic, and you along with it."

Yes, the tunnel, the explosion, and the water that followed. "Thank you for helping me escape. I regret placing you in danger. I had no idea WaterStone would try to kill you."

She shrugged and returned to sharpening her sword.

I searched about the lake, eager to see a merchant ship, perhaps a galleon from Yaggon, its purple and gold sails full in the wind. Through the mist, I spotted the shore, a thin gray thread veiled by the morning fog, and behind it, mountains that rose in all directions, but no boats. Jagged rocks, larger than our ship, jutted out of the water, sharp and unnatural. My eye connected a dozen of them in a straight line. These were no doubt the pillars of the great bridge that had once crossed the lake.

To come this far, we must have sailed through the night and against the winds, a credit to Aesop's skill. He was at the rear of the craft, tending the rudder. Water steamed from a dark wool cloak wrapped about him. He nodded to me, then turned his attention back to the winds and waves.

Smoking Bear ran the whetstone along the outer edge of her sword with great care. It was an unusual double-bladed invention, twin parallel sabers, spaced two finger's width apart, that tapered and joined at the tip to form a single point. The metal had wavy bands of dark and light steel folded together, and it appeared more natural, almost like wood, rather than manmade. I wondered how she sharpened the inner edges?

I felt awkward sitting silent next to her, so I asked, "What happened back in the tunnel? It should not have flooded as it did."

"Magic," she explained and ran her thumb over the edge, then inspected the drop of blood that welled from the cut. "It always attracts its opposite. That's why the place filled with water after Aesop summoned his flames."

"The fire, did it kill everyone?"

"I hope so," she replied without looking up, still fascinated with her bleeding finger.

I let that sink in. It was a criminal act, yet I did not

regret it. After hearing WaterStone's plans for me, I only felt relief to be gone from the Abbey.

She ran a cloth over the twin blades, then sheathed them. "I got some new clothes for you. Your robe was ruined, so I put some of Aesop's old things on you. It was either that or run around naked, and Aesop wouldn't care for that —not that he has much say in the matter. By the way, do they really cut off your . . . I mean your commission."

I realized my robes were indeed gone, and that I wore a pair of baggy leggings, a set of sturdy boots, and a silk shirt the color of sand. "Yes," I told her, "they castrate every acolyte when he receives his commission. It keeps their minds focused on scholarly rather than worldly matters." It also kept the acolytes from becoming too ambitious . . . which made me wonder why WaterStone was so dogmatic.

The breeze shifted and pushed the boat away from the shore with an invisible hand. The sail swung over Smoking Bear and me as Aesop brought us about. Small whitecaps tipped the water, dancing in the wind. We ducked and allowed the boom to pass over us before she asked, "That's a little severe, isn't it?"

"Yes." I shifted uncomfortably at the thought of my narrow escape, then changed the subject. "Have we passed the Flames of the Ward?"

"The what?"

"The Flames of the Ward. The great copper dish filled with a magic oil that burns yet is never consumed. It is carried by two enchanted birds, a dove and an eagle."

Her puzzled look told me she did not recall the famous artifact, so I continued to jog her memory. "The torch is a beacon for ships that enter the port. Weather conditions shift radically as the portals on the lake open to the various parts of the world. One instant it can be sunny, the next foggy, or even snowing on the Summer Solstice."

"You're crazy, little acolyte. Either that or you've been on that island too long. There are no copper dishes carried by birds, and the portals on this lake are only fairy tales.''

"But I have read of it, in several texts, cross-referenced and . . .''

''And just how old are these books you've been sticking your nose into?''

''Old? I do not know. The Abbey's records are slightly confused when it comes to matters of time. After the collapse of the great bridge, we were isolated.''

She yawned and stretched. ''No wonder then.''

When she stretched, I noticed she was all muscle and well proportioned. Despite a few scars, her skin was flawless, smooth, and an olive color. How old was she? And what was her relationship to Aesop? Wife, or perhaps younger sister? She might even be younger than me, but those things were difficult to tell. It was odd that she did not see the magical flames on her journey to the Abbey. Could my information be so out of date?

She got up in one fluid motion, then went below, and left me wondering.

We slipped closer to the shore, sailed between columns of stone that stood four meters out of the water—more remnants of the great bridge. About their bases, the pillars had tangles of algae that swayed back and forth in the waves. Schools of silver fish lingered under the green cover. They darted away when we approached. The columns formed a neat triple row all the way to the shore. There, the beginning of the bridge lay, a mountain of cut stone that spilled into the lake.

Five smaller fishing boats, gathered in those rocky waters. Their crews sang lusty ballads while they cast their nets upon the lake. They waved to Aesop and shouted greetings as we passed. He gave them a curt nod that barely acknowledged their friendly gestures.

Where were the larger boats, the great merchant vessels? There should be dozens, but I had yet to see one. I also could not find the long docks of metal and stone that reached across the bay. There was only a single wooden pier.

Aesop trimmed the sail and pointed the craft toward

the lone stubby dock. It was in a state of disrepair, rotting wood held together with tar and rope. Several of the supports had decayed completely through.

This could not be Sestos, yet how could I explain the ruined bridge? Perhaps we were in the wrong part of the bay, the wrong entrance. Yes, that must be it. This part was too shallow to allow the deep drafts of the laden merchant vessels to pass. No wonder I failed to see the Flames of the Ward, or any other signs of civilization.

Smoking Bear came on deck and helped Aesop lower the sail. Our momentum carried us to the broken dock. She then jumped across with a rope, pulled the boat in, and tied it off.

A man ran out to meet us. His strides made the structure sway dangerously. No grey touched his hair, yet his face held many years; sun and toil lined his skin and made it leathery. His left arm was loosely bound in a sling, and it clearly pained him to move with the injury, but he did so nonetheless. Despite his pain, this beggar managed to smile at the De Marcos.

"My lord," he said and dropped to one knee.

Aesop climbed onto the dock and scattered a few silver coins before him. The poor man went on all fours to gather the money. He was unbalanced with the injured arm; some of the coins escaped his grasp and disappeared between the cracks.

My heart went out to this fellow.

"What news?" Aesop demanded.

"M'lord," he said clutching the remaining coins in his right hand. "My son and I have seen no sign of the creature you described."

"Excellent," Aesop said to us, "then we have plenty of time. Let us get something to eat and rest a spell."

"Yes," Smoking Bear agreed, "white fish. I'm starved."

Sestos lay at the end of this dock. A few steps and I would be in the city of my afternoon daydreams. Should I stay with the De Marcos, or head out on my own? I had promised my services as a linguist to them, yet I felt an irresistible urge to explore this wondrous place on my own. No. Wandering the streets penniless and hungry was not how I wished to begin my tour of the merchant city. I would stay with the De Marcos for now.

More coins exchanged hands as Aesop arranged for his bags to be carried by the beggar and his son. We then crossed the dilapidated dock and left the blue sail of the De Marcos' boat behind.

We passed a row of tattered hovels, and emerged in a slum. I looked about confused—this was not Sestos. This place was no more than a village, and a poor one at that.

No secret gardens surrounded marble palaces here. There were only ruined buildings, little more than broken stones and weeds. No elephants crossed the blue-stoned plaza. The only creatures in this market were tiny silver fish drying on racks in the sun. There were no finely knotted carpets lining the alleyways, only trash, rubble, and filth. I saw no princes clad in silks atop their famous spotted horses, nor street performers who breathed fire and made coins vanish, nor exotic slaves clad only in jewels and whispery veils that hid delights barely left to one's imagination.

These people were as shattered as the ruined bridge and as tattered as their rotting dock. Their faces were weathered by the elements and full of suspicion. This changed however, when they spotted the De Marcos. Their expressions brightened into hopeful, yet pathetic, smiles.

Many approached Smoking Bear and Aesop to beg for food or money. The De Marcos ignored all of them. Had I possessed any coins, I gladly would have given them to these starving people. It was puzzling that the De Marcos, persons of obvious wealth, chose to ignore those we passed as if they were meaningless.

"This is Sestos?" The words rang hollow in my mouth.

Smoking Bear nodded to me, and kept her hand on the hilt of her sword.

Clearly, while I knew ancient history well, of recent affairs I had much to discover.

As we wandered deeper into the village, the peasants gave up, but not before Smoking Bear tossed a man from her path who demanded, rather than asked, for money.

Shacks of broken wood and smeared tar were scattered with no apparent order to their placement. The odor of excrement was thick in the air, and I had to cover my face to protect it from the flies that searched for their next meal. Across the street, a baby's cries went ignored. This place was diseased, one step away from death.

Yet here and there, standing among the hovels, stone buildings stood intact. They were designed with an impressive architecture, long sweeping arches that revealed grandiose courtyards within. Layers of carved geometric designs, complex, subtle, and worn by time, adorned the outer walls. Beautiful as they were, all were deserted.

"Do not the people inhabit these buildings?" I asked Aesop.

"Haunted," he told me. "None can live in those accursed places. I would not suggest entering if you value your life."

I was tempted to visit these palaces and ignore his warning. I knew within must be remnants of this city's glorious past. One in particular caught my attention: a manor built from stone the color of the setting sun. Carved over the wide arch was the name "Horace . . ." in Eldrich. Through that entrance, in the center court, I saw a mosaic that spanned the inner walls. Constructed of a thousand tiny tiles, a faded centaur rode onto a pale field of pink and blue grasses. Tiny flowers, exact in detail, white with blue centers, were woven into his mane. Ivy covered the remainder of the work and obscured what the strange creature held in his hand.

Why had none removed the wealth from these places, here among those who were so poor? If Aesop, a mighty sorcerer, believed them to be haunted, then there might be more within those walls than I cared to discover.

The streets near these buildings were also curious. Large, seamless sheets of stone formed a road. The engineering that produced such wonders was beyond my thinking. Most sections however, had their foundations undermined, and were little more than gravel now.

My hopes that this was all a mistake, that this was not Sestos, died when I spotted a blue rock the size of my thumb. This was one of the stones that paved the marketplace. My books had not lied. Sestos had been here, with wonders and delights, but had not survived as I thought.

I almost wished the city had never existed. Better that than to see my fantasy reduced to this fishing village. How long? How long had it been since the Abbey was built and the wars began? How long since gold passed between jeweled fingers in this plaza?

After the Golden Age, the magical portals must have disappeared, and with them the commerce that made the city thrive. Sestos was nestled in a formidable mountain range. Deprived of magical transportation, no merchant could journey here. And without trade, the city of merchant princes would be no more than a village.

I plucked the tiny blue stone up, then followed the De Marcos. They strode to the only large wooden building in the village. It was constructed of pine, worn white with time, and its shingled roof covered in moss. Over the doorless entrance hung a sign that proclaimed: THE WHITE FISHE.

My two companions entered, in spite of, or because of, the fishy stench that caught my nose ten paces before. We walked into a dark and deserted common room. In the far corner was a cold hearth, smoke stains above it on the ceiling. Aesop and Smoking Bear sat at a table in the back, which was an old door supported by two barrels.

A stout man came from the kitchen to greet us. To say he was ugly would have been humane. A mass of scar tissue served as his face. He smiled and exposed his toothless mouth in the process. The rags he wore for clothes were stained with unidentifiable blotches, yet about his waist was an apron of pristine white linen.

"M'lord De Marco," he slurred, and bowed low. "What is your pleasure today?"

"Two white fish with mussels, if you please, Phio."
He looked at me. "Make that three."

"And three Golden Fire ales," Smoking Bear added.

"I am not particularly hungry," I said, and hoped the
smell in here was not from Aesop's order.

"I highly recommend the cuisine here," Aesop said
to me. "Even Smoking Bear, with her gentle palate, can
stomach it. Why, the White Fishe is half the reason we
came to this dreadful little corner of the world."

Smoking Bear shrugged when I looked to her for help.
"Fine," I replied. "Make it three orders."

Phio nodded, smiled crookedly at me, then went back
to his kitchen. Sizzling sounds along with smoke and
steam billowed out when he opened the doors and yelled
to his assistant.

"How long do you estimate before your brother
monks decipher the Sarteshan poem?" Aesop asked.

"Oh, immediately," I answered. "I know four other
acolytes that can read Sartesh fluently."

He frowned.

"Do not worry. They may be able to translate it, but
they will never understand it."

He raised an eyebrow. "Why do you say that? It is
the same translation we have."

"Also," Smoking Bear said turning to Aesop, "they
were working for Morgan as we feared. You heard that
White Robe brag about the Bishops paying for our bodies. Once they get a hold of the translation, they'll know
where the statue is as well as we do."

That name, Bishop, brought a chill of recognition. I
was forgetting something, something from my dreams.
Another name surfaced, Rhodes, but I failed to associate
it with anything significant.

"I think there is little the two of us can do about it
now," he told her. "We shall take our young friend to
the clan house. He will be happier and safer there. Then
we must travel east with all haste if we are to beat Morgan—and his pets."

Smoking Bear looked to me and waited for my com-
plaint, but I sat there smiling.

"What are you grinning about?" she demanded. "You ought to be angry we're not taking you. I thought you wanted to tag along and see the sights. That was our bargain, and we just broke it."

"What would you give," I said still smiling, "if I could effectively nullify your enemy's advantage, this Morgan Bishop?" I did not know who this man was, or even the nature of their conflict, but I knew I could help them. Indeed, I had already helped them. The De Marcos were merely unaware of it.

"I do not see how you can accomplish such a thing," Aesop said with a hint of suspicion. "Nevertheless, if you could save me trouble from Morgan, I would pay you one hundred gold stars."

I nodded as if I knew what he offered me, then, "I have a far more useful suggestion. Allow me to accompany you to Sartesh. I am a scholar well versed in the ancient languages and histories. I could be invaluable to you there."

"That is highly impractical," he said. "It would be . . ."

Smoking Bear rested her hand on his arm, then said, "Let's hear what he has to say."

He shook his head and started to protest again, but she focused her eyes into a stare that silenced him.

Interesting. Was she in charge of this expedition?

"If you do not take me," I continued, "you will never find what you seek, at least not with that translation."

Aesop looked puzzled at this declaration, and Smoking Bear irritated.

"I understand why you do not want me with you. You feel I am young and perhaps may even become a danger to you."

I paused in the middle of my explanation and suddenly recalled that I must not leave Sestos. I was to meet someone here. I was certain. But whom? I knew no one except the De Marcos. The feeling remained, however, so I squeezed my memory for more information. Nothing.

"Go on," Aesop said, interrupting my thoughts.

I blinked twice and the anxiousness faded, then was forgotten. "Do you recall what I said earlier about the Sarteshan priests?"

"What was that?"

"They took great pains to hide their secrets from outsiders. And the measures they took to protect their religious documents is legendary. One would have to be a scholar not only in the language, but knowledgeable of their religions and histories to understand them."

"I am beginning not to like this," Smoking Bear muttered.

"Before I say any more, you must agree to take me with you. I must also insist on something more substantial than your word this time."

"Very well," Aesop sighed. "I swear on my family's honor to take you with us, *if* you manage to prove your worth."

I did not completely trust his word, but once he heard the truth they would have to take me. "When I decoded the document," I said, "I creased it so the stains formed the shape of a butterfly. But I neglected to inform anyone that the butterfly is symbol for the Sarteshan deity, Jexer."

"So?" she said, and removed a large cigar from her pack, then lit it. The smoke covered up most of the fish smell and replaced it with its own aromatic qualities. She obviously was becoming less and less pleased with me. Tough.

I felt different today. Yesterday I might have stammered out the explanation, taking whatever deal the De Marcos had to offer. Now I bargained with them, almost as an equal. Where did this courage come from? It was almost as if I had another set of skills to draw upon, as if there was another me. A flash of images touched my mind: a burnt book, a gold yin-yang, and a hand made of stone.

"Jexer is the Sarteshan god of fools," I explained. "He was the deity responsible for the jokes and farces chronicled in their history. The butterfly was a ruse. It is the easiest to find, and, it provided a false translation.

I am confident there are several alternate foldings, each yielding a different passage.''

"And I suppose you will translate the poem again in exchange for exploring Sartesh with us?'' she asked.

"Exactly.''

"Just what is to stop you from providing us with another false translation?'' Aesop inquired.

"One more reason to take me along. If one translation does not work, I can refold the document until we find the correct interpretation.'' An aroma disrupted my thoughts, fish and garlic.

"Ah,'' she said, "our food is here.''

Phio waddled out to our table, balancing three steaming plates with one hand, and holding three overflowing mugs in the other. He set them down, one for each of us.

"Mind the bones,'' he warned us, then returned to the kitchen. His apron was no longer white.

A fish, head and tail draped over either side of the plate, stared back at me. Its flesh had a coat of thick white sauce. Aesop unfolded his napkin and placed it on his lap, then carefully cut into the creature, removing the smallest bones as he ate. Smoking Bear devoured hers immediately, skin and all, with no such formalities.

I took one small taste, most of which was horseradish, and politely spit it into my napkin. The ale was palatable, smooth, rich, and cold, my first taste of such things. The bubbles left a stinging sensation on my tongue when I swallowed, but I did not mind. I finished the mug, which dulled my wits, then tried the fish again. It was still lethal.

Neither of them noticed my untouched meal, until Smoking Bear, who finished first, asked with a mouth full of fish, "You eating that?''

I shook my head. Gods, my tongue was aflame and my stomach in knots. How did they stand it?

She reached past Aesop and took the fishy delight away from me.

He finished his meal, then took one small sip of ale, and said, "I can not argue that you have us in an intriguing position.'' He stared into his mug and considered for a moment, ''I can reward you lavishly, if you are as clever in finding what we seek as you were with the translation. Understand, however, that the moment you become a burden to us, we must leave you behind.''

''I accept those terms.''

It was unlikely he was serious. After all, I was the only one who could read the document. I waited for Smoking Bear to comment, but her attention was still fixed on my fish. ''What exactly are you looking for?''

He cast a glance about the room, then whispered, ''Each royal family had one relic from the Golden Age. It is said that a man, a survivor of evil times, seeded each of the families existing presently. It is also said he bequeathed to each clan one powerful relic, with which they might prosper. The device my grandfather possessed, a small statue, half man and half beast, was reputed to have great powers over nature.''

''And you believe this statue is somewhere within the Sarteshan Empire?''

''I know it was hidden there to protect it from falling into an enemy's hands. If another clan ever retrieved our relic, they would have the power to attack us, and win.''

Another clan? From somewhere, perhaps a book read long ago, came a list of names, Pritchard, Rhodes, Bishop, and Chandler to be added to the family name of De Marco. There were others, but I had forgotten them. These were the old and noble families of Meredin, families of sorcerers who competed and warred among themselves.

''You look a bit ill,'' Smoking Bear commented, sopping up the remaining white sauce with a crust of bread.

''Just the fish,'' I answered.

Phio returned to collect his plates and settle the bill. Aesop lavished praise upon our revolting host for his equally revolting meal, then paid him with two gold coins.

We left the White Fishe, Phio, and his stench behind. Outside, waiting with our packs, were the beggar with the broken arm and his son. Smoking Bear hefted the packs, then decided which was heavier and gave it to me.

I slung it over my shoulder, unaccustomed to the weight. My experiences at the Abbey insufficiently prepared me for carrying loads such as this. I was a scholar, not a laborer.

Aesop gave the beggar what I assumed to be a small fortune in silver from his expression, then told him, "We may return this evening, if any ask."

"Of course, m'lord," he replied, then both he and his son bowed low.

We hiked out of the village toward the direction of the rising sun. Once in the forest, Aesop stood still for a moment, listened, then changed direction, heading north. Smoking Bear followed with her double blade drawn.

For the first few kilometers, I enjoyed the walk, in spite of the burden on my back and my burned hands. It troubled me deeply that Sestos lay in ruins. All the information I had of the world was drastically out-of-date. Was the Sarteshan Empire also destroyed?

Aesop, ahead of me, seemed distracted, as if he were searching for something. Occasionally he glanced into the sky, or stared into the forest. I considered initiating conversation with him, but saved my breath for the hike.

The Forests of Anac were wild. No traces of its previous cultivation remained. What happened to the exotic beasts the merchant princes allowed to roam these woods? Did they too die out, or had they survived? Thus far, the only wild creatures I had spotted were an occasional sparrow, or the numerous blue-tailed squirrels that dashed across the trail.

Spruces and pines filled the forest. They swayed slightly as the winds from the lake chased the rising sun. Sunlight filtered through the canopy, golden shafts of radiance, in which motes of pollen swam and left curious designs hanging in the air. In the shadows, crops of ferns, taller than I was, flourished. We trekked through a grove of silver-barked trees that smelled of vanilla. All the while, our steps fell silently upon the blanket of needles that covered the ground.

The forest thinned as we climbed the mountain. More rocks, black stones, broke through the ground, growing larger and more prominent the farther we ascended.

Smoking Bear signaled to Aesop, and we halted. "Rest," she announced.

I had no words, only sweat and a desire to lie down. My stomach rumbled from the ale, from the two morsels of white fish, and from its emptiness.

She removed the canvas bag from my shoulder and told me, "Try wearing it like this. Look, you already have a blister." From my pack she unloaded a satchel of pine nuts and a small crossbow.

She shoved a handful of the nuts into her mouth, then said, "Let me check your hands."

I sat and offered her my bandaged hands. She unwrapped them, and to my shock they were apparently whole. Only a slight greenish discoloration marred my otherwise healthy skin. No trace of the burns remained.

"The salve I put on your hands works well for minor burns," she explained. "A handy thing to have when you travel with Aesop."

I flexed my fingers once, and they felt stiff, but otherwise normal. "Thanks."

"Know how to work this?" she asked, and pointed to the crossbow.

"No, but I have seen some of the older monks practice with them."

"OK, I'll load it for you. Try not to shoot me in the back with it." She poured more of the nuts into her mouth, then offered me the bag.

For some reason I felt strangely attracted to this dangerous woman. She was rough, but good-natured, a bully, yet distinctly female somewhere under all that armor. I ought to be wary of these feelings, as she was likely married to Aesop, a man not to play games with. Inexperienced in these matters, I decided to err on the side of caution and merely be polite to her.

"Are you listening to me?" she asked.

"Sure, safety here, firing trigger here. As I said, I have seen them used before." I avoided eye contact with her, and instead glanced at the combat spikes riveted on her shoulder armor. Were those bloodstains?

"If you have to use it, take your time and aim. Don't bother trying to reload it. You probably can't. If whatever you hit doesn't die, I suggest you try running."

I nodded.

After washing the unsatisfying snack of nuts down with a gulp of water, we resumed our climb to the pass. I felt as if I would never make it over the top of these mountains, but my pride gave me a small burst of energy. Even Aesop and Smoking Bear began to show signs of wear, and they slowed their pace. The winds increased when we climbed above the tree line. My legs cramped, uncramped, then began to shake rhythmically.

We marched on.

The higher we scaled, the more desperate my breaths became. It was as if the Gods of Meredin were stingy and neglected to put an adequate supply of air on their mountaintops. The sun sank from its apex, and the sky took on its traditional cloak of ambers and reds. Streamers of fire traced the sun's last arc.

Without preamble we stopped.

Aesop pointed to the mountainside, then mumbled to Smoking Bear.

"Are you positive?" she asked him. "I don't recall it being there."

He shrugged, then approached the mountain wall. I sank to my haunches and watched while he cleared brush and stones away from the entrance to a hidden tunnel. He entered and lit a torch with a touch of his hand.

Smoking Bear and I followed him in.

Inside, was a cavern, one room, with a ceiling that stretched up into darkness. No wind followed us in. Crates, cots, and barrels of water filled the back portion of the cave. Aesop immediately inspected a large blue box with clouds stenciled on its side. Next to that was a basket, capable of holding five men, with room to spare.

I threw myself onto a cot, eager to sleep, too tired even to remove my boots. This was better than the straw pallet I was accustomed to, but not the bed of feathers I had hoped for in Sestos.

"Not yet, little acolyte," Smoking Bear told me. "You get first watch."

Too exhausted to protest, I dragged my numb body to the entrance and sat down, back against the wall. The sun set and left one final burst of gold in the east and deepening shadows across the mountains. Despite the cold and the absolute hardness at my back, I fell asleep.

5

A firm bed supported my back. I drifted in and out of consciousness, then realized I was not on the fold-out bed at home, nor my sleeping pallet at the Abbey, nor in the mountain cavern with Aesop and Smoking Bear. It always confused me when I woke up in a different bed. This one was more extravagant than I was accustomed to, with a down comforter and soft, stuffed pillows. It felt perfect.

I was up.

It took me a second to recall were I was, and which Roland I was. I remembered far more of my dream than ever before: sailing to Sestos, the shock of seeing the city's true condition, hiking up the mountain, and the cavern. There were still minor gaps, blank spots in the events, but most of it was there. It no longer possessed that dreamlike quality, insubstantial and distorted, but was now as solid and real as my waking world. Would I remember as much of this realm when I slept tonight?

Last evening, Eugene and I arrived at his desert estate. It was a guarded complex, complete with ivy-covered walls, acres and acres of manicured lawn, and straight

white columns, three stories high, that supported the ter-
races of the colonial mansion.

I had several questions for him, but recalled his re-
luctance to answer them. Yes, I still had to prove that I
was part of his family with a test of magic.

I had seen sorcery, in both worlds: the wall of flames
Aesop conjured, and the hand of stone summoned by
Eugene. It was not a question of *if* I believed in magic.
I did. It was a question of my generating such effects. I
held out my hand as Aesop had, then willed a tiny flame
to spring forth. My palm remained cool and empty.

This worried me, because if I was not a sorcerer, not
really the one Eugene sought, things could get much
worse for me. I pushed that thought aside. Clearly, if
magic did exist, there had to be more to it than just
willing it to happen like some comic book hero.

I rolled out of bed, stretched, and stepped to the high
window on the east side of the room. Four squares of
sunlight poured through the glass onto the floor. Two
stories beneath me sprawled a hedge maze, framed by
rows of flower beds awash with the blues of lilac trees
and the blood red of roses. Eugene and a woman strolled
through the labyrinth. Her arm rested on his in a polite
manner. Who was she?

My stomach rumbled once, a reminder of my last
meal over a day ago. I decided food was my next course
of action and looked for my dirty clothes. It wouldn't
do for me to wander about Eugene's mansion naked.
Unable to find them, I searched the closet. Several suits,
slacks, and dress shoes occupied the space. I dug deeper
into the back and found a new pair of blue jeans. I showered quickly and slipped them on, then found a pair of
hiking boots and a white shirt. The boots fit well enough,
but they were new and needed to be broken in.

I paused in the hallway. A small bronze statue caught
my eye. It had its own niche in the wall, a place of
honor. He was a baseball batter frozen mid-swing, and
wore an expression was pure determination—poised to
hit a home run. From his baggy uniform and curled mustache, I'd say he was from the turn of the century. He

bore a striking resemblance to Eugene. There was a name engraved on the base: Theodore.

My stomach complained again.

I descended the stairs and ventured into the garden, hoping to find Eugene, his companion, and food. There, I only saw the gardener, who informed me they had retired for breakfast. He gave me directions. My hunger and curiosity led the way.

Through glass French doors I went, into a marbled atrium that held a mosaic of light and reflection upon its polished floor, then through a formal dining hall filled with a hundred chairs and a mahogany banquet table. I pushed open the door to the servants' kitchen and halted. The same woman I saw with Eugene was here. She sat in a breakfast nook, examining a newspaper, unaware of my presence.

She was perfect, alluring and sensual, despite her blond hair drawn tightly back and the conservative gray business suit she wore. There was a strength in her face, but it was well hidden by her soft feminine features.

I'd been attracted to other women in my life, but nothing like this. It was more than physical; it was emotional, spiritual . . . something else too. I couldn't place my finger on it. Why was I acting this way? I was no boyish acolyte who had never seen a girl before. I tried to speak, to move, to even think straight. My will had fled me, however, and I could only stand and watch and wonder at her beauty.

She looked up from the paper and her eyes locked with mine. Her face changed in response to my presence; she smiled. It stunned me. Wave after wave of raw sexuality pounded into my flesh. There was a primal force emanating from her, something basic to the nature of man and woman. My heart stopped, then compensated by pounding recklessly. I stood frozen.

She broke the spell, and said, "You must be Roland."

Her voice was exactly what I expected: sweet, liquid, and musical. I shook the cobwebs from my brain. This was no way to make a first impression. I returned her smile, lowered my voice an octave, and managed to speak: "Uh, yeah."

"Sit," she said, "please." She placed her hand on an adjacent chair.

Part of me wished to sit far away from her, the rational part, but the effect of that initial moment lingered. I took the seat and leaned slightly toward her. I didn't feel fully in control.

She wet her lips, then said, "I am your cousin, Sabrina."

I wanted to embrace her, demonstrate my passion in pure physical terms. I checked my motion, and emotions, then mentally stepped back a pace from this chaos. I slowed my breathing and relaxed.

"Eugene mentioned you," I said, "but not how lovely you were." Much better, I assured myself. Keep your cool.

She lowered her eyes briefly. "It is not every day that one meets their long lost cousin. We must find the time to become acquainted."

The temperature rose a degree or two.

"I'd like that," I replied, and cleared my throat.

"Grand." She smiled even wider. "I shall arrange some minor expedition for us to get lost on. Perhaps lunch? This afternoon in the garden?" Her voice had a slight accent, it was familiar, but I failed to place it.

"It's a date then," I agreed, "provided Eugene has nothing planned for me." When I spoke his name, I recalled the test I was to take this morning. That thought sobered me, and I regained some control over my emotions. As the initial insanity of her first smile passed, I experienced the same sense of familiarity as when I had seen Eugene, and the bald killer.

"I heard rumors that you were in trouble." She dropped her voluptuous smile, and placed a comforting hand on my forearm.

The manner in which she touched me was nothing suggestive, yet it felt hot as fire on my skin. The sensation raced along my nervous system and numbed my brain. Alarm bells rang inside my head. What was she doing? At this point I didn't care, euphoria clouded everything in a pale haze.

"Trouble?" I smiled foolishly at her. "Yes, some, but Eugene helped me out. Everything seems to be under control now."

She nodded her head. "Tell me more of your family, Roland. Your mother, is she still alive?"

"My mother? Well, she's . . ." I stopped, distracted by a figure in the edge of my peripheral vision. I turned and saw Eugene. He watched from the doorway and glared at Sabrina.

Sabrina removed her hand. "We can talk later," she whispered. "Eugene, I believe, wishes to have a word with you."

She arose, smoothed out her suit, then greeted him with a kiss on the cheek.

A flash of anger passed through me. Jealousy? Already I missed her presence by my side. The heat from her touch dissipated, however, and my thoughts noticeably cleared. They exchanged a few hushed syllables and smiled to each other. She gave me one last glance that caused my pulse to race, then left us.

Eugene, dressed in a neat wool business suit, sat next to me.

"I am sorry you had to meet your cousin Sabrina unannounced, and alone."

"Is she your daughter then?"

"No, she is of the Bishop clan. At the moment we are allies." His face was unreadable.

Bishop? I knew that name. It was the Bishop family that WaterStone allied with. It was Morgan Bishop that wanted the De Marcos killed. He was after their magic heirloom.

If I was working with the De Marcos, and Eugene was friendly with the Bishops, then what precarious political position had I gotten myself into? I would have to be very careful what I revealed to either Eugene or the De Marcos of this.

A chef wearing a white linen apron entered from the kitchen. He offered me oily sausages, hot croissants, and a bowl of cantaloupe, then disappeared. Eugene poured the dark aromatic tea himself. After that white fish in Sestos, I rated this breakfast superb. The tea, very strong, jolted my awareness after the thorough fogging Sabrina caused.

"You must be cautious when dealing with Sabrina," Eugene explained and stabbed a sliver of apple with his knife. "It would be best, actually, for you to avoid the other families until you are fully briefed ... especially Sabrina. She can have a strong effect on an unprepared mind."

"Was it magic?" I asked, then licked the sausage grease from my fingers.

"Who can say for certain? If it is, it is a Bishop family secret."

He sipped his tea and we ate for a few minutes, then he said, "My men failed to locate you in Sestos last evening. What happened?"

I looked into my plate, slightly embarrassed, and replied, "I forgot. It was so clear when I fell asleep last night, but I got caught up in events. It just slipped my mind."

"Has your memory improved? Do you recall more of your dream?"

"Yes, I can remember *almost* everything. I am traveling with two merchants. We hiked into the northern mountain range, and are camped inside a cave." I purposely omitted the fact that the two merchants were the De Marcos, not knowing how he would react.

"It is a good sign—that you recall more. People may dream of Meredin, visit briefly, but they are not true dreamers, not part of the royal families. Their existence in that realm is irregular, truly dreamlike."

"What do you mean? I thought you said only our immediate family could journey there."

"Yes, however, true dreamers have an effect on those they spend a large amount of time with. These mundane persons are drawn to the other realm along with the true dreamer. Your mother, for example, may be able to dream of Meredin, but she would view the event only as a vision, vague, memory erratic, and her existence there partial.''

''You mean I might be dreaming of Meredin because of some echo effect?''

He nodded. ''It is possible that you are your mother's son by a previous father, and your dreams are a mere shadow of Clay's existence.''

I couldn't believe that. Last night was too real. ''What is it like for you when you dream?''

Eugene pondered while he chewed a bit of apple, then answered, ''Meredin is as real to me as this world. I can no longer distinguish between the dream and the real. That is what it shall be like for you too, if you are a true dreamer, one contiguous existence.''

I offered him a confused look.

''You will understand more of this later, after the test.''

I was about to continue my meal, but Eugene then asked, ''Are you done? We have a half-hour drive ahead of us. If we do not hurry, it will be over a hundred degrees when we get there.''

I gulped the rest of my tea, popped the last sausage into my mouth, and nodded.

Outside, his Mercedes waited, running with the air conditioning on full blast. We drove farther into the desert and away from his estate.

''Tell me more of what occurred last evening,'' he said.

''I am traveling with two merchants who came to the Abbey seeking wisdom.'' When I spoke of the dream realm, my personality slipped naturally into the other Roland. It was strange. He had another set of skills for me to draw upon, another intellect, and another set of morals. Would the two eventually blend together? Or would I forever possess this split in my personality?

''When we arrived in Sestos, I discovered it was only a fishing village.'' I paused, uncomfortable with the loss of my city. ''I read of Sestos at the Abbey. It was a wonderful merchant city-state. Portals filled the Lake of the Prophet, and all manner of beings traded there, from all parts of Meredin, even different worlds.''

"I have heard of such things," Eugene said after a moment. "That was during the Golden Age of Meredin, and long before my time."

"You don't know what caused the city's decline then?"

He shook his head.

Eugene pulled onto a dirt road and headed into a field of oil wells. All the rigs were working, all pumping rhythmically up and down, and all bearing the curious gold yin-yang symbol of Rhodes Industries International. He drove past these constructs, over a hill, and into a barren valley.

"This is the place," he announced and pulled over.

I got out. A blast of heat enveloped me. A few rocks jutted out of the sand at unnatural angles. The trees and bushes in the valley had been plowed up, then piled together in one large heap. From the charred remains next to this mound of vegetation, I guessed it would be burned later, and the valley left devoid of life.

A slight breeze pushed the hot air. I glanced at my watch, a blaze of gold in the sun. It was only ten o'clock and already my sides were sweaty.

"Let us begin," he said, donning a pair of sunglasses, "by discussing what causes magic. Did you take elementary chemistry in college?"

I nodded, listening carefully to his words. My life was likely at stake.

"Then I shall describe sorcery in similar terms." He bent over to draw in the sand. "You are familiar with the battery? How essentially there are two chemical reactions that power the positive and negative portions of the cell?"

Again I nodded and studied his diagram in the sand. A box, divided in half, one side labeled with a negative sign, the other with a plus.

"Now," he continued, "one may tap into the stored energy within the cell, but only in a specific manner. If you touch the positive terminal alone, or only the negative, nothing occurs. But if you touch both simultaneously, then a current flows between them. Place a device in this flow, such as a light bulb, and the energy excites the filament to produce light."

"You mean converting the stored chemical energy into work?" I patted myself on the back for remembering that. Why did I only get mediocre grades? Probably the calculus, I always struggled with the math.

"Something like that," he said and smiled. "There are differences, however, between magic and physics. In physics, work may be derived from a single force like gravity. With sorcery, the forces must always be used in pairs of opposites, like the positive and negative in our example."

"OK," I said. "So far, I follow you."

"When a sorcerer practices magic, he taps into these paired forces. He does not produce the flow of energy, any more than the wire connecting the two terminals of a battery does. He only directs the flow into a useful form."

"Sounds easy enough."

"It does *sound* easy, but it is not. The type of magic produced is related to the forces you manipulate. Take the elemental force pairs, fire and water, or earth and air, for example. If you wish to produce fire, you first must concentrate on the elemental force of fire. Then the opposite is required, the other terminal of the battery if you will, the elemental force of water. Concentrate on both forces, and the energy flows from one to the other. You may then divert the power to produce the magic you desire."

"What happens to the energy that flows from the fire, into the water side of the two elements? Do they cancel out?"

"Good, you grasp the difficulty involved with such manipulations. The energy does not disappear. The more you concentrate on producing the effect, fire, the less you can direct where that energy goes. The extra energy converts itself into water magic, of which you may have no control. Remember, you do not directly command the energy, you only use the flow between the paired forces.

A good sorcerer must split his concentration between the effect he wants, and the effect he does not want.''

"And if he doesn't? If he only concentrates on one of the magical energies?"

"There is a cancellation phenomenon. The two forces prefer to be at equilibrium. Say you are trying to light a fire and ignore the energies that flow to the water magic. You might douse your flame by creating a small storm.''

Now I understood what had happened in the tunnel . . . Aesop concentrated solely on the result, the fire. He then lost control of the energy that flowed into the water. That's what caused the tunnel to flood.

"Can you give me a demonstration?''

"That was my reason for bringing you here," he said and gestured to the valley about him. "This land is one of the highest yielding oil fields in the nation.''

"Oil? I thought there was no oil in Arizona.''

"That is precisely the point. There is little natural oil here, but several miles south, in Mexico, lie rich and plentiful reserves. For years, I have slowly altered the underlying geophysical structure and forced the petroleum to seep from the oil bearing shales, across the border, and into my lands. Today, I shall tap into a portion of those reserves. Doing this will save me the cost of exploratory drilling. If I am successful, the oil will surface here, where I shall set up another rig and collect it. Pure profit.''

"So you will first tap into the earth magics, then its opposite . . . air? And from the gradient of forces you will power your sorcery?''

"Perfect," he said. "It also helps to have knowledge of the forces you wish to manipulate, in this case, the geological patterns, the physics of stress and flow, and the mineralogical properties of the rocks. The more you know, the more efficient your use of the magical energies.''

"Now it's starting to sound difficult.''

"Watch and learn.'' He then bent over and touched the sand with his index finger. A grimace of concentration appeared on his face, but nothing else happened.

Three or four minutes ticked by and I observed nothing.

I almost interrupted him when a cool breeze materialized in the midmorning heat. This breeze grew and sand took flight. Small dust devils sprang into existence, then drove themselves toward us. This was the byproduct of his magics, the wind part of the paired forces. It must be.

I shielded my eyes from the dirt. It was difficult to see even a few feet in front of me. The flying sand stung the exposed parts of my body. Wind boiled about us. One final burst of fury, then it abruptly died.

I shook the dirt from my hair and down my back. My feet were buried a good three inches in the earth.

Eugene stood up and smiled from ear to ear. He was clean, not a speck of sand on his wool suit. "Come," he said, "observe for yourself the result."

I noticed nothing extraordinary about the patch of ground he claimed to magically alter. Then, slowly, a portion turned wet, no black, and a dark liquid spread through the sand. This blackness oozed from where his finger touched and formed a puddle. A tiny fountain then bubbled from the center, and the foul stuff expanded into a dark and strange-smelling pond.

Eugene closed his eyes again. A gust of wind raced through the valley. The black fountain slowed, then stopped.

The Roland of the Abbey knew magic existed, but he was in the dream realm. Sorcery, was it real? As real as my dreams? Even if Eugene set this up, and had a hidden tank of oil buried in the earth, how did the wind come up exactly when he wanted it to? I recalled what he said yesterday, . . . *you will learn to accept the reality of your situation . . . that or it will drive you mad.*

"Now," he said in his commanding voice, "I believe you grasp the fundamentals. I suggest for your first attempt you pick a reasonable objective."

"You want me to do something like that?" I pointed to the crude oil pond. "I can't."

"You do not have to manipulate the same forces. Pick your own. But you must try. It is the only way to prove you are Clay's son. If not . . ."

He allowed me the luxury of filling in the blank on my own. If he wanted, he could summon a hand of stone to crush and bury me, another body forever hidden in the desert.

"What are my choices? You mentioned earth and air, fire and water, are there others?"

"Of course, sorcery is limited by the rules I outlined, but the magics are only restricted by your knowledge and imagination. Any pairs of opposite forces will suffice: truth and illusion, life and death, light and darkness. Your options are virtually limitless."

"Maybe I should stick with what I know. I had two years of college biology. I'll try life and death."

"A strange first choice," he said, "and not one I have extensively experimented with. Yet it is as viable as any other. What do you plan to do?"

Good question. There was practically no life in this little corner of Hell. Plenty of death though. All that vegetation had been killed, then piled together, awaiting its transformation into a bonfire. That gave me an idea. "Could I use the death in those trees and restore some life to this valley?"

He shrugged. "I cannot say for certain. I would urge caution however, as there is one aspect of sorcery I failed to mention."

"Which is?"

"One of the benefits of magical manipulation is the abundance of energies for any task. Unfortunately, that is also the greatest danger. The most common mistake a young sorcerer can make is to conjure too much power. The more energy tapped for the magic, the greater the concentration required. If you recall the battery analogy, it would be as if you pulled too much current through the completed circuit. In sorcery, though, there are no circuit breakers to protect you. You could easily suck the life force from your body as you channel the energies of life and death."

"Or I could easily incinerate myself with fire magics, or crush myself using earth magics?"

"Yes," he admitted. "Every branch of sorcery has its inherent dangers."

I hesitated for a second. Life and death did sound absolute. As certain as my demise if I failed, or refused to even try. Did I really travel to Meredin, or was it only a dream? Now, with so much at stake, I was unsure. I grasped for a memory, some specific event that anchored my existence in that other realm, but the years at the Abbey slipped through my fingers. The harder I tried, the less I recalled.

The rubbing. Yes, the rubbing I took of the archway in the Oracle's tower. I still had it with me. It was the only thing that was truly mine, my sole possession of worth—that and one blue stone taken as a reminder of the glory of Sestos. Memories flooded back then, all linked, and all associated with one another.

I *was* there, sleeping in the mountain cavern. I could almost feel the cot beneath me.

Slightly more confident, I strode over to the mass of trees and weeds compacted into in a heap. Joshua trees, covered with long serrated needles from top to bottom and coated with layers of sand, composed the bulk of the pile. Dead plants, sage and creosote, and a few desert wildflowers were crushed underneath.

"Joshua trees," Eugene stated. "Not very attractive."

I did not let him dissuade me. This began to feel right. "What do I do now?"

"First," he said, "visualize the two forces in your mind. It would be better if you had a picture of the plant tissue, but use whatever image you can think of."

I called upon the Roland of the dream realm to help me. He had better powers of visualization and a higher quality imagination. Yet I did not summon him in his entirety. I retained a portion of me, the real Roland. I still needed the scientific knowledge of the tree's physiology. That was something my other self could not know.

I closed my eyes. The little biology I had years ago

provided me with a picture of the cells. Tiny chloroplasts produced energy; photons danced in a chemical soup; carbon dioxide reduced to cellulose; protons shuffled back and forth. Life.

"Next visualize the other force," Eugene said, sounding farther away, "the death within the plant."

This wasn't easy. Holding two images in my mind at the same time? No wonder I never *accidentally* caused magic to happen.

I tried to see the plant, how the lack of water dried up its interior, and how the machines ripped it from the earth. With no vegetation, the soil had eroded and left a lifeless rocky dirt. Oil seeped from below and further destroyed the natural processes with its sticky, suffocating presence. It was more than the lack of life I felt from the image; it was a dark, smothering thing. Death.

Still holding that grim vision, I imagined how this valley was in the past: a stand of cypress trees, birds building their nests there, small rivulets crisscrossing a field of grass, wildflowers blooming, and worms and insects burrowing into the dark loam.

A very peculiar feeling built within me. It was not easy to see both the images. Indeed, I wanted to hold on to the more pleasant one and discard the other. I had summoned some force, however, and I had to direct the energy that flowed through me. I discovered it was easier for the dream Roland to hold on to the picture of life, while the real Roland concentrated on the death. The flow felt like an electrical current, a slight tingle of power.

I focused on the image of life, the meadow. Somewhere in the background were the dead trees, but I shoved that image to one side and made it small and dim. The picture of life was clear. It grew larger and brighter: another tree, a black oak, and there, a nest of owls living within it, and in the field, water bubbling from a spring.

More energy flowed between the pairs of opposites, and the electrical sensation increased. It became painful. My hands and legs were filled with pins and needles, numb, yet sensitive to the flow at the same time.

Just at the edge of my awareness, I heard Eugene call to me, "Roland, not too much." He sounded a mile away now. "You are channeling too much energy into the enchantment. Remember to split your concentration equally between the two forces."

Yes, death. That was the image way back, nearly invisible in my mind. The picture of life was powerful, but I still had to direct the flow of the darker part of my two forces. I needed to shape the death, before it took a form of its own. Already I felt the dark power attracted to my life force, and a portion of it seeped in and chilled my body. I quickly shifted perspectives.

It was not a pleasant picture, those broken trees. I wanted to remove them from my imagination. In my mind's eye, I forced the trees to decompose. They turned gray about the tips, then mold and fungi covered them. I'd use the trees over, recycle them, use their deaths to refresh the land. The remainder of the summoned power, I channeled into the scene of decay. The Joshua trees collapsed into dust. The entire pile putrefied, rotted, and sank back into the earth whence it came.

Eugene shook me. He said something in the distance of my perception.

Slowly, I allowed both pictures to fade from my mind. I let the magical energies settle on both sides of the equation, newly balanced. I opened my eyes.

The dead trees were gone.

In their place a small patch of grass grew. No, not only grass, there were flowers too, just now rising from the soil. In a corner of the living area, tiny shoots of green poked through the earth. They were trees, small ones, but new trees. The soil was moist, darker and richer than the surrounding sand.

The growing slowed, but underneath, I sensed the force of death, the decomposed trees, and the life that fed upon them. How long it would last, or how far this tiny wilderness would grow I could not tell, but it certainly had changed. I had changed it.

Satisfaction pulsed through me. The magic worked!

That meant everything else, the families, the dreams, they were real too. I wasn't crazy. I was Roland of the clan Pritchard, a prince among the royal families of Meredin. I was a sorcerer.

"Outstanding," Eugene said, "absolutely outstanding, but dangerous. You manipulated far too much power. I do not know how you accomplished it, but I am impressed."

I allowed a grin to spread across my face.

Eugene saw this and his expression dropped. "One must always be cautious when working with magic," he warned. "I have known more than one sorcerer to die from their impatience. If you learn only one thing today, it should be this: when you cannot concentrate, do not use magic. Remember, the forces tend to cancel each other. More often than not, you become caught in the middle and canceled with them."

My happiness dropped one or two notches. I stopped smiling, at least outwardly.

Eugene was correct. I did feel the power of death hovering close to me, waiting to feed upon my life. This power was more dangerous than a loaded gun.

"Is everyone in the families a sorcerer?" I asked.

"Everyone who is genetically related. Your mother would not be able to use magic," he explained, "but if you had any children, they would inherit the ability." He then wiped the perspiration from his face with a clean handkerchief.

I again noticed how hot it was and suddenly felt ill.

"Come, you have earned a rest, and so have I."

I was weak and my vision dimmed. Was it the death that I absorbed, or did all sorcery drain you like this? I had plenty of questions for Eugene, but settled instead for sleeping on the dusty ride back to the mansion.

6

Sleeping was impossible. I did not care that the cot was too soft and sagged, but there were noises, voices, and a pounding that demanded my attention.

In my dream, I was too exhausted to do anything but stumble back to my room and fall asleep on that comfortable bed. That's probably why I was up early here.

I peeked over my wool blanket and saw Aesop hammering apart the box with clouds painted on the side, the source of the noise. He appeared like a storm god hurling his hammer against the calm blue sky in anger.

"I am pleased you are finally awake," he said. "I require assistance."

I felt and smelled like Phio's fish special, head and tail hung over each side of the cot. My new clothes were wrinkled from sleeping in them, and they carried the odors from yesterday's exertion.

"Take this." Aesop handed me a cup of steaming coffee.

I sipped and regretted it—hot acid and coffee grounds.

"It is not for you," he said with contempt. "Take it

out to Smoking Bear. She has been on guard duty most of the night while you slept.''

Guilt, that was a familiar emotion thanks to Hestor. I stomped outside. If I wanted to dissolve my stomach, I'd get my *own* cup of coffee.

My dream, rather the real world, proved to be extremely interesting last night. I remembered everything. It was as if I just closed my eyes, relaxed, and slipped into this realm. I was eager to test my new magical abilities, see if they worked as well in this realm as in the real one.

Smoking Bear stood a pace back from the tunnel's entrance, outlined in the predawn sky. The air was transparent to the west, leached of color while the sun climbed behind the mountains. Beneath us, fog covered the lake and the valley. I could not discern the small fishing village of Sestos.

Why were we bothering to post a guard at all? We were far from the village and concealed in a mountain cave. I seriously doubted that the Abbey would pursue Aesop after his display of pyrotechnics.

Smoking Bear turned when she heard me approach. Her eyes locked onto the tin cup in my hands. I stopped complaining to myself and handed her the deadly coffee. ''Can you use this?'' I asked.

''Thanks,'' she yawned, then took a sip, and a longer one, then drained the cup.

''Have you been up all night?''

''Most of it,'' she said. ''I got a few hours sleep, but Aesop woke me up. He's all fired up to get an early start. Said he had a bad dream.''

Aesop had a bad dream? As a member of the royal families, he too led a dual life. If he had a ''bad dream,'' that meant trouble. Perhaps there was a good reason to post watches, even here.

''Any more?'' she asked and handed the cup back to me.

''Let me go check.''

I went into the cave and returned with another cup of Hell's own brew.

Smoking Bear again drained it.

Cold tendrils of wind reached into the tunnel, and goose bumps ran across my arms. We were above the tree line, and over the cavern's entrance, a good deal of snow clung to the cliffs. I stomped my feet to get the blood circulating. How warm could Smoking Bear be after standing here all night?

"Let me get you some more coffee," I said, trying to hide my shivering.

I retreated into the warmer cavern and filled her a third cup. The fumes from the dark mixture were enough to wake me. I shuddered to think what it did to her insides. Again, I was curious if she and Aesop were married, or lovers, so when I handed her the cup I asked, "You and Aesop, you are not . . ."

"Not what?" she asked and sipped.

"Married?"

She coughed up a mouthful of swallowed liquid. "Gods, no!"

"Then you came on this expedition only to find the statue?"

"Yes, part of it's the statue," she said and wiped her mouth, "but it's an escape for me too. I have problems I'd like to avoid, and Aesop always has a dangerous excursion planned. There's usually a fight involved." A moment passed as she cradled the tin cup in her hands, extracting its warmth, then she added, "It takes my mind off things." She pulled her double blade out a few inches and dropped it back into its scabbard. "When I was younger, I needed no reason to go out on my own, but now things are . . . complicated." She looked back to the valley filled with a bright blanket of fog.

"What about you?" she asked, and handed her half-filled cup to me. "Why did you leave the Abbey?"

To be polite, I took a sip. It was not as bad as the first time, an earthy taste that warmed my insides.

"Aesop was correct when he called it a scholar's paradise," I told her. "Our libraries overflow with books, ancient art, architectural designs, everything of worth from the Golden Age . . . knowledge no one has seen in centuries.''

Smoking Bear listened to me, but her eyes scanned the sky. What was she looking for?

''Yet it was not enough for me,'' I said. ''I was too curious, too thirsty to see these wonders for myself. I believed the world would be just as it was in my books.''

''Are you sorry you came?''

''No, I am glad I can be of help to you and Aesop. Perhaps with this statue of yours, you might restore your lands as they were in the Golden Age, as they were in my books. I would like to have a part in that.''

She turned to me with a strange look on her face, confused. ''You sound like someone I knew a long time ago.''

From inside the cavern, Aesop shouted, ''Some assistance would be appreciated.''

The look of curiosity vanished from her face, and she flashed me a smile. ''He means you.''

She was different, warm and tough all at the same time. I did not want to leave her, but neither could I ignore Aesop.

Inside, I found him standing over a coil of silver metal, half his height and about a meter in diameter. In one hand he held a single loop of the same metal. With his thumb and index finger he brought the two together, and a bead of white-hot metal ignited where they touched. It was impossibly bright to look at, yet he stared directly at it, and rolled it back and forth between his two fingers. When the two pieces melted into one, he removed his hand. The spot cooled rapidly. It faded from pure white to blackened silver.

He looked up at me, and I swore I saw rivalry in his heated gaze. But that too faded. Was he jealous of me talking to Smoking Bear?

''You may assist me with the basket,'' he said. ''It is in need of repair.'' He walked to the back of the cavern, not waiting for my response, and I followed.

A large basket, tapered slightly at either end, lay on its side in the shadows. ''Observe,'' he said, then pointed, "here and here. These sections are frayed and must be made whole again."

"I do not know . . ."

"I will show you, once."

He removed a handful of cloth patches from a sack and strode to the campfire. A pot of viscous material that smelled like vinegar boiled next to the coffee. Aesop took the cloth and dipped it into the mixture. "Make certain the patch is soaked with this resin." He then pulled the steaming cloth out with his bare hands. "You must use a stick rather than doing it this way, I should imagine. Now, before it cools too much, but enough so you can handle it, stretch it over a damaged section." He did so. "Then smooth it out and allow it to harden." He wiped off the excess resin and repeated the process, applying another patch to the inner surface of the basket.

"I think I can do that," I said, "but why do we need such a large basket? Are we carrying something in it?"

"In a manner of speaking, yes." He sat down and poured himself the last cup of the coffee. "It is part of a balloon."

"A balloon? You mean a hot air balloon?"

He raised an eyebrow. "How is it you know of such devices?"

I shouldn't have known about hot air balloons. The Roland from the other realm knew, however. "There were records of these vehicles at the Abbey," I lied, "but I thought them to be only a legend."

"I see," he said, and gave me a suspicious look. "You had best get busy or such vehicles shall remain legendary."

That was close. I would have to watch myself in the future. I did not want the De Marcos to know I was a true dreamer, not with Eugene being my patron in the other world. I owed them both for saving my life; Eugene for rescuing me from Mexico, and the De Marcos for getting me off the Isle of Knowledge. How friendly would we all be if they knew I was associated with the other?

If not for the Bishop clan, my situation would be simpler. But with Eugene allied with them, and Morgan Bishop after the De Marcos' heirloom, I was in a sticky position at best. Was the friend of your enemy, your enemy also? I needed to find out how things worked in the royal families, but carefully.

I dipped three of the cloth patches into the boiling mixture and gingerly poked and prodded them with a stick until they absorbed the gooey sludge. One by one, I then applied them to the holes in the basket. I burned myself twice.

While I did this, Aesop unpacked a roll of silk and a large net from the crate. The silk he spread out on the floor of the cavern. It was a balloon with orange flames embroidered on a red field, not exactly a comforting image for a balloon (especially a balloon powered by a fire sorcerer). He then untangled the net and pulled the silk inside it.

How was he going to get hot air into that thing? And why were we setting the balloon up *inside* the cavern? I concentrated on fixing the basket, rather than bothering him with my questions. I might let on I knew more than an acolyte should.

It took me most of the morning to repair the basket. It might hold our combined weights. Never having flown in a plane before, let alone a hot air balloon, I would discover if I was afraid of heights once we were aloft.

Aesop attached a wooden spar to the front of the basket, then, onto this, a mast fitted into place. Together we raised the sail, a slender triangle of blue. I stepped back to admire our handiwork. It looked like a wicker boat.

Aesop warmed up to me as we worked together, and let whatever jealousy he felt fade. "The sail," he explained, "shall give us additional propulsion and the ability to steer the balloon. Of course, it will be impossible to travel into wind. The balloon's cross section is far too large for this tiny sail to enable us to tack."

He then told me how the hot air in the balloon was lighter than the surrounding cold air, and how it would rise up as a bubble through water.

I nodded, pretending to be fascinated by what I already knew.

"How do you plan to get the hot air inside the balloon?"

"Sorcery, air magics first, although I am not as skilled with that element as I am with fire." He glanced at the tattoos on his arm. "Once it is filled, then I shall heat the air within and we may leave."

I envisioned a blast similar to the one in the tunnel and could only speculate about the flame design on the balloon.

Aesop tied the metal coil to the basket's frame with a white braided rope. Asbestos? We then heaved the assembled basket onto one side and attached the balloon. From the netting, four slender cords hooked into place, one in each corner of the basket.

Aesop walked into the shadows at the far end of the cave, leaving the balloon fully assembled but lifeless on the stone floor. He turned a wooden wheel, which groaned in response. At the top of the cavern, twin doors parted to reveal the sun and a few wispy clouds above. Wind whistled through the entrance and up the hole in the ceiling.

Clever. He planned to take off within the cavern.

"Now, if you could give me a hand," he said, "I shall try to inflate this. I admit though, my air magics are a bit rusty . . ."

Smoking Bear jogged in and announced, "We have guests. You better look."

I dropped the section of silk I held and followed them out onto the cold mountain slope.

She pointed high into the sky.

I saw nothing but a patch of high clouds.

"Two of Morgan's pets this time," Aesop said, staring at the same clouds.

I then saw what he did, a creature flying in the distance. Perhaps there were two of them, as I discerned two snakelike heads. Flying snakes? That was impossible. It must be an optical distortion, warm air rising like a mirage.

"Demons," she said.

Demons? I knew the legends of these creatures. No two took alike, and all were deadly. When I translated *The Terror Chronicles*, I learned they were the original inhabitants of Meredin, here before man. Our two species warred for a thousand years before the Golden Age, then man destroyed them. They were supposed to be extinct. Evidently not.

"I shall ready the balloon," Aesop stated, then returned to the cavern.

"Good," Smoking Bear said, and removed her sword with an economy of motion. "I'll try to buy you some time."

"We are going up in a balloon with that thing flying around?" I asked.

"It's better than waiting here," she said. "Don't worry, when Aesop powers the balloon with his fire magics, he'll summon a storm to cover our trail. Just like the water that flooded the tunnel, the clouds will be attracted to his flames."

Of course, the water part of his magics. "Very well," I agreed. "What can I do to help?"

"Against that?" She shook her head. "Probably not much."

"What about your crossbows?"

Smoking Bear considered for a moment, then, "I'll load a few for you, but try not to shoot me by accident." She quickly loaded two bows, then flipped the safeties off. "Can you really handle these?" She was not being condescending. It was an honest question.

"I think so." I only wished I knew more sorcery to be useful. Although the weight of the crossbow felt reassuring, it was nothing compared to the power Aesop or Eugene might wield.

She loaded one more and set it by the cave entrance. Then from her own satchel she removed a vial of phosphorescent yellow. "Poison," she explained, "colored so there is no mistaking it for anything else." She placed her double bladed saber on her lap and removed a tiny screw from the tip. The two blades parted, and she slipped the glowing vial into a groove, then reassembled the blades.

"Let's see where they are now," she said.

We walked outside again, ready. It was not good news.

The demons were indeed close now, and I saw more details than I cared to. The flying creature *did* have two snake heads. Two fat triangles, each followed by sinewy twisting serpent body that merged into a giant bat. How could such an unaerodynamic creature fly? There was a rider mounted atop the snake-bat. He looked to be a man and carried no obvious weapons. He wore a great helmet that was formed from two metallic gold wings which spread to cover and protect his face.

I took cover in the entrance of the tunnel. Smoking Bear positioned herself a few meters ahead, blade out, waiting for the demons to close.

She did not wait long.

The bat folded its wings, coiled its two heads as if to strike, then plummeted toward her. The rider held the reins in one hand and reached out with the other as if he could touch her from afar.

I raised the crossbow and took aim. I would wait until the last moment to fire. The earth then shifted, rippled slightly, almost unnoticeable at first. Before I realized what it was, the ground heaved and tossed me outside the cavern.

A shower of snow cascaded onto me from the cliffs above.

Smoking Bear had also been thrown aside by the earthquake.

The demon bat struck the rocky slope where she had stood a fraction of a second before, barely missing her. Its wings beat against the ground as it pulled up, leaving a cloud of snow hanging in the air, a frozen fog.

From within the cavern, I heard Aesop curse.

I shook off the snow, picked the crossbow up, and fired.

The bat twisted out of the bolt's path. The right head snapped about and caught it with unbelievable speed.

I dropped the crossbow and retrieved another from the cave. My only chance to hit the thing would be when it got closer. I couldn't believe it dodged, then caught the bolt. This thing was fast.

The creature twisted in the air and dove again.

Smoking Bear stood. She braced herself and raised her sword above her head.

I waited and watched the falling demon, then aimed a meter above Smoking Bear, released the firing mechanism, and hoped. The missile landed solidly in the snake's left head, just below the eye. It did not slow it down a bit.

The bat slammed into Smoking Bear. Its claws lifted her off the ground, but only for a moment. She too had delayed her strike until the last second.

I heard the crack of bone and spotted a flash of yellow.

The demon screamed with an inhuman rage from both snake heads and raced skyward again.

Smoking Bear lay on the ground. Next to her, one of the bat's legs—cut clean through.

A thin line of the poison glowed on the underside of the bat as it struggled to regain altitude. It faltered, but managed to fly even with such a wound. Incredible.

I dropped the worthless crossbow and ran out to her. She lay in an unnatural position in the snow. There was little left of her right arm. The impact of the demon, together with her suicidal strike, had shattered it. Several places in her armor were pierced by shards of bone. I tried not to look at it and dragged her back to the cave.

The snakes screamed and again it dove. The rider laughed while they plummeted.

For a moment, I considered leaving her and making a break for the cavern, back to safety and the power of Aesop. He certainly would have no trouble dispatching these demons. So why was I still dragging her? What good did it do? We would both be slain, but I couldn't just leave her here, helpless.

I let her body rest in the snow and stood over her. In desperation, I prepared myself to summon whatever magic I could to defend us. My mind searched for some pair of life and death forces to tap into. I failed. All I could do was watch as the demons plunged closer.

A deep vibration shook my body. Was it the magical power I called upon, or was I shaking from fear? It turned out I was mistaken with both guesses.

A wall of powdery white fell in front of me. It folded back and extinguished the light and the life from my body.

Cold, dark, and unable to move. Was I dead?

A good rule to follow: if you can ask you're usually not. I knew I was still alive because Smoking Bear, or rather the warmth of Smoking Bear, was under me. One of the spikes from her shoulder armor dug into my ribs. I tried to shift, but above me the weight of a thousand snowballs crushed my body.

The warmth leaked from me, my breath slowed, and I began to fall asleep, forgetting who I was, and why I was here.

Far away in Arizona, at Eugene's mansion, I felt the weight of the down comforter on me, warm, soft, and white.

Warmth. Somewhere was warmth and wetness. Consciousness came first, then light broke through, and then heat.

Aesop pulled me out of the snow (his hands were hot, steaming), then Smoking Bear. He had melted his way through from the cavern entrance.

I sneezed and tried to stand closer to him as he radiated warmth.

He ignored me and inspected the body of Smoking Bear. "She will live," he said to himself. "But we must leave here immediately."

"What . . ."

"This is my doing," he said, turning to me angry. "I tried to fill the balloon too rapidly and lost control."

He wasn't really talking to me, but I understood what he meant nonetheless. He used air magics to get the balloon partially inflated. That explained the tremor, the uncontrolled earth magic. Then when he heated the air inside the balloon, he lost control of the paired forces of fire and water. In this case the water was snow, the snow that fell on us.

"It was a good thing the avalanche hit us," I told him, teeth chattering. "Smoking Bear and I were defenseless. She was already unconscious. The demons were about to finish us off."

"You mean I did not do this to her?"

"No, she waited until they were on top of her before she struck."

His painful expression disappeared. "Did she kill them?"

"I don't think so. The bat is wounded. One leg is cut off. The rider is undamaged though."

"Come, we must hurry. Demons are quick to recover from any injuries."

We carried her to the balloon. It was fully inflated and ready to go. And even under these circumstances, I could not help admiring the pattern of amber and yellow flames that licked the circumference of the balloon. From a distance it looked as if it were on fire.

We climbed in, cut the ballast, then lifted into the air. I unfurled the sail, and Aesop placed both hands on the metal coil. It glowed a dull red, orange, and finally, a brilliant yellow. I did not understand how he was able to touch it without burning himself. One of a myriad of questions I had yet to ask him about his sorcery.

The balloon slowly rose as the air warmed within it and provided lift. We drifted past the trap doors in the cavern ceiling and out into the cold open air. The sun cast a dim light, veiled by a set of darkening clouds in the west.

"Are you doing that?" I asked him, and pointed to the clouds.

"Yes," he replied, eyes closed. "The clouds will hide us and the wind will aid our escape." He then returned his attention to the coil.

Our sail caught the winds preceding the storm and the basket careened dangerously from side to side. This was definitely no elevator ride. I looked at the four cords that connected the basket to the balloon and hoped they held. They looked terribly thin.

Smoking Bear was unconscious. Her arm bled profusely. Could I repair the wound with my magic? I would need a pair of forces, life and death, as I did before in the valley. She was full of death, but what to use for the life portion of the paired forces? There was only Aesop (who was controlling the balloon) and myself. There was no place to direct the unwanted death magic except into my own body, and I admit that I was too much of a coward to attempt it.

I tried not to panic. OK, forget magic. What about first aid? I took a deep breath, relaxed, and tried to remember. The Roland from the real world knew what to do. First, I had to determine the extent of her injuries. She had more than one open fracture and a nasty-looking bruise on her forehead. One of the most important things I recalled: do not move the victim. Fine, already blew that.

I found a thick-bladed knife and used it to cut away the leather from her arm. The limb was remarkably discolored, looking like an overripe banana with a splash of blue thrown in. Two bones broke the surface of the skin. I did not touch them. Instead, I removed my shirt and applied pressure over the area to control the bleeding. I placed her arm on a coil of rope, elevated it, and hoped the bleeding would stop or slow.

"How is she?" Aesop asked.

I shook my head. "Her arm is shattered, and she sustained a blow to the head. I think I can get the bleeding under control."

He released the metal and looked for himself. The coil dimmed from brilliant yellow back to a dull silver, cold again.

"If we are in such a hurry, should you not be heating the air?"

"It is not wise. The more I warm the air, the more the storm intensifies. I want it to provide cover, but if it becomes too strong, it could tear the balloon apart." He paused and scanned the skies about us. "I have not seen the demons, yet."

I glanced at the wall of clouds behind us. The winds pushed the balloon ahead, but the storm still gained on our position. Lightning flashed within the great dark structure. The entire western sky was the color of coal and advancing on us.

Aesop tended the sail and occasionally glanced at Smoking Bear. If I did not know better, I'd say he looked at her lovingly. Was I jealous? They were probably siblings or cousins. What right had I to be jealous?

He noticed me watching him and said, "Keep a sharp eye out for anything unusual."

He meant the demons. I turned my back to him and examined the clouds below. The gusts from the storm had already pushed us to the far side of the mountainous valley. There was nothing below, no signs of pursuit, only reflective clouds. "We will need to gain altitude if you want to clear the mountains," I told him.

He nodded, lashed the sail in place, and touched the coil. The metal heated again, and its warmth was welcome on my body.

The clouds turned an inky and somber color. Within, lightning cracked but never touched the ground. These jagged fingers of electricity did not illuminate the sky; instead the light was instantly absorbed into the darkness of the storm.

Another bolt of lightning. I saw the flying demon's silhouette. How had it recovered so rapidly from losing its leg? They vanished, again lost in the storm. Did they see us? I'd bet money on it.

"The demons," I informed Aesop. "Below and to the south."

He turned and squinted. "Turn the sail about," he shouted over the wind. "Bring us into the storm."

"Are you crazy? If the storm doesn't tear the balloon apart, the demons certainly shall."

"Do it, Roland. It is the only chance we have. We cannot escape such a creature in this craft. We must battle it or lose it in the storm."

I agreed, reluctantly, and changed course. The sail protested when I brought it about, flapping in the wind. It did little to slow our progress, just enough for the storm to overtake us. The distance between the balloon and the opaque wall of clouds then closed to nothing. We were enveloped.

Inside the thunderhead, seeing was impossible, even within the basket. Aesop poured on the heat. Through the haze, the coil heated to a white flash, outlined in a halo of mist. I heard him mutter about blackbody radiation and running out of quantum states, but I ignored that. I listened instead for a clue to the location of the demons through the winds and clouds. All I heard was thunder; all I saw were the impenetrable curtains of gray.

The frenzied air currents forced the basket up and down recklessly. I grasped the sides with both hands and hoped Smoking Bear was secure.

A light filtered through the mist. Had we gone above the storm? No, this light originated from *beneath* the balloon. A hole, a few meters across, opened through the clouds and revealed the landscape below. At the other end of the tunnel, through the mist, I spied the mounted demon, his hand outstretched as I had seen him do before.

He motioned with that hand and the hole widened near him. The tube through the clouds expanded, racing from his position to ours. A portion of the distortion overlapped our basket. That part, one of the corners I repaired, boiled away along with the clouds. He obliterated it with a single gesture!

Had we been a meter closer, the center of the basket and the balloon would be gone. We would have been gone.

Aesop cursed, and the coil ignited with an unbearably intense light. The heat from it blistered my back, which minutes ago was nearly frozen.

There was a pause while nothing happened, then the balloon overcame its inertia and shot straight up. My stomach fell to the valley below.

The cables that held the basket to the balloon

stretched and creaked from the stress. I heard the damaged wicker tear further from the strain. Our basket deformed from the acceleration and threatened to spill us to our deaths.

Aesop was an outline now in the blaze from the coil. About us the storm intensified. The mast snapped and our sail fluttered away. Lightning and darkness increased as the magical energies flowed from the element of fire to that of water unchecked. I could no longer watch the painful light of the coil, nor could I hear anything but the roar of the storm unleashed. Beyond the balloon were walls of solid blackness, the fury of lightning. I crawled to the bottom of the basket to shield the unconscious Smoking Bear from the weather.

Without warning, the sounds ceased and the natural brilliance of the sun replaced the flashes of lightning and the hot radiance of the coil.

We made it through the storm.

Aesop collapsed next to me, exhausted. The upper portion of his tunic was gone, burnt away, although he did not have a single blister. His tattoos were alive and seething with activity. Flames of permanent ink crawled across his arms and over his chest, glowing with dull reds, eerie greens, and ebon blacks. I felt heat emanating from them.

The coil was gone.

"How is the basket?" he asked after a moment.

I cautiously inched closer to the destroyed end of the basket. There was a hole about a meter in diameter in the wicker. Five separate rips radiated from it and made one entire side of the basket dangerously weak. "It might hold for a while," I told to him, "but it will never survive another storm."

Through the hole, I glimpsed the storm beneath us, driven to an unnatural state. Lightning flashed continuously. Each cloud seemed to have a personal vendetta against the sky, desperately attempting to shatter it. They churned, moving faster than I thought clouds could. More charcoal thunderheads poured into the valley from the east to add to the elemental battle, and to balance the forces the fire sorcerer had unbalanced.

Uncertain of the strength of the basket at this end, I crawled back to Aesop and Smoking Bear.

Even this high above the storm, the winds blew with a fierce intensity. We were far past the mountainous valley, far from the Abbey, and hopefully, far from the pair of demons. I watched the skies below us but could not locate our pursuers.

We had lost them, for now.

7

I awoke early in this realm, because I exhausted myself in the other searching for the demons. We never saw them again. Aesop insisted I rest, and assured me he would wake me the instant he spotted them. Smoking Bear was feverish, still unconscious, her arm swollen to gross proportions. That bump on her forehead didn't look any better either. I needed to help her, so I slept.

I got up, dressed, and wandered into the garden, into the hedge maze in which I had seen Eugene and Sabrina yesterday. There was no one here, save the gardener, and he ignored me. I entered the maze and lost my way while I thought of a way to save Smoking Bear's arm. First, I needed to locate a source of life to attempt a magical healing. Next, I required a picture of what a normal arm looked like. I knew there were two bones in the forearm, and dozens in the hand. That was the extent of my medical expertise.

This hedge maze was no simple path. Usually, one can solve these puzzles by picking one wall and following it completely through. Not so, I soon discovered with this particular one. The shrub walls were only waist high. I could jump them and get out if I had to, but that would be admitting defeat. Tiny white thorns, small clusters of dense leaves, along with my pride, were as good as walls of stone.

I floundered through the maze for half an hour, and only got myself deeper into the labyrinth. The gardener came in and rescued me. He told me few people could find their way through the maze. His serious tone almost made me laugh. Almost. I asked him where the library was. He gave me directions, then returned to pruning his lilac trees.

Past a white-domed entryway, through a hall filled with the morning sun, and over the faded details of tan and red Persian rugs, I walked. Eugene's desert estate was simple in design, but nevertheless elegant, ornate in just the right places, with a gold-framed oil painting of a girl on a swing, and opposite that a porcelain vase covered with microscopic cracks. To my left was the library. Three of its walls held the dark leather spines of books, and a ladder on tracks provided access to the topmost shelves. The fourth wall contained a grand display case filled with crystals and other geological oddities.

There was no time for browsing, however. I needed to find a specific book. I searched though geophysical texts, chemistry books, and other such stuff, then discovered what I wanted, *Grennford's Anatomy and Physiology*.

I sat at the reading table, which was a single piece of fossilized wood streaked with the lines and knots of a long dead tree, and scanned the old text. I found a cutaway view of the human arm. There, in as much detail as I could stomach, was the architecture of the bones, the muscles, the ligaments, and the connective tissues. With this picture I had a blueprint to repair Smoking Bear, provided I found an appropriate source of life to fuel my sorcery.

I looked up, startled, when I heard the sound of china set upon the stone table. Eugene sat across from me, yawning, his tea steaming in wide bone china cup and saucer.

"You are up early," he said, then yawned a second time. "I assume that means all is not well in the Meredin?"

"Yes," I answered, "we were attacked yesterday and barely escaped. One of my comrades is seriously wounded." I glanced to the open book. "Two demons pursue us even now."

"Demons?" He looked surprised. "Are you positive they are demons?"

I frowned and nodded.

He matched my frown, then whispered, "Morgan. He is the only one proficient at summoning and controlling such creatures. But why would he attack you? He knew I was searching for you, protecting you . . ." He struggled with that thought for a moment and tapped his fingers on the table, then asked, "Are you in immediate danger?"

"I don't know," I admitted. "We may have lost them. I believe we are in the Nomious Hills or near them."

Eugene's eyes widened when he heard how far we had traveled. I made a note to limit what information I revealed to him, at least until I knew if he and the De Marcos were enemies or friends.

"I shall contact Morgan immediately and see what this is all about." His voice, that smooth baritone, contained a touch of anger, some outrage, and a generous helping of confusion. "There is a chance the demons act of their own accord." He said this more to himself than me.

He waited for me to offer more information, and when I said nothing he continued, "Now that we have confirmed that you are a true dreamer, and part of our bloodline, there are things you should know about your father, his political alliances, his friends, and his enemies. More lessons in sorcery shall follow, but it appears that this information may be more important given your situation."

I pushed the book aside. "Why should I care who my

father's enemies and allies were? That was twenty years ago. Can't I stay neutral?"

"No," he stated flatly. "Because you are a Pritchard, the political lines have been drawn for you. If you wish, you may go against such traditions, but your family's enemies may not necessarily honor your choices—as you have seen from the failed attempt on your life."

"That's ridiculous. You mean I must honor the alliances and feuds of a man who has been dead for twenty years? That makes no sense." It made sense, but I didn't like it. How else could I explain the killing of Sam? Someone wanted me dead, and for no other reason than revenge.

"These blood wars have been waged for generations," Eugene explained. "The hatreds and lusts for revenge are not easily quelled. Not only have you inherited the ability to dream, and the power of sorcery, but also your family's enemies and allies. You cannot walk away from it so easily."

I sighed. "Can you explain to me how this all started?"

"I can only tell you what I know. Clay Pritchard was a secretive man, and while we were friends, he never revealed the details of his political schemes." He sipped his tea. "It began with your father's father, your grandfather Horace, who was a great sorcerer, skilled in the magics of stasis and change."

Horace? I had seen his name before. Where? The other Roland recalled something . . . too bad I couldn't get back to the Abbey and look the name up in the central library. Another clue to this puzzle would be welcome.

"Horace revenged an old dishonor when he stole an item of great value from the Francisco clan. I never knew the specifics of the encounter, but the Franciscos rallied against him in an attempt to retrieve it. Horace panicked and went into hiding, but before he did so, he passed the Pritchard family heirloom on to your father."

"Family heirloom?" Aesop told me all the families had one of these relics from the Golden Age. It had never occurred to me that my family had one also.

"Forgive me," Eugene said, "a family heirloom is an ancient device capable of magics no mortal could produce. They are extremely rare." He looked to the watch on my wrist. "That is your family relic, the Cartaga you wear."

"My watch?"

"Part of the relic. The real magic was contained within the band of leather. When I first saw you, I only detected the faintest traces of that power in the watch. Without the band, I am afraid the Cartaga has little value."

I touched the heavy gold. There was something there that felt like electricity, no more than a feathery sensation. Eugene was wrong when he said it had no value. It was the only link to my past, my father and family.

"With Horace gone," he said, "it fell to your father to take up his battles with the Franciscos. He was successful, and eradicated the entire clan."

"He killed the whole family? What kind of man was he?"

"You must understand, Roland, if Clay had not removed the six members of the Francisco family, they would have murdered him. As it was, he merely postponed his demise for a year before allies of the Franciscos avenged them . . . and who they were is unknown to me."

"What happened to the rest of my father's watch? The band?"

"Gone. That is why you must look for it immediately."

"What does it do? How does it work?"

He shrugged. "No one knows. Your father never discovered how to operate it, else he might be alive. You must dig into your family's past and find out what happened to it."

"You mean my grandfather didn't tell him how it worked?"

Eugene smiled. "Relics do not come with instruction manuals. It often takes years of research to learn how they operate." He paused, frowned, and added, "That, or you can seek out one of the ancients, but that is fraught with perils of a different nature."

"If I can't use it, why the urgency to find it?"

"Merely possessing your family heirloom may cause your enemies to reconsider their actions. If you do manage to find it, I shall provide you with a safe haven so you may discover its secrets. Until then, you will only be a target for your father's enemies . . . your enemies."

I sighed again. What were my choices? I could stay here under the protective wing of Eugene (whom I trusted, but not absolutely because of his alliance with Morgan) or I could go out on my own. Perhaps it wasn't such a bad idea to ask Hestor a few questions, see if she knew anything about Dad and his missing watchband.

"I don't see any harm in looking for it," I agreed. "Besides, I need to check in on my mom."

"Excellent, I shall make arrangements for us to fly there this afternoon."

"With all due respect, Eugene, it might be better if I saw her alone. In her state of mind, I don't think I'd get any useful information from her if she had to cope with meeting you." After her reaction to his letter, what would she do if she met him in person? Burn the hospital down?

"Very well," he said, "but consider taking someone with you, as the other clans know of your existence. Sabrina would be a wise choice. She is an experienced sorceress and well versed in the intricacies of family politics."

Sabrina? Yes, I would like to get to know her, but hadn't Eugene warned me away from her yesterday?

"OK, I'll consider it. One other thing . . ."

"Anything."

"Could I borrow some cash for a taxi?"

"I shall see to that immediately."

"Thanks, Eugene. If there is any way I can repay all you've done for me . . ."

"There is," he said and set his tea down. "A day will come when you and I may not be on friendly terms.

This is the nature of family politics. I would have you remember my favors at that time to temper your judgment of me.''

I almost outright denied his prediction. Yet, with all the Machiavellian maneuvering I'd seen in such a short time, who was to say?

He got up. ''But, I see I have interrupted you. Please go on with your studies.'' He started to leave, then added, ''I hope your friend recovers from his wounds.''

I wound my watch a few times. It felt reassuring. ''Yeah, so do I.''

He left me to study the diagram of the arm, but all this talk of Clay, of magic, and of politics kept surfacing in my thoughts. I summoned the concentration of the other Roland to help me focus on the text. He had mastered harder subjects and by candlelight no less! This could be no more difficult than deciphering a passage from *The Terror Chronicles*.

I memorized the anatomy and went on to learn how the skin and fatty tissues were structured. I had to get this right. I did not wish Smoking Bear to be deformed, or worse, killed by a mistake on my part. After a while, my eyes grew heavy and my mind saturated.

I took the book with me, returned to my room, showered, then vacillated whether or not to take a nap. Sleep no longer represented rest, though, but a journey back to the balloon and whatever dangers were there. I stayed awake and packed.

There was a quiet tap at my door and it opened. It was Sabrina.

''Am I interrupting?''

As soon as I saw her, I felt a tidal pull, an attractive force, and a touch of static. I resisted this magnetism, fought back my adrenaline, and controlled my senses. ''No,'' I replied. ''I was just leaving.''

She looked different today, less businesslike, more relaxed. Her hair was down, slightly past her shoulders, blond, a few streaks of brown and bleached ivory. If she wasn't so pale, I'd have guessed she spent a good deal of time in the sun.

She entered, sat down on the bed next to me, and crossed her legs. "I am not accustomed to men standing me up," she said. "It has happened only once before. Nevertheless, I shall forgive you as I understand yesterday you exhausted yourself with your first sorcery."

"I see there are few secrets around here." Eugene must have told her. I didn't understand his behavior. First, he warned me to stay away from her, then he suggested I take her with me.

"That is true," she said and smiled. "The families love to gossip. We thrive on any tidbit of information about one another."

I avoided her gaze as I put a few dress shirts, still in their wrappers, into a traveling bag. They'd be wrinkled, but at least they were clean.

"Must you depart so soon?" she asked.

"I'm afraid so. My mom is sick and I must see her."

"This may be terribly presumptuous of me, but would you allow me to accompany you? I'd be disappointed if you left before we had a chance to chat."

"I don't know. I'll be seeing my mother and she's not especially social. I'd hardly call this trip a vacation." I forced myself to concentrate on packing and not look at her. She affected me, magically or naturally, and definitely clouded my better judgment. She was part of the Bishop clan; I couldn't allow her to come with me. Her family was responsible for the two demons sent after the De Marcos.

"I appreciate your loyalty to family," she replied and inched closer to me, "but you need my protection and my advice. Eugene told me of your superior magical abilities."

"Superior abilities?"

"The meadow you created in the oil fields."

"I would hardly call it a meadow. It's just a small patch of grass."

"Then you have not seen it recently? The 'small patch of grass,' as you call it, covers several acres now." She spread her hands over the down comforter to demonstrate, leaning forward in the process.

I could not help looking at her hands, delicate, and perfectly formed. Again the emotional madness surfaced. I battled it back and won, then returned to my packing.

"Although its rate of growth has diminished, it continues to swallow more and more land. Eugene has a team of biologists there right now to study it." She let that sink in. "You have a great talent, like it or not."

"OK, let's say I have talent, all the more reason for me to go on my own. I can take care of myself."

"On the contrary," she said, "it is because you are capable of such power that you must take me with you."

"I don't understand." I stopped and turned to face her. It was a mistake. Although there were no flashes of heat or passion, her eyes had a hypnotic quality to them. I lost my train of thought and carelessly tossed my apprehension aside.

"The more power you control," she explained, "the more likely you are to mess things up. To be successful at this magic business, you must concentrate on several things at once and have intimate knowledge of your subject. It can be overwhelming for a beginner."

That was true. Even Aesop lost control filling his balloon, covering us in an avalanche. He saved us, but nearly killed us in the process.

She continued, "Let me go with you. I can tutor you in some short cuts and get to know you all at the same time."

Should I take her? Maybe . . . There was no basis to trust her, especially after the unusual circumstances of our first encounter, and especially since she belonged to the Bishop family. On the other hand, she was a stunning woman, and I found myself deeply attracted to her, although that could be distracting. But perhaps I could turn her family alliance to my advantage, and find out where the Bishops stood with respect to the other families. She would certainly be more accessible than Eugene. I couldn't think of any other disadvantages, just a soft tinkling deep at the base of my skull: a muffled fire alarm screaming to be noticed. I ignored it.

"All right," I said, "I'd like very much for you to come with me. Who knows? It may be fun. Why don't you pack and meet me out front in twenty minutes."

"That's better." She smiled. On her way out, she leaned over and kissed my cheek, a polite cousins' kiss. Her heat washed over me, and the fringes of my vision blackened. "You won't regret it, cousin."

Somehow I thought I just might.

Her perfume lingered.

I stuffed my new shirts and two pairs of slacks into the small bag, then went to call a cab. I stopped and glanced through the window. Sabrina pulled around front in a low green car. It was an antique convertible Jaguar with the top rolled back. I always wanted one of those. I hung up, grabbed my small bag, and went to meet her.

A large straw hat covered her head, tied in place with a sea green scarf. She wore a thin white dress that moved of its own accord in the morning breeze, and white gloves that covered the last bit of her flesh from the sun. All that she needed was a parasol, and Sabrina would look like a Southern belle from the turn of the century. She bore a strong resemblance to the girl I had seen this morning in the painting by the library.

"Would you like to drive or shall I?" she inquired.

"I'll drive, if you don't mind."

"Be careful," she warned. "The clutch is touchy."

We drove off, and she was right about the clutch. I ground the gears into second, then back into first and halted.

"Here," she said, and set her hand over mine on the gearshift, "the order of the gears is reversed from the American standard." She shifted through the sequence, forcing my hand as she went. Her hand remained on mine a moment longer than was called for, then she withdrew.

What would it feel like to lace my fingers through hers? To hold her and kiss her? I could feel the warmth of her flesh even through her gloves. Stop, I told myself, this was no way to be thinking about a woman who was my cousin. Yes, but how far removed? First cousin, second, or further?

To clear my head, I double-checked the map Eugene had given me to get to the hospital. It would take a day, maybe less in this car. I decided to take the coastal route.

"Before I forget," Sabrina said, "Eugene wanted me to give this to you." She handed me a thick envelope with a gold yin-yang embossed on it. "He had to leave this afternoon to track down my uncle." She said "my uncle" like someone might say "that roach." Interesting.

Inside was a substantial amount of cash, all large bills, and three credit cards. Two days ago, holding a pile of money like this would have made me ecstatic. Now it was just paper. Strange how a few attempts on your life changed your outlook.

"If it's all right with you," I said, "I'd like to make a detour, and take a look at the oil field I was in yesterday."

"Tell me, was that *really* your first attempt at magic?"

"Yes. I'm surprised you didn't manage to pry all the information about me from Eugene."

She blushed, then asked, "Why did you wait until now to practice sorcery?"

"I've been . . . away for a long time, isolated from the families."

We rolled onto the road and away from the mansion in the desert. Already heat rose from the asphalt in wriggling lines of convection.

"I only ask," she said, "as it is unusual for a dreamer to discover his magical talents so late in life. Most family members begin their instruction early, lest they stumble onto the power accidentally. It can cause all sorts of havoc." She removed her hat and let the wind blow her hair back. Her neck was muscular, near statuesque perfection in form. I had to actively concentrate on driving.

"Do you believe, then, I'm at a disadvantage for starting so late?"

"In a way yes, and in a way no. You were born with

whatever abilities you have. The amount of magical power you manipulate remains constant, fixed by genetics. It's both a blessing and a curse when a child demonstrates superior abilities. It means more to control, more of a chance to be harmed by one's own magics." She brushed a lock of hair from her face. "My mother died by sorcery—just lost her concentration."

"I'm sorry."

"It happened a long time ago. Don't concern yourself with it."

We bumped along the road until it broke apart into dirt and gravel, then she said, "Everyone needs to practice, though. Most of us have our entire lives to develop strategies and tricks to balance the magics. You need to master those quickly to survive in the families. Take this turnoff here."

I did my best to drive slowly and not get dirt inside the car or on Sabrina. We passed the oil wells, then over a hill and into a green valley. But this was not the same place Eugene brought me. I must have taken the wrong road.

"Stop the car," she said.

"This isn't the place."

"But it is," she corrected me. "See, over there, that is Eugene's new well."

I noticed a series of stems and valves stuck into the ground, capping the spot where Eugene had squeezed the crude oil to the surface. She was correct. It was the right place, but it was changed.

The trees that were hardly saplings yesterday, now stood taller than me, and birds nested in their arms. Knee high grass covered the field, and only stopped near the edge of Eugene's well. And flowers! Flowers were everywhere. The land was completely transformed . . . altered by me? A breeze flowed over the grass and made it undulate like a sea of green.

"Look over here"—she got out of the car—"these blossoms. I heard Eugene's biologists claim they'd never seen the species before." She picked one and handed it to me.

"But I didn't even see these flowers in my vision," I said examining it. It had white petals that darkened to a royal purple center. A single stamen, covered with silky pollen, bobbled about the center. I smelled their fragrance; it reminded me of freshly cut grass and lemon peel, not what I expected. "How did I dream these things up?"

"It is possible you produced a new species from your subconscious."

"If you don't mind," I said and presented her with the flower, "I'll name them after your blue eyes and call them Sabrina's Passion."

"Thank you," she said, accepting it and blushing slightly. "I don't think anyone has ever named a flower after me."

Her smile fired off a pulse of pleasure in my brain, a rush of heat and excitement.

We wandered into the field to further explore my enchantment. It was just as I had pictured it in my mind the other day. Under a large rock, a spring bubbled forth, and carved rivulets through the grass. Tiny black fish darted into the shadows of the creek when we approached. Part of me was in this meadow; I absorbed part of the death here, and gave it a fraction of my life force.

Sabrina slipped her arm through mine. "It's wonderful," she said. "You have the potential to become a great sorcerer."

It would be easy to stay here, easy to waste the afternoon walking with her, but I forced myself to recall the reason for our journey. "We better continue," I said, wanting an excuse to feel the rush of wind on my skin again. "By the way, you never mentioned what sort of magic you practice."

"My sorcery is more subtle. I think it would be better to explain later, when you understand more."

Just like that, I let it drop. I wanted to ask her more but something restrained me. Was this part of her magic? No warning bells, though; they had long ago been turned off.

We drove away from the mysterious field of Sabrina's Passion. I'd come back later, alone, and attempt to discover how I had accomplished this.

She wove the flower into her hair, looking like a foreign princess, exotic, then asked, "Did you say you were married?"

"Married? Me? No, I'm too young."

"I don't think so. Would it surprise you to know that I have been married twice?"

I raised an eyebrow, but wasn't really surprised. "Are you married now?"

"No, my last marriage soured me on the possibility of ever doing it again." She paused, then, "Are you involved with someone?"

This line of questioning reminded me of a conversation one might have with a new and jealous girlfriend. I didn't mind, though; ever since I left college I had no one to discuss such things with. "There was one girl," I admitted. "I was serious about her for a time."

"Was?"

"She wrote me every day like clockwork, and for a time, I responded."

"Then what happened?"

"My life was full of problems. I didn't want to drag her into it all, so I returned her letters less frequently, then stopped altogether. The last thing I got from her was a birthday card a few months back."

"Are you going to pursue her now?"

"I don't think so. In my situation, anyone I became involved with could be threatened by the other families." Look what happened to Sam and that was only an accident.

"Yes," she whispered. "I have encountered that before. Turn here; we can catch the highway."

The desert ran up to the hills; grapevines replaced the creosote bushes along the roadway. Small ranches and farms appeared in the countryside, no order to their placement, traditional rather than planned. By afternoon, we reached the coast. The sea breeze, full of unfamiliar smells, brought with it a freshness that the desert lacked.

I decided now would be as good a time as any to try my luck and find out more about her family, so I said, "I have heard many things of your clan, especially Morgan."

"Morgan," she scowled. "All anyone can talk about is Morgan. He is a sloppy sorcerer and worse at diplomacy. I apologize, but he is the black sheep of our clan. No one likes the man, but he is family and, therefore, tolerated. I hope you shall not judge the rest of us based on his nefarious reputation."

"You mean your family doesn't necessarily support him? I thought all the royal families stuck together."

"Is that what Eugene told you?" She laughed once. "If we stood behind Morgan through half his bungled exploits, our name would be ruined."

"I just assumed . . ."

"Rule one in family politics: never assume anything from a relative—you'll live longer."

This was good and bad news. The good news was that Sabrina was not absolutely linked to Morgan. She was therefore a potential ally. I liked the thought of that. The bad news was the political connections between the families were much more tangled than I had originally perceived. Only in the grossest sense was it family against family; it was more like every man for himself.

The sun was red and touched the ocean when she said, "Just ahead is a pleasant resort. If you wish, we can rest this evening and get an early start in the morning."

Yes, I was tired after the day's drive, and I wanted to be as fresh as possible for my encounter with Hestor. I pulled into the parking lot and killed the engine. The resort sat on a cliff overhanging the ocean. It was supported by long concrete and steel legs that extended to the beach below. If I read the map correctly, the hospital was less than an hour away. Perfect.

I unloaded my bag and the smaller one Sabrina brought (although it was heavier), and lugged them into the lobby.

"Two rooms," I said to the clerk.

"Please," interrupted Sabrina, "two adjoining suites."

I started to object to the cost then recalled Eugene's gift. Certainly it would be expensive, but heck, it wasn't even my money. I pulled one of the credit cards from the envelope and made sure the clerk noticed the pile of cash. He accepted the platinum credit card, then called for the bellboy.

Our rooms, at the very top of the resort, provided me with an unwanted view of the ocean. After my balloon ride, the last thing I wanted was a high panoramic view.

The bellboy dropped my bag on the bed and asked if he could do anything else for me. I'd almost forgot to tip him. Usually I neglected this, as I was dirt poor. This time, however, I felt obliged, as I had all that money on me. I opened my wallet: only the hundred was in there. The envelope contained no bills less than a fifty.

Sabrina walked in from her suite. "The rooms are adequate," she said, "but I shall require an extra set of towels, a bowl of fresh fruit, and coffee immediately." She handed him a folded hundred and he jumped to carry out her orders.

"I always like to stay at this place," she said, strolling out onto the balcony. "Reminds me of home."

My suite had two rooms, a spacious bathroom, and, of course, the wide balcony. Sabrina disappeared onto the balcony outside; I assumed that this was how our rooms adjoined.

I reclined on the bed and closed my eyes. It would be easy to fall back into old habits, eating in front of the television, drifting off to sleep. Maybe I should unpack first, unwrap those shirts so they would have a chance to unwrinkle. I dumped the contents of my bag onto the bed. The anatomy book, borrowed from Eugene's library, spilled out among my clothes.

It was a good old book. A first edition with genuine hand-stitched binding, hand-drawn plates too. It reminded me that I had much to study tonight; it reminded me that I couldn't fall back into my old, comfortable habits. I was a prince of the dreaming realms with responsibilities and friends in need of my help.

I exhaled and lay facedown on the bed, opened the book, and read to gain further insights into the mechanics of life. It frightened me that tonight I would work magic on a person. The field was one thing; if I messed up, it was no big deal. If I failed with Smoking Bear, she could lose her arm or even die. I doubted Aesop would be pleased if that happened.

Sabrina reappeared upon the balcony and all hopes of concentrating vanished. She entered and left the sliding glass door ajar. Behind her, I heard the rhythmic ocean. A shadow of the feeling generated at our initial meeting lurked there. I wasn't sure she magically caused it, but I steeled myself against the sexuality that exuded from her anyway.

"Thanks for the help with the bellboy," I said in a hopeless attempt to discuss another subject.

She shrugged and sat on the bed, not too close, but not too far away from me. She had changed into a revealing silk shirt the color of the ocean at night. Her eyes fell to the book opened on the bed, then she asked, "Are you in trouble?"

"Is it obvious?"

She smiled, "That book, I've seen it before. It's used in desperate times by desperate people. Funny that there's never been a doctor in any of the families."

"As long as you know, yes. A comrade of mine is wounded . . . by a demon."

"That is serious," she said in a not-so-serious tone. "Normally wounds inflicted by those creatures *never* heal."

Never? I hoped Smoking Bear's bones broke from the impact, not the creature rending her. I replayed the scene again in my mind. It happened too fast, a blur, then she was down. "I still must try."

"Noble of you." She inched closer to me. "I happen to know a few things about demons. Things that might help you and your wounded friend."

"Might?"

"You are refreshingly new at this, aren't you? Don't

you know that no one in the families does anything for
free? Not even Eugene. He has helped you now only to
harvest favors from you in the future.''

I refused to believe that, but listened nonetheless. If
this was the way others within the royal families operated, I had to learn.

"OK," I said, taking the bait, "what *do* you know
about demons?''

Her eyes widened, and in a whisper she told me,
"Theirs is an alien intellect. Demons have the ability to
possess those with weak minds. They can split their essence, place it within a living or inanimate object, and
thereby be in two places at the same time. They are both
magically and physically potent . . . And they are never
to be trusted.

"But most important for you," she said and smiled,
"they have secret names. Knowing this name gives you
the power to influence a particular demon—not any
great power—but it may listen to you before it eats
you."

Her perfume, heavy and dark, reached me. I unthink-
ingly took a deeper breath to sample more of her fragrance, wild orchids and honeysuckle. "I assume the
demon who wounded your comrade is still alive?" she
asked. "And perhaps hunting you? If you describe it for
me, I may know its name.''

"There are two creatures," I said sitting up, trying to
think straight. "The first looks human, but he wears a
gold helmet that obscures his face. The second is a huge
bat with a pair of snakes in place of its head." I held
my hands up to mimic the shape of the creature.

She considered for a moment. "The rider, I do not
know him, but the bat creature, his name I do know.''

"Then tell me. I could save my friend's life—my life
for that matter.''

She leaned over the bed and closed the distance between us. The warmth I felt from her was natural, nothing magical about it.

I drew her to me, and we joined in a protracted kiss.
Her touch was fire and consumed my mind and soul.

Past the balcony, the ocean crashed against the beach to match the surge of blood within me.

The anatomy book fell from the bed.

"Later," she whispered.

8

A gentle rocking, back and forth, lulled me to sleep. A tearing sound I heard. I opened my eyes. I was in the balloon again, not embracing Sabrina under cool sheets and listening to the ocean a universe away. That sound was the basket ripping, damaged by the demon. An awesome power that: to gesture and make matter vanish. What pairs of opposite forces could cause that?

Aesop clung to the snapped mast, still searching the clear skies for our pursuers. The sail was gone, so our craft was at the mercy of the native winds.

"Don't you ever sleep?" I asked, then yawned.

"I would like nothing more than to sleep as much as you," Aesop replied, "but someone had to keep us aloft, and it was clearly not you. Please check on Smoking Bear's condition for me."

I crawled over to her. The bleeding had stopped, but her arm was still swollen and bruised. There was a faint odor of sickness about her. "Her pulse is strong," I offered as a bit of good news. "She could be in worse shape."

"If infection sets in, we may have to remove her arm."

Her arm . . . I knew, or thought I knew, how to repair it. If only I had the anatomy book with me to be certain. "If you set us down, I might be able to do more for her."

"Down?"

"Yes, down," I insisted. "Aside from Smoking Bear, this basket will not last much longer." I pointed to the torn section. The hole was twice its original size, and half the basket sagged. "The part the demon destroyed will certainly unravel if we continue."

His brows furrowed at my insistent tone, but he nodded, then looked over the side for a place to land. "These are the Nomious Hills," he informed me. "The remains of the Sartesh Empire should not be far from here."

Remains? I knew historically that the Sartesh Empire was a place of learning. Sorcerers and religious men, shamans and prophets all gathered there. I cautioned myself, however, that my perceptions of the world were centuries old. The Sartesh Empire could be no more than a village now, as Sestos was.

Our balloon, unaided by Aesop, slowly sank. Black dots grew into boulders; vast stretches of sand with crisscrossing tracks of water-eroded scars rose to meet us. With his hands raised, he gave one final burst of heat to cushion our landing. Smoking Bear was jostled about on the bottom of the basket, unknowing and unconscious.

These rolling plains that extended from the Nomious Hills were known as the Fields of Fire. They were called this because in the spring, wildflowers bloomed here in countless numbers: the wondrous Firestars with brick-colored petals, laced with a shimmering pollen that caught the wind and appeared as a fire storm upon the plain. Now, sadly, the land was barren. It was nothing but blowing dust, soil long washed away, fractal patterns left where water once flowed, and an occasional weed, barbed and hostile, clinging to life. I was not shocked to find it thus after my experience with Sestos, only disappointed.

We removed Smoking Bear from the basket and car-

ried her to the shade of the only tree in sight. Our footsteps conjured dust clouds from the powdered earth
where we stepped. Behind us, the Nomious Hills,
strange pieces of volcanic rock, were thrust up at uncomfortable angles into the sky.

The tree, which resembled a Norway spruce, had needles that were brown and brittle, scorched by the harsh
environment. It was, however, the only thing here, besides Aesop or me, that I could drain the life from. I'd
probably kill it. It was the last of its kind on this lonely
plain, the last reminder of another age.

The wind dragged our partially deflated balloon along
the ground, and sent a great plume of dust into the air.
Aesop looked at it and frowned. If the demons were
anywhere within miles, they would see it.

"I must tend to the balloon," he told me. "Please
make Smoking Bear as comfortable as possible."

I nodded.

He hesitated, looked a moment longer at Smoking
Bear, then left me alone with her.

I had no desire to do this. Yet, if I took no action,
she might lose her arm or her life. Better I had remained
asleep and with Sabrina. We were together until the
moon sank into the ocean. She then released the name
of the batlike demon to me, Bakkeglossides, which in
Eldrich meant: blooming night flowers. I gladly paid her
price and would do so again if she requested it, but could
not help considering the ramifications of our lovemak-
ing. Certainly it meant an alliance of sorts between us,
or perhaps it was a simple act of passion. No. Sabrina
did not strike me as someone who engaged in thought-
less acts. I suspected she had planned this the moment
she knew about me.

Why was I thinking of her? I needed to concentrate
on Smoking Bear. All these distractions, all these other
thoughts from other worlds must cease. I cleared my
mind and imagined her arm, how it should look according to *Grennford's Anatomy and Physiology*. The bones,
how they moved, the ligaments that joined muscle to
bone, and the muscles that powered motion, contracting,

pulling in concert to provide a universality of actions. Thankfully, her hand remained undamaged. There were too many bones, and too subtle a structure for me to put back together.

I propped her against the trunk of the tree. One last glance at Aesop. Good, he was unloading the balloon. I needed time alone and uninterrupted. I sat next to her in the dust and carefully took her broken arm in my hands.

How did I work this yesterday in the valley? I had two forces, opposites of one another, life and death. I had to concentrate on those simultaneously, allow them to flow into one another. From that flow of power I would create the effect I wanted, a reshaping of the life and death. This time I would be especially careful to pay equal attention to the death, lest it flow into me and do harm.

I closed my eyes.

In my mind, I stood between the twin forces: life and death, the tree and my friend. The paired forces appeared the instant I thought of them. The energy began to move from one to the other. A river of magic passed through my body and with it the tingle of static through my hands.

Next, I clarified the two images: Smoking Bear's shattered bones and the struggling tree. The tree had life, while Smoking Bear lay veiled in a haze of death. In the tree I saw the flow of water and sugars through a cellulose matrix, and tiny photon driven machinery within the needles. It was far from healthy. Was there enough life to heal her?

Then to the arm. In my mind's eye, or perhaps I *actually* saw all this, were the two broken bones, the radius and the longer ulna. Shards from the broken ends pierced the muscle and cut into the ligaments. I mentally pushed each chip back where I thought it belonged. Her bones, I noted, were slightly different from the picture in the textbook, reinforced about the styloid process and solid inside rather than the normal spongy construction. No time now to wonder why.

Back to the tree. The flow of magical energies increased, and where I held her arm it felt like fire, a numbing cold fire of electrical current. I channeled much of the death from her into the tree. I pictured the root system shriveling, drying, and decaying. I heard the tree creak and feared my healing would be undone by it falling on us.

Smoking Bear sighed and began to stir.

I returned to my picture of her arm, placed bone in contact with bone, and fused them with an imagined pressure. From a great distance away I heard the bones as they moved, an unsettling grinding sound.

Next, to her head. There I saw fluid near the injury, building pressure. I drained this away, then repaired the bones of her skull. There was something unusual about the construction of her head. It was thicker and didn't quite look like the skull in the anatomy text. I couldn't be certain, however, as I spent most of my time studying the structure of the arm.

I compared both pictures then: the death in the once living tree, her healed arm, and head once broken. The flow of magic slowed. The tree had little life left to fuel my sorcery.

With the trickle of power that remained, I eliminated the infection. Within her body swarmed the means to undo all my sorcery; tiny rogue bacteria oozed in tissues where the bones broke the skin. I stopped the flow of energies and reversed them, now sucking the life, the remaining sturdiness from the tree, rather than merely using it for a sink to dump the unwanted death into. I drew the strength of the tree into her, and killed the seeds of disease. In my mind, the infection flared a pale blue, then faded.

I eased off and returned to a lucid state. The flow between life and death slowed, then stopped. I experienced none of the exhaustion as before in the valley. I was tired, but only from the intense concentration.

I opened my eyes and examined her arm. It was not attractive, still yellowed and bruised from shoulder to wrist, but it was in one piece and approximately whole again. The swelling was down too.

This was fantastic. I had worked magic on a living person, successfully. How far could I push my new healing abilities? Mending bones might be only the beginning. Could I also cure diseases? Perhaps even raise the dead?

My elation was cut short when I detected a wisp of smoke and an unnatural heat behind me. I turned and saw Aesop.

He was watching me. Within his hand, he held a white flame similar to the one he conjured in the tunnel under the Abbey. I knew what he could do with that.

"Step aside, sorcerer," he commanded.

"Wait," I said. "Let me explain."

"No. First move." The flame flared, and the light made shadows spring to life behind us, ghostly flickers of dark on the sunny plain.

If I moved away from Smoking Bear, then what was to stop him from unleashing his magic? "I prefer to remain right were I am for the moment."

His eyes narrowed. "What family do you belong to? I do not recognize your features."

Could I get away with a blatant lie? If he saw me heal Smoking Bear, there would be no denying I was a sorcerer and member of a royal family. The problem was I did not know if his family had a grudge against mine. Very well, I would try the truth and see how that worked.

"Pritchard," I said, and carefully watched his reaction for anger or acceptance.

He frowned, puzzled. "I thought the Pritchard family was dead." He lowered his hand slightly. "Why did you wait until now to make yourself known? We needed your magic when the demons intercepted us."

In lieu of a better story, I continued with the truth— how Eugene in the real world sought me out with the letter, then rescued me, and how the assassin tried to kill me. From the glower that appeared on his face when I mentioned Eugene, I gathered they were not friends. I went on explaining that I had only recently learned to manipulate magic. I told him of the rejuvenated field and how I was up late last night studying the anatomy text to help Smoking Bear.

"So you claim ignorance of affairs both here and in the other world? If you really were our ally, you would have used your magical powers back at the cavern."

"I told you," I said, becoming annoyed, "that I just learned the basics of sorcery. If I were your enemy, I would not have healed Smoking Bear."

"True," he admitted, "unless you wanted to lull us into trusting you. For all I know you could have originally sent the demons after us. The Rhodes *are* allied with the Bishop clan, and I think it unusual that you escaped our battle with the demons without injury."

These people were paranoid (although admittedly with justification). "For all I know," I countered, "*your* family could have sent the assassin after me."

He made a sound of disgust through his teeth and shook his head.

"He's right," Smoking Bear said, and slowly sat up. "It could have been one of us."

"You are well again," Aesop cried, and let the flame in his hand die. He rushed to her side.

I exhaled and realized I had been holding my breath.

"Some"—she rubbed her arm—"mostly." She then turned to me. "Thanks, Roland."

"Can you move it properly?" I asked. "I only had a day to study the anatomy and physiology."

Smoking Bear curled her arm in, then stretched it out. "It's a little stiff, but I'm not complaining." She rubbed her head and remarked, "I got a splitting headache though."

"You heard him then?" Aesop sneered. "This Pritchard?"

"Yes, and I believe him. Aside from him looking very much like his father, I felt his control of the life-and-death magics. They were sloppy, amateurish, not that I'm criticizing you, Roland. He came dangerously close to siphoning a good portion of my death into himself. I can think of no sorcerer in the families who would do such a thing on purpose. Can you?"

"No," he said reluctantly. "I agree he is a new sorcerer, but what about his association with Eugene Rhodes?"

"If he is new to the families, then let's give him the benefit of doubt."

"I know you lead our family in these matters, Grandmother, but I strongly question your judgment on this issue. You could have been influenced by this sorcerer while unconscious."

"I've decided," she told him. "If you have problems with it, take it up at our next clan meeting. Until then be quiet."

Grandmother? Smoking Bear was no more than twenty years old. Aesop easily looked thirty-five, perhaps older. Could magic have slowed her aging process? Curious. Now I understood their relationship, how Aesop could be concerned and slightly adversarial at the same time. They were relatives.

"Roland," she said, "are you still willing to serve as guide through the Sartesh ruins? I'll tell you right now we're no friends of the Rhodes clan; in fact, quite the opposite. If some of our family knew of your potential alliance with them, they might have set up that assassination attempt."

I considered. I appreciated the candor of Smoking Bear. She gave me the opportunity to back out and wait here for Eugene. If I was in her position, would I be as generous? There was Aesop to consider, hot-tempered, well suited to know the ways of fire. He had saved my life back at the Abbey and I owed him something for that. I hoped he let me live long enough to prove it.

"I will go with you," I told her. Besides, I wanted to see for myself what became of the Sartesh Empire.

"Then you must swear," Aesop demanded, "that you shall not reveal our position or actions to the Rhodes clan." From the tone of his voice, I gathered that if Smoking Bear was not here, I would be unwelcome, at the very least.

"I understand."

"We have the means to check if any information

leaks to that family,'' Smoking Bear added.

"I assumed that." Spies spying on spies.

Aesop sighed and Smoking Bear clapped her hand, the good one, on my shoulder. The tension between the three of us relaxed. We were allies, of sorts, for the moment. That meant whatever occurred in this realm, I was obliged to tell neither Sabrina nor Eugene, the apparent enemies of the De Marcos. I balanced on a high wire, on the one side the De Marcos, on the other, the Rhodes and Bishops.

The tree, dead and rotted to the core, tilted slightly as the winds pushed it. It would topple over eventually, not even capable of returning life to the destroyed soil.

"Pity about the tree," she said. "This entire area was once a vast garden."

"What happened to the Fields of Fire?" I asked her. How old *was* she?

"Something similar to what you just did. In those days, there was a vast campaign staged on these plains between two families, the Bishops and the Franciscos. Their battle continued for weeks as each side had sorcerers specialized in the powers of life and death." She found a cigar in some hidden pocket, cut off its end, and lit up. "Where was I? Oh yes, each side used up the life from this place to heal their soldiers and replace their ranks. In the end, both battled to a draw until most were dead and this place killed in the process. Too bad neither wiped the other out, that happened much later at the battle of . . .''

The Bishops were enemies of the Franciscos. Since my father also opposed this family (Eugene claimed he had wiped out the entire clan), that suggested my family and the Bishops were possibly on friendly terms? I'd ask Sabrina about it tonight.

"We are wasting time," Aesop politely suggested. "I shall gather our equipment from the balloon, then destroy the remains so nothing may track us from the air. Perhaps I can also coax those clouds to give us additional aerial cover. If in the meantime, young Prince

Pritchard, you would be so obliging as to decipher the Sartesh manuscript . . .''

"Of course," I replied.

From the balloon, he brought my bag and the Sarteshan poem, still inside its protective case.

I unrolled it on top of my pack and examined the water stains for clues. "The statue," I asked. "You said it was a beast?"

"Half man and half horse," Smoking Bear replied while she examined the smoke flowing from the tip of her cigar.

"If it is nature this relic controls, then it may be associated with the goddess Cylarus of the Sarteshan pantheon. She was often depicted as a great tree."

I removed a roll of thin paper and traced the outline of each watermark. If I creased the old manuscript dozens of times, it would likely fall apart. There were twenty-two stains, some small, others large, and one the size and approximate shape of my thumb. I laid the tracing out and began the tedious process of matching the marks together, forming shapes.

Aesop destroyed the balloon with a fire so hot no smoke escaped. In response, the clouds that comfortably rested on the other side of the mountain range, crept over, eager to balance his magic. With any luck they would hide us from the demons.

Smoking Bear, who was initially intrigued with my efforts, soon became bored and watched the darkening skies for signs of the demons. She flexed her arm twice and winced in pain. There was nothing more I could do for her arm, however. To fuel my magic I required life, and these hills had none left to give.

Returning to the manuscript, I discovered the outlines of a snake, an hourglass, and several others that looked as if they belonged in a phychological inkblot test. Finally the image I wanted materialized, a tree. It looked unsettlingly like the spruce I had just destroyed. If I were the superstitious sort, it would have bothered me.

"Come here," I asked both of them. "Does this look like a tree to you?"

They both glanced at the outline, then to the tree behind me.

"Yes," said Smoking Bear slowly, "it does."

I turned the creased parchment and found a block of Sarteshan characters aligned on the front. It read:

> *Starchaser the Wanderer,*
> *Life of his undying skin,*
> *Copper, gold, and silver,*
> *Changed by the Dragon.*
>
> *Beneath the sea he lies,*
> *Protected by the earth,*
> *Sleeping to fortify and husband*
> *The minds and dreams of men.*
>
> *Pointing the way, he waits*
> *Within circles of stone.*
> *Subtle melody on his harp*
> *Sing, exchange, live!*

"Does that mean anything to either of you?" I asked.

"There is a dragon," Aesop said, "an ancient one, who lives in the mountains far to the north."

Smoking Bear shook her head and said, "We're positively not going there again."

"This line here," I said, " 'Beneath the sea he lies.' Is there a lake or river nearby?"

"No," she replied.

"Let us continue to the ruins and make camp," Aesop recommended. "We may then search them in the morning to discover the meaning of the poem."

"Makes sense to me." She flicked the butt of her cigar, mostly ash, onto the dead ground.

Where the balloon once was, only a blackened stain remained. Soon that would vanish too, covered by blowing dust. The clouds smothered the sky and hid the sun from us. I gathered up my small bag, the vellum document, and a large pack Aesop handed me, filled with food, a shovel, and other weighty equipment.

"It shall rain soon," Aesop informed us.

We hiked west and his prediction became fact. The rain came in large drops, meteorites that made the dust rise where they impacted the chalky earth, then turned everything into a fine mud. While we marched, I saw that even the stunted weeds had disappeared. Cracks appeared in the ground, carved by the water running to the lower elevations. We followed the runoff, down through the dead Fields of Fire, and into an equally dead Sartesh Empire.

I slipped once in the mud, and Aesop chuckled at my misfortune. Moments later he too, fell and covered himself in the grey sludge. Served him right. Smoking Bear laughed, yet he retained his dignity, brushed himself off, and ignored her. We wallowed along, allowing the rain to rinse the mud off us.

"What do you do?" I asked Smoking Bear. "I mean in the real world?"

"Real world? This is the real world," she answered. "At least this is the world I was born into. When I dream, I travel to an alternate realm, one called Earth."

"It is considered rude to ask such questions among family members," Aesop told me.

"Were you born here, or in another realm?" she asked, disregarding him.

"I always assumed in the real . . . in the other realm. My mother is from there."

"Odd," Aesop remarked. "You have the look of one who is native to Meredin."

I would take that as a compliment. That was the closest thing to a friendly gesture Aesop extended to me all afternoon.

If the sun set, I couldn't tell through the clouds and rain that covered the plains in a sheet of gloom. The light did, however, diminish, and a cool wind whistled through my soaked clothes, chilling me to the bone. Smoking Bear led us north for a time, into rockier terrain and off the muddy flats.

We stopped among a large group of rocks huddled together. Aesop threw his pack down and sat, wet, weary, and worn. I sat beside him and detected no signs of friendship. I would settle for courtesy. It was what I got.

"We could continue into the ruins tonight," I suggested. "There's certain to be better shelter."

"Haunted," said Smoking Bear.

It was the same response they gave before in Sestos. "You really believe in ghosts?"

"I don't know if they're really ghosts," she replied, "but they are something to be careful of. I've seen them walk through walls as if they were no more than paper. You can't fight a creature like that."

"If we venture into the ruins tonight," Aesop added, "we shall not return. They are most active then."

"There are more dead than living in these cities," Smoking Bear said to me. "Give me a hand with this tarp would you?"

I helped her stretch a canvas over the boulders to provide a measure of shelter against the rain. The storm, as if it sensed our attempts to elude it, increased in intensity. Large drops stained the canvas, slowly soaked in, and disappeared into the fabric.

"Where do they come from, these dead?" I asked.

She crawled beneath the flimsy shelter and I followed. "Some claim they are guardians or ghosts from the Golden Age. Who can say for certain? All I know is that they are real, and we'll be lucky if we don't run into one tomorrow."

"I have heard rumors," Aesop said, "that they are impervious to normal weapons, harder than any substance known one moment, ethereal and smoke the next. Let us hope they are not immune to fire."

"I'll trust my steel." She patted her parallel sabers. "I've never failed to at least annoy whatever I took a stab at."

Perhaps there was a way I could use my magics to affect such a monster. Life and death . . . ghosts seemed to contradict the natural progression of those forces, living in a manner after they had died.

Aesop gathered several stones. He appeared to be par-

ticular about which ones were acceptable and which
were not. After ten minutes, he had a sizable pile of
smooth black rocks. He closed his eyes, concentrated,
and touched the stone on top of his pile until it glowed
cherry red. He set this down in the center of our shelter
and repeated the process with the remainder of the
stones.

"Are we setting watches tonight?" I asked Smoking
Bear.

"Sure," she said, trying to ignite a damp cigar from
the glowing stone campfire. "Since you asked, why
don't you take the first one. Wake me when you get
tired."

I was already tired, but said nothing.

A rumbling overhead suggested thunder and things to
come. The temperature dropped rapidly, and a breeze
blew the warm air out of our shelter. I secured the canvas better with a few rocks.

Aesop touched the stones in his pile again and made
them glow. The rain pelted harder on the fabric above
us, attempting to cool the rocks. It was the water portion
of Aesop's magic trying to cancel the heat. A few drops
eventually seeped through overhead, fell, and sizzled on
the stones.

We stayed warm, however, and mostly dry.

I had more questions about ghosts, about family, and
about the nature of the De Marcos' statue, but I kept
these to myself.

Aesop, awake all last evening in the balloon, lay exhausted, breathing heavily. Smoking Bear huddled close
to the heated rocks and cradled her newly healed arm
close to her chest. Her eyes were closed, and a damp
cigar smoldered in her hand.

I listened to the raindrops and waited to fall asleep,
waited for Sabrina.

9

She left no trace behind. The only evidence of the night's passion were the cold rumpled sheets and pillows scattered on the floor. I was alone, which was both a relief and a disappointment. A relief because I swore to the De Marcos to reveal neither our location nor actions to their enemies. I didn't need Sabrina asking me what happened in Meredin the first thing when I awoke. It was a disappointment for a variety of baser reasons, among them a healthy dose of wounded pride.

I rolled out of bed and started toward the balcony. The morning fog had yet to burn off, a layer of slate over a grey ocean. Tiny beads of moisture dotted the wooden slats of the deck. I checked my motion, recalling how high that balcony was. The view brought back the unwanted memory of the disastrous balloon ride, the demons, and my new dislike for heights.

I'd shave and shower instead. Hestor always liked me clean-cut, and there was no need to get into an argument over four days' worth of beard. I turned on the shower, then jumped in without letting it warm up first, to shock myself awake. Standing there shivering and letting the cold water soak my body, I traced the connections between the family members I knew of, to see if I had missed anything obvious.

Eugene was loosely allied with the Bishop clan, who were the enemies of the De Marcos. OK, so far that was simple enough. Yet, this Morgan Bishop seemed to be disliked by Sabrina, his own niece. And Eugene had showed no great pleasure when I had mentioned that Morgan's demons were hunting me. Of course, I omitted that I was with the De Marcos at the time, the real targets of the demon's attack. How would he react when Morgan told him he sent his demons after Smoking Bear and Aesop? The De Marcos confirmed they were not friendly with the Rhodes family. Where did that leave me? In the middle. Confused.

I didn't know what to expect from Eugene. There was a kernel of truth in Sabrina's warning that no family member helped another from the goodness in their hearts. What did he want from me? So far he had given me everything, my freedom, money, a new life, yet he asked practically nothing in return. In contrast to the cautious behavior of the De Marcos, it seemed out of place and something to be wary of. Aesop and Smoking Bear were at least transparent in their motives: they needed my knowledge. I knew where I stood with them. The water warmed and I shaved without the aid of a mirror.

Sabrina, sensual and intelligent, what did she desire from me? She had a way about her, and I found it difficult to refuse her anything. She was a powerful ally in that regard, dangerous for the same reason. For now, however, she was my best source of information, so I decided to trust her.

This second-guessing everyone's motives could drive me crazy. Soon I'd be seeing demons around every corner. That reminded me—I had to make sure that Hestor received the best medical treatment at this private hospital. She was possibly my only unbiased source of information about Dad, even if she was insane. If anyone knew what happened to the original Cartaga watchband, it was her. The only problem was getting the woman to tell me.

I heard a knock at the door, then a rattling sound. With a towel wrapped about my waist, I opened the door. It was the bellboy bearing a carafe of coffee, Kona, and two plates of eggs Benedict. I wrote in a generous tip on the bill, which I noted had Sabrina's name on it, poured the coffee, and took a bite of the egg, Canadian bacon, and hollandaise mixture. The coffee had a naturally sweet taste to it, and I finished my first cup in the bathroom while I dressed.

When I returned for a refill, Sabrina was there waiting. This morning she was dressed for business in a light grey suit with a white rose embroidered upon her lapel, and her hair drawn back tight.

"Did you sleep well?" she asked. "I do hope you were able to dispatch those two demons."

What happened in my dreams was the one thing I could not tell her. I bent over to kiss her good morning and received a tepid response. It had none of last evening's intensity, nor was it completely frigid. "Fine," I replied. "Everything turned out fine."

She leaned forward, eager to hear more, but I resisted the temptation. She poured some coffee for herself, a warmer for me. "I mapped out the quickest route to the hospital on this." She handed me a folded road map. "It ought to take us no more than forty-five minutes to drive there. I also called this morning and inquired about their visiting hours. They are not open until this afternoon; however, I managed to convince the attending doctor to let us in early."

I didn't want to know how she did that. A mild compulsion to tell her all that had occurred last evening with the De Marcos washed over me, but I remembered my pledge of silence. It was similar to the feelings I had experienced the first time we met, a lack of control, that giddy gut-wrenching sensation that I initially thought to be love at first sight. I focused on my coffee, watched the steam rise, and resisted this pressure. If she *was* using magic, I had to break her concentration before my will collapsed and I told her everything.

"Tell me," I struggled to ask, "what do you know of my father, Clay?"

The intense feeling disappeared and she looked startled that I had a question of my own.

"Clay? He was very handsome as I recall and on friendly terms with our clan, very friendly with some." She gazed into the distance, then looked back to me and smiled. "His father, Horace, was involved with my Uncle Morgan in some wild scheme, but what precisely, I don't know."

"And how were your dreams last night?"

Her smile disappeared and she sipped her coffee, still gazing at me. "I've the pleasure of attending the annual carnival at the Rhodes' castle by the Great Inland Sea. Do you know where that is?"

I nodded. "So you are with Eugene?"

"No," she replied. "Eugene left to personally look for you and your friends. He was worried."

That was useful information. Smoking Bear would not be pleased to know the Rhodes followed us.

"We better get going," I said, drained my cup, then stood and waited for her. The longer I lingered with her over breakfast, the more likely it was that I'd spill my guts about events in the dream realm. My suspicions were confirmed as I was again tempted to speak, unnaturally so, and this time at a greater intensity than before. I countered by asking, "Are you ready?"

"Yes," she said, and set her coffee down hard. "Yes, of course we should be going."

Something had changed between us. She was the same person, and I was still attracted to her on many levels, yet there was an undefinable quality missing from my feelings toward her.

She took my arm and we strolled together down to the car. Then onto the coast highway and through the fog we drove. Sabrina proved to be an efficient navigator. I admired that; she was smart and wasted no time. I envied those abilities and found myself liking her, despite her magic, and despite the subterfuge.

It was still overcast when we arrived at the hospital. A delivery truck blocked the entrance to the parking lot, so I parked the Jaguar in the shade of a towering Norway spruce and we hiked up a gravel path to the entrance.

The hospital was a converted Victorian house, designed with ornate lines and tall arched windows with ivory lace curtains. Only a small wooden sign on the lawn gave away its true nature: Oceanview Private Hospital.

We mounted the stairs of the porch and entered. A stale, sterile, medicated odor greeted us when we passed through the door. The attending doctor—Anderson was the name pinned to his lapel—welcomed Sabrina and me. He could hardly take his eyes off her, and a bit of jealousy pooled in my stomach.

"Please, Mister Pritchard," he began, still looking directly at her, "try not to upset your mother. We have made such progress in calming her these past few days."

"What is she . . . sensitive about?" I asked. "Sensitive" meaning what topics might change her into a raving maniac? I hoped there was a fire extinguisher handy, just in case.

"She has blocked out the events of the last week or so," he explained. "That's something I'd like to discuss with you after you have seen her. An unspecified trauma has triggered this episode."

"Sure," I replied. "Now if you could show me which room she's in . . ." I didn't have time to waste explaining her life history to this doctor.

Anderson escorted us down a blue and lavender tiled corridor past carts piled with plates full of leftover breakfasts, then stopped at room number twelve.

"If you don't mind," I said to Sabrina, "I'd like a moment alone with her first. She might be a bit shy around strangers just now."

"Certainly," she said, looking slightly wounded.

I braced myself for the worst and went in.

Hestor stood by the window and gazed intently at the ocean. From the look of her, you'd never be able to tell anything was wrong. She wore her favorite nightgown, the flannel one with roses on it. She looked younger, her black hair shiny, her dark eyes clear and intelligent, and the lines on her face gone. This was not the crazy woman I had cared for the past three years. Maybe this private hospital gave her the professional attention she really needed.

"Roland?" she whispered and turned from her ocean view. There was no tearful greeting, no crushing embrace. It was as though we were still at home and nothing had ever happened.

"Mom?" I gave her a hug, which she returned, but not with the strength she usually did.

She looked past me at the closed door. "I heard you talking to someone out there. Did you come alone?"

"No, I brought a friend, someone . . ."

"Not some relative?" Her eyes widened and her voice strained on the word *relative*.

Did she remember Eugene's letter? "No," I lied. "This is a female friend, someone special."

"That's fine." She released me from her grasp. "How is work, OK? Has Sam given you any day shifts? You know I worry about you working nights. So many strange people come out at night."

"No. Not yet." Sam wasn't in any condition to give out day shifts. "I thought I might look for a new job soon."

She smiled and sat down on the edge of her bed. "You look nice and clean," she said, running her hand over my cheek. "Tell me about your friend, the girl."

"She's just someone I met at school." I sat next to her and took her hand. "Mom, do you remember why you are here?"

"Here? You mean the hospital? The doctor told me there was an accident in the apartment." She strained to recall the incident for a moment, then gave up. "I don't remember what, though." She turned to examine the wallpaper: tiny blue parrots and green palms.

I had to be careful. I wanted to direct our conversation toward Dad and the missing watchband. However, if I blatantly asked her, she'd lose her composure and I'd learn nothing. I didn't expect her to know much. She was not a true dreamer and couldn't possibly know about the complex interactions of the royal families. "Mom, do you remember anything *before* the accident?"

"Oh, far back?" She ignored the wallpaper and fixed her gaze back onto me. "I remember when I was young. It's the latest thing I've been working on with Dr. Anderson. Isn't he a wonderful young man? He's very pleased with me." Before I replied, she rambled on, "Mother and I, that's your grandmother, God have mercy on her soul, lived on the other coast. I worked in the factory then, that was before I had you." Something clouded over her face then vanished as quickly as it had come. "You don't remember that factory?"

"I wasn't even born yet, how could I?"

"That factory, it was so busy . . . so many things to plan. They never knew I ran it all. Heaven forbid a woman should hold any power or have authority. Why we'd just barely got the right to vote. The railroads too, they . . ."

What was she talking about? Right to vote? That was during the turn of the century. This was likely another one of her delusions. I'd go along with her fantasy for a while, see if she eventually wandered onto the subject of Clay by herself.

"Who didn't want you to have any authority?" I asked.

The same darkness that crossed her face before returned. "That was the problem with those two, always up to something. Oh, it started out as friendly competition. Then he wanted to take the money from the diamond mines in Africa and buy that damn railroad out West." She shook her finger at me. "That's when it started, with that railroad. Too much competition between those two . . . Too many roosters in the henhouse."

I was losing control of the conversation. I had to risk a more direct question. "Mom, have you seen Dad's watchband lately? I've been looking for the original strap.'' I turned my wrist so she could see the Cartaga. The light reflected off its gold and jet surface, casting amorphous patterns upon her face.

She stopped rambling, closed her eyes halfway, and looked about suspiciously. In a whisper she said, ''You know they wanted me to tell them where his garbage is, where I threw it all when he left me for her. I wouldn't, though.'' She stood and walked to the window. ''They've done everything to me to find it. Drugs, hypnosis, shock treatments, they've tried it all.'' She clung to the curtains like a child might cling to her mother's skirt, then giggled. ''They just don't know who they're dealing with. They have no idea . . .''

She was one step away from hysteria. This wasn't working. ''Mom,'' I said in my best calming voice, ''I don't think . . .''

''That's your problem,'' she cut me off, her eyes full of tears, ''you don't think, Roland. I've had to do all the thinking, all the planning, and all the hiding. Haven't you figured out that car accident was on purpose? Don't you know they're looking for us? They almost found you in that college and it's all because of the junk. OK? Why didn't I just burn it all when I had the chance? Yes, burn it. That's what I should have done.''

The accident was on purpose? She had killed two innocent people on purpose? Hestor cut up dollar bills, worried about demons in the refrigerator, and set the apartment on fire, but she was no murderess.

''They wanted that stuff,'' she said. ''They wanted his body, and they wanted you.'' She blinked and released her tears, then looked at me, just now realizing where we both were. ''You must go and hide,'' she pleaded. ''Stay away from this place. Roland, why did you let them bring me here?''

''Mom, please sit down.'' She was entering the first stages of her irreversible paranoia. I had to pacify her quickly before she started seeing things. ''Where is this 'stuff' you mentioned? I'll move it so *they* won't find it, then you'll be safe.''

"If it were that easy I'd do it, OK? Clay was furious when I hid it from him. It was all worthless. No one knew how to use the damn thing. I was so jealous when she came around. She had some nerve, even wanted to play with you. I tried to hit her once. Your father laughed at me. She felt like . . . like something not alive, like stone . . . like death."

"Who are you talking about?"

Her voice dropped, almost inaudible, "She told me she'd kill me if I ever said her name. She meant it too. If you could see her eyes when she said that, 'I'll kill you.' She had *demons* in her eyes." Hestor paused to look out the window, then smoothed out her gown and returned to the bed. "She killed people all the time . . . Clay too. Your father is no saint."

"Hestor," I said, losing my patience, "he's been gone for years now and you know it." That was the wrong thing to say. I realized this before I spoke, but it just came out of my mouth with a life of its own.

She stopped the instant I said it, reality smashing into her fantasy. Rather than face the truth, she did what she always did. She dropped to the floor, grabbed her knees, and began a rocking back and forth. I'd seen her do this twice before. She might stay like that for hours or days.

Damn, I should have kept my mouth shut about Clay. I'd need help to snap her out of this. Could I heal her magically? I succeeded with Smoking Bear, why not my own mother?

I opened the door. "Sabrina, give me a hand please."

She entered and looked about, perplexed when she didn't see Hestor.

"Here on the floor," I said. "Help me lift her."

When she saw her, she shot a curious look at me as if I had done something wrong. I grabbed Hestor's shoulders, Sabrina took her feet, and we moved her onto the bed. She weighed less than eighty pounds, a mere skeleton under her gown. I'd seen her starve herself before, but never this badly.

"Close the door please."

Sabrina complied and I looked to Hestor's head.

Something was drastically wrong in there and it was time I found out what. I had the ability. I'd use it.

I set up the balance between life and death without finding an appropriate source of life to fuel my sorcery. I'd use the life in my body. I didn't care what happened to me. This was my fault. I had to try something.

There in my mind, I saw her. Fragile and dim, close to death, her body veiled in a pale green haze of narcotics and depressants. I focused behind her skull, on the tiny capillaries that fed the grey matter. Yes, something was amiss there. Portions of her psyche were dark and dead, or perhaps they were never there to begin with. I wasn't certain, it might have been my imagination, but it looked like the sections that were there were all jumbled—parts of a jigsaw puzzle forced incorrectly together.

I touched her forehead and let the magic flow. The death from her streamed into me, and simultaneously, my life drained away. There was the tingle of magic, an electrical surge. It rushed between us faster than I anticipated, intensely painful. I jerked my hand away. Still the magic flowed undiminished. What was I doing? I knew nothing of the brain or nervous system. Pain shot through my left hand, the hand that had touched her. Death burned every nerve; a flash of white heat coursed up my arm and across my chest. Don't panic, I told myself, concentrate.

Again, I focused on her brain and saw that the dead areas were illuminated, moving, filling with life. The collapsed circulatory pathways opened; fluids rushed in, and more life flowed. Connections reestablished themselves. I felt thoughts exchange between them; caught a glimpse of Clay when he was younger, laughter, the taste of champagne, a horse-drawn carriage on the streets of Paris, the scent of manure and perfume, Idol Crags covered with mist, and then gone.

The parallel images of life and death within my mind momentarily faded. Pain throbbed through my body, beating to match my slowing pulse. I had to stop the flow. Too much life had been removed from me. Soon

I would exhaust myself, lose whatever concentration I still possessed, and my life would be forfeit.

I tried to back off. The flow between the paired forces was strong, almost too much to stop. I abandoned the images and focused solely on the flow, restraining it, then eventually bringing it to a halt.

I opened my outer eyes. Sabrina physically supported me and kept me from falling. I felt a surge of strength from her. She set me down on the bed next to Hestor. I was dizzy, but I remained conscious.

Hestor looked peaceful, different, more vital. It was the first time I'd ever seen her like this.

"Is she all right?" Sabrina asked.

"I think so. Parts of her mind were dead. I repaired them."

"Are *you* all right? I've never seen any sorcerer channel so much death and live."

"Roland," Hestor muttered and reached up to touch her forehead. Her voice was different, powerful and controlled. I didn't recognize it.

"Right here, you're going to be fine."

"That's good," she said, then rubbed her temples and squinted at the light. "I could really use some sleep though."

"Yeah," I agreed, "so could I. What do you remember, anything?"

"I remember it *all*," she said with certainty. "Go ahead, you do what you think is best with Clay's possessions. He would have wanted that. Just be careful. And trust no one, especially the families."

Sabrina backed toward the door as if this last comment applied to her personally.

"You know that place," Hestor continued weakly, "the storage facility by the farmers' market downtown? That's where Clay's stuff all is. I used a different name, Fischer, and they have a security code for it, your birthday." She motioned for me to come closer, "You better go though, they'll be looking for you. And don't say her name or she'll kill you, OK?"

"I won't."

"Don't say her name," she whispered. "Don't tell anyone it was Judith."

Sabrina gasped when Hestor said this. What did she know about her?

"I'm going to have a word with the doctor," I told Sabrina. "Stay with her until I return."

I was lightheaded, barely able to stand, but I had something to settle with Anderson. I found him smoking in the lounge, and flirting with a younger nurse.

"Are there any problems, Mister Pritchard?"

"Problems? You bet there's a problem. My mother is severely underweight and doped up on narcotics. I want her off of those drugs immediately."

He started to say something, but I cut him off. "I'll return in a few days to check up on her. She had better gain some weight back," I told him and pointed my finger at his chest, "or you'll have a malpractice suit to contend with." Maybe I'll just drain the life right out of you, I thought. Yes, that might feel good.

He stood and retreated a step back, fearful, as if he could sense the death that still shrouded me. "Of course, Mister Pritchard," he stammered, dread in his voice.

I left him there trembling and staggered back to room number twelve, barely able to stand. Sabrina took one look at me and put her arm about my waist to help me from the room.

We made it out into the hallway. "You'd better drive," I said, then blackness filled this world.

It still rained upon us, a light drizzle that pelted the tarp above. I inched closer to the pile of heated rocks. They were only a tad warm now, so I drew the wool blanket about me. It was itchy, wet, and cold. Smoking Bear whispered to Aesop, but I could not make out what she said. I turned over and went back to sleep.

Crossing the void again, I heard laughter.

Blood pounded in my ears. I cycled through dizziness, nausea, and disorientation, then repeated the process. My tongue stuck to the roof of my mouth, while the leather seat stuck to my backside. I managed to open my eyes then. Several other cars, all empty, surrounded us. We were in some sort of parking lot. In the distance, the roar of a thousand lions echoed. It did not improve my disposition.

"We're at the Oakland airport," Sabrina explained. "How do you feel?"

"Fine," I lied. My left hand was covered with phantom red ants that bit me. I flexed and tried to shake them off, but the little biters remained.

"I have known several masters of life and death sorcery," she said, "and none channeled death into their own bodies. It is very foolish. You're young and vibrant, a magnet for the death. It could have killed you." It wasn't motherly concern in her voice, but annoyance, as if my death would have inconvenienced her in some small way.

"What are we doing here?" I asked.

"I've booked us a flight back to San Diego. I assumed you'd want to check out this storage facility your mother mentioned."

I nodded and concentrated on slowing the spinning of the earth about me. "How much time before we board?"

"Thirty minutes."

Good. That gave me time to orient and take stock of what Hestor said. "What do you know about this Judith? You recognized that name in the hospital."

This time she did not react. "What do you mean?"

"I mean you were so surprised you nearly fell over when you heard her name. What significance does it have for you?" She knew I had seen her. Why was she trying to hide it?

"It's the name of my aunt." Sabrina shifted uncomfortably in her seat. "She disappeared a long time ago. No one has seen her for two decades. I doubt it could be the same person your mother referred to."

Doubt? I was certain it *was* the same person. All these family connections were tangled and intertwined like the

Gordian knot. I'd remember that name—Judith. Perhaps Eugene knew more about her, or the De Marcos.

She opened the door. "Come, we better go or we'll miss the flight."

It was obvious Sabrina didn't want to discuss the matter, so I let it drop, for now. I didn't feel up to a verbal or magical battle with her.

Sabrina took my hand, the injured one, and led me through the terminal. I stumbled through the aimless waiting crowds, up twin escalators, through a metal detector, and then we boarded. Had I the time to think of it, I would have insisted we drive. My luck on recent flights was all bad.

Once on board, I was no longer able to quiz Sabrina about family matters. This was a public place, not fit for the discussion of murders and family conspiracies. It was nice just to sit and relax for a while.

I no longer felt ants attacking my left hand. I felt nothing at all. It moved, responded to my commands, but there was no sensation from it.

The plane's engines roared to life and we taxied out onto the runway. I closed the window shade next to me. No more heights, please, and no more looking for demons. A deafening roar, the plane angled up, and we were airborne.

Had I traded healing Hestor's neurological tissues at the expense of my own? I hoped it wouldn't last long. I sat there and held a can of soda in my hand, trying to feel the cool metal. Nothing.

I forgot my hand for the moment and again attempted to make sense of what Hestor had told me. Were her claims of the hospital abusing her true? I knew she *thought* it was the truth. For a time when we were together, she had told all the neighbors that I locked her in the closet every night. That was hard to explain, especially when the police came by to check on her story.

I resolved to take her out of that place, though. Eugene did me a favor when he moved her to the private hospital, but now too many families knew where she was. If anything went awry, she could be taken hostage, or worse.

I couldn't think anymore; too much death had flowed into my body. I set my drink aside and fell asleep listening to the drone of the plane.

10

Smoking Bear's snores were louder than a jet engine.

I barely recalled stumbling through Lindbergh Field in San Diego, then taking a taxi to the Hilton. Sabrina made no amorous advances. I was asleep before my head hit the pillow, and immediately woke up here.

I got up, stretched, and walked away from our camp. Aesop was awake too. He watched the clouds with their fiery bottoms of gold drifting across the western sky. All was silent save the hissing and popping of the soil as moisture steamed from it and left tendrils of fog over a cracked mosaic of earth. Farther north lay whatever remained of the Sarteshan city-state. I saw black clumps, perhaps buildings in the distance, and the glint of metal or glass, but nothing else.

I flexed my hand. It was still numb. It was a small price to pay if Hestor remained sane, but I would never channel the death directly into myself again. Strange that the injury should translate into this realm. All the scrapes and bruises I had received before never materialized on my body here.

I retrieved the poem to double check the translation. The Sarteshan language was composed of symmetric and asymmetric geometric symbols, tiny squares, broken triangles, and fractured polygons. A small error in the alignment of these characters could form an entirely different translation. Thrice I creased the parchment to confirm the poem. The phrase, "Beneath the sea he lies," bothered me. The word was positively *sea*, not river or water. That made no sense because we were a hundred kilometers from the Ocean of Frost, and the Great Inland Sea lay on the other side of the mountains.

"Checking for inaccuracies in your translation?" Aesop asked, and strolled over to me. "I hope it is correct. It would be unfortunate to waste time following a false trail."

Behind me I heard Smoking Bear's snores cease.

"The translation is correct," I replied, ignoring his insult. "But I do not understand its significance."

"Something to eat?" He offered me a piece of dried meat, an unexpected gesture of civility.

As I reached for the jerky, Smoking Bear intercepted it. She tore a piece off, then passed the remainder to me, keeping the larger portion for herself. "Morning," she said, seeming happy and alert.

I echoed her greeting, then pretended to continue my analysis of the document. It was hard to believe she was Aesop's grandmother. It made me uneasy and uncertain how to treat her.

She said to both of us, "I wanted to talk about this poem before we go into the ruins and search randomly. If possible, I want to be out by sunset."

"Why is your family heirloom here?" I asked. "You mentioned it was hidden on purpose?"

Smoking Bear dug into her pack and found a cigar. She held it out to Aesop, who touched the end and made it smolder. "There was such unbridled suspicion in the families during the dark times," she replied. "No one trusted anyone, *especially* another family member."

"You mean like now?"

"Worse," she said. "The family heirloom was traditionally held by the eldest. He kept the workings of the device a secret until he handed it over to his successor. That way he had some protection against outright assassination."

"He couldn't trust his own family?"

"Back then, the clans were much larger than they are today. If you were a member in a family of three dozen, then it wouldn't hurt to bump off a few of your relatives to get what you wanted. These days you have to be careful whose throat you slit, being as there are so few of us left."

Aesop prepared three bowls of oatmeal from our rations. Smoking Bear declined, content with her cigar for breakfast. He gave one to me and set the extra bowl aside.

"So the elder died," Aesop said, continuing Smoking Bear's story, "or more accurately, he was assassinated by his children for the relic."

"Why hide it then?" I inquired around a mouthful of warm oats.

"In their zeal to obtain the heirloom," he explained, "the children failed to determine its operation. To be specific, the elder died before they could torture the information from him."

"Do either of you know how it works?"

"No," Smoking Bear replied, "but we know someone who will tell us—Xuraldium. He is an ancient one, a sorcerer from before the Golden Age, and a general pain in the ass. In addition to selling us the scroll to locate the relic, he also agreed to show us how it works."

"So that is why you risked coming to the Abbey? This sorcerer could not translate the poem for you?"

"Yes," she answered and blew smoke into my breakfast. "Where was I? Oh, the children who had the relic feared for their own lives. Their family and the other clans learned they had no idea how to work the heirloom. It was only a matter of time before someone else would kill them to get their hands on the thing."

"So they hid the statue in these ruins," Aesop added. "It was worse than useless to them; it would actually attract their enemies. They even went as far as to have their servants hide it for them. That way they could not be hunted down and coerced into revealing its location.''

''What happened to the servants then?''

''Xuraldium claimed the document was created by one of the servants of Sarteshan ancestry. I can only surmise these slaves wanted the statue for their own purposes.''

''That is why it was heavily encrypted,'' I said. ''So none but those of Sarteshan ancestry could find it.''

''Yes,'' Aesop said. ''Suffice it to say that the statue is ours and it is likely to be in the Sarteshan ruins. Now, instead of the history lesson, let us get on with analyzing the poem. You said the symbols on the back of the parchment represented various deities?''

I nodded. ''Yes, the false translation was the butterfly mark; that's Jexer's symbol. What I believe to be the true translation has a tree image which aligns the text, and that is the image of Cylarus, the goddess of nature.''

''Then the reference to the sea that puzzles you so,'' he said, ''may refer to a sea god, rather than a literal ocean.''

''There was a Sarteshan sea goddess—Arthusa. She was a sister to the nature goddess.''

''Tell me about these gods,'' Smoking Bear said. ''I've never heard of them before.''

''The Sarteshan mythology tells how the land was made by the deity Cylarus,'' I began. ''At the time, she was only the goddess of the earth, not of nature. The goddess formed the earth from her own body, made the salt from her blood, the rocks from her bones, and the soil from her flesh. When she finished, mountains towered over the continent, and plains spread from the hills to her sister, the sea.

''Cylarus was pleased by her accomplishment, but she sensed some element was missing—life. When she first attempted to create life from the earth, the salts and other minerals within the soil poisoned her creatures. The sea goddess heard her sister's cries of frustration and cleansed the soil for her. She washed over the earth and dissolved the salts, taking them into her own body.

"So, once again Cylarus cultivated the earth, but nothing grew, as there was no moisture to nurture her creations. Arthusa saw her sister weeping, trying to wet the earth with her own tears. The sea goddess again aided her. She asked her brother, the air, to carry away some part of her as a gift to their sister, what we now call rain.

"Finally the earth goddess created life within the realm. She became not only the earth deity in the Sarteshan pantheon, but the nature goddess as well. So grateful to the sea was Cylarus that she decreed shrines be constructed in each of her temples, so all would remember her and give thanks to the original source of life on Meredin."

"Then if there's a nature temple in these ruins," said Smoking Bear, "we can assume there's a sea shrine too. And I'll bet that's where our statue is."

"Then let us hurry," Aesop added. "We shall never find the statue by discussion alone."

The three of us gathered up the supplies and began our hike. Smoking Bear walked ahead with her sword drawn, Aesop went unarmed, and I readied one of the crossbows.

As we hiked, I noticed that the ground was littered with shards of glass of a dark volcanic variety. The farther north we traveled, the larger and more frequent these remains were. We proceeded with caution, as they appeared lethally sharp.

I spotted a toppled wall, and next to that, the foundation of a building and a broken piece of road, all made of the same smoky glass. The Sarteshans must have discovered a method to shape and fuse the volcanic material; perhaps they had even constructed entire buildings from it. More shards lay shattered upon the ground still wet from the evening's rain. Droplets of water pooled atop them and reflected the sun off their irregular surfaces, breaking the light into a thousand fragments tainted with the black-green color of the stone.

Kilometers of glass followed—one giant beach party with no trash can. More structures appeared the longer we marched: curved walls, a clear fountain with black stone fish swimming in the collected rainwater, and the disembodied hand of a titan statue curled about the broken pommel of a sword.

It was noon when we stumbled upon a virtually invisible amphitheater. It was hidden from view, constructed below ground level, a hemisphere that appeared like a crater in the surface of the city. Row after row of seats sloped at a gentle angle, and wide aisles ran to a center stage. From the amount of rubble in and around the theater, I speculated a dome had once covered the building.

Smoking Bear decided we would rest here and eat lunch. I saw none of the ghosts the De Marcos feared, so I entered the amphitheater while they lolled in the shade of a broken wall and ate.

I carefully removed the glass fragments from one seat and sat, expecting it to be hard and uncomfortable. It was not. The artist who had carved this was a genius, one skilled in knowledge of the human body. It fitted the shape of my lower back perfectly. Below, what must have been two large statues flanked both sides of the stage. One was only a broken pedestal now, the other a pair of feet. I swore I could almost hear the crowds applaud long-dead performers, and almost see a pair of giant statues hold the dome aloft while the noon sun was captured by the glass and refracted in kaleidoscopic patterns beneath. Fantastic.

What caused the destruction of this civilization? Wars, disease, magic, or all of the above? Whatever happened, I didn't care. I wanted it back. This was my world as much as any of the other royal families'. I vowed to myself, sitting there among the specters of the past, somehow to restore Meredin to a fraction of its Golden Age glory.

I wanted to stay and explore further, but the De Marcos were nearly finished. I returned and ate briefly with them.

"Let's get out of here," Smoking Bear said as she chewed the last bit of jerky. "This place is haunted."

I couldn't agree more. It was haunted, not with ghosts, but with the memories of an extraordinary community, lost.

We trekked north, searching and picking through the debris as we went. We found some intriguing relics, a piece of coiled metal, more statue parts than I could count, a few silvery hexagonal coins with their markings worn off, and a severely rusted knife, but no signs of the earth temple.

The afternoon shadows were long when Aesop spotted it, part of a building and a low wall that bore the unmistakable carvings of a giant tree, the same tree as on the poem. Most of the structure was missing, blasted away by an unimaginable force. Only a few meters of wall remained and these were covered with spiderweb cracks and deep fractures. There was no doubt, however, that the tree was the goddess Cylarus, and we had found her temple.

"I urge caution," Smoking Bear said. She looked worried and that in itself gave me cause to be concerned. From where Aesop stood, I felt the temperature rise.

The crossbow I held was a flimsy thing compared to her blade or the sorcery of Aesop. I had proved to be ill trained with it back at the cavern. It was just as likely to be useless here in any supernatural battle.

Because I injured myself healing Hestor, I was reluctant to use my magic again. I tested the magical waters, so to speak, and hesitantly thought of the abundant death here and the life within my own body. I was careful not to allow any of the power to flow between the two.

Initially I saw nothing but a blank darkness. My mistake was believing the darkness was nothing. It was not. The death here was a dam filled to capacity and overflowing. I perceived through my sorcerer's vision just the three of us, three tiny sparks and nothing else. It required all my concentration to maintain the imbalance, to keep the death from smothering our lives. I slowly disengaged from the image, from the magic that wanted to rush forth. Slowly, glacially slowly, the power, the death of the place faded into the imperceptible background.

"Take a look at these," Smoking Bear said, and handed me several pieces of petrified wood. They had tiny branches with knots and convolutions only nature could design.

"I also found these." Aesop gave me a handful of coins the same hexagonal shape as before, but made of gold rather than silver. Trees, barely visible, were struck onto the surface of the metal.

"Again," I said, "the symbols of the nature goddess." We were on the right track.

"What did you discover?" Aesop inquired. "I saw you concentrating and summoning your power."

I shook my head, "This place is filled with death. Filled is not the correct word, saturated is more accurate." I paused. "Healing is absolutely out of the question. If I attempted it, any life would be extinguished faster than I could save it."

Aesop frowned and we hurried our search.

The shadows from the black glass lengthened and melted together as the sun lowered itself. We split up, each searching through the rubble of the demolished temple. I found a stairwell, but unfortunately it was caved in and impassable. Smoking Bear found another, and Aesop discovered a third downward-sloping passage. Both of theirs were clear.

"Which one do we take?" I asked.

"Let us search the area," Aesop suggested. "Perhaps we shall find a clue indicating which entrance was closer to this sea shrine."

I unearthed a few more coins and pieces of petrified wood but nothing of significance.

"I've got something," Smoking Bear declared. She handed me a greenish bowl. "This was near the stairs Aesop found."

The bowl was magical. I knew the moment I touched it. The fragrance of the sea came to me, a scent of freshness and salt. An ocean spray misted my face while I gazed into the vastness of the sea contained in the bowl.

I sensed the power of water within, waiting to be tapped by any with the ability. I declined, knowing nothing of this element.

Aesop noticed us examining the bowl and came over, curious. "Let me see that," he demanded.

"Aesop, I wouldn't . . ." I warned.

Too late, he grabbed it from my hands. Instantly the color drained from his face. There was the sound of fire and water mixing, steam hissing and sputtering. He let the bowl slip from his dripping wet hands and it clattered to the ground.

"Damn it, Aesop," snapped Smoking Bear, "you should be more careful. This thing is full of water magics."

"My powers," he whispered. "I cannot access the elemental source of fire."

"You're extinguished," she told him, and shook her head. "It'll pass. Don't worry, I've done stupider things and lived."

Aesop appeared uncomforted.

"So," she said, "we either go down there now, or we leave and come back tomorrow when it's light. I for one don't want to wait another day with those two demons on our tail."

"We go," Aesop said.

With his fire powers gone and the death in these ruins overwhelming my abilities, what was going to protect us against the ghosts the De Marcos were so worried about? Yet Smoking Bear did have a valid point about the demons and the families closing in on us. "OK," I agreed, "let's go in."

"We'll need a light, though, if we want to go down there." Smoking Bear tore her pack apart. She fashioned a crude torch from the canvas and wooden frame, then lit it with flint and steel. "This won't last too long."

"I shall lead," Aesop said, and took the torch from her.

We then descended single file into the stairwell.

In places, the tunnel squeezed together and we had to push our way through. I had the sensation of being crushed. It was as if the guardians of this temple watched us, waited until we were far enough in, then would collapse the tunnel upon us.

The passage ended abruptly, blocked by a huge stone. There was an opening near the floor, too low to enter standing. One person at a time could pass through by crawling on his hands and knees.

Aesop handed the torch to Smoking Bear and went through. We waited for seven heartbeats in the dark. There were no sounds of panic, no bone-crunching death. Smoking Bear then tossed the flame before her and went in.

I followed quickly.

The crawlway narrowed and I scraped my shoulders to pass. For a moment, I was stuck between the rocks, stuck in the dark. Panic rose in my blood and I frantically pulled myself through.

I stood again in a large cavern filled with surprisingly fresh air.

Limestone formations of unbelievable variety decorated the walls, the floor, and ceiling as far as our torch illuminated. Strange natural curves and folds of stone clung to the walls; long daggers dripped water; clear pools with bulbous columns rose into shadows; spirals of stone stretched upward; veins of gold glistened in quartz; wide swaths of green and blue ores cut through the floors and walls; sparkling crystalline formations caught our light, stole it, and sent out their own brilliance.

"Observe," Aesop said, pointing to the near wall. "These formations are unnatural. One should not find gold deposits in a limestone cavern. This must be a special chamber, a holy place of sorts for the earth temple."

A myriad of passages left the grand chamber, most of them small, a few large enough to walk upright in. I counted ten of them.

"Which one?" she whispered. Even Smoking Bear was awed by the place. We all were. To speak was an intrusion, a violation of the serenity of this sacred vault.

Yet something did speak, and loudly. At first it made no sense. Smoking Bear whipped about to locate its source as the sound echoed about. Crazy shadows danced from the torch and made me dizzy.

The voice spoke again, in a Sarteshan dialect I knew. I told this to the others and replied in the standard dialect saying, "We come in search of the De Marco clan's statue."

Silence, then, "De Marcos? Are you family members?"

I replied to the shadows that we were.

"All the more pity you must die."

A figure emerged from the outer rim of illumination cast by our torch. Its outline blended into the surrounding rock. It wore a hooded robe of earthen colors with gold threads embroidered across each arm. With every step it took toward us the floor trembled slightly. For the briefest of moments I caught a glimpse of its face behind the cowl, a featureless surface of grey.

"I guard this temple from infidels," it explained, echoing throughout the cavern. "I protected it in life and now in tortured death." It walked forward with its granite hands outstretched.

"What did it say?" Smoking Bear hissed.

"It says we're in trouble," I told her, then released the firing mechanism of the crossbow. The bolt flew true to its target only to bounce off.

Smoking Bear pitched the torch to Aesop, then stood before the creature with her blades raised above her head.

It appeared unconcerned and advanced.

She brought the doubled blades down in a blur. There was a crack and sparks flew. Its robes were cut, but underneath was seamless stone, barely marred by her steel.

As the stone ghost approached, tiny cracks opened in the earth and dust fell from the ceiling. The air in the cavern moved suddenly, as if a door had been opened.

Of course! It was an earth sorcerer. I could counter its magics by using the powers of air, but I knew little about them. If I tried, I would likely do more harm than good. I'd have to find a way to use the magics I knew.

I shifted perceptions from mundane to magic and braced myself for the rush of death. This time, however, the powers of life and death were more evenly balanced. This temple was alive and still a source of power. The death in the ruins above I could sense; it was the greater of the two forces, but I could work magics here.

I saw the cavern with my inner vision, represented in the colors of magic. Before, when I healed Smoking Bear's arm and Hestor's mind, I thought the lights and color was pure imagination. Now I knew they were real. On my own I could never think of all these variations, all the subtle forces that played on the rocks and crystals. Masterworks of magics, all earth-related and all beautiful.

But I couldn't let the aura of this place distract me. I looked to the ghost. Within it were crystalline patterns of radiance. Hidden in this matrix was a lightless form, a smudge on an otherwise flawless design, death. Still holding the image in my mind, I eased off to see what was occurring physically in the cavern.

The ghost reached for Smoking Bear, but she danced out of the way. It was off-balance and she lunged back, connecting, causing small chips of stone to fly. Given enough time she might defeat this creature; she was faster and could damage it slightly.

A portion of the ghost's earth magics vibrated in harmony with those in the chamber's ceiling. I saw power being drawn from the temple, and a section of cavern collapsed.

Smoking Bear heard it rumble, then fall, and moved with blinding speed out of harm's way. A mass of stone landed dangerously close to her, thudding into the floor. I noticed a flash of magic from her, but did not recognize its source.

Our torch flickered as the dust from the cave-in choked the air. I didn't know how proficient a warrior Smoking Bear was, but I ventured she couldn't fight this thing in the dark. With Aesop deprived of his sorcery and our torch almost out, we were likely to lose this battle. I needed to try something.

I focused again on the magics, on the power of death within the ghost. How did it maintain such an imbalance? How did it isolate the death without life to balance it? I looked closer. There, a small thread, a vein of magic extended from the ghost and into the earth. I followed it with my mind. I left my body.

When I passed through the stone floor, my perceptions fogged. About me were tons of stone, an unthinkable density that crushed my spirit, but I could still see in a fashion. The earth magics pulsed mightily here. I ignored them and continued to follow the thread of death. Four meters below the surface, the line of magic terminated in a buried body.

The corpse was stone, petrified, and wrapped in crumbling cloth. Isolated within the remains was a pulse of life. The death flowed into the body through the thread of magic. It interacted with the life, beating with the opposite frequency. One pulse of life, then one of death. Both forces flowed, yet neither canceled the other so perfect was their cadence.

The Roland from the other realm recognized what this was. It was an alternating current, cycling between positive and negative forces. I knew how to stop it.

Using the abundance of death about me, I channeled some of it into the life force. It only required a small difference to shift the death pulse slightly out of cycle with its counterpart. The pulse of life came a fraction of a second early and annihilated a part of itself when it combined with the death. With the next beat, more of the preserved life force vanished. A few more cycles and it would be completely annihilated, leaving only the death.

I returned to the cavern to see how we were doing.

Smoking Bear had a nasty cut on her forehead. Aesop concentrated. His hands smoked from the effort, but he was still under the influence of the water magic in the copper bowl.

The ghost slowed and turned to me. "You," it said,

pointing. "You have disrupted the enchantment."

I sensed another pulse of death and more of the life force vanished. Some of the stones that built its ghostly arm fell from the mangled robes, dead rocks.

"I cannot allow you to proceed!" it screamed. "The statue must not be removed." He turned to Smoking Bear. "You know that!" More stones fell as its other arm collapsed, gravel on the ground. The earth shook with a renewed force. The air whipped about the cave. Our torch flickered.

The ghost of stone stumbled away from Smoking Bear. When it turned, she brought the parallel sabers down. There was the sound of steel ringing. Its body shattered. I sensed the line of magic connected to its buried body snap.

We stood silent a moment, breathing heavily, waiting to see if the thing would reanimate. It remained on the floor, lifeless and inert, no more than a pile of rocks.

"Are you injured?" I asked her.

"No, not really," she said, then touched the blood on her forehead. "A stone caught me in the head. It's nothing serious." She turned, "Aesop?"

"I am undamaged," he replied softly. "I still cannot produce a flame. Perhaps in a few moments."

The torch crackled and dimmed.

"We don't have much light left," I said. "Should we continue or return to the surface?"

"We go on," she said, "but which tunnel? There must be a dozen of them. By the way, Roland, nice job with the ghost."

Aesop stiffened, his pride wounded. I knew it would be difficult to recover any friendship now that I had succeeded where he had failed. What was I to do? I was certain he possessed more skill than I did. I just thought of it first.

"There are ten tunnels other than the passage we entered," he noted.

"So which one?" she repeated.

Were there any clues to the statue's location in the

poem? What had it said? "Pointing the way, he waits within circles of stone." Ten tunnels?

"I believe I know which one." I pointed to the seventh passage from my left.

"How do you know it is that particular one?" Aesop asked.

"We don't have too much time left," Smoking Bear urged and looked at our dying torch. "Let's just try it."

Aesop appeared unconvinced, but yielded and nodded his head. He handed me the torch.

The passage I chose was three meters above the cavern floor. Both Aesop and I boosted Smoking Bear up into the tunnel. She lay on her stomach, then gave me a hand up, while Aesop pushed from below. He followed, climbing on his own.

I could barely stand upright in this tunnel. The left wall shimmered and glistened with a vein of gold and quartz. Had I more time, I would have investigated, but the torch was nearly gone.

Two twists and twenty meters in, the passage ended in a solid wall.

Aesop announced his displeasure, "You have wasted our time and torch. Now we must return to the surface and fashion another one before we may continue."

Smoking Bear had already started back.

I had the torch so I followed. What had gone wrong? I was certain I had unraveled the clue in the poem correctly.

I was about to hand the light back to Aesop, when I noticed that the vein of gold did not extend into this section of the tunnel. Just ahead it disappeared into the earth. I thought these Sarteshan Earth worshipers followed the lines and contours of the earth. The main chamber was not a perfect shape. It preserved and enhanced the natural beauty of the cavern. It was odd that this tunnel followed the vein of gold for so long, then turned from it halfway through.

I scrutinized the wall where it angled away from the quartz deposit. I ran my hand across the section, and the earth gave a bit. It was not stone at all, but packed earth.

Aesop and Smoking Bear returned to see what the delay was. My hand was fully through the camouflaged section and extended into another chamber. They helped, and, in a few moments, we uncovered a hidden passage. The vein of quartz curved along, following the hidden tunnel.

Aesop said nothing.

This passage was smaller than the first. We had to bend over to make our way through. Then the torch sputtered one final time and died.

All I could see now were the dying embers glowing on the torch, winking out one by one.

"Aesop," she whispered, "do you think you can light up? I'm getting a bad feeling in here."

Smoking Bear and I waited. In the dark, my fears of being watched returned. If there were more guardians like the one in the main cavern, I didn't want to meet them here. An encounter in this cramped space was certain to be fatal.

First came a heat, then a dull glow. I saw Aesop's face full of shadows and concentration—a man obsessed with fire. A smoky flame caught in the palm of his hand, died, then sparked again and burned steadily. His tattoos flared to life and slithered across his arm.

"The effect from the water bowl has worn off," he said, triumph in his voice.

It grew hot quickly in the cramped passage so we moved on. The tunnel continued for ten meters, then emptied into a chamber two meters in diameter.

A basin of alabaster filled this room. Water dripped into it from the ceiling above, overflowed, and drained back into the earth. There, sitting in the center, upon its own pedestal, was a centaur statue made of gold. It was the De Marco family heirloom.

11

~~~~~~~~~~~~~~~~~~~~~~~~~~~

*R*olling over in bed, I nudged Sabrina from her sleep. She returned to her dreams, but I was awake. Better here than camped in a cold dark cavern in the middle of the Sarteshan ruins.

I stumbled into the bathroom and grimaced at my own face in the mirror. It was too bad we left the Jaguar in Oakland. I would have enjoyed the drive down the coast, and it would have given me more time to think. However, the quicker we investigated this storage facility and got out of town, the better. The police might be looking for me.

My left hand was still cold. Just when I forgot it, I touched something and felt nothing. My lack of concentration and forethought caused the injury. I should be grateful it was only my hand that went numb, and not a vital organ.

I stepped into the shower, but it could not rinse the feeling of politics from me. Everything I felt and touched, even Sabrina, had a taint of suspicion. I longed for simple answers and enemies who would make themselves known.

The dreaming part of me almost enjoyed this puzzle,

but my waking self was terrified. Somewhere in the middle of these feelings of curiosity and fear were my true emotions. The two personalties, dream and real, were becoming blurred. Their individual talents and traits were still there, but compounded: the real's suspicion and turmoil symmetric to the dreamer's patience and precision. Both had their place, their limitations, and together we had a strength I was unaccustomed to.

When I reached for a towel, Sabrina entered the steam-filled room. She ran her fingers through her hair, through colors of gold, platinum, and white, then stretched in a sensual rolling motion. I wanted for there to be more than politics between us; however, Sabrina had her own goals within the family hierarchy. I could only guess how I fit into her plans.

"Eugene wishes to see you," she said.

No pleasure before business? That was fine. I could play it cool too. "What's the urgency?"

"Didn't say, but he was extremely irritated."

"Did you tell him about Hestor?"

"No . . . I didn't think that appropriate. I thought I'd let you speak for yourself."

I was thankful for her discretion. Hestor staying at that private hospital still bothered me. The more I thought about it, the less I wanted any of the clans to know her location. I replayed the scene of Sam getting his brains blown out again in my mind and decided to move her tomorrow.

I stood there, dripping in the shower stall, formulating questions for Sabrina. Before I asked them, though, she stepped in and turned the hot water all the way up. Soap lathered and our frictionless bodies moved over one another. For the briefest of moments all thoughts of family, of plots, and of politics were washed away. This lasted as long as the hot water did, then the cold water of reality doused us.

Sabrina ordered a late brunch from room service while I toweled off. She appeared pleased. Was I completely under her spell now? No, I felt in control of myself. There came no unusually powerful feelings, nor the magical stimuli I felt before in her presence. What then? Where exactly was this relationship going? Later, I told myself, after I sorted out where I stood within the clan structure, then I could examine my growing feelings for her. Who was I kidding? I already knew I was falling for her, and without understanding how the families operated, whom I might offend, that could be dangerous.

"You know," she said, "manipulating life forces as you have been must give you extra energy in these basic life processes."

"Basic life processes?" I said puzzled.

"Reproduction," she purred, and reclined into my lap.

"Don't tell or all the women in the clans will want me."

Her eyes grew wide and darkened. "No, I think I'll keep this our little secret. At least until I grow bored with you." She smiled.

We kissed again and likely would have continued had not room service interrupted us. Cursing their early arrival, I went to the door.

When I returned, Sabrina was in the bathroom getting ready to depart. I sighed and abandoned my fantasies of staying all day in this room with her. Duty called, and a prince of the realm could not allow his personal feelings to interfere with politics. Bullshit.

The traffic downtown was heavy. Sabrina drove the rental car, and I had to admit she was better than I. She found a parking spot the size of a postage stamp and parallel parked perfectly the first time. The storage facility had rows of windows, painted black, and covered with grime and heavy security bars.

Two bums, camped by the side of the stairs, snickered to themselves when we walked up to the steel door entrance. There was a short hall that ended in a second steel door. Embedded in the wall next to this was a barred window, and on the other side sat a clerk. He was busy paging through a *Playboy*.

The clerk ignored me and fixed his attention upon Sabrina, asking, "What can I do for you, Missy?"

"First," she replied, "my name is not 'Missy.' Second, your business is with Mister Pritchard." She slid a fifty under the bars. It disappeared.

"So what can I help *you* with, Mister Pritchard?" He pulled at his mustache, evidently pleased with the transaction thus far.

"Is there a room here rented under the name of Fischer?"

"Now I can't let you know that unless I have the proper identification or a security code." He glanced past me to Sabrina, no doubt hoping for more money.

I told him the date of my birth. He checked the number's validity in a moldy book, then returned, disappointed. The code was correct.

"Lot 43," he told me, "it's the second from the last on the right-hand side." He pressed a button and the steel door buzzed with electrical current.

I pushed my way through and inhaled the scent of rot and mothballs. Every seven paces along this inner hallway, a sturdy iron door was set into cinder block. Water stains on the walls and rust on the doors indicated that little, if any, upkeep was provided. As we wandered farther back, the air cleared a bit, the doors appeared cleaner, and patches of disintegrating carpet covered the warped hardwood floor. Second from the end was a door numbered 43. It was free of corrosion and smelled slightly of machine oil. The lock was a sturdy old-style combination with three separate dials.

"Any ideas what the combination might be?" Sabrina inquired.

I shook my head and crouched closer to get a better look at the lock. "Hestor kept the security code simple enough," I said to myself. "Was the combination my birthday too?" It had three dials, possibly one for the day, the month, and the year. I turned them into the proper positions. Nothing, it held solid.

What about Hestor's birthday? No, that didn't work either.

One last birthday to try. I dialed in the numbers and pulled. The lock clicked open. Happy birthday, Clay.

"Was the combination your birthday?"

"No." I wasn't in an informative mood about my father either, so I kept the secret to myself.

The door swung inward and a sliver of light penetrated the darkness. Half-formed shapes lurked within the shadows. I took one step in and fumbled for the light switch. A solitary light bulb covered with dust, cobwebs, and dead moths flickered to life and shed an uncertain glow. It was a pack rat's dream come true. Rotting cardboard boxes, paintings covered with stained paper, and canvas bags stenciled with faded letters were stacked along the walls and floor of the room, in some spots all the way to the ceiling. A path through the center had been cleared, but disappeared ten feet into the artificial cavern of junk.

"It's going to take some time to get through all this stuff," I said to myself.

"What can I do to help?" Sabrina asked, then covered her face with a handkerchief to ward off the rising clouds of dust.

"We'll have to organize all this somehow, and I'll need your help to identify anything with family significance."

"Allow me to arrange the rental of another room," she said. "We can spread this around and have a bit more space to work in."

I nodded and she left, presumably to bribe the clerk again. I stepped in and made my way through what Hestor claimed were my father's belongings.

Rather than search the entire room by hand, I decided first to look magically for any signs of the watchband. I glanced about for a likely source of death. Near the door were several animal heads, hunting trophies. They had little death in them, merely the outlines of once-living creatures, but they'd do. For the life part of the paired forces, I'd have to use myself. I flexed my left hand, the dead hand, and had second thoughts. No, as a sorcerer I must master these simple manipulations. If I was constantly afraid to use my powers, other family members would view me as weak and as a target.

So I cautiously pictured both life and death images: the slain creatures, hunted, stuffed, then mounted upon wooden plaques, and myself, blood flowing, pumping life through my body. The power came, but I refused to let them rush together and cancel one another. I held them apart and gazed about the room.

A faint glimmer in the back. It shimmered as sunlight upon clear water, motes of light vibrating and crisscrossing, and reminded me of the copper bowl Smoking Bear had found. There was nothing else in the room, so I dropped the gradient of forces.

Just when I relaxed my grip over the magics, a flickering in the shadows caught my attention. It was back in the farthest corner. When I took a closer look, however, it vanished. Had I imagined it? No. I dropped the magic. Curiosity had replaced my concentration. I went to search by hand.

Crawling over unidentifiable bundles, I got to the first of the two magical sources. Eight crates were neatly piled along the back wall, stamped with the name, *Storm Dancer*. They were nailed shut, but each had a list of its contents tacked to the side: mainsail, forecastle, rudder. It was a boat, disassembled like a giant toy. I tried to open one. No luck, though; the nails held tight.

In my peripheral vision, there again was a blinking of faint magic in the same corner. That was impossible though. I hadn't set up any life and death gradient of powers. How could I see any magic? Ignoring the boat, I pushed my way over there. A large black square crouched in the corner, half my height and twice my width. I rearranged a few boxes to clear the area. It was a safe.

Chipped gold letters on the safe's door proclaimed ALDUSIAN GOLD MINE. A dial faced me and was numbered from zero to one hundred. I dialed the three birthday combinations, but the lock was uncooperative. I knocked on its side. The thick metal returned no sound. I'd need sophisticated tools to get inside this. If my father's watchband was anywhere in this forgotten chamber, it was in this safe. What else could produce enough magical energy to register through inches of steel plate?

Eager to gain access to the vault, I hastily made my way back to the center of the room. On my way, I accidentally kicked a sack, which I discovered contained an extremely heavy object. My foot throbbed from this revelation, so I sat on a crate marked WINTER BRANDIES to massage it. Curious, I unwrapped the toe-crushing substance to see what it was.

Within layers of oily cloth was a bronze bust free of oxidation. The head had a traditional strong Roman nose, a stare of nobility, and a slightly bored expression. Something was familiar about his face. Remove the curls, add a mustache and a baseball cap, and he was the same bronze baseball batter in Eugene's mansion. What was his name? Theodore? Sabrina might know who he was, perhaps a distant family member. His strong jawline and chin reminded me of Dad's, or mine for that matter.

The sole light bulb in the room flickered, flashed, then went dark. Suddenly the door looked farther away than I last recalled. Fear rose in my throat, and it was as if I was inside the earth temple again, watched by spirit guardians. Was this place protected in a similar fashion, with ghosts? I shifted again to view the place magically—nothing but the ship, the darkness, and my imagination. Relax, I assured myself. Hestor was the one who had stashed all this junk here, and she possessed no magical abilities. Nevertheless, I made my way toward the door before some mysterious force slammed it shut and trapped me.

Sabrina met me half-way down the corridor. "I bought two more rooms," she informed me, "lots 54 and 56, about the same size. I paid in cash so none of the credit cards could be traced."

"Great," I said. "We're going to need tools and a few lights before we can continue."

"Tools?"

"I'll explain on the way to the hardware store."

It took forty-five minutes before we returned with seven battery-powered fluorescent lights, a small generator (guaranteed to be silent), a high-torque power drill with several carbide bits, a roll of industrial strength tape, a cheap camera, and lunch.

We sorted the items into the three rooms by priority. Items that caught our immediate attention stayed in lot 43, those things that looked moderately interesting went into lot 54, and lastly either junk or broken items went into lot 56. Most of the hunting trophies went into this room except one which neither of us could identify. In appearance it was similar to the Greek Sphinx, although in size, it was closer to a German shepherd. Its face was not human, but not an animal's either; there were disturbing similarities to both. A pair of golden eagle wings lay folded, one on each side of the lion's body. They looked real and not merely sewn on. We took a picture of it and kept it in the top priority room.

The Sphinx watched us the remainder of the morning and far into the afternoon while we toiled, rearranged, and cleared the piles of accumulated junk. Most of the interesting things were heavy, like the safe and the boat, so they stayed in lot 43. There was a wide variety of materials to be sorted: crates of French wine long since spoiled and cloudy with particles, a brittle leather saddle with tiny silver stars hammered in place, a crystal chandelier stained from an untold number of candles, a rolltop desk frozen shut, a box of ballroom dresses, Civil War uniforms, and tuxedos, a carved ivory totem, perhaps Alaskan, a carton of antiquated motor parts, several round tin disks with square holes punched in them, and books sporting colonies of mold—Steinbeck, Hemingway, some in Latin, *A Discourse on Human Emotive Volatility* (I hadn't read that one before). More boxes, crates, and bags followed in a blur. We began arbitrarily to cart the things off to lot 56, the least valuable room, to examine later. I was in reasonable shape; still my back ached and my muscles were exhausted when we finally finished. Sabrina, like me, was covered in grime, sweat, and dust.

Tired, but no less curious, we started our inspection. The first thing I wanted to open was the safe. Sabrina agreed. She told me the Rhodes may have owned this Aldusian Gold Mine at one time. Perhaps this was one of the companies Eugene and Clay jointly owned.

I fired up the generator (which was not quiet), hooked up the drill, then broke three bits on the vault door. The fourth made it through the lock and opened the unyielding door.

Within, were several shelves on the top and three larger compartments beneath them. I examined the smaller shelves first. Most obvious were the rows of gold bars stacked in the upper right-hand corner. Next to these were solid gold coins with eagles stamped on one side. They were in mint condition and likely worth a fortune. A flash of greed passed through me, but my scholarly half reminded me that this was not a game of money. If Eugene was an example of how sorcery could be used to gain wealth, then riches would follow surely enough. What *was* important was discovering exactly what happened to Clay and who my enemies were. I set the gold to one side.

The next shelf held an iron box secured with a tiny lock. There was no key, but one short burst from the drill worked just as well. Inside were miniature envelopes, yellowed with age, paperwork of some sorts. I set this next to the gold.

Sabrina immediately picked them up. A smile spread across her lips when she opened the first tiny paper sleeve. She emptied the contents onto her dirty palm. A pile of not-so-small diamonds spilled from the paper. This was no paperwork—they were jeweler's envelopes. She picked out a stone the size of a dime and held it in front of a fluorescent light. It gleamed with white rainbows.

"Are they real?" I asked.

She nodded and her smile grew.

I watched while she carefully opened each one, inspected the contents, then returned them. There were more diamonds, some fancy yellow, others pale red, even brilliant black ones, uncut rubies, and watery sapphires.

One envelope was shoved beneath the others. It bore a wax seal of a triangle contained within a circle. Sabrina picked it up like the others, broke the seal, and removed a single stone. The thing was a long emerald-cut jewel the length and width of my little finger. Cold indigo at one end, it faded through the spectrum to a canary yellow at the opposite. In the center it burned a fire of pure living green, which caught the illumination from our lamps, trapped it, and grew darker. She held it between her index finger and thumb and stared into its depths.

"What is it?" I asked.

She said nothing and continued to gaze at the gem, enamored by the colors.

Something was wrong. Several seconds ticked by and she had not moved.

I viewed the gem magically. There was power inside it, a dozen pairs of opposites. Some I recognized—life and death, fire and water, earth and air—but the rest were unknown to me. Each pulsed within its own section of the gem. It reminded me of Hestor's mind. All those parts seemed to fit, but they were jumbled like a jigsaw puzzle forced incorrectly together.

Its magical fields of power rippled, aligned, and synchronized. My own life and death forces, static before, now oscillated with the identical pattern. *It* was influencing them.

A thought crossed between us, carried by our coupled fields of power. A dozen tiny voices spoke: "HELLO."

I backed off quickly, stabilized my paired forces, then dismissed the magic. How could an inanimate object speak to me? Was it Sabrina playing a practical joke? No, she didn't appear to be communicating with it, but mesmerized by it.

I pried the stone from her fingers, replaced it in the envelope, then stuffed it into the front pocket of my jeans. It was cold, a sliver of ice.

She didn't move for a few moments, still gazing at her empty fingers. Then she returned to the last envelopes and continued to identify their contents, emeralds and black opals, as if nothing happened. Curious.

While the unusual stone merited further attention, I would investigate later, when I was alone. It had a hypnotic effect upon Sabrina, yet not me. And it was alive. Better to be safe on this one point. Eugene might know what it was. He was the expert on stones and things related to the earth.

The last of the smaller compartments was empty, so we proceeded to the larger bins. The first held only fine grains of sand jammed into the corners, vacant. In the second was a heavy box that I removed to examine. It was crafted from mahogany and a simple brass clasp held the lid secure.

"It's a Safety Box," Sabrina said, running her finger over its polished surface.

"Safety Box?" I echoed.

"A box enchanted to give one a measure of protection from one's enemies. Within it you place an item stolen from your greatest opponent."

"Does it really work?" Considering my father was dead, I doubted it.

"Sometimes. It is a relatively minor magical device. Most of the family members do not bother with such things today."

"Too simple for the complicated schemes of the modern clans?"

She raised an eyebrow, but said nothing.

I set it close to me, almost fearing what might be inside. I had made friends in every family except the Chandlers, whom I had yet to meet. When I discovered whom my father believed to be his enemies, then their motives and friendship would be suspect. I wanted to trust them all: the De Marcos, my partners in adventure in Meredin; Eugene, who had befriended me and saved my life; and Sabrina, for whom I was developing profound feelings.

Opting to be a coward a while longer, I looked to the last bin. Within were two unframed photographs. The first one, slightly yellowed about its edges, was a picture of Eugene and my father standing by a river. They both held up a pan full of gravel and were shaking hands. They looked dirty but happy. Behind them, several men all panned for gold in the same river. Either this photograph was a hoax or it was taken many years ago, possibly during the Alaskan or Californian gold rush. Eugene looked five or ten years younger than when I saw him two days ago. My father appeared as old as he was in the picture of him back at the apartment.

"Do you know anyone in the families to possess unusually long life spans?" I asked and handed her the picture. Smoking Bear was much older than she looked, why not Eugene and Clay too?

She nodded. "I have heard rumors of such things. But if any have found the magical means to lengthen their lives, they have kept it a well-guarded secret."

I made a mental note confirming that Clay and Eugene were friends. That was reassuring. At least I knew a portion of Eugene's story was accurate.

The second photograph was printed on tin and one corner was badly bent. Dad and a woman were on a balcony, toasting champagne. From the angle of the picture, I could make out the city behind them and a partially constructed Eiffel Tower. Etched on the bottom were the words, CLAY AND JUDITH AT THE FAIR. As chance would have it, the young woman had turned during the exposure. Her face was a blur. Even distorted she seemed lovely, though, shining blond hair, a tightly laced bodice, and fine, delicate hands that held the champagne flute up to the light. This was Judith, Sabrina's aunt, the woman Mom was terrified of.

"Your aunt?" I handed the second picture to her.

She examined it carefully and straightened the corner. As Sabrina was pale to begin with it was difficult to tell, but I swore even more color drained from her face.

"Yes," she whispered, "this is she."

She paused considering for a moment, then said, "I suppose you ought to know the rest of her story as she was obviously involved with your father." She tried to meet my eyes, then looked away quickly, embarrassed. "Judith had liaisons with several men in the various families. This was unheard of in those days as birth con-

trol was neither reliable nor practical. As I understand
the rumors, she became pregnant by a man on unfriendly
terms with our family. My Uncle Grant, the head of our
clan at that time, decided that she be exiled. She never
returned. Whether she still lives in seclusion or was murdered I know not." Sabrina returned the picture to me.
"Since it was a very long time ago, I would assume the
latter."

"What happened to the child? You said she was pregnant? Is it possible I have a half brother, the child of
this woman and my father?"

"I am sorry. That's all I know. Judith is not spoken
of often in our clan. Interfamily relations are a delicate
matter . . . If you wish, however, I shall delicately ask
when I return home."

"Please."

I filed the two pictures back into the bin. The possibility of an older brother intrigued me. Eugene certainly
knew more than he was telling. I recalled his explosive
reaction when we had first met, when I mentioned my
mother, and he had thought I meant Judith. He had
clearly been alive when she had been. It was one more
thing I had to ask him.

Reluctantly, I then opened the Safety Box. A mound
of rotten royal blue velvet lay within. I pulled the bundle
out, discarded the cover, and found a dagger underneath.
It had a simple blade that tapered to a fine point. Several
scratches marred the blade, and I wasn't certain but it
looked bloodstained. The pommel bore an enameled device: two nebulous shapes, one white, the other black,
swirling about one another. It was a distorted yin-yang,
the symbol of Rhodes Industries.

Why did Clay consider the Rhodes family to be his
enemy when Eugene was his friend? It didn't make
sense.

"It is a dueling weapon," Sabrina informed me. "I
have seen them used before in ritual combats."

"This symbol—the white and black design, it's the
Rhodes crest, isn't it?"

She nodded, "An older version, yes, I believe so."

It couldn't have been Eugene my father had feared. In the picture they looked like the best of friends. I looked again to the dagger and speculated on whom it might have been used. That picture of the two of them had been taken a long time ago. Anything could have happened since then.

But why would Eugene bother to find me and save my life if he had been my father's enemy? What could he want from me? The watchband? It made sense, sort of. He might just be using me to get Hestor to reveal where she had stashed it. After I found the relic, I'd return to his desert estate and he'd have the magical relic and me. So why bother to teach me sorcery? There was also the assassination of Sam to consider. That was another loose end I couldn't figure out, the mysterious bald killer.

"Be careful of Eugene," she urged. "He has allies in many places, political power, and wealth beyond belief."

"I've got to get my mom out of Oceanview. If Eugene is my enemy, I don't want her where he can reach her."

"I can move her for you," she offered. "It may not be wise for you to return there."

Sabrina could get Hestor to a safe place. Release forms or not, she had power over the young Doctor Anderson and would likely be more tactful about it too. "OK," I agreed. I had to start trusting someone in this realm. It might as well be her.

"Don't worry about your mother," she assured me. "I'll take care of her."

"How much help can I expect from your family, or from you," I asked, "if Eugene is hostile toward me?" I hated to use our relationship in such a way, but if he was my enemy, I'd need allies quickly.

She pushed her brows together and sighed. "I'm not in a position to speak for my entire clan. The head of our family is my Uncle Morgan. I shall delicately put the question to him, but don't expect much. We have a long-standing alliance with the Rhodes. Both our families enjoy the benefits from such a treaty. You may, however, rely on me for whatever you need." She caressed my left hand.

I didn't feel it.

"Let's call it a day," I said, and squeezed my eyes shut, gritty with dust. Between moving several tons of antiques and the shock of finding the Rhodes' dagger in the Safety Box, I was drained both physically and mentally. "We've found everything here that's magical anyway."

"How can you possibly know that?" she asked, and laughed softly.

"I summoned a pair of magical forces and restrained them from flowing into each other. Certainly you've done this before?"

She looked at me unconvinced. "You cannot summon a pair of opposite forces and put them on hold as if they were a phone call."

I shook my head. "I'm telling you I did it ten minutes ago."

"Amazing. I've never heard of anyone who had this ability before. You actually can *see* the pairs of magical forces?"

"At first I thought it was only my imagination. But recently I envisioned the details of an enchantment, then used that knowledge to defeat a ghost. I could never have imagined such a resonance between the life and death forces on my own."

"I'd be careful to whom I told this, Roland." She got to her feet and brushed the dirt off herself. "Some clan members might feel threatened by your unique abilities. Some might even take steps to see such talents eliminated."

I made a mental note to keep my mouth shut in the future. All I wanted to do now was get out of this place, out of the layers of dust and mysteries that had yet to be discovered among my father's legacy. I stuck the dagger back into the box, *my* Safety Box now, and returned it to the safe.

We then closed the three rooms up tight and left. It

was dark outside and the clerk had long since gone home. The outer steel door slammed shut behind us and its lock clicked into place.

We returned to the Hilton. I wanted to relax, stare at the TV, and mull over the information I had gathered.

Sabrina disappeared into the bathroom and ran the shower until steam bellowed forth into our suite. She then made her entrance covered in perfume, the fog from the shower, and little else.

A fine idea that. After all, we were filthy.

12

The De Marcos refused to trek through the ruins at night, so we camped in the central chamber of the earth temple. No additional ghosts of stone materialized from the walls to threaten us. Aesop still suffered from the magical effects of the water bowl and had a difficult time providing a campfire. It was a dark and cold camp we made. A far cry from the scalding hot shower I left in the other realm. As my brother monk, Booklight, might have said, "Life is full of missing pages."

In the blackness just beyond my reach, I heard Smoking Bear gently snoring. I knew she slept curled about the statue. Aesop had nearly lost his hand when he tried to sneak a look. She insisted we leave it alone until we knew more about it. Probably a smart thing.

I mulled over Sabrina's comments about clan members finding ways to prolong their lives. It explained how Smoking Bear was Aesop's grandmother yet looked like his daughter. It meant I could not accurately judge any family member's age or experience based solely on appearance, not even Sabrina's. Especially Sabrina's.

Aesop was up and conjured a small light. A tiny flame burst to life upon the rock floor, seemingly burning with-

183

out fuel. He appeared well rested and I hated him for that. Obtaining a good night's rest on a solid rock floor was a skill I had yet to master.

I moved over and warmed my hands before his magical fire.

After a moment, he broke our silence. "How were you able to decide which tunnel was the correct one?"

Since he had started the conversation, I assumed I was again in his good graces. That was good. I needed all the friends I could get now. "I guessed," I told him and rubbed my warm hands over my arms.

"Guessed? These passages are apt to be filled with deadly traps and more guardians. You guessed?" His voice rose a few decibels and Smoking Bear stirred.

"It was an *educated* guess," I explained in a deliberately lower voice. "Do you recall the verse from the poem? It said, 'Pointing the way, he waits within circles of stone.' Well, this cavern certainly qualifies as a circle of stone, and if you look it has eleven tunnels radiating from it."

He looked about and confirmed this number.

"Neglecting the tunnel we entered," I said, "that leaves ten, like ten fingers spread out. I guessed the pointing way mentioned was the right index finger. At least that's the one I point with." To demonstrate I poked at him over the fire. "If the tunnels correspond to the fingers on a hand, then the pointing finger was the fourth tunnel on the right. The one we took."

"Clever," he acknowledged, and his eyes narrowed in appreciation. "Dangerous, but clever nonetheless."

"Let's not waste any more time talking," Smoking Bear interrupted. "We have a long walk ahead of us. Is it daylight yet?"

I didn't even hear her get up.

"Yes," Aesop answered. "The sun rose seventeen minutes ago."

How he knew the sun was up, I couldn't guess. Perhaps he had some connection with that ultimate fire source through his magic. Whatever the reason, we gathered up our gear and thankfully left the cavern. I'm not claustrophobic, but just spend the night in absolute darkness, surrounded by tons of earth, and you'll know what I mean. Smoking Bear walked behind us, carrying the blanket-wrapped statue in both hands.

"Don't forget your bowl," she told me.

The bowl Aesop had dropped, the one filled with water magics, lay in the same spot. He averted his eyes when I picked it up. The sensation of the ocean, a refreshing mist, materialized as I held it. I shoved it deep in my pack, well out of sight from the fire sorcerer. He had no comment.

"Do you think we'll make it to the bell by sunset?" she asked Aesop.

"Perhaps, *if* we do not encounter any trouble."

"What bell?" I asked.

Smoking Bear answered: "It's sort of a calling card that Xuraldium, the one who is going to tell us about the statue, leaves for people. Ring it and he comes."

"Sounds simple."

Neither of them replied, which led me to believe that it was not.

We kept our discussion to a minimum while we wound our way back through the shattered glass ruins of the Sarteshan Empire. It was an Arctic field of black ice, one that the sun's warmth never touched.

Our eyes, however, were not concerned with this. We scanned the cloudless skies, a piece of clear glass itself, for signs of pursuit. Why the demons had not found us was a mystery to me. From the air they should have spotted us in the ruins yesterday. I found it difficult to believe they were that incompetent.

Heading one part east and one part south, we cleared the silent city and reentered the wasteland, the dead Fields of Fire. In a few hours, we could no longer see the city in the distance. I imagined how it might have appeared in ancient times. A traveler from this direction would see towers of colored glass that reached into the sky and a polished mirror black wall the height of six men. It was a city of wonder, a civilization composed of different races and different cultures that blended into one splendid mixture. Such a metropolis could support thousands of people and, if the surrounding fields were fertile, possibly more.

There were so few people in this realm. Was it as Eugene suggested, that the number of people here were linked in some fashion to the number of true dreamers? And as the families killed each other off, were they also destroying the ability of this realm to support a population? If that was the case, why was the other realm, the real one, so overcrowded? I had no answers. Perhaps this ancient one, Xuraldium, knew.

The rolling plains, even after the rain, were desolate. Scattered weeds soaked up the precious water, and too soon the sun returned to bake them. The drying earth puckered into a network of cracks. Our steps made an unsettling grinding sound as we crunched over it.

Dust began to blow again. The rain was forgotten.

Smoking Bear called for a rest in the middle of nowhere in particular. She looked up at the sun, kicked the dirt, and muttered something about time and distance; how we had very little of the former and too much of the latter. She sat next to the statue, negating any curiosity either Aesop or I had about it.

We gulped our water silently. I finished what was left in my canteen, but it did not quench my thirst. Aesop's water bottle was nearly full. I heard it sloshing on his belt, practically untouched. Come to think of it—I had not seen him take a drink since we left Sestos. He caught my eye on his canteen and wordlessly offered it to me. I nodded my thanks, and decided he was a good guy after all, at least as long as his water held out. I was just getting comfortable when Smoking Bear stood and began again toward the Nomious Hills.

"If I did not know better," I said, catching up to her, "I'd say we're in a great rush."

"The bell," she said, without looking at me to break her stride, "it's only visible during the shadowy periods in the day, just before dawn and just after sunset. We'll spend an entire evening out here in the cold, being chased by who knows what, if we miss it."

I increased my pace to match hers.

Four thousand three hundred and forty-two paces over the baked soil, and Aesop (I was convinced he was far-sighted) was the first to spot them, the two demons, a speck in the southern sky.

Smoking Bear scowled, then gently set her bundle down. She drew her saber. Aesop prepared his magics. I didn't have to look; I felt the heat.

There was nowhere to run and no terrain to use to our advantage. The demons had picked a very good spot, for them.

I viewed the area magically, using the abundant death in the wasteland and my own life as paired forces. The statue, even wrapped in the wool blanket, radiated enormous power. Some of the magics I did not recognize, but there were elemental pairs of forces, and a vast supply of life and death, gleaming brilliant white and inky black. Aside from the negligible life within the weeds, there was no other life source to power my magics.

Having no choice, I cautiously tapped into the statue's life magics to boost the radius of my mystical vision. The statue's magics were stronger than I anticipated. It took most of my concentration to keep the two powers from flowing together and canceling one another.

Far up and to the south flew the two monstrosities. A wealth of shadowy magical fields danced about them. The magics looked like life and death, yet were different, muted, shifting colors and intensity, insubstantial. The rider constructed shields about himself from the unknown sorcery. Within, I recognized a large reservoir of the normal life and death forces. That was bad. He could heal himself.

The bat sent forth a finger of its own magic along with a high-pitched chirp. The sound bounced off Aesop and returned to it. I noted that the claw, the one Smoking Bear removed, had regrown.

I knew the flying demon's name, but how to speak with it before they attacked? Shout? No, that was impractical as the helmeted one would not wait while we carried on a conversation. Had not the stone in my father's safe called to me? I remembered the patterns of force that emanated from the stone. It influenced my magics, then used our coupled fields of power to communicate with me. Could I do the same?

I maintained the images of the dead land and the life force within the statue, *and* simultaneously pictured the fields of power about the bat and myself. Continuing at an excruciatingly slow pace, holding four images in my mind, I perturbed my own magics. When it appeared to be similar to the jewel's pattern, a fourfold vibrating globe of radiance and shadows, I forced my magical fields of power into proximity with the bat's. They oscillated just as the stone had made mine.

One of the snake heads noticed this disturbance and smoothed its magics out, negating my efforts.

I pushed harder, intensifying the contact.

Annoyance vibrated through our connection, then it asked, "What is it you want?"

I got through!

I formed my reply, but the four images wavered and began to dissolve. I could not simultaneously hold on to the four images *and* talk. I had reached the limits of my intellect. How could I reorganize them and free a portion of my concentration to speak with the demon? I needed some mnemonic device, a physical representation of all the life and death forces, something alive and something dead.

My hands! The left was, for all practical purposes, inert from the death I had absorbed while healing Hestor. The right was alive and normal. All I needed was to collect the forces of life within the right, the death in the left. But how? I eased off, allowed the mundane world to superimpose over the magic, then reached out physically to touch the magic sources. The wasteland death, the sinister portions of the bat's fields far and away, I imagined touching, like a child might reach to touch the sun, not knowing any better. Naturally, I felt nothing within my inert left hand, but a chilling sensation raced up my arm as if it were submerged in ice water. I repeated the process with the living fields, and my right hand tingled, burned with the surge of electricity, of living magic.

With the images reorganized, I had freed a portion of my concentration. I could speak with the demon.

"Are you the one called Bakkeglossides?" I echoed along our coupled fields of magic. Pause. Then, "Hello, are you still there?"

The right snake head responded, "We take great offense at your reckless pronunciation of our names." A feeling of irritation twinged though the connection. "How is it you know them?"

"That is not important to our discussion. As I understand it, knowing your name grants me a measure of power over you."

They mentally chuckled in unison. "Power? No," the left head replied, "you merely have our attention."

What precisely does that mean? While I only thought this, it proceeded to tell me as if it had heard my words.

"It means you have the good fortune to bargain with us. If you can offer us a measure of worth, or a tidbit of value, then an exchange of favors may be possible. If not . . ." A feeling of hunger originated from the demon, then the sensation of something being swallowed, alive but paralyzed.

"I see. You are a capitalist. What would it take to make you go away?"

"Not possible," both heads answered. "We are bound by previous agreements to serve as mount until the statue is found."

"Once you find the statue, are you still compelled to serve?"

They considered my question while my heart pounded thrice, then said, "No."

"We have the statue." I ventured a glance at it. "The heirloom is there."

The right head looked down and sent a pulse of sound and magic at the bundle. It bounced off and the left head sampled the echo. "You are correct." As soon as it confirmed the statue's presence, one of its magical fields shifted from an opaque lavender to a translucent blue, nearly invisible in the air.

"Now are you freed from the previous contract?"

I sensed a twisted satisfaction from the right head. "Yes, we have fulfilled our contract to the letter." It scrutinized my magics and me, then remarked, "You know more of our kind than you originally allowed us to believe. Who are you?"

"Who I am is of no consequence." I quickly re-checked the pairs of forces I held, hoping to conceal my thoughts from the demon. I needed to stay calm and bluff him if I could. Let *him* worry how powerful *I* was. "What is important is that we reach an agreement before our companions battle one another."

"Yes, I ardently agree." The demon slowed the beating of its wings slightly. "What specifically do you wish?"

"I require that you not attack us. Perhaps you could even aid us in combat."

The right head laughed, or the equivalent gesture for the creature's anatomy. "Not attacking you is one matter, but to attack one of my brothers is another. You do not have the means to bribe me sufficiently, or do you?"

Both heads paused as the helmeted demon shouted orders to make a high pass over us. The right head measured the distance and navigated, while the left continued to communicate with me through the thread of sorcery. "We assume from the feel of your magics and as you are speaking to us thusly, that you are a necromancer ranked at the Azure level of competence?"

"Azure?" I kept my thoughts under tight rein. Honestly, I had little concentration left for emotions.

"Apologies if we have given offense," it amended hurriedly. "You have mastery over life and death?"

"Of course," I lied. Mastery was a rather subjective term.

"We may require healing in the future. If you grant us this onus, say on five occasions, then we would agree not to harm you or your companions, at this time."

"Five? I might heal you once, and you must fly us

all to the bell in the Nomious Hills.'' What manner of
healing did a creature who regenerated its own leg need
from me?

"No." The right head sent a pulse of sound off Smoking Bear. "We refuse to carry that one." The acid taste
of bile transmitted through our bond, a vision of Smoking Bear's sabers flashing, a quick midair dodge, and the
burning of poison though its blood.

"Very well, twice I shall attempt to heal you, as long
as it does not endanger my life. Furthermore, you must
not harm my companions or myself while I owe you
these favors or the deal is off."

Both heads considered, then, "You bargain well for
one of your kind. We have a binding contract." Another
portion of its magics altered, a morsel of brick red
flowed into a pale river of clear green power; they mixed
into café au lait. Part of this new magic oozed through
our coupled fields and interacted with mine. The air
about me buzzed; the hair on the back of my neck stood
tall; there was the feeling of water trickling down my
spine, and a sense of excitement, of . . .

. . . of sin.

Now I understood these shifts in forces. The tidal ebbs
and flows in the fields of magic about the demons were
the paired forces of good and evil, and the various
shades of morals in between.

I withdrew from the creature with a shudder. After we
confronted the helmeted demon, and if I survived, then
I would consider what I had just agreed to.

"Something strange is going on up there," Smoking
Bear said, shielding her eyes, trying to see better.

Bereft of my mystic vision, I barely made out the bat-
snake demon. It flew above us in slow lazy circles. In a
terrible way it was graceful. The two heads pumped up
and down, balancing the shifting rider and the beat of
its wings. The whole of its body was involved in flight.

The rider, on the other hand, was anything but graceful. He shouted orders, then hit the creature with a metal
rod that sent electric arcs across its body. The bat

winced, but continued in this circular pattern, spiraling down and away from us.

"Is the demon damaged in some fashion?" Aesop wondered aloud.

"It is not damaged," I confessed. "I made contact with it. For its pledge to leave us peacefully, I agreed to heal it."

"You bargained with that demon?" Smoking Bear demanded, her eyes wide with astonishment.

I nodded. "I thought it was the best thing to do."

"You're just full of surprises aren't you?"

"Look"—Aesop pointed—"it is landing. Shall I attack them both on the ground?"

"No," she stated flatly. "If the bat will not attack us, then let's not engage it unnecessarily. Bad tactics."

Aesop shot a penetrating look at me.

He didn't trust me? Of course not. I was family. In his place I would be equally suspicious. I felt the heat build within him and the humidity rise about me.

Bakkeglossides fell the last few meters onto the ground as the helmeted one touched the metal rod to him again. Electric flowers bloomed nearly a meter in height and the bat's midnight skin smoldered. Both serpent heads hissed and snapped at the other.

The rider leapt off his mount, raised his hand, and flipped the demon off. The bat shot off into the sky, becoming smaller and smaller, heading toward the hills, a black speck, then gone.

The helmeted one spat a curse at his rebellious mount, then approached us. "I do not care how you arranged that little coup," he said. "All I am interested in is the statue. How happy I was when I heard you went to all the trouble to deliver it to me personally. I dreaded the notion of searching those ruins by myself. All those ghosts and guardians, temples and hallowed ground . . . a very distasteful affair." He stopped and tilted his head toward Smoking Bear. "Always a pleasure to see you again, my dear."

"Why don't you go to Hell," she replied in a voice of pure venom.

He stuffed the silver rod into his belt and removed his black riding gloves. "At the proper time," he replied.

I recalled the power within his hands. With a mere gesture he had punched a hole in the clouds, nearly destroyed the balloon, the basket, and us.

Aesop jerked his head, a signal for me to move. He also circled, and the three of us spread out to form the points of a triangle about the demon. I suppose this was so he could not attack us without retribution from the others. I just hoped he ignored me.

The demon wore a light tunic of blue silk embroidered with silver stars, the constellations of Meredin. When he moved, I heard a jingle of metal beneath his outfit. His helmet was huge, twice the size of his head, and made of gold. It must have weighed ten or twelve kilos easy. A pair of sculptured eagle wings swept down from the crest to cover his face. The feathers were spread apart, slits for the eyes and for breathing. Small wormlike *things* wriggled behind them when he spoke.

"Sure," said Smoking Bear. "You can have the statue." She moved slightly to one side of the bundled relic, then planted her saber tip into the sand. "Why don't you come over here and try to take it?" She smiled, and I saw her muscles tense, her knees bend slightly.

A newly born spring welled up under my feet, the remnants of the rain trying to extinguish the mounting power of Aesop's fire. I risked a glance behind me and saw fat clouds sneaking over the rocky hills, more water.

"I have no wish to harm you," the demon cooed. "Surrender the statue and my master will be satisfied. It need not mean your deaths . . ." He let that final *s* trail off in oblivion.

I set up a very weak magical field, tapping into the statue's power again. Smoking Bear had a surprising amount of unknown magics about her, darting globes of fluorescent pink and apple green; Aesop shimmered with the intensity of a flare, all smoky reds and oranges; and the demon was surrounded by a kaleidoscope of colors, the shades of good and bad conscience.

He took one step toward Smoking Bear.

That was all the provocation the De Marcos required.

Smoking Bear whipped her sword into an en garde position, flicking a small amount of sand into his face. The helmet protected him, but he flinched.

Aesop took advantage of this confusion to loosen his power. White heat swelled forth, a compressed mirage of wavering air that boiled over the field. The earth melted, turned glassy, then cracked where the focused inferno chanced to touch. Pools of molten sand were sucked into the storm of fire and vaporized into a pearly cloud. In less than a heartbeat's span it surged to where the demon stood.

His tunic blasted away in a flash. Underneath his light outer clothes he wore a suit of metal rings. They too melted. Only his helmet remained, untouched by the heat, and shimmering gold. The superheated cloud cooled, and the gaseous sand precipitated into small crystals upon his flesh and helmet. He remained standing, to my amazement—a perfect human torso burned black. The outline of his armor, smoking metal rings, clung to his charred skin.

He whipped about to face Aesop. His skin cracked. Beneath the winged helm, I saw a thousand points of light the color of blood.

Smoking Bear darted in to finish the creature off before the heat subsided. Her leather armor began to smoke when she closed.

The demon heard her and turned again.

If they could keep this up, continually distract him, then he would never have a chance to use his powers.

She raised the double saber in a high feint, then, with mercurial speed, brought it down and up, cutting from inside the creature's guard. Her entire body followed through with the motion. It raised a hand, perhaps to attack, perhaps to defend; it didn't matter. Her blades intersected the demon's arm and severed it. There was a dry sound as if a dead branch had been snapped off.

How much damage could he take and stay alive?

From behind the helmet he laughed. It was a good belly laugh, not a fake one, originating deep within his body and echoing through my soul. Even Smoking Bear paused when she heard it.

He gathered his magic. The life and death within his shields flared with power. There was a flash of light as they flowed into one another. I blinked, slightly dazed from the intensity of the sorcery. When I looked again, his arm was whole and his skin was unblemished and pink. The severed arm still lay on the ground where it fell. He had grown a new one.

"I am disappointed," he said to Smoking Bear and shook his head. "You are becoming slow in your old age." As he spoke, there were more unsettling motions beneath the helmet. "Now allow me to demonstrate that *my* powers are as vital as ever."

I did not see his attack coming, not even magically, but somehow Smoking Bear anticipated it. From the demon's recently regenerated hand, magic gathered and burst forth. She jumped, faster and farther than any Olympic athlete. Some of the magic about her flowed. One of her pink spheres exploded as a sliver of his power intersected with hers.

The area where she had been standing a second ago was gone. A hemisphere in the earth, perhaps two meters in diameter, appeared. There was no heat, no explosion, nor had the earth been moved in some fashion. It just vanished. Sand cascaded into the hole. The demon chuckled.

"Very good, my dear. Hop about, provide me with some entertainment before I am done with you."

Desperate, I tapped into the energies the statue held. I could not identify the demon's offensive magic, but I knew he must be using life and death to heal himself. If I was lucky, I'd get a chance to use those powers against him.

From Aesop, I felt heat building again. I saw enormous energies play about him, dancing wildly, flickering in and out of existence as a fire does. The water magics splashed nearly out of control as he forgot them and focused solely upon his flames. He then released the power. A tightly formed pattern reached out, not to attack the demon, but to land squarely upon the earth under his feet.

The air leapt about the evil one. The earth beneath him flashed a bright white, cooled to a yellow, then a dull red. The demon flared as a torch would and writhed in pain. His new skin blistered, and he sank into the molten sand. He screamed and pulled one leg free.

When he tried to remove the other leg, Smoking Bear lunged at him. Her sword impaled his midsection and she ripped it free. He reached for her but she again danced away. Where she had been, another section of the field disappeared, this time over four meters in diameter.

Smoking Bear stomped her feet. Her boots smoldered from the brief contact with the glazed earth. Her magics were low. Only one pair of pink and green globes remained. Attacking the demon physically gave her no time to concentrate and rebuild her magical defenses.

No blood flowed from the demon's wound. One hand held his stomach, and the other rested on his free leg. He tapped into the life and death forces held in reserve. When he accessed them, they glowed prominently, no longer hidden beneath his shields of good and evil.

To counter, I switched power sources, fast. I siphoned his life force reserves and drained the power into the death, into the wasteland. The demon pushed more life through and tried to heal himself. Some magic did trickle through to repair the damage to his leg, but most spilled into the desolation about us. He finally caught on and cut the flow of wasted power, cursing as he did so.

Tiny weeds sprouted, along with yellow flowers and long blades of grass. The long dead Firestar blossoms burst forth and unraveled, their cherry red mouths covered in dusty copper pollen. With the water that collected as a result of Aesop's magics, this section of the wasteland had turned into an oasis.

The demon stood at an odd angle, with his left leg useless and his right supporting all his weight. Aesop collected his magic and prepared for another blast. Smoking Bear circled slowly to his back side.

The demon turned as best he could and faced me. He cocked his head at a curious angle, then shrugged, and raised his hand toward me. His magic, straight from Hell, rolled forth.

Smoking Bear shouted, "Move!"

I stood frozen, fascinated by the power, just as I had the first time I had seen Aesop's fire. I grasped for the life within the statue, the life within the land, anything to save myself. I panicked and lost control. The pairs of forces slipped though my fingers.

My mind slowed the events of my last moments. The destructive power closed to three meters, then two meters. I'd never see the dream realm as it once was, magnificent and healthy. I would die here in these wastelands. I would die as my father had. I would die the last of the Pritchards. Would the families continue to battle until only one remained? Then what?

One meter, then the wave of magic touched me. The first layers of my clothing disintegrated, consigned to oblivion. In the moment before I, too, vanished, I regretted the millions of things I had never done, but . . .

My consciousness snapped a universe away.

Next to me lay Sabrina in shadow, outlined by a faint glow originating to my right. I sat up, scratched my head, and looked about confused. Was I dead? If you died in one realm, what happened to you in the other?

From the floor, the muted glow brightened. I rolled out of bed and investigated.

My pants were glowing. I fished about in the front pocket and removed the stone that had mesmerized Sabrina yesterday. It was burning emerald in the center, one end midnight blue, the other the color of straw aflame. Magic was there. I didn't have to have a gradient set up to sense that. Cautiously, I imagined the life and death forces within it and instantly the vision came. Its twelve separate sections spoke to me simultaneously.

"ENTER," they urged.

Enter? Enter what?

"ENTER," they repeated.

I examined the jewel closer. On its facets and planes played a tiny drama reflected a dozen times: a demon stood, one hand pointed; Smoking Bear shouted a warning; and I stood and watched helplessly. The longer I observed the scene, the larger the view became until it was life-size, a window to the other world.

I stepped through.

The power rolled over the earth directly at the other Roland. I watched from a different perspective now, from outside my own body. I had no more feelings of panic. I had no feelings at all. Strange. With a clarity I rarely possessed, I delved deeply into the life the statue held, then readied myself, taking three slow breaths (even though there was nothing to breathe in this phantom form).

The demon magic touched the other Roland and dissolved the outer layers of his clothing. I waited, continued to watch, and conserved my power until the last moment. The skin on his right calf evaporated, exposing capillaries and fatty tissue. I speculated on how much that might hurt, then channeled the life magic into my other body. I did not try to stop the demon's magic, rather concentrated only on repairing the damage as quickly as it occurred.

The destructive forces poured over me, acid upon my skin. My sorcery was not enough. I had only slowed the dissolution of my other self. Another layer of flesh peeled away. Muscle lay exposed on the calf; the skin on his thigh disappeared; the right boot was nearly gone; tiny bits of white bone poked through his foot.

I squeezed more life from the statue into the other Roland, focused only on tapping more power, more power to counter the demon's, more power to save my life. The two canceled one another, boiled about, one seeking superiority over the other. The image was a distorted yin-yang. My healing life force swelled to embrace the dark rainbows of chaos streaming forth from the demon's hand. More power, and the first few layers of connective and fatty tissue reappeared on his calf. More power, and patches of skin knit together. I was winning!

The destructive power abruptly ended. I ceased draining the statue even though my leg was still bleeding. The energy level within the De Marco's heirloom was nearly gone. I stepped back into my body. The contact with the stone in the other realm severed.

Events resumed their normal speed. I first felt pain from the open wounds on my leg, then relief that I was still alive.

The demon stood staring at me, his mouth agape. This time he brought up the other hand and again pointed at me. Perhaps I was too hasty in returning to this body. I braced myself. Damn.

Smoking Bear slashed from behind. In his zeal to eradicate me, he had ignored her. Bad mistake. Her parallel blades were raised as high as she could, fully extended, then they sliced through the air, leaving a twin mirror trail. The sword bit into his neck and passed clean through. His head, helmet still on, left his body. It executed a slow arc through the air then bounced twice on the scorched earth. A sigh escaped the demon's body and it collapsed, blood finally flowing from his wounds.

Aesop approached the helmet and kicked it off the disembodied head. He then melted the earth about the wings of gold and watched while it sank into the molten grave.

I tried to stand. My injured leg gave and I lost my balance. Only the back half of my boot and leggings remained, and blood oozed profusely from where the skin was peeled away.

Smoking Bear jogged over to me. "That was an impressive little trick. Are you OK?"

There was genuine concern in her voice and something strange in the way she looked at me. Worry? From Smoking Bear? No, only a reevaluation of my powers.

I smiled, just happy to be here. "I am fine," I said as I held my leg and tried to slow the bleeding.

From Aesop's pack she removed bandages and attended my leg. The dressing was uncomfortable, too tight, but it did stop the bleeding.

Aesop helped me up with his arm about my waist.

I glanced at the demon and my heart stopped. He was standing, his head again on his shoulders.

"Your enemies apparently underestimated you," said the demon to us. His unhelmeted head was a mass of worms, tiny white translucent tentacles, under which lay a smooth surface of flesh. No eyes, nor mouth, nor nose were there; these were shrunken and tangled, multiplied a thousand times on the tips of the squirming fingers of flesh.

"I do not understand your young friend," the demon said, "but I know when I am outmatched. Another day, my dear. I look forward to the occasion." He bowed to Smoking Bear, gave me an appreciative glance, then pointed to himself and vanished.

"What happened? Where did he go?"

"Apparently," Aesop replied, "he took Smoking Bear's suggestion and returned to Hell."

"Can you walk?" she asked me. "It'll take him a long time before he recovers, but I want to get to the bell just in case there are more where he came from."

I tried. It hurt, but I managed to take a few steps.

We resumed our march, now slowed by my leg. It was clear we would not reach the bell, and comfort, by sunset. Once in the Nomious Hills I had to rest more frequently as the terrain became rocky.

When the sun touched the eastern edge of the land, a bloody pink grapefruit cut in half, she pointed to a cliff and announced, "There."

High up a smooth rock face, some twenty meters up, hung the bell. It looked to be of oriental origins, large and cylindrical.

"You feel up to the climb?" Aesop asked her.

She answered by setting the statue down and removing a thin knotted rope from my pack. The shadows in the hills lengthened and a cold wind blew. She walked to the face of the rock, carefully examined it all the way to the top, then climbed. It took her ten minutes to reach the top. Twice during her ascent, she stopped and backed down, unable to continue by the route she had chosen.

When she got to the upper ledge, the shadows just covered the niche where the bell hung. It was no longer there.

Curses rained down upon us from her perch.

"I shall start a campfire," said Aesop.

I sat on the hard ground and prepared myself for another uncomfortable night.

13

I woke up tired from the battle, tired from our hike across the Fields of Fire, and tired from Sabrina last evening. I vaguely remembered her departure when it was still dark. Our plan was for her to move Hestor from Oceanview, while I continued to search through my father's belongings. Tomorrow we'd meet back at the resort by the sea and compare notes.

How did the family members go for so long without REM sleep? My life was becoming one nonstop existence. I never truly slept anymore, but I didn't feel the way you'd expect to after staying awake all night. This was different, a cross between a caffeine high without the jitters and the exhilaration of running three miles on a cold morning. I thought people who never slept went crazy. Maybe it only happened to nondreamers.

I was doing a bad job of shaving when a polite knock at the door came. It was probably the bellboy with breakfast so I ignored him. Had I really stepped through the stone last evening?

I tried to communicate with it again, but it stubbornly lay in my palm, inert and silent. Perhaps the stone merely showed me what I already knew how to do—

leave my own body. Hadn't I extended my vision and found the ghost's body beneath the earth temple? And when I spoke with Bakkeglossides flying kilometers away, he appeared as close as I was to my own reflection in the mirror. I was, however, grateful for the thing's assistance. Whatever its powers and motives, it had saved my life.

Again came the knock, this time more insistent.

Wiping the lather from my face, I went to peer through the peephole in the door. A small man, his features distorted by the lens, stood there. I didn't recognize him. He wore a three-piece suit and looked like he wanted something. It was the "wanted something" part of his appearance that made me hesitate, yet there was a familiar quality to his face that prompted me to open the door anyway.

His expression was one of recognition.

"What can I do for you?" I asked.

"Good morning, Mister Pritchard. Roland?" He extended his hand and offered a weak handshake. "My name is Lloyd. I am Eugene's son, your cousin." He spoke with a faint English accent.

How had this Lloyd tracked me down? Did that mean Eugene also knew where I was? "Come in," I suggested.

He did and sat in one of the two uncomfortable chairs in the room. I sat on the bed facing him, still in my robe. He looked concerned rather than friendly.

"I have limited time here," he continued, "so let me get to the heart of the matter." His voice was civilized but had an edge of annoyance to it. "It has come to my attention that recently you discovered certain properties belonging to the Rhodes family."

"Oh?"

"Yes."

"Exactly what properties are you referring to?" I inquired.

"Do not be coy with me. I know you broke into an old storage building last afternoon. As I understand it, you destroyed certain irreplaceable antiques in your rampage."

"Are we talking about the same place? All those things are mine. My mother put them there herself."

"Ah, then perhaps this is all a misunderstanding. I have heard your mother is not at all well."

"Don't bring my mother into this." And how did *he* know about Hestor?

He raised his hands, and said, "I offer my apology."

I didn't like this guy. Eugene's son or not, I wanted to pop him one right in the face. His hair was slicked back too perfectly, and he was too neatly dressed in that charcoal grey pin-striped suit too early in the morning for my liking. "Just how did you find me?"

"That is of no consequence. We were talking about those items which you removed from lot 43."

So, he knew exactly where Sabrina and I were yesterday. Maybe I was the one who was mistaken. Maybe I *had* searched through the Rhodes' belongings. On the other hand, I had the proper code and combination to get in. Whose property was it? "I was under the impression that Eugene gave me permission to search for . . . a certain item belonging to my father."

"Then you had best get on with that search, but first return what you took."

Took? The only thing missing was the one peculiar stone and that was staying right where it was, in my robe pocket. Unless Lloyd went to lot 43 and expected the place to be packed to the rafters . . . The other two-thirds, the less interesting things, were in lots 54 and 56. That might be the source of his confusion. "I better call Eugene and find out what this is all about."

"Feel free." He pointed to the phone by the bed.

I picked up the receiver. It was dead. I slammed it back down. "I'm tired of playing these games. Who sent you?"

"You are making a grave, perchance a fatal, mistake by not cooperating with me."

Suddenly this Lloyd didn't seem threatening or powerful at all. He was trying to bully me, and I hated bullies. He reminded me of a scaled-down version of the detective who dragged me down to Mexico, not in his dress or mannerisms, but in the way he expected me to jump when he gave a command.

"You will be taking on the entire Rhodes empire," he stated calmly, "the entire family and all our resources, mundane and magical."

"It seems to me, if you were so powerful, you'd just take whatever you wanted without asking."

"It does not have to be this way. I know my father has taken a liking to you, but if you persist in this course of action, we shall be forced to take steps."

"Then you'd better take a few steps out of here right now," I said, standing, "or I'll give you some help." This Lloyd was no match for me physically. I hesitated a second and glanced at him magically.

He rose from his chair also.

Forces sprang to life around him. Crystalline patterns of magic solidified from his golden aura. The magic not only surrounded him, but it reached deep beneath the floor, deep into the earth. Before the magic fully formed, however, before he attacked, the power suddenly dissolved.

"No," he whispered, "this is unnecessary. I am by temperament a peaceful man." He rubbed his temple and the color in his face drained. For a moment, I thought he would faint. His body swayed but he steadied himself with one hand on the chair. He looked about puzzled, then blinked a few times, and declared, "I look forward to our next meeting, Roland." He even had the nerve to hold out his hand—as if I'd shake it.

I glared at him.

He shrugged and withdrew the chivalrous gesture, then left, closing the door gently behind him.

I sat back down on the bed, relieved. I thought I'd be in another magical battle. Sabrina was correct when she said I'd have to learn the magical and political ropes quickly to survive.

Lloyd was strange. His personality oscillated between the civilized country gentleman and an abusive busi-

nessman. Was this typical behavior for him? Schizo-
phrenic? And Eugene's part in this was increasingly
mysterious. The dagger within my father's Safety Box
was there for a reason. I could not help suspecting Eugene of a more sinister role. Did he send Lloyd to
threaten me? Lloyd might be acting on his own. Just
because they were both Rhodes didn't guarantee they
had the same political motivations.

Before I acted on any of this speculation, I'd call Eugene and ask him personally what was going on. I
picked up the receiver and this time it worked, so I dialed the desert estate. A servant answered, stating that
Mister Rhodes was out of town at the moment on urgent
business.

"Just tell him I called," I said. "No, there's no number where he can reach me, thank you." I heard several
clicks through the line before I hung up.

I decided then to move from the hotel. A nagging
feeling that something bad was about to happen came
over me. One more call to make, though. I threw a few
things in my bag while I waited to get through on the
phone to Oceanview Hospital. I reconsidered and hung
up.

Now *I* was being paranoid, but if the Rhodes empire
had vast resources, it would be a simple matter to trace
or tap one phone call. And I didn't want anyone to know
what Sabrina and I were up to. I'd have to trust that
everything was well with her. What was I worried
about? She could take care of herself and the young
Doctor Anderson. I should be worrying what my next
move was. I nervously wound my watch until the stem
would turn no more.

I packed one change of clothes and left the rest in the
room. In case anyone searched later, I wanted them to
think I'd be returning. I was not.

I took the stairs; the elevator looked too good a place
for an ambush. Pausing in the stairwell, I listened for
any signs of pursuit. Silence. Outside I caught the bus
on the corner and took it downtown. There, I got on the
trolley and rode it in circles for an hour. When I felt

certain no one had followed me, only then did I go to the storage building.

I scanned the street once for any trace of magic. Nothing. The two bums that had camped by the building yesterday were still there. There were drunk, and smiled and waved to me as I went in.

"I'm moving the contents of lots 43, 54, and 56," I informed the clerk with the mustache.

"Is there a problem, Mister Pritchard?"

"No," I lied, "my family is moving out of state." I folded two fifty-dollar bills in front of him and pushed them under the barred window. "This may take care of any inconveniences."

He took the money without comment and stuck it into his magazine. President Grant censored a scantily clad woman.

"Would you mind calling some reputable movers for me?"

"Certainly, Mister Pritchard," he said, then buzzed me through the security door.

Twenty-two hurried strides down the dirty hallway, then I halted at lot 43, crouched over, and turned the lock. It felt gritty, and made a pinging sound when it opened.

I flipped the light switch on, forgetting that the bulb was dead. It remained dark. Yesterday we left the portable fluorescent lights just inside the door. I fumbled about for them, but they were gone. My eyes adjusted to the faint light, and I saw there was nothing within the room. I double-checked by looking magically. All my father's possessions, the safe, the disassembled boat, they were all gone.

Lloyd, it must have been Lloyd who took it all. I should have punched his face when I had the chance. At least I still had the gem. I touched it in my front pocket to reassure myself it was still there. I would get Dad's property back, even if I had to fight for it.

Next, I checked lot 56, the room containing the least interesting items. Those too were gone.

Mad as Hell, I checked lot 54. The lock on the door

turned smoothly. Inside were all the items we classified as of intermediate interest. The rolltop desk, the bronze Roman bust, the stacks of oil paintings, the books, the ivory totem, they were all still here.

Why had Lloyd removed the most and least interesting items, lots 43 and 56, but left this one untouched? Was he still in the process of removing the contents? It occurred to me that he might return before my movers got here. I would almost welcome the confrontation. I felt violated, ripped off. The only links to my family's past had been stolen. Someone was going to pay.

I packed a few of the loose items and waited. Every few minutes, I heard footfalls in the hall, but it was only my imagination. Twice I was so certain, I prepared my magics, ready to do battle with Lloyd. He never showed.

I finished packing what I could, then went to the front desk.

"Has anyone else been here this morning?" I asked the clerk.

"No. Is there a problem, Mister Pritchard?" He appeared to be telling the truth, but with good liars one never knew the difference.

"No, no problem." If I told him about the stolen lots, there would be questions, and he might call the police. That was the last thing I wanted.

My movers soon arrived in a faded red delivery van. Tacky orange flames were painted on the front and billowed across the hood. Letters had once been stuck to the side panel proclaiming: ON THE BALL MOVERS— MOVE A.S.A.P! Most of these had long since fallen off, leaving only outlines in faded paint. It read: ON E BALL O S—O A.S.P!

I asked them to load everything up and move it to a place north of here in Mission Valley. Phil, the man in charge, slightly overweight but with a kindly smile, gave me an estimate. It was roughly half of my remaining cash. Whatever the cost, it would be worth it to protect my property.

I helped Phil and his assistant load the van. By noon, all the remaining items were shuffled to the new loca-

tion. This one was outdoors and guarded by dogs. I paid
for three concrete cubicles, which could barely contain
everything from lot 54, then I was dead broke.

With my family's possessions secure, I'd catch a
plane and rendezvous with Sabrina. I hoped she had better luck than I did today.

Phil dropped me off at a bank close to the airport. He
asked if I was in any trouble, then offered me a few
dollars. I thanked him, but refused. It was heartening to
know there was one good person out there. When I became as wealthy as Eugene, I promised myself I'd find
Phil and hire him. I could use an honest man working
for me.

From the bank, I took the maximum cash advances
on all three credit cards Eugene had lent me. If he traced
the cards, all he'd learn was that I was at this bank, and
not where I was going.

The short walk to the airport gave me an opportunity
to organize what I knew as fact, rumors, and my guesses
about recent events.

Fact One: Sam was mistakenly killed at the Gas n'
Mart in my place. That meant one of the families wanted
me dead for reasons unknown.

Fact Two: The police picked me up, questioned me,
then planned to turn me over to this enemy family. Whoever it was, he or she possessed considerable influence.
More evidence that it was one of the royal families.

Fact Three: Eugene rescued me from this unknown
enemy. There was a purpose attached to his motives, but
I'd save that for my guesses.

Fact Four: Hestor hid Clay's possessions. Lloyd
claimed they belonged to the Rhodes. But since lot 43
was filed under the name Hestor gave me, and the combination was Clay's birthday, it was probably my family's.

Fact Five: A Rhodes' dueling dagger was in Clay's
Safety Box. Sometime in the past, he and the Rhodes
family had been enemies. The important question was
which Rhodes? Eugene? Lloyd? Lloyd appeared
younger than I, but who knew how old he really was?

Last Fact: My property was stolen, either last night or early this morning. I didn't tell anyone about it, and Sabrina was with me all night. So how did Lloyd find out?

Now to the rumors.

First, there was Judith, who supposedly was involved with Clay. Sabrina claimed she was dead, but she was suspiciously tight-lipped about the entire affair. I suspected she knew more. Hestor even knew the mysterious woman. She had whispered her name to me at Oceanview. Judith must have disappeared sometime in the recent past if Hestor was around to see her. Somehow she was connected to the stuff in lot 43. Another round of questioning with both Eugene and Sabrina seemed in order.

Then there was Lloyd. His behavior was curious, civilized and hostile at the same time, as if there were two personalities within him. The real mystery was why he came to my hotel *after* he had stolen the two lots.

For my speculations, I'd begin with Eugene. He might be using me to get the Pritchard family heirloom. If he failed to extract information from Hestor, then I would be his only chance to find the missing relic. Even if this was true, who was trying to kill me? Certainly not Eugene; he wanted me alive for whatever reasons. He claimed Clay had killed the entire Francisco clan single-handedly. If any of them still lived, or their friends, they'd be spoiling for revenge.

I was so deep in thought, so entangled in these knot-like connections, that I was nearly run down by a bus driver in the white loading and unloading zone. By reflex, I flipped him off, then entered the terminal.

Picking an airline at random, I bought a ticket on the next flight to Oakland, to Sabrina, and hopefully more answers. I had thirty minutes to kill, so I grabbed a quick bite to eat, a slice of cheese pizza, then made my way through the X-ray machine and to my gate.

The stewards at the check-in counter announced that all first-class passengers should board the plane first. I had a coach ticket. As soon as the rich and famous were on, all the economy passengers were then told to board. I got up with the rest of my fellow travelers and stood in line, waiting to get on the plane and wait some more.

It was hard to miss him when he jogged up to the check-in counter, a man easily weighing 250 pounds. He was not fat, but bulky, and stood a good head taller than me . . . a good bald head taller. It was the bald assassin, the one who had shot Sam. He was five paces behind me.

There was some difficulty with his ticket at the counter and he had yet to look my way. If I got out of line, I'd have to walk right in front of him. He was certain to spot me then. And do what? This was a public place. He couldn't just shoot me and expect to get away with it. Besides, it was unlikely he carried a gun into the airport.

So what was I worried about?

I was worried that my enemies were well connected with the police in this town. Enough so that he might kill me here and get away with it. I was worried about his huge hands. They looked like they could easily fit over my head and crush it.

He received his blue boarding pass, first-class seating, and got in the back of the line. I quickly turned around so he couldn't see me.

If he was in first class and I was in coach, then there was a chance we'd never see each other. I would get on the plane before him and deplane after he was off. I handed my green boarding pass to the steward and walked onto the plane, as far back as possible.

We took off and I was trapped.

I couldn't believe that the assassin was coincidentally on the same flight, going to the same place as me. He might be after me, or maybe Hestor. Probably Hestor, since no one knew I was here. Who knew where my mother was? Eugene and Sabrina. Did he work for one of them?

The stewardess came by with a cart full of drinks and offered me a soda. It was warm. I sipped it and wondered if Sam's killer was drinking champagne up there in first class, while he plotted Hestor's murder. My stomach suddenly turned as I recalled parts of Sam spattered against the back wall, soaking into the powdered doughnuts, and how the assassin enjoyed shooting him over and over.

I got up, to the annoyance of the person sitting next to me, and went to the bathrooms in the rear. There, I washed the perspiration from my face and tried to forget the pizza, now sitting heavy in my stomach. If I panicked now, I was dead. Was there some way I could attack him magically on the plane? Not with all these people around. I didn't have the resources to engineer a cover-up like the other royal families might. That's all I needed were problems with the Oakland police.

The door rattled. A fist hammered on the other side. Someone wanted in.

My heart leapt into my throat and pounded to the beat of my pulse. The insistent shaking continued. Had he spotted me in line? I put my hand on the latch and held it closed. I was staying in here where it was safe.

"Excuse me," said an urgent female voice. "I *really* need this bathroom. The ones in front are out of order."

Feeling foolish, I released the latch and stepped out. "Sorry for the delay," I said and blushed.

She rushed in past me and closed the door.

Exhaling a breath of relief, I turned to walk back to my seat . . .

. . . and ran right into him.

"Pardon me," he said. His voice was the same oversmoked gravelly rumble I had heard on the video. "I didn't even see . . ."

We froze and made eye contact. He then smiled at me. It was the same smile you'd make on Christmas morning opening presents. He placed one of those massive hands on my shoulder and whispered, "Why, excuse me, *Roland*. I didn't see you."

He held me for a second, then let go. I stumbled down the aisle away from him. The strength in his hand, it was powerful enough to snap my shoulder. And he knew me, by name. No mistakes this time.

I crawled over into my seat, ignoring the complaints of the person next to me, then took three deep breaths. I summoned my magic, imagining my own life force, then the death stored within the stone. The pulse of my life beat out of control. I was in a flight or fight mode, barely able to concentrate and hold the two paired forces apart. If I didn't relax, I'd never be able to use my sorcery.

The person sitting next to me was a smoker. I saw the death, a blackened film suspended in his lungs like exhaust. I borrowed an invisible portion of it (he'd never miss it), and let it flow into my body. It cooled the life within me. My pulse immediately calmed. Now I could think.

I had to see what the assassin was up to. Perhaps I'd use the stone again to leave my body. I didn't need its help, but last night, when I had had its assistance, I was reassured and unemotional. It aided my concentration. I had the feeling I'd need it.

There were a dozen pairs of opposites crystalized within the gem: life and death, air and earth, fire and water, and nine others unknown to me. They flickered and undulated upon the stone's facets, a rainbow of shifting hues, lapis lazuli, jade, aquamarine, cat's eye, and fire opal. And coupled to each pair of opposites, a glimmer of something else, fragments of memory, pieces of another existence . . . an alien existence I could not fathom.

Through this maze of rainbows, I willed myself. My consciousness was repelled, however. Why wouldn't it let me through? It occurred to me then that last night I had been *invited* in. This time I was trying to force my way. Curious. I attempted to communicate with the stone as I had with Bakkeglossides, but it refused my connection. Stubborn little piece of . . .

The life and death forces within it pulsed rhythmically. Inspecting my life and death forces, they too pulsed, but they were slower and larger, matching the cadence of my own pulse. The stone's forces were compressed, and cycled much faster—a blur of sinusoidal absorbance and radiance. We were out of phase with one another.

Could I alter their rhythm? Make the stone's forces beat like mine? I drained a small portion of the death in my body and channeled it into the stone. There was more power there than I had thought. Nothing happened.

Maybe I couldn't alter *them*, but I might be able to alter *my* life and death patterns.

I let the life force within the stone flow into my body. This made my life and death fields oscillate faster and with a smaller amplitude. My blood raced, pressure built within me, and my heart strained to keep pace. Still I was slightly behind the stone's rhythm. I let more of its power into me, and the fringes of my vision blackened, nerve endings fired electrical flashes across my skin, and blood pounded through my ears.

Our two pulses converged . . . and time suspended.

I was sucked into the stone.

Twelve pairs of magic enveloped me. Together we pulsed to the same primal rhythm, a cosmic force that seethed back and forth. We were harmonious, and suddenly we more than thirteen; we were a thousand, and the thousand fractured a thousand times, a million more, until my personality submerged into a continuum of power, of personality, and of existence. We were nearly everywhere at once, seeing, touching, hearing, smelling, and tasting this world, the dreaming world, and countless others I did not recognize. I was consumed.

The millions of others surrounding me, they scrutinized me, debated my worthiness, then accepted me as one of their own. My thoughts dissolved, reshaped, and remolded, then gone. Transcendence and bliss . . .

"Sir? Please wake up. You must have your seat belt on before the plane lands."

"What? Aesop, just a few seconds more."

"I'm sorry sir, you must wake up. The plane is about to land."

Plane? I rode the heavens on a horse of quicksilver. What did I care for a mere plane?

Reality walked through the door and slapped me across the face. We were landing. I was not in Meredin, but still on the plane and about to land in Oakland. I snapped my seat belt together and the stewardess left me alone.

Something crucial had just occurred, with the stone, but the memory was elusive. I couldn't remember.

The plane touched down, taxied to the gate, and stopped. The pilot wished us a pleasant day and encouraged us to fly with them again. Fat chance.

The bald killer was getting off this plane before me, perhaps with enough of a head start to arrange trouble. I had to get to Oceanview before he did, and make certain Hestor was not there when he arrived.

The first few people in the coach section stood up and waited to deplane. I immediately rose and pushed my way through, ignoring the colorful curses and sharp glances from others.

Once off the plane, I sprinted through the terminal, only slowing near the X-ray machines and the airport security who eyed me suspiciously. I had not seen the bald killer yet.

I ran outside and hopped into the second cab waiting in line. It was an older American car with a large V-8 engine, no fuel economy, but fast.

"You know where Oceanview Hospital is?" I asked the driver.

He was younger than me, skinny, nervous, and looked liked he was on speed. "The place down the coast? Sure," he said. "It's a good drive though, an hour easy."

"There's an extra hundred in it for you if you get me there in thirty minutes."

His eyes lit up, the dark fire of greed. "You gotta deal, mister."

We sped out of the terminal and got onto the highway. I looked back and checked if we were being followed. There was no one. I relaxed, slumping back into the slick vinyl seat.

What had happened on the plane with the stone? I felt

for it within my front pocket but it was gone. Dread poured into my stomach. Had I dropped it?

I shifted to view magically, and carefully tapped into the driver's death. As I suspected, his blood and tissues were laced with a blazing red material, amphetamines I guessed.

Inside my body, just beneath my sternum and close to my heart, lay the stone. Its magical rhythm beating a perfect five times for every one beat of my heart. I felt my chest but there was no scar tissue, no point of entry. Yet it was there.

I was certain now this stone was sentient. It had called to me the other night and saved my life. It had resisted my efforts to penetrate it forcefully. It had even greeted me the first time I saw it in the storage room. What was it? I had forgotten something, something that happened while I was *inside* the thing . . .

The driver slowed.

A police cruiser behind us, single red eye glaring, was the source of our decreased speed. I glanced at the speedometer. It read eighty-five, falling rapidly. OK, no problem. We were just going a little fast. The cop would write this guy a ticket and we'd be on our merry way.

We pulled over to the side of the road and sat there for a minute, then two cops stepped out. One approached the cab, while the other went to the rear of the taxi and watched.

"Please step out of the car," the first cop ordered the driver.

He did and offered some comment about how his luck and offal were of a similar nature.

The officer told him to place his hands behind his back, then cuffed him.

This was not normal. I prepared myself and shifted to a magical perception. How could the assassin have found me so rapidly? Maybe I just picked a winner of a cab driver with a criminal record. But I found it difficult to believe in coincidences lately.

I looked back. The other officer approached the car with a black oblong device in his hand.

Something much more interesting caught my eye, however. Inside the police car, in the backseat, were two magical fields I had seen before. Muted colors, ever shifting, the forces of good and evil. The bald assassin stepped from the cruiser. He was a dreamer, a user of magic—a relative.

The cop then threw open the rear door of the cab and pointed the black device at me.

I fumbled for my concentration, lost it, and tried to kick him in the face when he leaned in.

Two fangs exploded from the black device and stuck in my chest. A split second later, I received the shock of my life.

14

~~~~~~

The stars melted in the west, and the empty black sky warmed to the color of hyacinth, then faded to the clarity of lightly brewed tea. The darker shades fled across the dome of the sky before the sun's chariot.

Aesop and I had climbed to the ledge last evening because we feared missing the bell when it arrived again this morning. This was no small task considering my wounded leg, but with luck and a sturdy rope provided by Smoking Bear, we scrambled up the face of the cliff. I could have drained the life from the twisted scrub pines and creosote bushes in these hills to heal myself, but I wanted to restore this realm, not deplete it further. I'd start by allowing my injuries to heal naturally.

Only an outline in the dirt remained of the massive frame that held the bell. It truly had disappeared. We sat waiting in the predawn light. Aesop cooked over a small fire, and Smoking Bear dangled her legs over the ledge and watched the world whiten.

I had been awake since I lost consciousness in the other realm. Now I was either dead or held captive by the bald assassin. I didn't feel dead, though. If I fell asleep now, I was certain I'd wake up alive. The question was: wake up to what?

Aesop glanced at me over his fire. I knew he suspected something was amiss but he held his silence.

"Do you need help with breakfast?" I offered.

"Yes, thank you," he said, then handed me a spoon to stir the lumpy oatmeal. He waited a moment, then, "You are pensive this morning. Did your dreams disturb you?"

I frowned. Was I that transparent?

"If there is a matter in which you require assistance, merely ask."

Help. That was the one thing I dreaded asking for. Help is what Hestor always needed. I was forever there to help with her hospital bills, her soiled clothes, and extinguish her occasional fires. Helping her cost me a normal life and my education. Help is what Eugene offered, entangled with invisible strings. Help is what Sabrina gave me, embedded in suspicion and her magics. If I asked for your help, Aesop, what price would you make me pay? What political arrangements would be made? The De Marcos were my friends (at least I thought of them as such). I wanted their camaraderie, their trust, not their *help*. It came packaged with too many other things.

"I am in trouble in the other realm, serious trouble." I said the words quickly. "I was captured by the same assassin that tried to kill me a few days ago. Captured or worse."

"Tell me of this assassin," he said.

Without meeting his eyes, I explained the details: how I had hoped to elude him by boarding the plane first, how he knew my name, and how the fields of good and evil magic surrounded him.

Aesop took the oatmeal I had stirred into a thin paste during my narration. "We would be delighted to help you. Without your aid we would have never found our statue and defeated the demons." He paused, meditating a moment, then added, "If anything, we owe you."

"I would rather that we not owe each other anything but that we just be friends."

"Friends?" He smiled warmly. "Yes, that would be acceptable. It has been some time since I called any family member a friend."

Smoking Bear kicked a stone off the ledge. "This assassin sounds like Morgan Bishop. Bald, a few wrinkles on his head, and using good and evil? Who else in the families could it be?"

Bishop? Morgan Bishop? He was the one who killed Sam? That brought up a host of interesting possibilities. The Rhodes had an alliance with the Bishops, and Sabrina was his niece. No, I couldn't assume they were all against me. That *was* paranoid. Just as I didn't assume Lloyd was acting on Eugene's orders when he stole my father's possessions, neither could I assume Eugene and Sabrina were in league with Morgan. Not until I had some more facts . . .

"We must find out where he is holding Roland," Aesop said to her.

"I know, I know," she replied, pacing back and forth. "We'll have to bargain with the old lizard again."

I wanted to ask the De Marcos about the Bishop family, but a faint ringing cut me off. The sun was rising. The first streamers of light angled over the horizon. Aesop gathered up our equipment and Smoking Bear hefted the swaddled statue.

"Ready yourselves," she said.

A pure tone sounded with the first warming of the air, the first deepening of the shadows on the face of the rocks.

The outline of the frame formed first, dissolving in reverse. A polished wood with tiny carved characters then materialized within that outline. The details of the men and women chiseled into the frame appeared, and they bowed before the rising sun in supplication. The bell formed next, hanging in the center, a great thing fatter in diameter than I was tall. It was brass, unpolished, and engraved in a language unknown to me. I could not even make out from which language these symbols originated. The acolyte part of me forgot the plots of the families for a moment and was tempted to take a charcoal rubbing of them. Was that the Eldrich symbol for knowledge I spied? Smoking Bear stepped forward, however, before I could get a closer look, and swung a great beam against the bell's side.

A second tone, in perfect harmony with the first, the ringing of the morning, moved through the air. It was softer than I anticipated and produced faint ripples in the sky, a stirring of power. I shifted my perspectives to see magically. About the bell strange forces vibrated in complex resonances. I recognized none of them. It was technology from the Golden Age, sorcery strong enough to do what?

The space above the bell distorted. Sound and magic formed knots in the air. It twisted and sucked into . . . nowhere. A hole in the air, the inside of a worm, it tightened and pulled into a tunnel. The far end opened and light poured through, a shining liquid. The opposite side was bathed in the late morning sun. It was another place.

A pleasant voice, carried by the waves in the air came to us, "Who calls . . . who disturbs Xuraldium during his morning sun?"

Smoking Bear stepped forward, "You know very well who it is, old one. Now let us through before the sun rises and we wait on this miserable rock until sunset."

"As you wish," the voice said. The tunnel in the air, the passage to Xuraldium, bent down and touched the earth. Smoking Bear entered and vanished. I looked for courage to Aesop, but he was halfway in.

The sun was just breaking over the top of the mountains. I entered.

"Welcome, esteemed travelers," a parrot whistled from its perch of gold. It then turned to groom its metallic blue feathers and added, "The Great One shall arrive expeditiously."

We were no longer on a rock in the middle of desolation.

This was a palace built in the architecture of the Golden Age. Long sweeping columns of pink-veined marble, cast in the forms of trees, raised a dome above our heads. Branches of stone sprouted from these columns, and each was home to hundreds of carved malachite and jade leaves. The dome was a mosaic. Countless white, clear, and blue stones puzzled together the late afternoon sky. A sun, partially hidden behind a cloud of pearls, cast its warmth on the air with rosy pieces of bloodstone, amber, and other stones whose colors ran across in fiery rainbows.

Frescos adorned three walls. Upon the first, children and satyrs frolicked in the Fields of Fire and ran around a Maypole. A grey-green ocean crashed upon a beach of smooth rocks and shaded tidal pools on the second wall (Aesop moved away from that one). And the third wall was full of shadowy creatures that crouched in a dark forest of ferns and fungus.

The fourth wall was a rounded portal that led to the garden, cultured in some areas, wild in others, filled with jasmine trees and honeysuckle and roses. A tiny stream burbled from a fountain, meandered down terraced steps, then disappeared under the garden wall. Beyond those walls and a curtain of mist, I heard the churning of the ocean.

I stepped forward to explore this palace, what I thought might be the last piece of the dream realm as I had read of it in the Abbey's libraries.

Smoking Bear placed her hand on my shoulder and said, "Don't waste your time in that garden. I know it's beautiful, but you have a chance to question one of the greatest sorcerers alive. He'll not tolerate us long in his domain, so stick around."

"He is trained in numerous magical styles," Aesop explained, "but is best known for his mastery of information and ignorance."

Information and ignorance? That is a legitimate pair of magical powers? "I don't understand."

"He trades a bit of his hard-earned knowledge," he told me, "for that which he does not yet understand.

The more important the information sought, the more he forgets. He has long since discarded any politics or family allegiances. He has forgotten them.''

"Don't ask him any trivial questions," she added. "He's probably lost those memories, and it annoys him when he discovers something has slipped his mind."

The parrot squawked once and flew into the garden.

Xuraldium entered.

He was not a man but a reptile standing upright, a crocodile in a robe. A long leathery tail followed him and made scraping sounds on the marble floor. Rows of exposed teeth formed a permanent smile in his lizard head.

"Welcome," it said. "Do I know you?"

"Don't play games, Xuraldium," Smoking Bear answered. "You know why we've come."

"Yes, the statue. You must require more clues to discover it. Well, I am certain a reasonable form of payment may be arranged . . .''

"We have the statue," Aesop interrupted.

"So soon? How disappointing." He sighed. The great reptilian body expanded and revealed huge bunches of muscles beneath his robes. "Have we negotiated payment for my services?"

"Yes," she said, "and we've already paid."

"Are you certain?" he asked.

She gave him a look that was absolute.

"Very well, let us have a look at it."

She unwrapped the statue with the care of a new mother with her baby. For the first time I got a good look at the centaur figure that I had risked my life and soul for.

The horse portion was silver, speckled like a pinto with gold and copper patches. The mane and tail were metal wires so fine they drifted in the air like wisps of smoke. The whole thing was no larger than a cat. Xuraldium flicked his tongue over it twice.

"Starchaser the Wanderer," he whispered, "where have you been all this time?" Then to Smoking Bear he asked, "You would not care to part with it?"

She frowned and her stance tensed a little. "No."

"No, I did not think so."

The centaur held a small harp. The strings appeared tight, and I had no doubt that it would play. On his back he bore a tiny quiver of arrows and a bow. The bow curved gently on the ends and molded itself to the centaur's human back.

"I will need the Sarteshan document translated before I tell you of the statue's workings," he hissed.

"We have that," Aesop stated. "Roland, could you please?"

I rolled the vellum out and creased it into the proper alignment. The reptile watched me, and never once blinked his gold-slitted eyes.

I reread the verse.

"Outstanding translation, young human. You misinterpreted the character for Live, however, it should read *Sing*, *Exchange*, *Exist*. Your name was . . . ?"

"Roland."

"Do you require employment? I have need of an assistant with your talents."

"Perhaps later," I said.

He removed his gaze from me and returned to the centaur. "Yes, I remember now. Starchaser was an eccentric even in the Golden Age. He was always running about, saving villages, rescuing damsels, or planting forests. Near the end, he prophesied the end of this land and changed himself into this inert form; rather, he requested the Dragon of Aetna to change him."

"What does it do?" Aesop inquired.

"Quite simply, it *is* Starchaser. You must find a volunteer to trade places with him and he will return."

"Assuming we find a person willing to become a little statue," asked Smoking Bear, "then what?"

"Starchaser had great abilities, knowledge, and magic. He can heal your lands, restore your crops, and rejuvenate your forests. What you then do with such lands is, I suppose, up to you."

The De Marcos raised an eyebrow at each other.

"To call him forth, sing the translated poem and play

the following on his harp." He plucked the harp's tiny strings with one claw. He was no master musician, but the melody was simple enough. I matched the music to the verse in my head. Yes, they went together.

"Is the person trapped forever as a statue?" Aesop asked.

"Until someone else replaces him," Xuraldium replied. "You must understand Starchaser did this voluntarily. He knew that the wars and reckless use of magic would continue unabated until there were few families remaining. He chose to do this because he knew he would be needed in the future. He will help you, yet he has his own distinct motivations.

"So," he continued, "have you any other business for me, or may I return to my morning sun?" He glanced to his garden. "It is very nearly gone."

"We have more business for you, old one," Smoking Bear said, "if you are interested."

"Business? I am ever interested in opportunities to do business. What did you have in mind?"

"We need a few questions answered. First, we need to find out where Roland is in the other realm. His life is in danger."

"And what is it you propose to trade for this knowledge? I cannot give away information, you know. I would be forever besieged with endless inane inquires. I have my solitude to think of, my peace of mind."

"Roland, show him your bowl."

He returned his attention to me. "You are a strange one. You are not of the family De Marco, yet you travel with them on a vital quest. From your features, I would say you are a Pritchard, but they perished twenty years ago."

"My father was Clay Pritchard."

"Most interesting. I assume then you also have . . . questions for me. Let us see this bowl."

I dug deeply in my pack and retrieved the bowl. "We discovered this in the Sarteshan ruins."

"The Sarteshan Empire was destroyed?" he asked himself. "I must have forgotten that, how unfortunate."

"It is aligned with water magics, the ocean, and the goddess Arthusa." I handed it over to him. His clawed hand grasped for it, brushing the surface of my skin and leaving little scratches. I was glad I felt nothing from that hand.

"Intriguing. 'Truth lies in deep water,' " he spoke into the bowl in a very ancient Eldrich dialect. About its rim, long-tarnished characters glowed with sorcery. The bowl filled to the brim with water. He drank it.

Aesop backed away two paces.

"Marvelous, I shall take it. You two, please make yourselves at home. I shall divine the truth for you later. First Roland, you may join me in my library."

Aesop nodded and gestured that I follow Xuraldium. Smoking Bear mouthed a "be careful" to me.

I followed his tail through several rooms. We passed cases of relics from a time past, paintings of places that no longer existed, and statues of heroes long dead. It was a museum of sorts, a tribute to another age in this realm. I would have paid much to explore his palace and have this old one tell me all he knew.

He paused in front of a plain wooden doorway. "As a fellow scholar," he said through his sly fixed smile, "I hope you appreciate my humble library." He then pushed open the door.

The library was simply the largest room I had ever seen. It was a rectangle that stretched beyond the limits of my vision. Books lined the walls, solid books, held in place by little rails. Ladders on rollers ascended to the ceiling, which was a series of translucent panels that allowed the natural light to filter through. I could spend a lifetime in here, perhaps longer, and happily would have had he allowed me. Maps of this realm and others lay unrolled in crystal display cases. Suits of armor stood guard in recessed alcoves like metallic insects in their lairs. Reading tables, overflowing with volumes, scrolls, and the remnants of spent candles, were arranged in geometric precision down the titan corridor of knowledge.

He sat on the thick carpet, then adjusted himself into

a lotus position. I picked a comfortable chair, which creaked slightly, and faced him.

"I wanted you alone," he whispered, "as I may say things that are best kept secret between the two of us."

"I understand." Politics springs eternal.

He said nothing. Did he just want me to start asking questions? There was an uncomfortable moment of silence, then I said, "As an acolyte at the Abbey of Glossimere, I studied the histories of this realm. I have traveled the lands, yet they are not as they once were. The land is devoid of life, and the people, the people lack spirit and nobility of character . . . and there are so few of them left. What happened?"

Xuraldium hissed, "That is not a question. It is a matter of history, of tradition, and of stupidity. The family blood feuds drained the life and soul from the land to fuel their magics without a thought to the consequences. The families were, and still are, the powerful seeking more power. Those who would oppose such philosophies are quickly disposed of in our circles. Those who are reckless in their ambitions are similarly weeded out. What is left is the middle, the cunning, the quiet, the plotting, and the politically correct family members. They are the ones who use caution as their adviser, and planning as their mistress. They are the troublemakers. They are the ones who have been successful over the years.

"Now," he said, calming down a bit, "why don't you ask me a *real* question? Why don't you ask of important matters, something worth knowing? It is after midday, and I tend to slow down a bit after midday, so be quick."

"Very well," I said. "Can you tell me about my father?"

"Clay? What do you wish to know?"

"You can start by telling me why he died and who killed him."

"Ruah-vindicare." He pronounced, rolling the first *r*.

"I beg your pardon?"

"Ruah-vindicare, the spirit of revenge, the death duel.

It is a formal proclamation between family members announcing their intentions to kill one another. It is a declaration of war, on a personal level, and was an honorable form of carnage practiced by your foolish family ancestors for generations.''

"This duel, with whom was it fought?''

"Eugene Rhodes.''

"Eugene?'' His name hung there in the air, and my mind refused to accept it. Had he only helped me to locate the Pritchard family relic? Deep down, however, I was uneasy with this explanation. He had seemed so sincere when he rescued me in Mexico, and he had gone out of his way to teach me the principles of sorcery. Those were not the acts of a man who was my enemy. After seeing that picture of him and Clay panning for gold, I couldn't believe they'd fight a duel to the death.

"What caused the two of them to come to such terms? I thought they were friends.''

"They were,'' he said, scratching beneath a polished scale with his razor claw. "Their friendship forged an alliance between the two clans that lasted nearly a century and gained the fear and respect of all families. Unfortunately a woman came between them. She loved them both. And your father vowed to have her or die.''

"That was Judith?''

"Correct. Then you must know the rest of the story.''

"No, please continue,'' I urged and leaned forward.

"Judith bore a child with one of these two men, who specifically I am uncertain of. Some assert it was with Eugene, while others have speculated it was Clay's progeny. The Bishop family became infuriated and lost much prestige over the incident. The child was naturally destroyed, or so the reports indicate.''

"Destroyed? Why?''

"That I shall explain momentarily. Be silent while I recount the tale.'' His tail swished back and forth once in annoyance. "Your father embarked on a quest similar to the one the De Marcos recently completed. His family heirloom was complex, powerful, even his father and grandfather failed to understand its operation. Many claim the relic was Theodore's own personal talisman, but that is idle speculation.''

''Theodore?'' That was the name on the figurine in Eugene's mansion, and the same man whose bust I found in Dad's belongings.

''His is a different tale,'' Xuraldium explained, ''and for sale at a higher price. Do not interrupt me again, please. Your father came to me seeking information regarding his relic. He was fearful and apparently losing his battle with Eugene. Yet even with all these books and all my knowledge, I failed to divine the heirloom's operation. It was a very stubborn piece of magic. You do not have it with you?''

I shook my head.

''Regrettable. I believe your father became desperate thereafter. Stories filtered back to me that he struck out for the Abbey of Glossimere to bargain with the mad one who dwells there, the Oracle.''

Was that why I was at the Abbey? Clay took me with him? ''And . . .?''

''And he never returned from the Isle of the Knowledge. One may only assume he was unsuccessful with the Oracle.''

How many times had I passed the entrance to the Oracle? Once a day, twice? How many times had I passed my father, dead and unknown, within that hollowed tower? Did the Elders know? Of course they did. All who wished to see the Oracle were required to petition the council first. The petition was always granted, it was a mere formality, but they knew and never told me. WaterStone knew yet never spoke a word. He had wanted my loyalties to belong to the Abbey; he had allowed me to believe my father had abandoned me there. I had to find my father and remove his body from the tower at once. He might have also left some clue there to indicate where the watchband was.

''How does the Oracle work?'' I asked.

''If you wish to confront the Oracle, reconsider. As I remember, only one individual ever tested the mad one and returned to tell of it. Dozens have tried, but only Eugene has survived the test.''

I said nothing, awaiting his answer. Eugene mentioned that he was at the Abbey before to visit the Oracle. Did he go there before or after Clay died?

''The answer to your question is: I do not know how the Oracle operates.'' He was irritated, either at my insistence or by the fact he did not know. ''Now I shall answer another question,'' he hissed, ''but hurry, it grows cold. I am tired.''

What I needed to know was where my father's watchband was, and how to work the thing to aid me in this power struggle. But Xuraldium had already confessed he didn't know these things. ''You said Judith's child was killed. Why?''

''You do not understand? No one has explained this to you?'' His golden eyes went wide and he sighed a great sigh. ''For you to comprehend, I must first educate you in the basic principles of sorcery.''

''Another has already shown me how to summon a pair of opposite forces. There is no need to explain.''

Xuraldium hissed three short times, a laugh? ''No, the fields of power about you are random things controlled by emotions and a primitive intellect. Have you not seen the greatness of the Golden Age sorcerers? Can you cause people to turn into statues and back again? Can you make water fill a tiny bowl no matter where it is? Can you command passages to form and cross vast distances in space and time? You know nothing of magic. You are simply trifling with it.''

He was right. One lesson with Eugene did not make me an experienced sorcerer. ''My apologies, ancient one, please tell me.''

He nodded. ''Let me tell you then *why* magic works. You are from Earth, correct?''

''Yes, of course.'' I almost said ''isn't everyone,'' but I had the feeling not everyone in this room was.

''You have few sorcerers there, I believe. Why?'' He paused to flick his black tongue out, catching a scent. Then, before I answered, he said, ''Dualities. Duality, is the first principle that drives all magics. You know that you must set up a duality of forces to practice the most basic of sorceries. Have you ever wondered why you may do this and others may not? The answer is: duality."

"I do not understand."

"I know," he said. "Allow me to continue, young man. You exist simultaneously in two different worlds. Your very existence causes a sort of power gradient between yourself here, and yourself back in your home world. It is this self-duality that enables you to step between magical forces and manipulate them. Nonsorcerers may never produce magic, for they possess no significant dualities. They are forever trapped in a limited existence. They are the half people, the distorted ones, the lost souls."

"So as long as this duality exists, I may continue to conjure magics?"

"Correct."

"And if I were to die in either realm, I could no longer practice sorcery."

"Correct again."

Then the stone ghost we fought could use sorcery because of the enchantment within his buried body. The resonating life and death forces granted him a limited duality, enough to manipulate the powerful earth forces within the temple.

"There are other dualities an experienced sorcerer may acquire," Xuraldium said. "The duality of living in two planes of existence is the most common, but there are others. It is these other dualities that the royal clans wish to discover and study. They increase one's power and allow access to abilities far beyond the reach of simple 'pairs of opposites.' "

"Other dualities, like what? And what does this have to do with Judith's child?"

"One of the best," he said in a lowered voice, "was the practice of inbreeding between clans. The child of such a union has a greater effect over the cosmic forces for he has an additional duality—the duality of being the child of two dreamers.''

"That's a duality?"

"I forget you are from Earth, where science is the rule rather than magic. Allow me then to offer an alternative explanation—one you may find more philosophically palatable. The genetic code that allows a dreamer to exist in both realms is a doubly reinforced dominant gene that is passed down from generation to generation. When two dreamers join, their genes form what your scholars call a supergene, and the resultant child has superior influence over magical forces.''

I nodded, partially understanding. Was that why I could stop the flow of power? Why I could see the forces of magic? Was I the offspring of Clay and Judith? And if so, why did Dad marry Hestor on Earth?

"This practice, however, is strongly frowned upon by all the clans in this age. Aside from the cultural reasons and biological hazards, family members usually succumb to their fears of an imbalance of power and permanent alliances forming from such a union. The offenders and their offspring are disposed of.''

"Is that what happened to Judith?"

"Yes. I believe they burned her at the stake . . . although my memories of that decade are somewhat foggy.''

Was I also at risk? Was that why Morgan wanted me dead? Because I was the child of Clay and Judith, two dreamers? I didn't even know if Judith was my real mother. If I was, it explained why Dad had left me at the Abbey, to protect me. It also explained why he took a second wife in the real realm . . . to cover the fact that I was Judith's, and to shield my identity from the other dreamers. On the other hand, if I was Hestor's son, there had to be another explanation for my enhanced magical powers.

"Are there other dualities?" I asked. "Other than this genetic one?"

"Yes, of course," he said, irritated, "but you must discover those for yourself. I do not desire a full-time student. Now if you will excuse me, I must catch the last few minutes of good sun before it is gone. I enjoyed our little talk. Please feel free to stop by anytime.''

He shook my hand and left more scratches on my skin, then escorted me to the simple wooden door, and shooed me out.

Smoking Bear waited in the hall for me. She had bathed and wore a dress of cream silk that clung tightly to her muscular torso and hung loose about her legs. A simple belt of iridescent pearls wrapped about her slim waist, and her ebony hair was set with a comb of gold. She was lovely, every bit a princess of the realm.

"What did you two discuss?" she asked in a whisper.

"Family matters," I replied, "mostly my father, and some advice on sorcery." Had I not been so preoccupied with the revelations recently thrust upon me, I would have taken a greater interest in Smoking Bear. Her beauty rivaled Sabrina's, and I found myself attracted to her in other, less physical, ways. Her directness, her experience, and her courage were all qualities I admired. But, like I said, my mind was clouded with other matters.

We walked back through the mazelike palace, back to Xuraldium's grand entrance room. Either my eyes deceived me or the frescos were different than when I had last seen them. The children and the satyrs had danced a bit farther about the Maypole; the ocean had inched its way farther along the battered coast; and the shadows lurking in the dim forest had shifted.

"You look asleep on your feet, Roland. Why don't you get some rest?" She gave me a gentle push through the circular door and into the gardens.

"What about Morgan? How are you going to get Xuraldium to . . ."

"You leave the old lizard to me. If anyone can persuade that pompous ass to spill his guts, I can. Now go rest, you've earned it."

I wanted to argue, but she was right. I was dead on my feet, and perhaps literally dead in the other realm.

There was a hammock tied between two lilac tees. I

rolled into it and sighed. Hummingbirds flitted from flower to flower and drank their fill of nectar. There was a scent in the air, the perfumes from a hundred blossoms mingling with the tang of the ocean. The waves broke beyond the palace walls in a soothing rhythm, a never-ending cycling in which I found solace. Long after the families annihilated one another, the ocean would still be here. Arthusa would still caress her sister's shores to comfort the loss of her creations.

I closed my eyes. For the first time in a week, I had no thoughts of family, of demons, or of dreams.

15

Numb and dumb. My body was a thick sponge, a cloud floating over the earth, floating through the day; my consciousness diffused into thin cirrostratus trails of water vapor. Something was amiss, however. The clouds condensed, sank, grew darker, heavier, and piled into ominous cumulonimbus, into thunder and lightning.

The faintest perceptions slipped through. I sensed the sheets over me, the hum of machinery, the stench of cigarettes, but little else. My body was warm, no hunger crawled through my stomach, and my bladder was empty, so with these basic physical needs taken care of, I decided to return to the clouds and see if I could make that storm go away.

But there was something I forgot, something I had to do here. *Brain*, I suggested, *why don't we wake up*?

Out to lunch, gone fishing, or back in fifteen minutes, it replied. *Take your pick.*

One should never argue with one's primary mental functions, so I dismissed the silly feelings of unease and turned back to my clouds. Unfortunately they were no comfort, now black and solid, veiling the countryside of my mind with sheets of rain. Lightning flashed over the subconscious terrain, informing me of its displeasure.

Very well, my ego said to the superego and the id, *you two argue this out. I'm going to take a look around and see what this is all about.*

The lightning of my superego struck, then it rolled out the big bass drums for thunder. My id sighed, rolled over, and ignored both of us.

Life and death, I needed a pair of forces to power my sorcery and leave my body. I knew I could use my life and the death stored within the stone, but my thinking was sluggish.

Concentrate. First, picture the air rushing through your lungs, how the oxygen exchanges for carbon dioxide through capillary membranes, how every breath recharges the hemoglobin, the medusa-like protein cage, reverses its veiny blue to blood red, the color of life. Next, an image of death swelled from my silicate campaign: a mound of bodies bulldozed over, a mass grave, and the odor of decay . . . It was an image from a place I had never been.

The gradient was there. I struggled to keep the forces from flowing.

I sensed a buoyancy, a lifting of my spirituous matter if you will. In my mind's eye I sought the gem. It was a tiny window of clarity in this fog, still beating its five-fold rhythm to the marching of my heart. I mentally touched its glowing center and slipped though unchallenged. There came none of the psychedelic intensity as before on the plane, only a feeling of reassurance.

Notably my thoughts cleared.

With a puff of smoke, my storm vanished. I became aware of my surroundings. I floated above my body just short of the ceiling. Below me, I breathed deep slow breaths, wore a gown, and had an IV stuck into my right arm.

This place was a hospital room, yet not exactly a traditional one. There were the usual things you'd expect, an adjustable bed, machines to monitor my heart and respiration, round analog clock with a second hand, and an IV bottle dripping. In the corner were two chairs, a low table with a plant, and an ashtray overflowing with cigarette butts. The plant was a bonsai, a tiny Norway spruce. It was trimmed to look as though it blew in a phantom wind. There were two cigarettes ground into its soil.

What I found disturbing was the rough-tiled floor and the grated drain in the center of the room. On the wall was a spigot, an attached hose, and a spray nozzle—the kind you'd find in any garden. This brought to mind all manners of uses for this room, and the ease with which any evidence of sinister activities might be washed away.

I glanced at the clock, and it informed me I had slept most of the day away. I had to snap my body out of this coma and get out of here.

Examining my life forces, I found the source of my lethargy. There was a thick pea green material that clogged my veins and clustered about my brain and spinal column. Some of the gunk coagulated in my kidneys, but most of it passed through unaltered and congested my body. This was similar to the stuff in Hestor's body, a tranquilizer or sedative, but more powerful. I'd need another life force to restore mine to the proper level.

The bonsai had strong life within it. Decades of growth and energy were stored there. It was the only thing to channel the death magics into and drain the life from. I'd probably kill it. That saddened me, but I had no choice. It was either that or wait until Morgan showed up.

I focused on the pair of forces I'd need: the life in the tree, and the death, the drugs in my body. When I did this however, my consciousness slipped away. I drifted closer to my physical form. I forgot! I had to maintain the first gradient of forces to remain outside my body and remain lucid. So, straining, and concentrating on the four images concurrently, I let the death from my body surge into the plant, while I simultaneously drained its life.

My kidneys burned with a magical life and destroyed the poison. More magic flowed, and I loosened the clumps of toxic material about my brain. The tree dropped its needles onto the table. A branch dried and withered.

I dismissed the second pair of forces. Most of the contamination had been purged from my system, and the tree still possessed a fraction of its original life. I hoped it survived my abuse. Double-checking myself, I discovered a trace of the drug lingered in my bloodstream, in the hard to metabolize fatty deposits, but that would take care of itself in time.

Floating directly above myself, I reached through my chest and touched the stone. I was pulled through. There was a rush of blood. The sensation of breathing returned.

Sitting up, I took stock of my senses. I wiggled my fingers and toes feeling all of them (except on my left hand). I got out of the bed and looked for my clothes. They were thrown into the closet. I just pulled on my jeans when I heard voices outside the door.

It unbolted and the bald killer walked in.

The odor of stale smoke, sweat, and expensive cologne entered with him. He wore a white turtleneck and a black sport coat carefully tailored to hide his massive frame. I recalled the power in those monstrous hands. He was strong enough to walk over and snap my neck like a pencil. And it occurred to me that he just might do that.

He pulled the cigarette from his mouth and demanded, "How the devil did you get up?"

I summoned my power, collected the life and death forces from the stone, the tree, and even myself into my living and dead hands. The stone swelled with magic, seeming more than willing to help battle him.

When I conjured my magic, I saw fields of power circling him, seven pairs of gossamer veils, shifting between translucency and solidity, between color and shadow, the spectrum of morals between good and evil.

"Drop your magics," I told him, "or I'll be forced to drain the life from your worthless carcass." I didn't know if I could really do this, but I was mad enough to sound like I could.

"How do you know I have . . ." he started to say.

"Just drop them."

His power faded.

I eased off on my own magics. I couldn't keep that level of concentration up forever.

"The stories of your magic haven't been exaggerated," he remarked nonchalantly.

"Are you surprised, Morgan?"

"You know who I am? Never mind, obviously you do." He flicked his cigarette onto the floor. It sizzled, leaving a dark brown spot on the tile.

"Roland, why don't we start by putting our cards on the table? I know you and Eugene have something up your sleeve. That's fine with me. Hell, I even expected it. I just want what's rightfully mine. Hand over the stone and we'll call it even."

"Stone? I don't know what you're talking about."

"You shouldn't try to lie to a master of good and evil," he said, and wagged his finger at me. "It's bad for your soul."

"OK," I said. "Assuming I have this stone of yours, why should I give it to you?"

"It belongs to me!" he shouted. Morgan relaxed, then continued, "Look, I have no real beef with you. It was your grandfather that stole the Matrix from me."

"Horace?"

"Now I'm not trying to point fingers at anyone, so I'll tell you the story straight. Demeter from the Francisco clan, your grandfather Horace, and myself got together to make that stone. We found a dozen separate pieces of the . . ." Morgan paused, then considered his next words with deliberation. "We used one of a kind items, things you just can't find anymore. It was a once in a lifetime deal. You know what I mean?"

I nodded, even though I wasn't sure what he meant. The remark about a dozen pieces, however, that caught my attention. I already knew the stone had a dozen of something alive in it. What, yet, I didn't know. Morgan did.

"So, the day after we finished the job, Demeter tells

me Horace got greedy and swiped the thing. Well, Horace came to me next and claimed the same of Demeter. Naturally, neither of them owned up to having the stone. I didn't want to get involved in any Ruah-vindicare, so I stayed on the sidelines to watch the fireworks.''

"I know the rest of this story," I said, not wishing to appear completely oblivious of political matters. "Horace disappeared and my father took up the feud with the Francisco clan. He won, and you think he passed the stone on to me."

"You got it," he said and smiled. "Now if you tell me where it is, I'll forget this little double-cross you've engineered with the Rhodes family."

Double-cross? What was he talking about? "So you found out about that," I said, trying to draw more information out of him.

"Found out? How could I miss it? Eugene breaks our agreement and steals you for himself? Tell me''—his voice dripped with sarcasm—''did he do it from the goodness of his heart, or did you trade Clay's heirloom for his protection?''

"Neither," I replied. "And while we're on the subject of double-crosses, why don't you tell me how you found out where my mother was?"

"Sorry, my sources are confidential. But if it makes you feel any better, I never touched your mother. She was long gone by the time I got to Oceanview. Don't ask me how, cause I don't know."

I breathed an invisible sigh of relief and thanked Sabrina.

"All right, Morgan," I admitted, "I've got your stone." His eyes lit up when I confirmed his suspicions. I baited the hook further by saying, "It's a beautiful thing, the deepest of blues at one end, yellow at the other, and in the center, a green fire that darkens the longer it's exposed to light. Is that it?"

Morgan licked his lips, then said, "You haven't . . . done anything with it, have you?"

"Done anything?"

"Used its powers. Or talked with it?"

"No, *that* would be foolish, using powers I know nothing about."

His smiled deepened to the same predatory grin I saw on the cop who beat me. "Roland, how stupid of me to try to force your hand. Anyone can see you're too smart for that. I've done this thing all wrong. You have as much claim to the stone as I do. Why don't we *share* it?"

Beneath my skin, next to my heart, the stone shifted. I sensed an emotional discomfort through our empathic bond. *What would Morgan do if he knew you were hiding in my flesh*?

"Share it with you? Not after you drugged me and murdered my friend. You were even going after my mother next! Think again Morgan."

His smile never faltered. "The punk at the convenience store? He was a nondreamer. What could he matter to you? Besides, Eugene and I had to play it that way, one good and one bad."

"One good and one bad?"

"Ah, so Eugene didn't tell you? No, of course he wouldn't. Let me fill you in then." He fished his cigarettes from his pocket, tapped one out, and lit up. "Want one?" He held the pack out.

I shook my head. "No. Thanks."

"Eugene concocted this scheme to find Clay's heirloom. He knew you and the Pritchard relic were in one of the two realms. We searched Meredin first with no luck there, but got a break when his investigators found Clay's grave in San Diego. The plan was to scare the devil out of you by blowing away your friend—make you think someone was out to get you. The cops would kidnap you, beat you a bit, and soften you up. Then after a few days or a week, Eugene shows up to save the day. We thought that you'd be so worn out that you'd spill your guts, and tell us everything."

It made sense. Why else would a family member risk killing a nondreamer personally and get videotaped in the process? How else could Eugene have talked with my captors before he killed them? Simple answer: he knew them.

Eugene apparently came earlier than expected, though. He then taught me how to manipulate sorcery, and sent me out on my own. Sure he originally wanted the heirloom, but something or someone changed his mind. Why? Morgan didn't know. He thought we had made a deal on the side, a deal excluding him.

"Morgan, you're scum. Just because Sam wasn't a true dreamer was no excuse to kill him. What was your cut in this scheme? Eugene got the watchband, and you took the stone? Well, I've got a news flash for you: the stone is mine. I plan on keeping it. I get the feeling it doesn't like you anyway."

His face and bald head flushed. "Enough of this talk." He reached into his sport coat, removed a gun of large caliber, and pointed it at me. "I've tried to play it nice with you, Pritchard. Now you'll tell me where the Matrix is or I'll take care of you and start searching from scratch."

I knew he'd shoot me, maybe even enjoy doing it, as he had with Sam. "Go ahead and pull the trigger," I said. Miraculously my voice sounded solid. "Please," I added, "it will give me the death I need to drain the life from your overstuffed body into mine. I could use a little pick-me-up this afternoon." I doubted I could heal myself after being shot. It would be impossible to concentrate. Still, it was a good bluff.

"Life and death sorcerers," he said, then saw the withered bonsai and spat out his butt, the cigarette butt. "I hate you guys. OK, there are other ways to get what I want, slower forms of persuasion."

An explosion rocked the building, then another, then a smaller third one, like sonic booms one after another. Several screams followed. Guns fired nearby. Men shouted with panicked voices.

Nine seconds glided by on the analog clock while Morgan and I strained to hear more. Then outside the door I heard, "This one?"

This was answered by a pathetic: "No?"

The door splintered off its hinges and nearly landed on a startled Morgan. A man flew through the open doorway, arms strangely loose about his sides. He landed badly on the floor, both arms broken, snapped in several places. When I say he flew through, I meant he was thrown, thrown by Smoking Bear.

She stepped in and said to the unconscious man projectile, "You should never say 'no' to a lady." Starting from her feet and going up, she was dressed in cowboy boots, black with silver star spangles, a white zippered jump suit (which hid the bulk of body armor beneath), aviator sunglasses, and a black baseball cap with golden MacArthur style scrambled eggs on the brim. Aesop followed her in, tattoos still in motion, still on fire from the recent use of his sorcery. In this world, he sported a neatly trimmed beard, blond shot with red and silver. He wore a red flannel shirt, jeans, hiking boots, and on his shoulder carried a duffel bag.

Morgan pointed his automatic at her, then to Aesop, then back at her, unable to decide which was the more threatening of the pair. "Ms. Bear," he snarled, "I don't know how you got in here, but take one more step and I'll shoot."

"Shoot who, Morgan? Me?" A short laugh escaped her. "You're not seriously going to use a *gun* against *me*?"

He frowned, deepening the wrinkles on his bald head. "Hell," he muttered and lowered the weapon.

"That's much better," she said sarcastically. "We wouldn't want anyone to get hurt. Now shut up. The more you talk, the less I like it. Roland, are you OK?"

"I'm a bit shaky. I was drugged, but I think I've recovered." It was strange to see the De Marcos in this realm. They were the same people I knew from Meredin, but with distinct touches native to Earth. Smoking Bear had a perfectly done set of nails, blood red naturally, and wore matching lipstick. Aesop chewed gum.

"What happened outside?"

"That," Aesop answered, "was the last of Morgan's personal bodyguards." He then turned to him. "You really must hire better-quality help. Most of them ran before they fought. Must say something about their love for their employer.''

"Have a seat,'' Smoking Bear ordered Morgan and grabbed his gun. "You're not going anywhere. Roland, get your things. We're getting out of here in a big hurry.''

"You know me better than this," Morgan said, and sunk into a chair. "I was going to release him.''

"You expect me to believe that?'' she said.

He shrugged.

I took a step forward and grew dizzy. Black dots swam before my eyes. My knees gave out.

Aesop caught my arm.

"Thanks,'' I said.

"Hang on a bit longer. We will have you out of here shortly.''

"Why don't we talk this over?'' Morgan suggested. "I'm sure an agreement could be reached. A transfer of money might be arranged. Consider it a ransom.'' He reached into his coat and removed a cellular phone. "I'll just call my bank and . . .''

"I have a better idea,'' Smoking Bear said, and rested the gun barrel on his forehead. "I think I'll just blow your brains out. I didn't particularly enjoy those two demons you sent after us. Consider it a token of my undying affection.''

"No,'' he whispered.

"Happy landings, Morgan.''

"No,'' I echoed, "wait. You can't kill him like that.''

"Why shouldn't I? He sent those demons after us, nearly killed all of us.''

"Kill him and the remainder of the Bishops will be after us. We've won. You have the heirloom and know how to use it. Why make more enemies?'' I couldn't believe I stopped her. I wanted Smoking Bear to spatter his head against the back wall just as he had done to Sam. But two things bothered me. First, he was a dreamer; kill him and part of Meredin died too. There was also Sabrina to consider. If I was a party to murdering her uncle, then any hopes I had for the two of us would vanish.

"What do you suggest we do with him then?" asked Aesop.

"Let's take him with us. That way we can keep an eye on him and make certain he won't cause any more problems, in this realm at least."

"I don't think that will work out," Morgan said, standing.

He was halfway up when her knee connected with his solar plexus. The blow lifted him a good six inches off the floor. There was a crack, what I assumed to be ribs breaking.

"Whoooof," he said, doubling over and collapsing to the floor.

"Just a reminder of what I'm capable of," Smoking Bear hissed. "I told you to be quiet. Next time I'll break your hip or something less repairable." She rolled him over and stuck her face inches from his. "Easy or hard, Bishop, take your pick."

"How could I resist your . . . magnetism?" he grunted.

"Good." She glanced at her watch. "Aesop, tape his hands. Roland, are you ready?"

"Yes, but I've got to make one phone call first." I grabbed Morgan's cellular phone and dialed the number for Oceanview.

Aesop secured his hands with a thick utility tape, while I waited for someone to answer. He was barely able to stand after the blow she dealt him. I didn't feel sorry for him.

"Hello, yes. This is Roland Pritchard. I am checking on the status of Hestor Pritchard in room number twelve."

"One second sir." I heard a file cabinet open then slam shut. "Pritchard, Hestor, yes I have her file right here. She was released on her own recognizance yesterday."

"What?" I yelled into the phone. "That's not possible." Her recognizance was as stable as a raft in a typhoon. "Let me speak with Doctor Anderson."

Silence.

"Did you hear me?"

"Yes, I heard you, sir, but Doctor Anderson has been involved in an accident. He passed away last evening."

"Oh." I thanked the nurse and hung up. How did Hestor check herself out? I thought someone in her condition wasn't allowed to leave. Perhaps Sabrina altered the records to make it look that way. But what about Doctor Anderson? Did she arrange that too?

Smoking Bear glanced down the corridor and announced, "All clear." She went first, Morgan followed, then me, and Aesop guarded our backs.

The lights were out in the hallway, but Aesop glowed with twin fires—a white flare constrained to either hand. It smelled of smoke in here. Not the clean scent associated with the fire sorcerer's magic, but the tang of burning wood and the odor of scorched flesh.

"We'll take one of his cars," Smoking Bear said. "They may have tampered with ours already."

Morgan groaned.

We walked into the garage unchallenged.

Every car I had ever wanted was there, low-slung Italian beauties, classic British roadsters, American muscle, and more. Smoking Bear walked over to the station wagon parked in the rear of the garage. It was an ugly faded green, and had peeling wooden panels. She got in, reached under the dash, and started it.

Aesop pushed Morgan into the backseat, then got in after him. I took shotgun.

Smoking Bear pulled out of the driveway and onto a mountain road. Glancing back, I saw where I had been prisoner, a Swiss-style villa, well camouflaged by the surrounding trees. No one followed us.

"Where to?" she asked me.

"The Rhodes' desert estate." It was time to confront Eugene about his connections with Morgan, his son Lloyd, and Judith. Time for answers.

"Are you sure that's where you want to go?" Smoking Bear said. "We just got you out of one jam."

"I'm certain. Eugene and Morgan arranged my kidnapping. He may even have my mother. You two don't have to come along. I know it's asking a great deal, but I thought with the three of us together he'd think twice before taking offensive action."

"OK," she said. "We're on a roll. Why not take on all our ancestral enemies in one weekend?"

We wound through the highlands for another hour, then the mountains covered us in a cloak of shadow and we pulled off onto a side road.

"Why are we going this way?" I asked.

"I could drive all night, but I don't want to tax Xuraldium's hospitality by staying any longer. He's touchy when it comes to his privacy. We have to get to sleep, return there, and be on our way."

Too bad. I could grow accustomed to his library and fanciful gardens. Maybe when things calmed down, I'd take that job he offered. If things ever calmed down.

The station wagon bumped along a barely visible dirt road for a few minutes, then we stopped.

"I'll go find some firewood," she said. "You boys keep a careful eye on Morgan."

We opened the car doors and let the mosquitoes fly through. About us were pine trees, volcanic rocks, timeworn and crumbling, and a fine carpet of needles covering the ground. Curious squirrels darted from branch to branch, hid in the rocks, and inched their way closer to get a better glimpse of the intruders.

Aesop and I got out of the wagon to stretch our legs. The squirrels vanished.

"Aesop," Morgan said, "you're a good fellow. Why don't you remove this tape? It's starting to itch."

"My condolences, but I do not possess my grandmother's martial abilities. In a physical contest, I am afraid I could never beat you."

He sighed. "Fair enough." He turned his attention to me. "Roland, you never mentioned if you found your father's heirloom."

"You're right, I didn't."

He frowned. "Thanks for saving me from Smoking Bear. I owe you one."

"I had my own reasons for saving your life," I said, trying to mask my distaste and failing. "And they had nothing to do with liking you."

"No, of course not. But that has nothing to do with the fact that you did. Would you mind lighting a cigarette for me and sticking it in my mouth?"

I reached into his jacket pocket, got him a cigarette, lit it, and held it to his lips.

"Have you *formally* aligned with any one family?" he asked through the corner of his mouth.

"Formally aligned? No, but I am partial to the De Marco clan as you may already know." What was he up to? I shifted to observe him magically. He had summoned no powers I could see.

"Consider carefully before committing to a formal alliance. It will mean you have instant friends, yes. But you also get that clan's sworn enemies. The Bishop family has no sworn enemies. True, many people don't like us, but we are strongest among the five families."

"Five? I thought there were more."

"No, just the five," Aesop interjected. "Perhaps two dozen dreamers survive total, no more."

Five families left? How many were there in the Golden Age? The histories I read indicated there were dozens of families and hundreds of dreamers. This confirmed my theory correlating the number of dreamers and the population of Meredin. Yet with so many dreamers, wouldn't the opportunities for war escalate? My cousins, to put it mildly, were aggressive. With more families, the scheming and backstabbing would rise in geometric proportions. There must have been a radically different philosophy in the Golden Age, a political system that discouraged the clans from attacking one another.

"Our numbers are decreasing each year," Morgan added to my thoughts as if he could read them. "We need formal alliances so one family, excuse me, one group of families, may survive."

"Once I know the facts," I told him, "I promise to give your offer the consideration it deserves."

"Perfect," he said. "I've nothing to fear then. When you are in possession of the truth, you'll see things my way." He relaxed his bulk in the backseat. He acted as if he'd just won some verbal victory. I checked again with magic—nothing.

He was convincing, almost magically so, but it wasn't sorcery, just plain psychology. He played on my fears that I couldn't trust any source of information, any family member. I wished for a source of knowledge above political motivations to call upon. The De Marcos claimed Xuraldium didn't care to entangle himself in family matters, but that didn't mean he was free from them either. He did, after all, do business with them.

Smoking Bear returned with an armful of deadwood. I went to help her. I knew Aesop was capable of making a campfire, but the price was rain. I'd settle for an honest smoky campfire any day.

"Any problems with our prisoner?" she asked.

"No," I replied. "Just talking."

She nodded. "He's cunning isn't he? Trust him, and he'd sell your soul—make you think it's the deal of your life too."

"For most of our relatives, that wouldn't buy too much."

She laughed. It was the first time I heard her do so without sarcasm or contempt. I liked it.

"He spoke of alliances. Made me think I couldn't trust anyone. Is there nothing but deception and intrigue in the families?"

She stacked the firewood next to a tree, and said, "What's there to tell you? It's the way the clans have interacted for generations. All I can offer you is my personal trust, my personal alliance. Any more would be a lie." She lowered her voice to a whisper. "I think you know that, though."

I sat beside her and pushed together a pile of pine needles, tinder for the fire, then gathered rocks for a fire ring. "I'll take your personal alliance. It's the best offer

I've had yet." I paused and looked directly into her eyes. Hazel, the color of steel, and flecked with silver stars. It was difficult to stare directly at her. For a moment I felt like prey, and she the hunter, then the tension eased. "I'd offer you my personal allegiance also, if you'd have it."

"Yes, Roland." She smiled for the briefest of instants and held my hand, the right one. "I'd like that."

Her hand was soft, disguising its true violent nature. It stayed where it was atop mine and we drew closer. She relaxed her martial poise, parted her mouth slightly, then closed her eyes. I felt her heart beat against my chest, strong, running fast.

A twig snapped. Aesop had come to join us. His timing was lousy.

She withdrew rapidly from our near-kiss, her cheeks slightly aglow.

"Do you require a light?" the fire sorcerer inquired.

Neither of us answered.

He touched the pile of tinder, then placed a few sticks on the flames. In moments the fire blazed with a pure and natural heat.

Smoking Bear retreated, and sat opposite from me across the campfire. Her face was masked by the fire-fed shadows.

Morgan joined us next, with his hands still taped and the cigarette nearly burnt down to the filter.

"Aesop," Smoking Bear said, "can you get my bag from the wagon?"

He went, then returned with what appeared to be a small doctor's bag.

"We all have business to attend to tonight, Morgan, so I'm not posting guards." She reached over and ripped the tape from his hands. "You know me, I'm if nothing else a fair woman." She then removed a small bottle and syringe from the bag. "I'll give you a choice: a mild drug to make you sleep soundly, or a blunt object across the back of your thick skull."

"Not much of a choice," he said, rubbing his wrists. "If I get a say in it, I vote you let me go."

"That's not one of the choices." She stuck him with the needle.

He stiffened, then relaxed.

"Make yourself comfortable while you can."

He did and was out two minutes later, breathing heavily next to the fire.

I almost wished Aesop wasn't here. I wanted to talk with Smoking Bear alone. Was that her real name? Should I even be entertaining the thoughts I had for her? My right hand still held the memory of her touch, soft, warm, not what I expected from one who loved conflict as much as she.

Sabrina was out there too. Morgan cast more doubts in my mind about her. Someone told him where Hestor was, and if it wasn't Eugene, then it had to be her. She had used sorcery when we first met, to enhance my attraction toward her. How could I ever trust someone like that? Someone who could pull your heartstrings on demand?

The only one who was innocent in all of this was Hestor. She'd probably been caught up in these complex politics from the time she met Clay. For the first time in years I felt sorry for her. No wonder she tried to hide me from the rest of the family. No wonder she went crazy.

I gazed up at the stars, envious that they had no such problems.

The fire popped. I watch the distant suns while they wheeled across the sky, and realized what I had to do. It wouldn't be easy, but I'd have the answers I longed for. I inched closer to the fire and relaxed.

Tonight would be a busy day.

16

Tall grass, fields of it, enveloped the road. The breeze played tricks with my eyes as the plants wavered and made the sides of the road seem to ripple like a flag. With this illusion, came the sighs of a million stalks of wheat in the wind. This green ocean rolling over the hills was part of the De Marco's ancestral lands.

"Xuraldium was kind to transport us so close to your castle," I said.

"He only wanted to get rid of us," Smoking Bear replied.

She mentioned nothing to me of last evening, of our aborted embrace. Was there a family code of honor against a simple kiss? Whatever it was, she was being tight-lipped about it. I hoped one moment of passion wouldn't ruin our friendship.

"Why doesn't Xuraldium record everything he knows?" I asked Aesop. "Then when he forgets something he'd be able to look it up."

"He does. His vast library is filled with such volumes. If he remembered which piece of information was in what manuscript, he could solve his dilemma." Distracted by farmers in the fields waving to us, Aesop paused to return their greeting, then added, "The maladies of sorcery are not easily overcome."

I flexed my hand, still lifeless, and agreed. "Are these all your lands?"

"Yes, this is one of our most ambitious projects. We employ crop rotation, an exhaustive use of natural fertilizers, aeration, and other organic techniques to maximize our harvest. It is expensive and difficult, yet we manage to feed all our subjects. It has been years since a surplus has been produced. With the statue that may now change. Many things may change."

The farmers here were a healthy lot, not fat by any means, but well fed and happy. They sang while they tended the fields. Children raced through the grass, hiding, playing in an imagined jungle. They were nothing like the diseased beggars of Sestos. Which family let that city fall into decay? They could learn a lesson from the De Marcos.

"Regrettably," he added, "we have had little success with the forests. Most of the game has vanished and the larger trees are dead."

A woman, in threadbare but clean clothes, approached us from the fields. "Pardon, m'ladyship," she said, "I bear bad tidings from the castle."

"What bad tidings?" Smoking Bear growled.

"The Lord Leonardo says you've gone off and died on us. He's taken the throne and now commands the royal family."

"Looks like your son is eager to cause his grandmother trouble," said Smoking Bear to Aesop.

"If it is Leonardo, we have little to worry about. He has the tactics and subtlety of a fish on dry land." Aesop dug deeply into the folds of his tunic and tossed the woman a silver coin. "Many thanks, mother of our earth."

She curtsied, then ran back to her fields.

"What was that all about?" I asked.

"When we leave on such expeditions," explained Aesop, "one of my offspring usually attempts to seize leadership of the clan. It starts innocently enough with claims of taking charge to preserve the peace, but it always ends in bloodshed.''

"Aren't you worried they have some treachery planned upon your return?''

"No," he said matter-of-factly. "We have made preparations well in advance.''

Smoking Bear halted and set the bundled statue of Starchaser down. The road forked. One path led higher into the mountains, while the other followed the contour of the land down into the plains.

"Roland, you can come no farther with us," she stated. "Your presence would be difficult to explain. Some of our family still has old debts to settle with your clan.''

"We could not guarantee your safety there," Aesop said apologetically.

"I understand.'' It was hard to tell what Smoking Bear thought. She wouldn't meet my eyes; either embarrassed or angry, I couldn't discern.

"We shall arrange for you to stay with a friend in the village," Aesop began.

"No, I cannot accept your generous offer. There are matters that I must personally attend to. Last evening, I decided there is only one source of information that could tell me what happened to my father and my heirloom. There is only one source that knows who my true enemies are: the Oracle at the Abbey of Glossimere.''

"Are you crazy?" she demanded. "It's too dangerous to return there. They'd crucify you.''

"I realize the danger, but I have no choice in the matter. Just as you must return to your clan and quell this uprising, I must tend to my family's troubles.''

It was not that crazy a plan. True, Aesop had killed WaterStone and the other monks who tried to murder us. But they were dead, so there were no witnesses. I'd claim the De Marcos kidnapped me and I had just now escaped. Then I could petition the council of Elders, a petition that historically had never been denied, and I'd be in. Eugene claimed to have faced the Oracle and survived. Tomorrow I'd discuss this with him, and if he really was an ally, he'd help. If he was unwilling to assist me, then I could either abort my journey to the Abbey or face the Oracle on my own. I hadn't quite figured that part out yet.

Smoking Bear sighed and shook her head. "Roland, it's suicide." She looked down. "I don't want you to leave."

If circumstances were different I'd be tempted to stay with her. Stay and do what? She was likely five times my age. There was also Sabrina to consider. Until I understood what was happening with the two of us, how could I involve myself with Smoking Bear?

"You still have my personal allegiance," I told her in a whisper. "When both our family matters are settled, I shall return. I promise."

Aesop stepped forward and shook my hand. "Do you require additional supplies?" He offered his pack to me.

I took it. "Thanks."

Smoking Bear left the statue where it was and came over to hug me with the strength of three. I kissed her there in front of Aesop, not a thing of passion, but of affection, and of farewell. She did not resist my gesture, instead returned it in kind, then withdrew from the embrace. From her weapon belt she removed a dagger, its blade the length of my forearm, and handed it to me. "You may need this." Her face was unreadable.

We stood there for a moment, neither party willing to walk away from the other. Smoking Bear then broke the spell, picked up the statue, and marched up the high fork.

"Luck to you," Aesop said. "We may need your assistance in the future. Politics are coming to a boil. I would like to know I could call you friend."

"I'd be honored. More likely I'll be calling for *your* help in a few days," I said.

He nodded to me, then followed his grandmother.

Taking the lower fork, I started off on my own. I looked back once, but already they had vanished beyond a turn in the road. I'd have to wait until this evening to see them again.

My leg was still a bit stiff from the battle with the helmeted demon. There was, thankfully, no swelling or infection, but I had to move carefully lest I tear the wound open. The next available life source I came upon I'd drain and fix it up. But not from the land. I made that promise to myself after seeing what it did to the Fields of Fire.

The road, now a trail, curved along the mountainside and revealed a view to the east of the Tyrrhenian desert, and beyond that, partially obscured by haze, were the Mountains of Cervin. This desert, as I recalled from my studies, had seasonal flash floods and was riddled with caves and sinkholes. It was a dangerous place to trek alone.

The trail forked again and I took the less traveled branch, a one-track path. To my left, higher in elevation, I spotted the forest Aesop had spoken of. It was thin, with many trees toppled over like broken twigs. I hoped Starchaser could help them.

I switchbacked down the mountain. The grassy hills gave way to bent scrub pines, then creosote, Joshua trees, sage, and an unusual species of cactus capped with a ring of violet blossoms. I made ten kilometers and dropped a thousand meters before lunch.

The desert was odd. Certain areas were dead and nothing more than sand. Other parts flourished with life, abounding with cacti and bees that gathered nectar from their open flowers. Ruby-speckled lizards soaked up the sun and occasionally chased a bejeweled insect for a crunchy snack. It must have rained recently. Perhaps the storm Aesop generated found its way here.

I shifted to a magical perspective to examine the different areas. The life was as drained in the dead spots as it was in the Nomious Hills. The life from the surrounding land only slowly seeped back into them. How long did it take the land to recover? Did it ever recover?

A shadow flashed just behind me. I turned but saw no one.

"Who is there?" I drew Smoking Bear's dagger. I had no idea how to use it. "Show yourself."

The shade crossed my path again. I looked up and saw the snake and bat demon, Bakkeglossides, circling high above me.

I used my magic to communicate with it as I did before—four simultaneous images spun through my thoughts. It was easier this time, though, either because it was willing to talk, or I was getting better at manipulating several mental images at once. Probably the former.

"It is time to fulfill your portion of our pact," the left head demanded. "We have need of your services." I sensed through the line of sorcery a satisfaction, as if it had fed recently. There was a faint aura of death about it, but nothing clearly definable. It hesitated a moment, fixed my position with sonar, then spiraled down to the ground and silently landed.

I had no idea how huge the creature was until I stood next to it. A bat's body the size of a school bus and all black, a black that absorbed the light and gave none of it back. There was a wasplike stinger that extended from its rear. The heads were fearsome things, twin fer-de-lance, fat serpentine triangles of unwavering stares, sensory pits above its molten bronze eyes, and cupped scaled ears, sonar dishes, a pair for each. These were mounted on long coils of muscular snake as long as its bat body, and covered in grey-mottled scales with serrated razor edges.

"What ails you, demon?" I thought in my firmest voice. Of course I was terrified, but I couldn't let either the snake heads sense that.

The right suspected, however, and said, "You are not as clever as we once believed. We were deceived earlier to think you an experienced necromancer of Azure ranking, yet rumors tell you have been a sorcerer for less than a cycle of seasons." A hint of contempt flowed through the link.

"Believe what you will," I replied, and pretended my thoughts were icebergs and locked my knees in place. "I shall keep my end of the bargain as best I can. Will you?"

I then sensed confusion from the right head, either at my unexpected courage or its indecision to allow an amateur to heal it.

"These . . . beetles," it hissed, keeping the right head glued on me while the left motioned to its body. "They suck the life from us."

"Beetles? I'll need to get a better look."

They did not reply, so I assumed I had permission to approach (not that I wanted to). It folded a wing and I climbed up. The bat portion had soft velvety fur, but beneath were the same razor scales on its neck.

"Where?" I asked.

"Underneath."

Gingerly, I pulled a scale aside and exposed its tough leather skin. There, a baseball-sized beetle was attached to the demon; its tiny head stuck beneath the skin. It was translucent yellow, and I saw the blood it sucked from the bat move through its internal organs. It squirmed a bit in the sunlight, but otherwise ignored the interruption.

If this was the source of the demon's irritation, I wouldn't even have to use magic. It would be easy. I prodded the beetle with the tip of the dagger.

"No!" The left head shouted into my mind.

The parasite burrowed deeper into the flesh. The demon shifted in obvious discomfort.

"If they were that simple to remove," the right hissed, "we'd not need your services." If a snake could clench its teeth, it would have. Rage and frustration coursed though our line of sorcery.

"OK, OK, let me try something else." So much for not using magic. I concentrated less on the complex sorcery that allowed us to talk and more on my own mystic vision. I wanted to get a better look at these things.

"What are you doing?" both heads asked, now sounding very distant indeed. "I sense power about you, yet no magic flows. You cannot do that."

"Apparently I can. Now be quiet, I'm trying to concentrate."

I counted forty-seven of the bloodsuckers. Six were

fat and full of eggs, ready to make more of their kind. Each released an oily orange spit into the demon. It was a force of death this secretion, slightly magical, and slightly evil.

Bakkeglossides thought something to me, but I ignored it, severed contact, and moved closer to the pumpkin shade of death. In my mind's eye, I penetrated the surface of the demon, through its body, deeper, until I saw the thing twisting its own coils of genetic material, splicing itself into the cell's machinery, taking control, replicating at an alarming rate. Viruses. Cells shattered and a thousand new viruses burst forth . . . no millions of them, and began the cycle anew. Death magic abounded here.

I backed out, rearranged forces, then asked the right head, "How did you become infected?"

"A curse," they both admitted.

"From the other demon, the helmeted one?"

"No. My brother understands the art of bargaining. Our former master, however, was not pleased, even though we followed his instructions to the letter. This was his reward."

Morgan. It figured.

Sorcery would be necessary to destroy these creatures, that or an extensive antiviral medication, of which I had none. The difficulty lay in what to use as a source of life. I did not wish to drain *my* life forces to replace the demon's. That was a mistake I'd only make once. The life in the land was also taboo. So what was left?

The beetles had set up their own little imbalance. They sucked the life from the demon and left behind death, the viruses. Could I use the life in the parasites to counter the death in the demon? It was worth a shot.

I scrutinized one on its left neck. I'd have to do very little as a gradient of power was there already. I pushed the death and made it flow backward into the gorging parasite. The paired energies collided and canceled one another. The freeloader squealed once, the viruses went inert, and both forces turned grey, then transparent, then gone.

I returned to my physical body and pulled the beetle from the demon. It left a trail of black blood behind.

The left head hissed at me.

"One down," I said, "forty-six to go."

Bakkeglossides was not pleased.

When I finished exterminating the last parasite, I was drenched in sweat. The sun was merciless. Despite the beetles providing the mechanism for their own demise, I expended energy concentrating and manipulating the magics.

"One final check," I sighed, then examined the demon's body inside and out in my phantom form. There was a strange division in Bakkeglossides's life force I hadn't noticed before. Half of it existed on the right side, the other half on the left. Sabrina had told me that demons could "split" themselves, exist in more than one place at the same time. This must be what she meant. The partition in Bakkeglossides was similar to those in Morgan's magical stone, the Matrix. But where the Matrix looked like a puzzle put together incorrectly, Bakkeglossides's parts fit together seamlessly. I would have asked the demon about this, but I had no wish to appear ignorant in the affairs of magic.

"You are clean," I declared.

"Many thanks, young necromancer," the two replied in unison. "We would like to know how you are able to leave your body and return so easily."

"You don't know?"

"We do, of course, but are perplexed at your doing so. Your kind for many cycles has not wielded such power. To remove one's consciousness from one's body is a common trait among your species, but to return is rare. How long have you practiced sorcery?"

I was too tired to conceal my thoughts from the demon. "Less than a week," I said, then sat in the shade of its body, and gulped water from my canteen.

The right head mentally nodded. "Then you must possess multiple dualities to hold the power at bay by mere thought as you do. We were wise to bargain with you rather than fight.''

I knew I had another duality—other than existing in two worlds at once. I was beginning to suspect that being the child of two dreamers wasn't the only way to possess a dual nature. Xuraldium hinted there were other techniques. Did Bakkeglossides's self-imposed ''split'' life force count as a duality?

''Tell me demon,'' I said, ''do you dream?''

''Sleep and dreams are weakness only humans have. We demons never sleep,'' both heads informed me.

Never sleep? Then they only existed in Meredin. They *had* to split themselves in this manner to manipulate magic. Whole, they had no duality.

While I was fascinated by this revelation, I had to keep moving. The Abbey and my answers were still far away. I rose, stretched, and picked up my pack. ''If you don't have any more work for me, I must continue my journey. I have a long way to go and it's not getting any cooler.''

The left head searched its body for any overlooked parasite, while the right inquired, ''You travel across this desert?''

An idea formed and I hushed my thoughts before I replied, ''Yes, it is unfortunate. I have heard tales of the sinkholes here that can swallow a man if his step is misplaced. There are also deadly burrowing scorpions, but they are said only to be active at night, so I should not have to worry about stepping on one.''

''It is regrettable your species is so fragile, especially since you have a propensity for self-destruction.''

''Yes, if I died, I would feel extremely guilty for not being able to fulfill our contract, the other healing I owe you.''

''Oh,'' the left said. Then after a moment the right asked, ''What did you say your destination was?''

''The Abbey of Glossimere, beyond those mountains.''

''Perhaps we would find it agreeable to transport you if, say, you heal us thrice more?''

"No, I am afraid I could not commit myself to such a one-sided bargain. Good day." I continued along the path deeper into the desert.

From behind me I heard, "Twice."

I turned, "Once, and under the same conditions as our first agreement. Also you must not tell any others of my sorcerous abilities or the deal is null and void."

"Such cunning in one so young," the left answered. "Yet as we are going that way in any event, I agree." The right then added, "You would make a fine demon."

"How long will it take?"

"I should have you there before the sun sets."

So fast? Assuming I had even found the pass through the mountains, it would have taken me three, maybe four days, to get to the Valley of Thought on foot. The danger was facing the Oracle before I asked Eugene how he had survived the experience. We were only a few hours away from his estate in the other realm, but I had no guarantee that he'd reveal the secret of the Oracle to me. Still, it was an opportunity I could not pass up.

I climbed on the back of the bat and it lifted into the air with a powerful stroke of its wings. The two heads shifted continuously as it flew, not haphazardly as I had once thought, but to change its shape as it plunged through the winds. The ride was smoother than Aesop's balloon.

The demon ascended to a dizzying altitude and the desert fell away. It appeared flat and featureless save the occasional ribbon of darker soil, proof of the recent rainfall.

"Tell me, Bakkeglossides, what do you know of what my kind calls the Golden Age and its collapse?"

The left navigated while the right thought back to me, "It was a time of high magic, when many species, not merely yours, inhabited this world. It was a season of great contracts, complex in loopholes, rich in language and ambiguities. City-states, portals to the other realms, and great philosophers were the order of that period. But then the wars began and the others left.

"We find the motives of your species incomprehensible at times. You are violent beyond reckoning. You humans hunted our race to the brink of extinction. Then when there were too few of us left to focus your attentions upon, the royal families turned on themselves. Anger and revenge spread from clan to clan like a fire, and destroyed this world. Only cinders remain today. It is all so senseless.''

''My species is violent?'' I cried. ''What of yours? I wouldn't call our encounter with your helmeted friend a social function.''

''Violent? No, we kill only by contract, by order, and by law. What could be more civilized?''

Far to the south, I glimpsed the Great Inland Sea. The sunlight reflected upon its surface like a mirror framed in the land. From this distance it appeared no larger than a pond, but I knew from my studies it was an enormous freshwater sea. Past that, I could almost make out the Ocean of Frost, just a hazy mist blending imperceptibly with the horizon. The view was nearly enough to distract me from the cold winds that blasted through my clothes. I dug my arms deeper beneath the demon's fur, warming them against its body.

We cleared the Mountains of Cervin as the sun dipped below the horizon and set the sky awash with gold and pink watercolors. Once over the summit, I was in familiar territory. I had seen this valley before from the balloon: a dimple in the mountains, the Valley of Thought, and cupped there, the Lake of the Prophet, within which floated the Isle of Knowledge and the Abbey of Glossimere.

''Land behind those hills on the far side of the isle,'' I said. I had no wish to fly directly into the Abbey on this demon. My welcome would be icy enough.

We touched down, a feather landing, silent as a leaf falling.

''My thanks again, Bakkeglossides.''

''You are most welcome, young necromancer. Perhaps when we meet again you will have learned the proper pronunciation of our names.''

It lifted into the air, a shadow in the darkening sky, then vanished.

The rocky hills on this part of the isle shielded the Abbey from the winds that blew across the lake. In the distance, I heard the two old men who tended the sheep that grazed here laugh. They were both drunks. Farther along, there were rows of shadows, the apple orchard that supplemented the monks' diet (although no lowly acolytes ever tasted any).

I had often come to these hills to escape my studies and the gossiping. None of my brother monks cared to explore the island, so it afforded me a measure of privacy.

The hills sheered away to form cliffs on the other side. Sometimes, I climbed to the very top and watched for merchant ships headed for Sestos. I was decades, perhaps hundreds of years too late, but that never stopped me from daydreaming. Then I would venture down those cliffs. There were plenty of handholds and ledges, so it was an easy climb even in my robe. Where the boulders touched the lake was a hidden cave. I would pretend to be a pirate, waiting to plunder the fat Yaggon galleons that dared to glide past me with cargoes of slaves and spices and silks. My imaginary crew and I would raise the sail of our equally imaginary cutter, crash along the waves, board the galleon, and battle their crew. We always won.

Down from the hills and into the groves, I went to pilfer one of the forbidden apples. It was a bit green but delicious nonetheless. I grabbed two more and devoured them on the path to the Abbey.

The Elders would not be elated to see me, especially since I planned to refuse my commission again. And especially since I planned to file a petition to see the Oracle—which they would consider suicidal. There would be questions and suspicions about the De Marcos and the murder of WaterStone, but I counted on tradition to protect me from any lengthy inquisition. Even criminals had the right to see the Oracle.

Mounting the final hill, I spied the vegetable gardens,

the twin towers, the library complex, the mundane dormitories nestled in the very back, and the ruins of the secondary library. It was all still as I had left it.

One week and a lifetime of change had passed since I was here. The grounds appeared smaller and less glorious than I recalled. Strange how that works, but isn't that the way of things? You hold onto the images of the people and places in your life, and as events and time pass, those memories blur to take on the scale of myth. Only when you return to your past do you realize how small your life has really been.

Two guards stood at their ceremonial posts by the entrance to the complex. There was really no need for them, but tradition was tradition, and it dictated that acolytes freeze their body parts while guarding against nonexistent intruders. One of the pair was sound asleep. I understood the arrangement; one slept while the other watched out for Elders. I had done this before, been caught at it too. That was a tradition of sorts also.

I walked up to them as if I belonged here. "Good evening."

The one asleep jerked his head, suddenly awake, and his helmet clattered to the ground. The sound alarmed the second guard so, that he dropped his crossbow.

"Allow me help you with that." I picked it up and handed it to him. It was unloaded.

The first guard, now awake, shook his head at the noise. An Elder was certain to show up and investigate. It meant extra duties for causing such a disruption. I knew him, my friend Booklight, so called because he studied well into the evening by candle. His hair was thinning, and rumor had it he was the oldest noncommissioned acolyte on the island.

"Roland?" He said, squinting into the dark.

I clasped his hand. "What has happened since I left?"

"Left? We heard of your capture by the two sorcerers that arrived last week. They killed many of our brothers when they were denied our knowledge. How did you free yourself?"

"I shall explain later, if I am able. Right now I need you to wake the council."

"Wake? The council? Are you mad?"

"I thought you never wanted your commission. This is your perfect opportunity. Go wake them. I wish to petition to see the Oracle."

The other younger acolyte dropped his spear again.

"You have some sort of death wish?" Booklight whispered.

"No, I am serious."

An Elder emerged from the hallway. "What may I do for you traveler?"

He called me "traveler," yet I knew he recognized me. It was SilentSpeaker, one of the few Elders I counted as just and noble.

The two guards stood at their best attention.

"I seek to petition the council, wise SilentSpeaker," I repeated.

He raised an eyebrow in astonishment. "Do you know that only one person in the last fifty-three years has seen the Oracle and lived? Why is your need so urgent?"

"I shall present my petition in accordance with tradition before the full council." I didn't mean to be rude, but I'd only get one shot at this. I wanted my case to be heard once, not echoed about the halls in gossip for a week before I saw the council.

He considered me for a moment in the darkness then said, "Come, you know I cannot deny you."

We walked together through the winding passages, through the dormitories, past my sleeping brothers, and into the council chambers. He asked me no questions, and said nothing of my departure. Surely he knew what had occurred in the tunnels when the De Marcos and I had escaped.

"Please wait here, Roland," he instructed me, then disappeared down the black-tiled hallway.

The council chamber was empty. This was my first visit to the famous room. Had I accepted my commission, I would have seen it a week ago. All things considered, I was satisfied with my choice. At least I was making my own decisions and had all my bodily parts.

There were only twelve worn wooden thrones here, but when the Abbey was first built, there were thirty-one council members. It is not widely known, but the number of Elders diminished as the years passed, just as the population of the dreaming realm did. Would there eventually be one Elder left, alone on the Isle of Knowledge with books that none read?

Above me loomed a dilapidated arched roof, cracked open in sections, and its murals water stained and chipped. Painted on the inside with a luminous substance were the forty-four constellations of Meredin. Through a hole in the ceiling, I saw the real stars twinkling in the clear night sky. I connected the dots; there was Magilian the Ogre, Phinerius the Executioner, Cylarus the Tree, Arthusa the Whale, and others I had forgotten.

A White Robe entered the room, interrupting my mental exercise. "Roland," he whispered, "how pleasant to see you again."

The voice was WaterStone's. He had survived Aesop's fire? "WaterStone, you live?"

"Yes," he replied and removed the cowl about his head. As he lifted the cloth I saw his hands, melted and malformed into slender shapes, covered in stained bandages. When the backlash of Aesop's fire hit me, I raised my hands to protect my face. WaterStone took the full force of that blast. His hands must practically be gone. The cowl fell away and revealed a face that had no hair; his majestic black beard was now a hoary scar upon his chin; and blisters covered his distorted head. He grinned at me—a fiendish twisted thing.

"You killed six of my favorite men last week," he spat past lips that were no longer lips. "The last died in agony two days ago."

"You are the one that forced that confrontation," I said.

"Is that your pitiful excuse? Do you think the council or I care what *really* happened? You escaped with valuable information, irreplaceable information. We almost had the De Marco relic for our own. Do you know what that was worth to us?'' He smoothed his robe with a bandaged hand. ''But I forget my manners,'' he said, changing his tone to a cordial one and sitting.

I heard shuffling in the shadows behind me. ''I have returned, not as acolyte but to petition the council.''

''The Oracle? You came back to seek your doom then.'' He shook his head. ''I am afraid we cannot permit such a promising young monk to face the Oracle. The loss would be unbearable,'' he said, his voice laced with sarcasm.

''I have already spoken with the guards and a full Elder. It will be a secret for about five minutes, then all on this island will know I have returned and my purpose. If you kill me, you violate one of your most sacred traditions. I *will* petition the council and you *will* allow me to see it.''

He laughed, then coughed. Fluid rattled about in his lungs. ''Very well, Roland, you will visit the Oracle. One death is as good as another I suppose. I only wish I could see it.'' He motioned to the guards, ''Take our guest to his room.''

Two monks, whom I did not recognize, emerged from the shadows. They held their oversize crossbows at my back. I made no sudden moves.

''When I am done with the Oracle, WaterStone, I'll come back to deal with you privately.''

He laughed again and this time coughed uncontrollably. He waved the guards to take me away.

Nice going, I assured myself, threaten one of the council members. That will do my petition worlds of good. Still, I felt some satisfaction in hearing him choke.

The guards led me below the Abbey to the holding cells. These were reserved for criminals and outcasts. I suppose I now qualified.

They slammed the door shut and left me alone in the dark.

My cell was cold, two paces by three, and smelled of urine. I sat in the moist straw and tried to sleep but could only think of the mad god in the tower.

How had Eugene survived? I hoped he would share

the secret with me tonight or I was doomed. Many
monks, all smarter than me, went into that tower and
failed to return. What did the Oracle do to them?

I sighed, ignored the stench, and relaxed.

Sleep came for me as she always did, dressed in a
gown of shadow and whispering comforting thoughts.
She took my hand and escorted me across the void.

17

It was overcast in the mountains, strangely incandescent as the sun tried to burn its way through the atmosphere. Fog rolled through the forest, a thick blanket that covered everything in its path with droplets of moisture. Our campfire was out.

The De Marcos and I were up, but Morgan slept on in a drugged stupor. I was tempted to kick him in the head—revenge for infesting Bakkeglossides with those parasites, but stopped as the demon's words echoed in my mind . . . *You are violent beyond reckoning.* OK, so maybe we were a bunch of vindictive hoodlums. I kicked a little dirt on him instead.

Aesop and Smoking Bear talked to one another in hushed voices by the station wagon. I made no attempt to overhear their conversation because I had problems of my own to consider.

WaterStone was alive and might nullify my petition for an audience with the Oracle. The question was: did he have the influence to sway a majority of the council? Would they believe him when he spoke his lies? Asking the De Marcos for assistance was out of the question. Even if Aesop had another balloon, it would take one

or two days to cross the Tyrrhenian desert. And any
delay of my petition would give WaterStone time to arrange for an accident to befall me. I could conveniently
slip on the slick dungeon floor, crack my head open, and
none would be the wiser. Even if the council did approve
my petition, I was gambling that Eugene would share
the Oracle's secrets.

I had Morgan's phone, so I dialed the number for the
desert estate.

A servant answered. He became excited at the sound
of my voice and said Mister Rhodes was frantic to locate
me. He was not there, but would definitely be in this
afternoon.

"Yes," I said, "you may take a message. Tell him
that I am coming to visit this evening. It's a matter of
life and death, so make sure he's there."

The servant then asked where I was and the nature of
my difficulties. I hung up.

Aesop returned from the wagon, doctor's bag in hand.
"Problems?"

"No," I lied. "Nothing I can't handle. What about
you? How did it turn out with your son?"

"There were difficulties," he replied, without meeting
my eyes. "Leonardo was more adept at intrigue than
either of us expected. I believe, however, that we shall
have everything under control shortly."

Smoking Bear returned and stomped the embers of
the campfire into oblivion. She smiled briefly to me but
clearly was preoccupied. She gathered her gear in silence.

Aesop and I then loaded Morgan's body into the back
of the wagon (where I hoped he'd be as uncomfortable
as possible).

We drove back along the dirt road and onto the rural
highway that wound through these mountains. In the
backseat, Aesop nodded off, and returned to the dream
realm. Smoking Bear kept a careful eye on him in the
rearview mirror while she drove through the bright fog.

Morgan finally came to when we cleared the clouds,
dropped in elevation, and emerged in rolling foothills.

"I hope you both slept well last night," he said, leaning forward. "I know I did." He rubbed where Smoking Bear had stuck him and muttered about the mosquitoes and the feast they had at his expense.

"I slept like a log," Smoking Bear replied. "And you'll be out again soon if you don't keep your mouth shut. Aesop is trying to wrap things up back in Meredin."

"A thousand apologies," he said unapologetically. "Roland, what happened to you? My spies tell me you didn't arrive at the De Marco's castle."

Smoking Bear raised an eyebrow when he said this.

"Where I am, and what I do, is none of your concern," I answered.

Unable to solicit any friendly responses, he shut up and scowled at both of us. I checked him magically to be certain he wasn't up to any mischief. Nothing.

We were well into the hills when Aesop returned, awaking with a start. He glanced out the window, mute, and watched the California black oaks, the wide fields of dried grass, and the cows that reflected his gaze back through their black blank eyes. He cracked a smile to Smoking Bear and me to assure us all was well, but I couldn't shake the feeling that something had gone wrong.

"Why don't we stop and catch a late breakfast?" Morgan cheerfully suggested.

"You can eat when we get to your buddy's house," Smoking Bear snapped back at him. "Besides, you could lose a few pounds."

Silently we glided down the hills onto the level sandy plains of the Mojave Desert. My ears popped from the change in elevation. The windows were tinted and the old wagon had a decent air conditioner, but the temperature still rose to an uncomfortable level. Smoking Bear increased our speed, shooting across the flat terrain.

I dozed several times, drifting back and forth between realms, between the stuffy warmth in the station wagon and the damp stone floor of the Abbey dungeon. Pre-

ferring the heat to the cold, I forced myself to stay awake
and in this realm.

Smoking Bear suddenly slowed down.

A traffic jam materialized in the middle of the desert.
Cars stretched as far as I could see with no visible source
to account for the delay.

Aesop wanted to speak with Smoking Bear, so we
traded places. I sat in the back next to Morgan, who was
covered with sweat and obviously miserable. Thankfully
he had nothing more to say to me.

The line of cars crept forward. I waited and hoped we
would clear the crash or whatever emergency held us
captive. If it was an accident, should I use my healing
magics to help? Did I have time? What sources of life
and death were at my command?

I found myself developing a magical reflex, summoning the power quickly when I needed to, and concentrating less on visualizing the forces. I almost felt the
sorcery, a liquid electrical sensation. Aesop certainly had
this reflex—summoning huge quantities of destruction
upon command. He was quicker to use his powers than
I'd ever be, a little haphazard also.

We inched forward, all of us straining to see ahead
and discover the origin of our sluggish pace. It took
forty-five minutes before I spied flashing police lights,
blue and white. They reminded me of the shooting at
the Gas n' Mart, and despite the heat, chills slithered
down my spine.

There were only police here, no ambulances or fire
trucks. I quickly counted thirty cops milling about, eating sandwiches, drinking sodas, watching, and waiting.
They were armed, but not with the familiar varieties of
side arms. These police had shotguns and automatic
weapons with extra clips of ammunition.

Ahead in the road lay a belt of metal spikes that covered both lanes. Any car crossing that would have its
tires shredded. Five more cops waited there. To the right
of the roadblock, sat two cruisers with their lights flashing. To our left, was a large van with a satellite dish on
top, apparently a command center. A dozen more heav-

ily armed men loitered there, looking anxious and uncomfortable in the noon desert heat.

A trooper waved the car in front of us forward. His partner stood ready, shotgun in hand. He looked inside, briefly spoke with the driver, then waved them around the barrier and motioned for us to pull up.

"Be ready," Smoking Bear said. "This is not what it appears to be."

"What do you mean?" Morgan asked.

"See those police cars back there? Take a careful look at the seal on the door."

Aesop stared, eyes forward, already concentrating.

Morgan and I squinted to get a look at the car. The seal appeared official, but in tiny lettering just below it was: ACRONITE SECURITY FORCE. They weren't police.

We pulled forward.

The trooper checked the license plate of the station wagon and whispered to his partner. He approached the driver's window and Smoking Bear rolled it down.

"Would you please step out of the car," he said. It was not a question.

Before she did anything, however, Morgan leaned forward. "Excuse me, officer, I'm the registered owner of this car. Why don't you look over *my* license?" He passed his license over Smoking Bear's shoulder.

The officer began to say something, paused, then took his license.

I glanced magically at Morgan. Seven pairs of diaphanous shrouds enveloped him. One caressed the trooper's hand when he took the license. It dissolved through his glove and into his flesh, into his soul. He examined the license and found the three hundred dollar bills beneath. Wordlessly he palmed the money then returned Morgan's license.

"I don't see anything out of order here," he said. "You can go on. Have a safe trip."

Smoking Bear rolled the window back up.

He was about to wave us through, when a man stepped from the van. I recognized him, dressed in a three-piece suit in this heat. It was Lloyd.

Lloyd likewise recognized us. He shouted orders to his hired cops. They raised their weapons.

The temperature jumped from desert simmer to inferno broil. Aesop opened a door to a volcano and drove the car in. The air shimmered and twisted about the wagon; we were surrounded on all sides by walls of heat. I only saw blurred colors and distortion—the stuff mirages were made of.

I shifted perspective magically, shifted through the Matrix and left my physical body. Outside, I saw Lloyd shouting to his men. The asphalt around us was on fire, boiling in patches. Behind us, a family abandoned their sedan, its paint cracking from the heat, the two front tires aflame. Our station wagon appeared as distorted from the outside as it did within. Storm clouds condensed above us out of the clear desert sky.

Lloyd's troopers fired, aiming at the walls of flickering red and purple heat. The man that Morgan had bribed was nowhere to be seen. Perhaps he had been too close.

I reflexively dropped to the ground (unnecessary as I wasn't physically there). Bullets whistled through me into Aesop's shields. Only after several hundred rounds were shot into the car did Lloyd call for a cease-fire.

I returned to my body and ducked behind the front seat.

The lead was molten when it struck the windshield. The impact lessened, yet it still turned the smooth glass into a network of spiderwebs. We were, for the moment, safe from their guns. But a shield of flames wouldn't stop Lloyd from burying us alive with his sorcery.

"Drop the section at ten o'clock," Smoking Bear said. She cracked the door and dove out. Although exposed to the exterior only for a moment, the blast of heat reddened my skin and softened the vinyl seats. I followed her out, without my body, sparing a glance at Aesop and Morgan.

Morgan was in a trance and covered in deep shadows of evil. They coalesced into a darker solid shape floating near him. Aesop had lines of force tethered to him, each one a Roman candle of magic, fiery rainbows that extended to his shields, and each mirrored by a clear fountain of magic ascending into the atmosphere, the water portion of his sorcery.

Outside, Smoking Bear charged the nearest man. Dozens of tiny globes of translucent pink and cool green trailed obediently behind her.

He fired his shotgun at her—hit her square in the chest. She fell, then rolled to her feet suddenly in front of him. It hurt, I saw the pain in her face, but it didn't stop her. I remembered she wore some sort of body armor under her jump suit.

Smoking Bear grabbed his gun, locked his arm behind his back, then threw him toward the car. He hit the inferno barrier and exploded into flame and ash. The spheres of magic caught up with her and began to spin about her like moons, increasing their angular speed, leaving smeared tails of color behind them.

She fired his shotgun, and dropped another man, then she struck a third trooper, using the empty weapon as a club, crushing his chest.

A strong wind blew; Lloyd faced the station wagon, concentrating. A hand of power reached into the earth and pushed something under the car. I barely noticed another line of power attached to him, a thin silvery cord that shimmered, covered in diamond dust, the likes of which I hadn't seen before. It wasn't his. There had to be another sorcerer.

Before I investigated, his troopers reacted to Smoking Bear's attack. She was beating a man into the ground, when a dozen of them formed a loose half circle around her. She threw the shotgun at the nearest man and caught him full in the face. I heard the splintering of bone.

They shot her.

The automatic weapons however, only hit her magic, deepening the globes' colors from cool green, to lime, to brilliant jade, and from translucent pink, to lobster, to solid brick. She killed them. She used her hands and feet, bounded from man to man like a tiger stuck on fast forward, broke arms, snapped necks, busted kneecaps, anything to disable her foes, seemingly growing stronger and faster the more rounds they fired.

Three of the remaining four fled before her. One man stood his ground and fired his assault rifle point blank into her. She finally fell, stunned, a mass of blood and puckered Kevlar.

I returned to the car. Aesop had to help her.

When I returned to my body, the edge of panic seeped into my voice and the sensation of adrenaline, biochemical lightning, shot through me. "She's down," I said.

The shimmering slowed and the walls of heat dissipated. "Where?" Aesop asked, as calm as a pool of water.

"About twenty feet from the front left fender."

He opened the door. "Take cover," he said, then stepped out.

I opened my door. Morgan remained motionless, deep in concentration. I tried to pull him out through my side. The asphalt stuck to my shoes, melting them while I dragged his weight across the seat. He became vaguely aware of my efforts and stumbled out on his own. I guided him behind a cruiser far from the road.

I left my body next to his and returned to the battle.

Lloyd shifted a fissure beneath our station wagon. The road tilted and cracked open. A sinkhole materialized under the road. It swallowed the station wagon and four cars next to it.

Aesop, melting his own path over the uncertain earth, distracted the remaining troopers. His heat forced many of them to retreat or be incinerated. A few shot at him, the bullets disappeared, melting and boiling away before they touched him.

Smoking Bear was just standing up, bloodied and shaky.

The smaller line of magic secured to Lloyd, the cord of captured moonlight, detached and wormlike made its way to her. It touched her and she froze. Her globes of sorcery disappeared.

The men not shooting at Aesop, then aimed at Smoking Bear to finish her off. Some charged her in a berserk rage, mouths foaming, eyes wide. A portion of the unknown sorcery that touched Lloyd also touched the men returning to battle. It prompted this senseless rage.

I interposed my ghostly body between Smoking Bear and the unknown magic to absorb it and give her a fighting chance. The fine silver coil attached to me, touched my brained, numbed it like ice, and froze my spine. It was fear.

About me I heard fighting, cries of pain and gunshots, Smoking Bear and the troopers, but I could do nothing more.

This was fear so great, had I a body my heart would have stopped. It filled me and paralyzed me. It was all the fear I ever experienced rolled into one giant feeling. The dread of living the rest of my life as Hestor's caretaker, fear of never having friends or a family of my own, fear of failure, childhood horrors, the things in the dark, the unknown sounds in the middle of the night that woke me, fear of growing old and helpless, the primal terror of death, all of them crashed into my mind. I couldn't think of anything but the fear. It had me. I cried out, wishing only to be gone. Death was better than living like this even for a moment.

A wave of blue flame boiled through me. Aesop launched an attack at Lloyd, who countered by raising a wall of earth to deflect the blast. The wall blackened, turned to glass and shattered. Lloyd was thrown backward. The command van nearly blew over, tottered, then fell back on all four wheels.

The line of magic attached to me dissolved. The intense fear vanished. Aesop's explosion had mercifully caused the anonymous sorcerer to lose control. I took a second to recover, to mend my spirit, then looked for Smoking Bear.

She lay facedown, covered in blood and powder burns. There were six dead or dying men. No one moved.

I examined her wounds and found countless tiny abrasions, cuts, bruises, a large puncture in her leg, and the most dangerous wound: a bullet penetrated just under her arm through a gap in the body armor. It must have rattled about in her rib cage, shredding the right lung, then nicked her heart and an artery. There was massive internal bleeding.

The only life forces available were from the men who tried to kill her. Had I the right to drain their lives to save hers? They were only doing their job. They may have thought we were criminals. No, they opened fire without hesitation or warning. They deserved what they got. Smoking Bear was my distant relative, and for whatever reasons, I felt more than a casual camaraderie toward her. She was a dreamer, more important than a hundred men of shallow existence.

I was angry now, angry at Lloyd and his unknown partner in this ambush. Revenge, sweet slow torture was called for, but not now. Now I pushed all those emotions into the deep freeze and helped her.

A sizzling rain fell; whirlwinds threw sand into the air; and the earth shook. These things were no more real to me than words in a book. I noticed them in an abstract fashion, but they could not touch me in this ethereal form.

Life. First the life I pulled from the least wounded man. One with a broken face, his brain dark in my vision, inert, but the remainder of his body in good shape, and another, sobbing with pain, a pair of shattered legs nearly pinched off at the knees. Yes, they'd do nicely.

Death. She had plenty to start with to balance their lives and make my sorcery flow.

I drained the essence from them. A trickle at first, then more, the warm pinpricking tingle of magic, channeled by my living hand into Smoking Bear. Quietly, the man with the head injury passed on. The other sensed what was happening and fought for his life. He was no sorcerer, though. I pulled harder and it came, flowing freely like blood from a fresh wound.

The power from their stolen lives I mentally ordered to repair her heart. It was a massive thing, twice normal size, with eight chambers with a double set of veins and arteries. It must be a mutation, a built in redundancy of the circulatory system. While I was intrigued, I silenced my curiosity and returned to the task at hand, knitting the muscle fibers back together, then closing the jagged hole in her second right pulmonary artery, and thickening the walls to withstand the pressure of her blood pounding through it.

Now her lung. I was running low on life, so I drained the remaining four men until they were no more. I did this suppressing my emotions, knowing I'd pay my guilt in full and with interest.

Her lung was torn in more places than I could count. Should I just close the tears up? No, it had thousands of microbranches, a giant inverted tree of minute detail. I could spend days trying to repair each tiny pathway. The left was in good shape; it had one large gash that I sealed with a thought. I pictured this in my mind then held a mirror to it. *This*, I told my subconscious, *this is what the mass of mangled tissue on the right should look like*. I concentrated on that picture until it was crystal clear, and beyond the magic, I sensed the healing begin. The life, the fuel for my sorcery, was almost spent. I slowed down and took a final look.

The lung looked good, a true mirror to its mate on the left. It filled with air and held. The bullet was lodged next to her liver, but there was nothing I could do about that. The smaller wounds and the hole in her leg would have to wait.

I defocused from the images. My power faded, and I returned to my physical body exhausted and sickened at what I had done. The power to kill came too easily. Now I understood how a sorcerous war got out of hand. The ease of revenge, by merely thinking of it, could strike any normal man down. Were these men less valuable because they lived in one realm only?

Next to me Morgan stood, and his face was full of tension. The air sparkled about him with golden motes of magic. I chanced a look over the police cruiser we hid behind.

Aesop and Lloyd confronted one another.

The van was nowhere in sight, only a smoking crater

remained. Tornadoes formed and sent black veils of sand and rock into the air. A broken water main spewed forth its contents, and elsewhere, scattered patches of rain deluged the desert. High innocent cirrus clouds darkened and fell, then spread across the ground, and enveloped the battlefield. More tremors shook the earth and cracks opened beneath my feet. Smoke filled the air along with the smells of burning asphalt, rubber, and flesh.

I took Morgan's arm (for he was still in a trance, full in his concentration) and guided him farther away, into the desert.

When I returned my attention again to Aesop and Lloyd, I saw something was wrong (besides their trying to kill each other). There was an imbalance of the magical forces—precisely what Eugene had warned me of. Aesop had summoned too much fire, heedless of what the water was doing. He had to because Lloyd threw caution to the winds, literally, and called on his earth sorcery, ignoring the fierce powers of the air. Was he crazy?

From Aesop's hand snaked forth a pillar of fire so bright it burned my eyes to watch. It ignited the sand and tore at the winds, this column of flame that whirled toward Lloyd. From the sand, the earth sorcerer manufactured a huge funnel of glass, curved like a broken snail shell. The tower of fire spun into the structure, began to melt it, but then was channeled through and redirected at its creator.

The fire twisted back and struck Aesop. He absorbed the heat and glowed as white-hot metal, melting all before him, turning the section of earth between him and his opponent molten.

Lloyd shifted the ground beneath him, piled it into an island, a hill of stone that was safe from Aesop's conjured Hell.

Where was Smoking Bear?

Fingers of stone, clear, giant, hexagonal crystals rose from the melted earth and grew to the size of telephone poles. They glowed orange, reflecting the molten sand. The stone columns then toppled over, slowly at first, but they quickly gained momentum. They were aimed at Aesop. He jumped, and barely escaped being crushed by the tons of silicon.

It was becoming impossible to see from my position. There was an explosion from where Aesop was last. I only sensed a wave of pressure and heat through the thickening walls of sand and rain that buffeted about their duel.

I felt Morgan finish whatever magics he had started and turned to look.

The ground opened at his feet, a perfect circular hole. Streamers of evil boiled forth and evaporated the balance of good in Morgan. I stepped back two paces. Rising from the hole was a demon: a huge rotating stone pyramid, larger than a car, with a single ruby eye glaring from the capstone.

"What is your wish, O Master of the benign and the malicious?" it boomed.

I couldn't hear Morgan's reply as the winds howled and drowned his voice. The demon responded, though, and floated into the battle. The elemental forces parted before it, parted like a curtain. I saw what it was after now—Lloyd.

He raised an earthen hand, partially molten, to halt the demon's approach. It merely passed through and ignored the stone structure.

Lloyd ran.

The floating stone hovered above him and landed.

Lloyd vanished.

The demon rose and started back.

"Get Smoking Bear," I shouted into Morgan's ear.

He nodded and closed his eyes, concentrating again. The creature coasted for a moment, red eye probing the mixture of elements, then made its way through the veils of dust, rain, fire, and wind.

When it emerged, Smoking Bear was held like a magnet to a refrigerator door on one of the pyramid's faces. Lloyd was nowhere to be seen.

Water welled up from the earth faster than it could be absorbed. Walking was impossible. Already I sank into the muck up to my knees. A full tornado touched down; I couldn't see it, but I *felt* it as it tore the ground to pieces and my ears popped from the painful change in pressure.

The demon bumped up against me, lifted me, and I lay stuck on its surface. It ignored the winds and carried us far from the unnatural storm.

I was blinded, and my skin stung from the wind-driven sand. Another explosion sounded and a wave of pressure passed over us. The demon's body shielded us against it, but then a blast of steam hit me from the front. I left my body, and the pain, and returned to help Aesop.

The desert was gone.

The earth exploded from the bedrock below, mixed with the water, then was carried into the air by the torrents of wind that raped the earth.

Magics, earth, water, fire, and air, were all out of balance. Each tried to cancel its counterpart; all fought in a battle of the elements. A tiny amber flame persisted within the center of the tempest. It was Aesop.

I moved forward, but the unbalanced forces batted me aside as if I were a moth, even though I had no real body. I could only observe from a distance as the wild magics collided, every time losing a fraction of their intensity, every time slamming into Aesop. The flame in the center winked out of existence, gone, as the wind snuffed it out, the earth smothered it, and the water doused it.

It rained hot mud. The giant hole in the earth overflowed with water where the road had been moments ago. I returned to Morgan and Smoking Bear, helpless to do anything but watch as Aesop died.

My mind was numb and filled with sand. I sat next to the pyramid of stone and watched while the storm slowly lost momentum. Black swirling clouds of dirt, water, and smoke blended into the overcast sky. The sun was gone, well hidden above those elemental blankets. Fires still burned, winking dull red in the distance, the last traces of Aesop's sorcery. The demon carried us a mile down the road, yet even this far away, boulders occasionally fell from the air, and the ground was alternately muddy and searing hot in patches.

"Let's get out of here," Morgan said. "It's still dangerous, too unstable."

No kidding. Of course it was dangerous, but I had to go back and retrieve Aesop's body. There might be a way yet to save him. What kind of life force would I need to restore him? What would be left of him after all that?

Morgan didn't wait for my reply and started marching along the broken road. The demon obediently floated behind him.

I followed. Who was I trying to fool? Aesop was dead. I couldn't raise the dead.

The road was broken, shattered, and lying at odd angles. No one would be driving this way for a long time. The cars were abandoned, windshields smashed, doors left open, and frames bent from the force. How many innocent people had died because they were caught in the crossfire of our family conflict?

"Morgan," I demanded, catching up to him and grabbing his arm, "why did your demon only pick up Smoking Bear and not Aesop?" Yes, this was his fault. Why hadn't *he* saved Aesop?

"I was in a trance the whole time," he stated, his eyes narrowing at my accusation and my hand on his arm. "I didn't even know they were there until you told me. I only knew Lloyd was the troublemaker."

Then it was my fault because I didn't tell Morgan? All I had to say was, "get Aesop," and the demon would have picked him up too? No, the runaway magics were too powerful. If I couldn't get in to help Aesop, and I didn't even have a physical body, what chance did the demon have? I didn't want to know.

I should have done something though, tried anything. I just watched Aesop in the center of the storm, buried, drowned, and ripped to pieces. What kind of friend was I? He trusted me, gave his all for us, and all I did was watch him die.

An aftershock vibrated through the earth.

Morgan held up his hand and the demon halted. "I can't control this one any longer. I better release it."

"Didn't you make a bargain with it? I didn't think absolute control was required."

"I never bargain with demons." He smirked. "They twist your words to serve their own purposes."

The demon's capstone eye, laser red, fixed upon him and glared. From inside there was a rumbling and sand showered from the base. Lloyd, without ceremony, dropped onto the ground. The pyramid then gently allowed Smoking Bear to slide off its surface, dipping one edge to the ground so she wouldn't fall. It then moved off to a dry patch of sand and sank into the earth, back to whatever Hell it came from.

Morgan sighed and sat down where he was. He rubbed his bald head to smooth the wrinkles out.

I inspected Lloyd. He had a few cuts and burns, but nothing I considered serious, and nothing I felt like healing. He'd live . . . maybe, but not too long after Smoking Bear found out what had happened. Why did he let his magic go wild? It was almost as if he was self-destructing on purpose, unthinking, like the men who had charged Smoking Bear.

For Smoking Bear, I dipped into my reserves, the life force of the jewel within me, to seal up the large wound on her leg and clean up any signs of infection. I was concerned about the bullet still inside her, but I didn't have the energy or concentration to extract it. I removed her armor, which was ruined, and made her as comfortable as I could. Her body was ugly with bruises, covered in dirt and blood that was not her own.

I sat there quietly, thinking of Aesop.

A light rain fell. The day rolled by overhead, hidden by the storm. I buried my head beneath my arms and tried to cry for my friend but had no more strength. Tears, along with my revenge, would have to wait.

Smoking Bear regained consciousness. She tried to stand, failed, then tried a second time.

I helped her up. "You shouldn't be moving yet," I told her.

She ignored me, took one look at Lloyd and snorted, "I assume we won? Where's Aesop?"

Neither of us said anything.

"Roland," she insisted, "where is he?"

I looked back to the storm still tearing up the desert. "He didn't make it."

"No, that's not possible." She started to hobble back toward the site of our battle.

I grabbed her arm. "There is nothing you can do now."

She spun to face me. "No," she repeated. Tears filled her steel eyes, then she collapsed in my arms, sobbing. I rocked her back and forth and could think of nothing to say. What was there to say?

"This one," she hissed and tore herself from me. "He's responsible." She moved to Lloyd's unconscious body to strangle the life from it.

"You're wrong," I said. "He was controlled by a second sorcerer. Kill him if you want, but he couldn't help himself."

She stopped, uncertain whether to murder him or listen to me.

"It was the same sorcery that used our own fears against us, the same magic that made Lloyd's men charge you."

"Yes," she whispered, "I remember that now."

"I thought it was strange for that little punk to be so aggressive," Morgan added. "Too gross for his subtle tastes, if you get my drift."

"We better continue," I said. "It'll be dark soon."

Morgan got up and threw Lloyd over his shoulder. Smoking Bear said nothing, following last. We walked by the side of the road, walked into the early evening. No stars tonight.

Two ambulances and four police cars drove past us in the dirt alongside the broken road. They didn't stop.

It was dark, and I didn't even know if we were traveling in the right direction, but I had to continue marching to keep my mind off Aesop.

Then, in the distance, I spotted a car slowly rolling through the desert and waved it down. When it came closer, I saw it was a large four-wheel drive pickup. A spotlight flared to life and pointed at us. The glare made it impossible for me to see.

The door opened and a man stepped out, outlined by the light.

"At last, Roland," the silhouette said.

It was Eugene.

18

I was back at square one, the Abbey. I was back in my Mexican cell, only inverted through a mirror in time and space. The same smells of urine and rot were here, the same darkness, and an equal amount of danger. This time, however, Eugene wouldn't be charging to my rescue. Last evening when I asked him to explain how he survived the Oracle, all he could do was apologize and keep silent. I was on my own.

It was strange that he had his doctors patch up my injuries, had Smoking Bear flown to the nearest hospital, and listened with apparent compassion when I told him how Lloyd had ambushed us in the desert, yet he wouldn't give me the simple information I needed to live. I argued with him, even threatened him, but he just sat there and said he was sorry. I almost believed he meant it too. Almost.

So where did that leave me? I had gambled on him and lost. That left me with three options. I could talk to WaterStone and convince him I erred when I left with the De Marcos. He wasn't stupid, though, and even if he agreed to forgive my past offenses, I could never be certain of his sincerity. Additionally, I'd have to accept my commission and stay here. Fat chance.

I could try to escape. Assuming I got out of this cell and eluded the guards, I had no idea how to sail a boat. Swimming was out of the question. The lake waters were bone-numbing cold, and it was kilometers to the nearest shore. In short: suicide.

That narrowed my choice to the Oracle. If I survived, I'd still have to deal with WaterStone, but it would buy me some time to figure a way off the isle.

I rolled over on my side and ran over the possibilities again. The damp straw barely covered the cold stone, and the chill did nothing to raise my spirits. No one brought water or food to me, so it was impossible to tell how much time passed in the pitch-black cell.

I was just dozing, just returning to the down comforter and my bed at the desert mansion, when I heard shuffling in the corridor. A thin line of torchlight leaked under the door. There was a rattle of keys and the door opened. Two guards, each holding a short, curved knife, dragged me out and into the upper passageways of the Abbey.

It was late afternoon; heavy shadows filled the corridors outside the council chambers like funeral curtains. My friendly escorts, without announcement, shoved me though the open doors. It was the same chamber I had been in last evening, yet different. Tired sunlight filtered through the cracks in the ceiling and made the painted constellations appear drab and artificial; the room seem small and unimportant.

All the council was here, twelve men, cunning and wise. The master of them all, Everus, sat at the head of the half circle table. He was old, his height diminished, skin wrinkled, and eyes cloudy, but his mind was the sharpest in the room.

I knew the rules in this ceremony. I could speak my mind only after the formal charges were read. One petitioning the council always had the temporary right of free speech within the confines of protocol.

Everus adjusted his reading glasses and glanced at the scroll before him. "Roland," he said in a somber voice, "you are accused of extremely serious crimes by members of this council."

Twelve pairs of eyes rested on me, gauging my response.

After facing demons and battling men with assault rifles, these old men did not intimidate me. I stood defiantly before them and stared at WaterStone, his melted face hidden beneath the cowl of his white robe.

"The charges are murder, assault, theft of properties belonging to the Abbey, destruction of properties belonging to the Abbey, and conspiracy."

Conspiracy? What deception did WaterStone plan to bury in his charges against me?

"Who brings these charges?" Everus asked. "Stand so the accused may face you."

WaterStone stood, coughing as he did. "I saw the aforementioned events," he declared, "and I have witnesses that may be called for verification."

I bet he had witnesses. Who would dare speak against the word of WaterStone?

Now, according to tradition, it was my turn to answer the charges. "These allegations are wholly manufactured," I said. "It is my belief that WaterStone is accountable for the same crimes, wishing only to pervert the truth and shift his guilt upon another. I, however, am not here to speak of these things. My true purpose is to . . ."

WaterStone interrupted me, "You must answer the charges first. We care little for your explanations at this point. I am certain my fellow brothers shall be eager to hear your account of the *truth*, at the proper time."

My temper flared and blood rushed to my cheeks, but I held my tongue. WaterStone was in his element here. Many of the council members were sticklers on protocol. If I didn't follow it to the letter, they might judge me prematurely. I kept my temper in check and picked my words with care. "My plea? I plead guilty to these charges. Guilty, if it is a crime to defend one's self from an unwarranted attack. Guilty, if it is a crime to leave the Abbey a free man before accepting his commission, then I am criminal and you must act accordingly."

"The punishment for murdering a fellow monk is death by crucifixion," WaterStone replied. "Are you certain you wish to enter your plea as guilty?"

"Yes."

The Elders whispered to each other. Everus called for silence, banging his limp hand upon a book. For a moment, he reminded me of an ancient monkey, some simian that had wandered into this chamber with his troop of baboons.

"Please, Roland," the High Elder said, "can you tell us why these events occurred?"

I sighed. Would they believe my story? I knew some would oppose my petition solely because WaterStone wished it so. I told the truth, though; these were intelligent men, able to recognize lies when they heard them. "I left the Abbey of my own free will to explore Meredin. When the De Marcos came to this isle, I traded my linguistic services for safe passage to Sestos. On our way to the dock, WaterStone and his men stopped us. He revealed that he was in the employ of the Bishop clan and had been instructed to steal the De Marcos' document. Aesop De Marco, the fire sorcerer, warned WaterStone to take no offensive action, and only after his men attacked us did he use his magics."

"A fascinating story," WaterStone said, appearing mildly amused. "But have you one shred of evidence to support this fable?"

"You may examine the passages under the docks. There should be traces of the battle there."

"But that only proves we were attacked, not the circumstances of the incident."

"True," Everus interrupted, "but you have yet to explain why you and six monks were in those tunnels, WaterStone."

Some of the White Robes nodded to one another, while others shook their heads. Political alliances and lines of war were being drawn by the subtle gestures of those about the table. I wished I knew who was on which side.

"Why have you returned, Roland?" Everus asked. "Is it to clear your name in this matter?"

"No, High Elder. I would like nothing better than to prove these charges false, but my primary purpose is to petition the council and gain access to the Oracle."

"And why do you seek this petition? Most die in the attempt to communicate with the mad god in the tower. What makes your need so great?"

"I am the last of the Pritchard family. In the past week traveling the land, I have seen much that troubles me. I have many questions for the Oracle that shall directly affect the balance of power among the royal families."

"A prince of the realm!" WaterStone exclaimed and stood. "You have no more royal blood in your veins than a fish."

"I could arrange a demonstration," I said, and narrowed my eyes at him.

"That will not be required," interjected Everus. "Who you are is of no matter when you face the Oracle." He shook his head, then said to me, "We allow you a moment to consider the ramifications, the risk, of your petition."

"With respect, sir, I need not reconsider."

"Very well, Roland," he sighed, "in that case, if you would please step outside while the council discusses your request."

I bowed and the guards escorted me to the small waiting chamber just outside. Technically they could refuse the petition. What perplexed me was WaterStone's attitude. He ought to be happy, knowing the odds of my survival. Maybe he just wanted to see me crucified.

Through the chamber doorway, I heard angry voices at odds with one another. Fifteen minutes passed, a very long fifteen minutes, then the guards returned for me.

"We have decided," announced Everus, "to grant your petition . . . provided that if you return from the Oracle, you account for the charges brought against you."

"My thanks to the council members for their wise decision."

"You should know," he added, "that many of the council were opposed to this. Your petition passed only by the smallest of margins. Any additional information you could bring to light would assist your case."

Everus's warning was serious, which led me to believe that some of the council thought I might survive the Oracle. Otherwise, why was WaterStone so opposed to my going?

I claimed to be a member of the royal families, and it was another such member, Eugene, who returned from the Oracle. He, however, revealed nothing to the Elders of his experience. If I lived, I might be able to buy my freedom with that knowledge. Interesting.

I nodded to Everus, indicating I understood his hidden meaning. "Again, my thanks to the council." I bowed and the guards led me out.

The pair silently directed me at knife point to the Oracle's tower and to the archway I so admired. The older one gave me a candle, then backed off several paces, almost as if he were afraid to stand too close to the entrance. There was no door, just a winding stairwell.

I lit the candle from an adjacent torch, then looked at the carvings on the mammoth arch for the last time. Warnings and death threats, which loosely translated from Eldrich said, GUARD DOG ON DUTY, NO TRESPASSING, SEEN BY APPOINTMENT ONLY, and NO SOLICITING. I mounted the stairs without looking back.

The light from my candle was a dim globe in the green-black spiraling passage. The stone used to build this tower was the same smoky volcanic glass in the Sarteshan ruins. Water covered the walls, stairs, and dripped from the ceiling. It got colder too. I counted the stairs to steady my nerves. Forty-five, forty-six . . . Dad must have come up the same way. . . . sixty-seven, sixty-eight, sixty-nine . . . What killed him up here? . . . eighty-three, eighty-four . . . I knew he came here to find out how the family heirloom worked, a desperate ploy to defeat Eugene in their Ruah-vindicare, but what then compelled Eugene to follow, to face the Oracle? . . . one hundred twelve, one hundred thirteen, and I paused to catch my breath. These stairs were steep, not made to be easily climbed. At one hundred sixty-three, a pale light trickled down from ahead. I snuffed the candle and turned the corner. I entered the chamber of the Oracle.

The room was not grandiose as I imagined it to be. It was a single chamber roughly six meters across, carved from the same featureless stone that composed the rest of the tower. There were no windows and it was very humid. In the approximate center was a pool of water where the illumination originated, formless lights beneath the surface that shifted color periodically. No basin contained the pool, the water just welled up from below, and its edges lapped the chamber floor. The light reflected through the water and cast dancing images, threads of crisscrossing luminescence, onto the walls.

The water and light were so mystifying I nearly stumbled over the skeletal remains on the floor. Bones littered the room. Some were intact; others were chewed, burnt, and broken. How many had died here? A dozen? Two? More? I licked my lips and was suddenly thirsty. Where was the Oracle?

"Hello?" My own voice startled me. I approached the pool, careful not to slip on the weird surface of bones and slick glass. I walked the perimeter of the basin. Nothing.

I cleared a spot on the floor of grinning skulls and ribs, then sat down. I would wait for a while, drink my fill from this pool and go, or better yet, wait until tonight and arrange for Smoking Bear to get me off the Isle of Knowledge. There was no Oracle here. It was long dead. No wonder Eugene had nothing to tell me.

"Your thoughts are untrue."

I turned. An old man stood on the opposite side of the chamber. A circle of gold leaves crowned his white hair, and a dark blue robe loosely wrapped about his naked form.

"Greetings, young Roland Pritchard."

I almost asked if he was the Oracle, but halted myself

from the obvious. "Greetings to you, Oracle," I replied. "I have come with questions."

"I know," he said. "However, there is little we can tell you until the enchantment of this place works its magic. This magic will affect you too . . . and it will kill you if you are not clever. While we wait, perhaps we shall tell you of ourselves? We already know you."

"Please," I said, not wanting to seem impolite, yet wary of his alluding to my death.

"We were once a thousand demons," the old man declared, "proud and arrogant, and eager to battle the humans that invaded our land."

"A thousand demons?" I said with a smirk. "Looks like you lost a little weight."

"Yes," he replied, "we have, but that was millennia ago. We are something else entirely now, greater than the sum of our parts. The war betwixt my kind and your ancestors, you know of it?"

I nodded.

"Simply put, you won and we were captured. Your ancestors did not kill us, though; they used our essence. They forced each of us to split ourselves ten thousand times, then placed these minuscule portions of our consciouness into paper dolls, and into grains of salt, and into motes of dust. The paper they burned and let the smoke drift over the lands. The salt they dissolved into the waters of the oceans, lakes, and streams. And the dust they scattered to the four winds."

"If you were split so many times," I said, "wouldn't that give you ten thousand dualities? Wouldn't it multiply your power?"

"It does and it does not," he said and sighed. "We demons must split ourselves to impose a self-duality, yes. When we do, however, our comprehension is correspondingly halved. Split ten thousand times each, we drifted for seven centuries, our intellect merely a whisper, power but no understanding. Then came the faintest stirrings of awareness . . . what your Zen philosophers call 'no mind.' Action without thought. With the passing centuries we learned. Our bits accumulated knowledge.

"This pool contains the largest of our fragments. Wherever our shattered essence dwells, that place may be seen upon the pool's surface. The sorcerers of this isle used these waters to learn of the other realms, of their friends and enemies, and of secrets best left undiscovered. Regrettably, they also learned that we still lived, and they came to fear us. So they erected this tower, and limited our freedom, such as it was. An enchantment so devilish holds us, that there is little hope we shall ever leave."

The water in the pool darkened a moment, then shimmered again.

"Morgan Bishop collected twelve of our fragments to tap our collective powers."

"The Matrix?"

"Yes. Parts of us are in the stone you carry in your native realm. We have watched you, and helped you when we could. Our awareness in that stone is limited, however. It is twelve parts scattered throughout billions. We hoped you would live to follow in your father's footsteps, and return here . . . return here and help us escape our prison."

"I am in your debt, Oracle. I never would have survived had you not shown me how to return to the dream realm, to my battle upon the Fields of Fire."

"You already knew how to translate between the realms," he said. "We merely calmed your emotions, and placed you in a meditative trance to clear your mind."

"What can I do to help you?"

The old man smiled, and tears glistened in his eyes. "You are not like the others, young Roland. You place our needs before yours. So trusting, so noble . . . There may yet be hope for these worlds."

I swallowed, and found my throat dry, my thirst growing.

"The enchantment begins," he cried. The old man warped, melted, and resolved into a fearsome green canine, mouth open and snarling, full of dog breath. Its front paw balanced on a golden globe, a world of foreign continents. "I must explain the rules quickly."

"Rules? I suppose I can't ask you questions and then you answer them?"

"Would that I could," growled the dog. "But let us not waste time—as yours is very short indeed."

I wanted to ask a hundred questions, but instead held my tongue and listened. I had a feeling my life would depend on these instructions.

The dog pushed the globe away, stood on its hind legs, thinned its body, and changed into an old woman, not quite mummified. "First," she whispered, dead skin flaking from her face, "there is a time limit. It is based on your stamina and your will. Do not attempt to adjust these magics. Others have tried, better sorcerers than you, young Roland. All have failed."

I checked. Mighty fields of power penetrated the room, originating in and about the water. These were forces on a cosmic scale, mightier than Xuraldium's tunnel in the air, mightier than anything from the Golden Age. They reached beyond this tower, beyond this world, and reached into the stars themselves, sorcery powerful enough to imprison a god.

"Second," the woman continued, "for me to answer your inquiries, you in turn must tell me something I do *not* know. I watch many worlds, many existences, so this will be difficult.

"Lastly," she explained, "failure to provide me with supplemental knowledge will mean your death. If you attempt to leave, I will be forced to destroy you."

I wanted to ask why. Why all these conditions, but rather concentrated on finding her some information so I could leave with my life. I might as well try to win this contest; it was, after all, what I came here to do.

"What are you likely *not* to know?" I asked her. "How much do you know already?"

Her form collapsed into a spinning mote of light, green, shining, filling the room with an uneasy radiation. "Since you are new, I shall treat this as *not a question*," said the light in a ringing voice, "but rather an elaboration of the rules. I know nearly everything of your world, Earth, and this world. There are several other realms I exist in, but you need not concern yourself with them. What I do not know are those things deliberately hidden either through extreme cunning or magic."

"This is an unfair test," I protested.

The light altered, cooling slightly to a bluer shade. "This is no test. I am imprisoned here by the dual forces of knowledge and ignorance. Until I know more than I do not, I must stay. I watch and gather as much information as I can, but it is never enough. As time passes, those secrets long forgotten become less and less probable to be discovered by the feeble minds of men."

I wanted to drink from the pool. My thirst was becoming a distraction, but I knew this was the enchantment. I purged all thoughts of the cool water and concentrated. What could I possibly know that the Oracle would not? "Let's see just how much you comprehend. The third president of the United States was . . ."

". . . Thomas Jefferson."

"The introductory passage of the lost manuscripts of *The Terror Chronicles* . . ."

" 'Evil is the natural state of all sentient creatures. One may argue that to deny this natural state is evil itself.' "

"The value of pi . . ."

"Approximately 3.1415926536."

"Approximately?"

"I could give you the exact number, but that would waste both our time."

"OK. A collection of peacocks is . . ."

". . . a muster of peacocks."

"The remains of the guardian of the earth temple in the Sarteshan ruins are . . ."

". . . 4.2 meters beneath the surface of the central worship hall."

"The variation of solitaire known as 'forty thieves' is also called . . ."

'Napoleon at St. Helena,' named thusly as The Little

Emperor played it constantly during his exile.''

"Xuraldium's original family name is . . ."

"Clever, young Roland, but you are not privileged with that information. My response would answer a legitimate question.''

This thing was too smart. My life was draining away, along with the water absorbed from my body with each word I spoke. It probably knew everything that I knew. We could go on like this for hours, yet I had only minutes left. This was hopeless.

"Your father is here among these remains," the light said. "He used similar tactics. They all do. It is tragic.''

"My father?" No, searching for him now would only waste my energy. Later, if I had the chance I'd look. Think, Roland . . . What did I know, what can I tell this creature? Gods, I was dying of thirst. I licked my lips, swollen and cracked. My tongue was dry. Without a source of life to tap there was nothing I could do.

I closed my eyes and banished all thoughts, all temptations to plunge my head into the pool and drink my fill. I slowed my life force, slowed the cycling back and forth of my essence and the death in this place. I couldn't stop it, but I could repress my own pulse, and the rate at which my life was stolen.

"Can I guess?"

"What?" The spinning light solidified and took the form of a samurai posed to strike. His gleaming katana was a graceful arc over his head, the blade reflecting the light within the pool.

"Can I guess? Can I offer you my theories of an event. If it is true, will you know, will you accept it as fact?''

"I will know the truth when I hear it," the samurai said, and sheathed his katana. A tiny drop of blood fell from his thumb and into the basin.

"Do you know who my enemies are?"

The warrior nodded and sat opposite me.

Let me try to reason it out. There are only a few possibilities: Eugene, Lloyd, Sabrina, Morgan, or any combination of the above. There was also the Chandler clan, an entire family I knew nothing of. The Oracle knew who my enemy was. But did it know why? "Do you know the motivation of my adversary?"

The samurai frowned, considered for a moment, searching for the answer, then, "No, that is hidden from me."

Success! All I needed to do was figure out why and then whom. I began at the top of my suspect list: Eugene. He wanted my family relic, and only rescued me to find it. –

"My adversary is motivated by a lust for the Pritchard family heirloom," I offered.

The Oracle metamorphosed again. A potted plant sat where the samurai once was. The branches rustled, yet there was no breeze. Tiger-striped orchids opened, and spoke, "No, you are incorrect."

No one wanted the relic? At least it was not the motivation behind the violence. Then what? More basic, why would anyone act against me? Power. It was the underlying motive in all family politics. I needed to be more specific though. The Oracle was certain to know the royal families craved power.

In what forms did power manifest itself? There was money, but I suspected all my relations possessed fantastic wealth. Magic? How could anyone increase their personal magical power? Sabrina said the power was fixed at birth, yet Xuraldium claimed dualities caused one's power to increase. These paradoxes, a person existing in two realms at the same time, or a demon splitting his existence, enabled him to interact with a balanced pair of forces and produce magic. How would any of my adversaries increase their dual nature by interacting with me?

It clicked into place then. I knew.

"I understand," I said. "I know why she did it."

The fragrance from the blossoms reached out to me, a light sweet thing, the tang of oranges and cinnamon, intoxicating.

My thirst raged on. When I spoke, my lips bled, and my voice croaked as a frog's. "Sabrina, she wants me dead now. The other family members tried to court me, isolate me, make me their allies, but not her. Her plan was more subtle. By interacting with me, she had an opportunity to increase her power many times, at least for a short while.''

The plant said nothing.

"She is pregnant, pregnant with the child of a dreamer,'' I explained. "Don't you understand? That gives her another duality. She is actually two dreamers in the same body. I'm willing to bet she's pregnant with twins. That would give her yet another duality. Of course! That's what her comment about me manipulating life forces when we were together meant. What could be easier than becoming fertile and pregnant by making love with a sorcerer who manipulates life?''

I paused, and swallowed the dry leather in my throat. My words were barely a whisper. "Now I am only a source of trouble to her. If the other families found out she was becoming more powerful, they'd eliminate her. I was new to the clans, ignorant of their taboos and customs, a perfect opportunity for her, a perfect target.''

I was just guessing, but it all made sense. "She needed me to interact with her on a physical level. Once she had that, I would no longer be needed, or wanted. One slip of my tongue, one trace of gossip about our relations, and it could kill her. She was the second sorcerer, the one who controlled Lloyd, and the one responsible for Aesop's death.''

"You are . . .'' The Oracle's form fluxed again to that of a hollowed rock; its inner surface covered with sparkling amethysts, each possessing a tiny voice. ". . . correct. We congratulate you on your deduction. Long has it been since we tasted the gift of new knowledge. This has explained much of the royal family's behavior. You may drink now. The killing magics shall not harm you.''

I crawled to the pool's edge and drank, drank to replenish my life, drank to soothe my throat, drank until I was glutted and could not move. The water had that sweet spring taste, that wasn't a taste but a pure cleansing sensation. I closed my eyes, lay next to the water and listened to it lapping at the stone floor.

I savored my success, bittersweet as it was. Sabrina used me. She had it all calculated even before we met. She had generated the lust I felt at our first meeting, made Eugene trust her, and completely dominated Lloyd. Her sorcery must control pairs of emotions: love and hate, trust and suspicion, anger and fear, and the gods only knew what others. And the worst part was that my artificial attraction to her lingered on. I still wanted her. Damn.

"Roland," the hundred crystals spoke in unison, "since your information was so exact, so intriguing, it warrants the resolution of three questions."

"First, I'm going to find Clay—that's not a question. I'll look for myself." I stood and let my water-filled stomach settle a moment, then searched through the bones. Here, were a few sections of spine, there, the metacarpals of a hand. They had chew marks on them, as if they had been gnawed upon by a hungry creature. Among the anatomy, I spied bits of cloth, broken pieces of jewelry, and armor. Then I spotted a strip of golden leather by the wall, the Cartaga watchband. Next to it was a skeleton. The skull was smashed in, and there was barely a whole bone in the lot. This was what was left of my father.

Curious that the band was here in the dreaming realm and the watch in the real world. Why did Clay separate the two? More importantly, how did it get to this side?

As for my father, it was strange to see his bones. Had he not fallen in love with Judith, none of this would have happened. How different would I be if I hadn't grown up at the Abbey? Involved in family intrigue from the beginning, would I be as suspicious and murderous as my counterparts?

"Perhaps things turned out better this way," I said to the bones. I tried to dredge up some feelings for him, but all I could do was recall the memory of a large man, his huge hands, and a strong voice. *Sorry, Clay, I'd bury your bones and say a prayer for you, but after all these years, I have no tears left for you.*

I collected his remains in a moldering cloak, at least what I thought to be his remains. There seemed to be several duplicate pieces in my skeletal selection.

I set the bundle to one side then examined the watch-band. It looked like leather but felt like metal—smooth and cold to the touch. What kind of creature did this come from? Each end had a pair of snaps so the watch could be secured. Checking it with my mystic vision, I found a tight knot of magic, but the longer I looked at it, the farther away it appeared. I defocused my powers, and it returned. Whatever I did, it seemed to move from my perception just when I thought I saw it.

"We are pleased you found your father. He tried so hard to give us information. He was brave."

"I had best leave now," I said. "It will be dark soon. I have much to prepare in the other world."

"What of your questions?" The rock melted and flowed into a new form. A scantily clad girl stood across the pool from me. Tight silken cords wrapped sinuously about her arms, outlining her shape. Transparent sea foam veils hardly covered her body, which I found very enticing, and a wave of white hair floated about her perfectly round face as if it were underwater. "Stay then a while," she pleaded. "Ask me a question."

I sat back down. When I returned to the Abbey, I would face WaterStone again. "Perhaps I should rest here and think things through."

She rubbed the palms of her hands together until a golden goblet materialized between them. "Accept this humble refreshment." She set the goblet down and walked away from it. I circled the pool and picked it up. She moved away from me as I did so, always positioning herself across the pool from me.

Even though I was full of water, I tried a sip of the dark liquid within, to be polite. It was wine and even my uneducated palate informed me it was superb; a smooth buttery texture rolled inside my mouth, the flavors of dark chocolate, raspberries; then it was gone, leaving the scent of smoked oak on my tongue. I finished the entire thing.

"I have thought of a question for you."

"It is because you drank the wine of decision," she said, toying with the cord about her arm. "Ask me."

"Hestor. She left Oceanview two days ago. What happened to her? Where is she now?"

"That is two questions," the nymph remarked. "Do you desire me to answer both?"

"No, wait. Just show me where she is now." Finding her and getting her to safety was the most important thing. Later, I'd find out how she got out of the hospital.

The surface of the pool smoothed, and upon it an image formed, a translucent reflection: my apartment complex in San Diego. Through a veil of smoke and steam, I saw it had been burned to the ground. Charred two-by-fours sticking up like black fingers, a hot water heater, and smoldering heaps of stucco were all that remained. "Hestor is here?"

"I am sorry, Roland," the Oracle quietly said. "The body of Hestor Pritchard is there, beneath the debris."

"She started it," I whispered to myself. It was not a question. I knew she did. I felt it. Whether she got caught in her own fire or committed suicide, that I didn't know, but I could see her, a can of hair spray in one hand, a box of matches in the other . . . a little gasoline, and things got out of hand.

Poor Hestor. She wasn't crazy; she was driven crazy by living with Clay—seeing demons and conspiracies around every corner. She had been right.

For a time, I cried. But mixed in with my tears of grief was a small amount of relief. Hestor started dying years ago. I think she got what she wanted, rest, peace, and one final happy dream. I touched the surface of the pool. The ripples made the fragile image of the other world vanish. *Good-bye, Mom.*

I wiped the tears from my face, and my resolve returned. "My second question," I said. "Tell me about my family heirloom, the watchband. How does it work?"

"It was Jexer's own talisman from before the Golden Age," the Oracle explained. "It is a great magic coiled

into a band. Some say that it is made from the hide of
the eternal serpent, upon whose back the universe rides.
Jexer may have lied about this . . . many of his words
were lies. The watch that goes with it is a mere orna-
mentation, only the band is magical. To put it simply, it
is a Möbius surface in the fabric of reality or of dreams,
if you will. It forms a gateway between the two worlds.
Rotate one end of the band half a revolution to form the
Möbius, then snap the ends together around an object
you wish to transport. It will follow you in your sleep.
I do not believe it can carry much volume or mass, but
if you ponder the unique items you may carry from one
realm to the next, you will understand the magnitude of
such a power.''

So that's how it got into this realm without the watch.
''Elaborate please. It can move anything? Like a gun,
or penicillin, or a book?''

She nodded.

This had a host of interesting possibilities. The snaps
were gold and riveted in place. I twisted it and snapped
the ends together to form the endless geometric loop,
then shoved it in my tunic. It was going back to the real
realm with me tonight.

''OK, my last question . . .''

She smiled softly at me, as if answering me gave her
pleasure.

I briefly allowed myself a forbidden thought of her,
then recalled this was no simple girl. ''The dream realm
is dying and diseased, and its population dwindling.
What can I do to reverse this, restore it to a second
Golden Age?''

''A mighty question for one so young.'' The Oracle
pondered a moment, then said, ''Come and I shall show
you the events that led to the collapse. You may then
draw your own conclusions.'' She touched the pool with
her finger, ''Behold.''

The ripples in the pool settled and revealed a landscape that I was unfamiliar with. No, wait, I had seen
something like this before in Xuraldium's gardens.

"The land of Meredin five millennia past," she announced.

Forests covered the land. Trees with black branches dangled heavy flowers that glowed with the colors of a sunset on a cloudy evening. Butterflies like bats came to perch on them, wings of silky silver and coral. Unfolding ferns and hollow grasses that whistled in the breeze grew along gentle meandering riverbanks. It was a fairyland.

The scene changed. Tall minarets of watery blue and pale red glass reached for the sky like fingers outstretched, grasping at heaven. Streets paved with grey and green polished stones. Scholars and sorcerers walked here, peddlers shouted to be heard through the crowd. Stranger creatures mingled with the humans: centaurs (like the De Marco statue), tall graceful peoples with pointed ears and wide eyes, short squat ones with bulging muscles and golden armor, winged humanoids that never touched the ground, and creatures with long, coiled octopus arms that lay suspended in tanks of water and pushed by servants; they all walked together. A huge dome, carved from volcanic glasses of various shades and clarities, picked up the afternoon sun and shattered it, a natural sculpture of radiance moving with the day.

"Sartesh?"

She nodded. "Look again."

The picture changed. The city of Sestos being built by thousands of craftsmen. The lake was covered with ships, triangles of vermilion, gold, and linen white that skated across the water. Some of them appeared out of the fog, and others disappeared in the same mysterious fashion. The great stone bridge spanned the lake and used the Isle of Knowledge as a steppingstone, then arched up into the sky and disappeared.

"Then," she explained, "Meredin was a center of activity, peoples from all realms visited here. All contributed, all enchanted this world with their unique cultures and their particular values."

"What happened?"

She sighed, "War and greed. First war with our kind,

the natives of Meredin, then your ancestors fought among themselves, unable to share even with their kin. Sides were chosen, lines drawn, borders erected, and battles fought over them. Ambitious sorcerers drained the magic from this place to fuel their ambitions. You have seen the plains near the Nomious Hills, devoid of life?''

"Yes."

"But you know this story already in your heart. Many of the other races died from war or famine or disease, while others simply chose never to return to the dream realm. Only the humans remained to fight their last battles. They did a very good job of exterminating themselves. At one point, there were only four dreamers left, and even then they fought among themselves. One of them was your direct ancestor, Theodore."

His likeness appeared in the pool—a heroic figure wearing a Roman breastplate, shouting orders to his soldiers, then charging into battle.

"The bust in the storage lot," I said, "and the figure of the baseball player."

"Yes, that is he. He seeded the other families, the ones alive today, so the tradition of dreaming could go on. It has continued," she added, "with an unfortunate similarity. As you may have *guessed*, it is the health and prosperity of the dreamers that reflects the health and well-being of the land of Meredin. When there was peace and harmony between the families, the dreaming realm experienced a Golden Age. When the families plunged into war and destroyed one another, so did the land wither and diminish."

"Then the population, the inhabitants of Meredin, they are definitely linked to the royal families."

"For every genuine dreamer, hundreds, perhaps thousands of others may follow his night's journey here. The number greatly depends on that dreamer's powers, his dualities. In a sense, a dreaming family builds its own kingdom, fashions the land with their magic, and the people from their dreams. These citizens of Meredin are never aware as true dreamers are, nor can they manipulate magic as you do, but their existence in the dreaming realm adds another dimension to their otherwise colorless lives.''

"Answer my question,'' I demanded. ''Tell me how I can restore the dream realm to a second Golden Age.''

She looked into the pool, then back to study me, then looked again into the pool, "Yes, you may be the one.'' She walked over to me and whispered the answer into my ear.

I could not believe it.

19

~~~~~~~~~~~~~~~~~~~~~

"Answers, Eugene, it's time for answers."

I had my back to him and the conference room we were in, a cavelike chamber, roughly hewn from a coarse grey stone. Instead of looking at him, I gazed out the window, past four inches of solid wire-reinforced glass, to the eerie outside. The sky was pure black, sprinkled with a million stars and no moon. Even though it was night, the sun blasted the surface of the barren earth with a harsh light. Craters of rock and powdered earth marked the landscape, reminiscent of the plains about the Sarteshan ruins. In the darkness of a crevasse far away, I saw what could have been the remains of a city, three pillars and the outline of a road, but then again maybe it was only the shadows playing tricks on my eyes.

I dismissed my speculations on the view and turned to face the mysteries in here, to face Eugene. I stuck my thumb in my front pocket and touched the Cartaga watchband. It followed me across the void of sleep, translated to this realm. Excellent, I'd need it soon.

"I know about Judith," I told him, "about Morgan and your deal, and what really happened to my father, the Ruah-vindicare, but I just wanted to hear it from you. No more apologies and no more delays. I know you had the chance to eliminate me several times, but elected not to. I want to know why. Why bother to help your enemy?''

Eugene shifted uncomfortably in his leather chair. ''Very well, Roland, I see I can keep the truth from you no longer.'' His voice was different. It no longer possessed the general-commanding tone, but was tired and slow. ''Your father and I were friends in the past, great friends. That much of what I told you was true. This was unusual given the nature of family politics at the time, but we didn't care.''

''That was back in California during the Gold Rush, the Aldusian Gold Mine.''

Remembrance glazed over his eyes. ''Yes, in California, and before that, the diamond mines in Africa.''

''So how did Judith figure into your friendship?''

He shifted again in his seat. ''That is a personal matter, and I would rather not speak of her.''

''You will tell me,'' I insisted. ''She was the one who came between the two of you, wasn't she?''

His lips strained into a single line, then relaxed. ''She and I were in love,'' he admitted. ''It was difficult for us, since our families were at war with one another. Our relationship was . . . precarious. She wanted to marry, but that was out of the question. Family members on both sides would be outraged. Then she wanted a child! We argued over it continuously. What was she thinking? The child of two dreamers would be a monstrosity.''

''A child possessing another duality and more magical abilities than normal? Ability enough to upset the normal balance of power between the families?''

''You have learned much in the last few days,'' Eugene remarked. ''Perhaps too much.''

I didn't like his tone, so I gathered my power about me, drew upon the reserves of death in the Matrix. Eugene, however, had summoned no forces. I eased off but kept a minimal amount of magic ready. ''We are talking about you and Judith.''

"Yes," he exhaled, "so we were. We had a falling out over this issue and she left me for Clay." He looked away from me and continued, "I never knew if she really loved him or if she seduced him to spite me . . . or perhaps merely to gain power. He was everything to her I was not. He gave her commitment, promises of a future together, *and* a child. He was a fool."

"Because he ignored the threats from the other families, or because he took her away from you?"

"Both. My best friend, he was a brother to me, yet he stole her nonetheless. I had no other recourse but Ruah-vindicare, the death duel."

"No recourse? You could have left them alone."

"You do not understand. Then, there were twelve families. You dared not show any weakness. To do so would have invited your enemies to gather and destroy you. It was not the actual power you possessed, but how others perceived your power. My honor and family name were at stake. I could not allow them to escape."

"That explains the dagger in his Safety Box."

"Yes," he replied, "my dagger. I loaned it to Clay when we explored the caverns of Idol Crags on the shores of the Great Inland Sea."

"What happened then," I asked, "after you challenged him?"

"He panicked. Clay was a brilliant financier, a great builder of things, but, unfortunately, only a mediocre sorcerer."

"He needed his heirloom's power to win your duel."

Eugene nodded. "He went to Xuraldium first to seek information. When that failed, he journeyed to the Oracle."

". . . and left me at the Abbey."

"When Judith discovered *she* provoked Clay's rash actions and caused the Ruah-vindicare between us, she left him in the hopes I would call it off."

"But you couldn't do that."

"I could have, but only at the cost of my reputation. I considered it, but by then it was too late. Clay had gone to the Oracle and perished."

I knew all too well what had happened to my father in the Oracle's tower. "If Clay was dead, though, why did you need to go to the Oracle?"

"I went there to retrieve his body. The thought of his remains lingering, food for the mad god, gnawed at my conscience."

"You must have passed the Oracle's test. What stopped you from telling me about it last night? I could have been killed."

He took a deep breath, then said, "I only made it halfway up the tower. After so many others had failed, I could not bring myself to face it. I sat on those cold wet stairs until my candle burned itself to nothing. Then I returned and claimed to have gained what I wished from the Oracle."

"Your reputation among the families certainly didn't suffer from the attempt."

"That is not the reason I went," he said and his voice hardened. "But you are correct, it did not hurt my status within the clans."

I was surprised none of the others had thought of this trick. Then again Eugene had to make the attempt before he discovered he could wait it out alone on the stairway. He couldn't have known that ahead of time. Maybe he had intended to go through with it. I'd grant him a small measure of courage for that. Very small.

"What happened to Judith after Clay died?"

"The Bishop clan found and killed her," Eugene said matter-of-factly. "They burned her at the stake."

"Her own family killed her because she bore a child with another dreamer?" No wonder Sabrina was so closemouthed about Judith—nothing like a cozy little murder to sweep under the family rug.

"The taboo of interclan relations is the strongest custom of the dreaming families. It had happened only thrice before with my lifetime, and in each case, the offenders were killed . . . their children too. The offspring of two dreamers is too powerful. If they were allowed to grow to maturity, they would most certainly overwhelm the existing families. No dreamer would tolerate such a child's existence.''

I took a deep breath, exhaled, then asked, ''Am I Judith's son?''

Eugene looked at me for a long time before he whispered, ''I hope not, Roland. I hope your superlative magical talents do not originate from your mother *and* father. Whatever their source, it shall remain a mystery. Clay took that secret to his grave.''

He stared out the window to the black landscape beyond. ''We shall never speak of her again. For both our sakes.''

Just our little secret, huh? ''None of this explains why you abandoned Morgan's plan.''

Eugene looked back to me and said, ''It is true that Morgan and I kidnapped you. We also conspired to murder your coworker at the Gas n' Mart. It was all to heighten the drama, to inspire you to trust me and reveal the whereabouts of Clay's heirloom and Morgan's Matrix.''

''But you didn't go through with it. Why?''

''When we met in my office, you reminded me so much of your father—and how poorly I handled the entire affair. The thought of you rotting in that basement across the border was more than I could bear. It reminded me too much of Clay's death, how I was responsible, and how I failed to retrieve my comrade's body. I could not go through with it again.

''After I rescued you, I had no choice but to train you in the basics of sorcery. First, to determine if you really were a dreamer since I risked Morgan's wrath, and second, with no knowledge of magic, you would have been helpless in the presence of any family members, let alone Morgan, who still searched for you.''

I sat there listening to his story, my head resting in the palms of my hands. There was no way I believed it all. How could I trust a man who allied with the same people that had murdered the woman he loved? Oh, he looked sorry enough, overflowing with the milk of human kindness. I just found it incredible that he'd double-cross Morgan to assuage his guilt over Clay. There was something amiss with his explanation; what, I didn't know, but it didn't ring true.

"Five days ago," he said, "after I retrieved you from Mexico, and after I taught you the basics of sorcery, you asked me if there was any way to repay me. I requested that you temper your judgment of me. That is what I ask of you now, Roland. Do not judge me harshly."

"I can't easily dismiss my father's death."

"Would you have done differently in my place?"

"Yes," I started to say, then held my tongue. I had not been raised within the families. Given the environment Eugene grew up in, it was amazing he'd done this much for me. Honestly, if I was in his shoes, I would have gone through with the plan he and Morgan concocted.

"Let's just call it even," I said after a moment. I wasn't serious with my offer. I'd never forget what he did to Clay, but until I found some indication that Eugene had something sinister on his agenda, I'd pretend to be his friend. Besides, I needed him for my plans.

He sat straighter. "Thank you, Roland."

"Now what about Lloyd? Did Smoking Bear tell you he attacked us in the desert?" I knew why Lloyd tried to kill us the other day. I just wanted to know how much Eugene knew of Sabrina and her control of his son.

"She did and I thank you for interceding on his behalf. He claims to recall nothing of the last week. I do not know if I believe him, so I confined him to the estate."

"You can believe your son. He has been under the influence of a powerful sorcerer."

"Who?"

"I cannot say. If all goes well, however, I may know soon." I couldn't tell Eugene it was Sabrina. If she influenced Lloyd, she might be able to influence Eugene too, especially if she was growing in power from her new dualities.

"I am pleased to hear he was not responsible. Of all

my sons, I thought Lloyd was the least capable of treachery."

"And Smoking Bear?" I asked. "Did your doctors have any problems removing the bullet from her?"

"She has recovered. The doctors say that aside from the bullet inside her, there was no serious damage. They were extremely puzzled by this. It appears that you have honed your magical skills considerably within the last week."

"Yeah," I replied with a slight amount of sarcasm, "it's from all the practice I've gotten patching myself together."

"She waits for you even as we speak." He frowned, then added, "The De Marcos and I are not on the friendliest of terms. If possible, she needs to leave my estate this afternoon. Her presence is awkward."

"I'm certain she'll want to leave as soon as she sees that I am unharmed. But we're not at your mansion, are we?"

"We are and we are not. It is difficult to explain. I brought you here last evening for security. The estate is only a short walk away; you can see more on the way there."

He rose from the chair and I followed him out of the conference room. We left through a circular tunnel that gently curved deeper into the earth. Strips of artificial lighting were placed every few paces. It was different from the room we were just in. The walls were carved to mirror smoothness from a mottled marble of cream and blue designs. It was as if the conference chamber at the end was added as a rude afterthought. The passage twisted through several turns, then opened to a courtyard, the center of activity for a city, a city that belonged in the dream realm.

These were the ruins of an older civilization, Roman or Byzantine, perhaps an amalgamation of the two. The houses that lined the streets had no space between them, just jammed together one after the other. Each had its own central courtyard that opened to the sidewalk, complete with fountains and soil where gardens might have once thrived.

The entire city sat in the bottom of a huge canyon and was capped with a clear dome, one that allowed the unusual darklight to enter. It reminded me of the shattered dome of the amphitheater in Sartesh, carved with identical geometric cuts except titanic in its proportions.

"Are we in Meredin?" I asked.

"No."

The city contained no natives, but there were crowds of people. Men and women were everywhere, and all wore coveralls bearing the yin-yang symbol of Rhodes Industries. They analyzed, collected samples, and photographed the ruins with scientific precision. I was tempted to engage one in conversation and find out more of the city.

It clearly had been empty for many hundreds of years, but I had never seen an archaeological site so well preserved. The streets were perfectly paved, not a stone missing. Carts could have rumbled across them yesterday. Columns swept from the floor to the ceiling, half in and half out of the walls, spreading fanlike across the clear dome. Closer to the floor, the images of gods were carved into each column. The gods stared at the workers, stared at nothing.

"Our tour can wait for another time," Eugene said. "I believe Smoking Bear is impatient to see you. I for one do not wish to keep her."

I agreed. Still, the acolyte portion of me would have been content to stay a while. This place was a city beyond the Golden Age of Meredin. It had somehow survived and developed in isolation. Could it be some earthly ruins? No, I doubted it. There were certain details that were distinctly from the dreaming realm. One god trapped within the column was Xuriphus, the Meredin wind god, yet he held lightning within his left hand, a feature definitely from Greek mythology.

Eugene cleared his throat and I had to abandon my theories for now.

He led me through curved streets choked with dust to

the opposite end of the city. Here the other canyon wall that cradled the city rose up at a right angle.

Set in the wall was a short archway and a tunnel that vanished beyond into the shadows of the earth. Two men, armed with rifles, flanked the passage. Eugene cast them a serious look as he approached and they snapped to attention. One offered him a clipboard. He took it, scanned the ledger, and signed the bottom.

While he did this, I noticed the curious capstone of the short arch. It was a clear grey rock, slightly luminescent, with the Eldrich character for sky etched onto its surface. The symbol was a twin set of three parallel lines that ran across one another. Most laymen thought the resulting pattern, four diamonds, was inappropriate to represent air, but I knew it was really six crisscrossing lines, one for each of the major winds that ran across Meredin. But what was this doing here? Before I could examine it for magic, Eugene proceeded into the unlit tunnel and I went in after him.

There was an itching static sensation as I made my way deeper into the passage, the mounting of sorcery about me. I summoned a gradient of forces and observed patterns of magic appear, twisting and warping the space about us. The design then collapsed upon itself, and I felt the same disorientation as when Xuraldium transported us to his palace by the ocean.

The dizziness, along with the magic, abruptly faded. Eugene was still ahead of me, still walking through the black avenue that was no normal passage. From ahead, I perceived light, tainted green, and a rustling of branches in a breeze. Fresh air brushed against my face carrying with it the scents of water, lilacs, and fresh manure.

I walked for several paces, and the stone roof overhead was replaced by a trellis heavy with thorny vines full of green and red leaves. Through this tube of vegetation shone the genuine, warm, and welcoming light of the sun, filtering through a patchwork of leaves and lattice. As we continued, the stone walls were gradually exchanged for flora, and I noticed a slight uphill grade

to the path. After a minute or so of this, the top of the
tunnel opened and we emerged in a corridor of barbed
hedges with walls eight feet tall. The dense shrubs had
tiny round leaves and clear white thorns.

We came to a four-way intersection, and Eugene,
without hesitation, took the left passage. I was certain
now that we trekked uphill. The height of the walls diminished as we meandered our way through the turns
and twists.

Finally I saw over the walls, and I knew where we
were: the hedge maze in Eugene's garden. I cast a glance
backward and the whole thing appeared as one level
plane. The labyrinth angled deep into the earth, but no
one could tell from the outside.

Eugene led me through the puzzle I had lost myself
in six days ago and into his garden. He paused to praise
the old ground keeper's work and suggested that he feed
the roses. The old man smirked at me and winked.

Another servant met us halfway to the mansion. Eugene ordered tea and a light breakfast to be brought to
us in the library. We walked quickly into the mansion
to avoid the desert heat outside, over Persian rugs, and
back into the library.

Eugene sat down at the table that was a single piece
of petrified wood and wiped the sweat from his forehead
with a handkerchief. I noticed the Greenford's anatomy
text was missing. The dreaming Roland experienced a
profound sense of guilt for not returning the book.
That's what twenty years being a librarian will do to
you.

"We can speak freely here," Eugene told me.

The tunnel under the garden maze certainly led to another place. I doubted the desert mansion was built atop
the ruins of an ancient civilization. And there was the
strange darklight of the city to consider. Unfortunately,
there were more urgent matters to discuss. Maybe after
this was over I could ask.

"Tell me how you survived the Oracle," he said.
"Did you really go up to the top and face the mad god?"

I nodded. "I'm sleeping there now. There is a test of

knowledge one must pass to satisfy it, and to live. Once that is done, it will answer your questions based on how well your information impressed it." I paused and shook my head slightly, then said, "The nature of that test, and how I overcame it, are things I'd rather keep to myself for now."

"Yes, of course."

How did this increase my standing in the eyes of the various clans? In reality, I had been the only one for hundreds of years to appease the Oracle. I checked my ego before it got out of control. I got lucky, nothing else. I easily could have ended up like Clay, a pile of bones.

"Now," I said, leaning across the table, "I require a few favors from you." This was the time to push Eugene; his supposed guilt was ripe, and I'd play my visit to the Oracle for all the influence it was worth.

"You have only to ask. What is it you wish? Additional money, training in sorcery?"

"First, and of primary importance, I need you to gather all the family members at your castle in Meredin tonight. At the minimum, I'll need the heads of the four other clans there."

"Gather all the families together? At one time and place?" He pushed his chair slightly away from the table. "I seriously doubt it is possible."

"I have confidence in your abilities of persuasion." This was it. If Eugene wouldn't do this for me, the dreaming realm was lost.

"I cannot believe that . . ."

"It is critical," I said with certainty, "both for your sake and the sake of the other families that you do this. The Oracle revealed to me the imminent destruction of Meredin. It also divulged the only way to prevent this catastrophe."

"I do not know if this assemblage of the clans would be such a wise thing." He paused, examined me, decided if I spoke the truth or not, then said, "However, since you have discussed this with the Oracle itself, I must trust your judgment."

"Also, no one must know that I am arranging this. I have enemies in the families who may try to stop us, or attempt to kill me, if it becomes known that I survived the battle in the desert."

"What reason should I give for them to come? What of Morgan? He knows you are alive."

"Tell them *you* went to the Oracle and have grave news concerning all the families. As for Morgan, I don't care what you do. Get him drunk, threaten him, whatever it takes to get him there."

"Do the Oracle's revelations actually merit such drastic actions?"

"Eugene," I said in my most serious voice, "what it had to say will change the way the families operate forever in the dreaming realm."

There was a soft knocking at the door, then a waiter rolled in a cart full of breads, pastries, and a complete tea service.

"Just leave it here," Eugene ordered him. "We shall serve ourselves."

The man nodded and left, closing the doors behind him. Pacing back and forth, I spied Smoking Bear waiting outside in the hallway.

"There's just one more thing I need," I said.

He handed me a fruit-filled tart, which I wolfed down immediately. My last meal in this realm was before Morgan grabbed me in Oakland: a slice of pizza.

"And that is?"

"The two businesses you and Clay owned," I said with my mouth full, swallowed, then continued. "I'll need a complete disclosure of my share of the past profits set aside in the trust you mentioned. If I am to compete with the royal families, I'll need to solidify my financial base as rapidly as I can."

He smiled and said, "You are more like your father than you realize. I shall make the proper legal arrangements for you."

The door opened and Smoking Bear strolled past a guard apparently put there to stop any unauthorized visitors. "Forget the formal introductions," she said, "just let me through.'' She pulled the seat next to me out, turned it, and sat down with the back facing the table. ''I'm glad to see you're in one piece. This guy hasn't threatened you, has he?'' She pointed at Eugene.

He glared back. ''Smoking Bear, you have stretched the hospitality of the Rhodes family to the breaking point. I could have easily eradicated you while you were in surgery, and gladly would have too, had Roland not been here. So count your blessings and try not to provoke me further.''

Neither of them had summoned any magics, but I knew that was only a matter of time.

''Maybe it would be best if Smoking Bear and I spoke alone,'' I suggested. ''We can go over the details of gathering the clans together later today.''

''By all means,'' he said, and rose. ''I shall be at your disposal, Roland.''

Smoking Bear closed the doors behind him, smiling as she did so. ''That one's so well-mannered. He'll shake your hand as he pulls the knife from your back.''

''I'm sorry about Aesop,'' I whispered to her. ''I wish I had been able to do something more.''

''You did plenty.'' Her smile dropped. ''Aside from patching my body back together, you kept your own skin in one piece. That was no small feat considering what was going on at the time. No one is blaming you for what happened to Aesop. He went out exactly the way he wanted to.''

She sat down next to me again. ''What's all this talk about a gathering of the clans? I couldn't help overhearing what you two said. Is it true about the Oracle?''

''Parts of it are correct. The destruction of Meredin is certainly going to happen if things don't change.''

''So you plan to get the families together in one place and talk them into making peace?'' There was a touch of mockery in her voice.

''Something like that,'' I replied, ''but not exactly.''

''You'll be lucky if there isn't a full-scale war.''

''There is a more important matter to consider: Sabrina. She is the one who manipulated Lloyd, and if she shows up at this meeting, things could go very badly. She is potentially, for the time being, the most powerful wielder of magic in the clans."

"And just how did she manage that?"

I told her.

Smoking Bear surprised me and laughed. "It figures. Didn't anyone warn you about her, or tell you about . . . you know? Sex in the families?"

"I believe she compelled Eugene to forget that little detail. And it never came up as a topic of conversation with us either. Unfortunately, I have no proof of what she has done. If I accuse her in front of the other families, it will be her word against mine. And we both know who would win a contest of influence between the two of us."

"Aesop will verify what happened. He saw her in the desert, hiding in that van."

"What? How could he? I thought he was . . ."

"Dead?" she finished for me. "He is, but only in this realm. He was born in Meredin, so his death here doesn't automatically cancel his existence in both worlds. If he'd been born here, then it would be over for him."

"How is he?"

"Shaken . . . He has no sorcery and can't sleep. It's only a matter of time before it drives him mad." She looked at the floor. "In a few weeks, it'll kill him."

No sorcery? Of course, he had no dualities to power his magic. "Then perhaps," I whispered to her, "Aesop can serve us better than any other. Do you still have Morgan's gun?"

"Sure. But what good will that do?"

"Listen, this is what we're going to do . . ."

She listened, but couldn't believe it.

20

~~~~~~~~~~~~~~~~~~~~

With the Oracle's aid, I contacted Bakkeglossides. The demon was happy to return and pick me up, provided that we bargained well with each other.

The Oracle's shape continually shifted. I didn't want to ask why, since that was a legitimate question and might begin the challenge again, but I suspected I knew what caused it. The mad god was bound to one spot, and that represented a great force of permanency, or stasis. To balance that magic, the opposite magical property had to be tapped, that of change. When it altered form, it fueled the magics of its prison.

I bade farewell to the Oracle as it mutated into a tan and orange striped spider of monstrous proportions, suspended over the pool in a giant web, covered with drops of dew, waiting to snare a bit of information and suck it dry. It wished me well with a ghostly voice and asked that I visit it again when I knew more.

Down the spiral of the tower I went, without the benefit of a candle, descending the wet stairs of glass. I slowed my pace, fearing I might slip and knock myself senseless. I laughed. To be killed after facing demons, battling insane sorcerers, and matching wits with a god, by tripping down a mere flight of stairs.

Near the bottom, beyond the massive archway, the light of a torch flickered. I poked my head cautiously around the corner. A lone guard sat on the floor, picking his nose, not expecting anyone to emerge from the tower. I did, however, and strolled past him as if I belonged there. For a moment, I thought he'd ignore me.

"Hey!" he said, then fumbled for the crossbow beside him.

Not wanting to answer any time-consuming questions, I sprinted down the black-tiled corridor and out into the central yard, where I hoped the demon was.

It was before dawn, and the only thing there in the cobblestone courtyard was a sundial and the statue of the founding Elder. I summoned a gradient of forces, scanned the skies, and spotted the demon perched atop the Oracle's tower. A wave of sound and sorcery bounced off me, then it spread its wings onto the morning air and floated down.

"Hey!" repeated the guard who chased me. This "hey," however, was not a command to halt, but a cry of fear when he saw the bat and snake horror fill the court and accidentally knock over the statue of His Eminence. The young acolyte fled.

I mounted the midnight velvet of Bakkeglossides. Whatever chance I had to prove my innocence to the council was gone. Not only was I skipping out on my own trial, but upon a demon. WaterStone could blame any conspiracy he wanted on me, and no one would challenge him after it was told how I escaped.

The demon lifted into the air and the Isle of Knowledge fell away beneath me.

Later, I would return, after this family business, to straighten WaterStone out.

"You are surprisingly punctual for one of your kind," the right head thought to me.

"Thanks. And thanks for picking me up on such short notice."

"I assure you there is no philanthropy in this action,

only the protection of our vested interests." It paused and struggled through an unusually strong gust of wind, then inquired, "You carry a metal object that reflects a great deal of sound and has a familiar odor to it. Do you mind our asking what it is?"

I removed the weapon from my tunic. "This? It is a crossbow of sorts. I retrieved it from another world last evening." The demon must have smelled Morgan on his gun.

"A crossbow? How did you . . ."

"I will be happy to discuss that with you another time, when I have less on my mind." As much as I wanted to trust the demon, it still was associated with Morgan, and thereby with the Bishop clan. I couldn't risk *this* bit of information getting back to them. It would ruin everything.

"As you wish," the serpents said together. A ripple of curiosity filtered through their thoughts.

I tucked the gun into my tunic, lest it fall into the lake. The watchband had translated two kilograms of mass from Earth to this realm. How much could it bring over at one time?

The demon and I crossed the lake, skimmed over the tops of the Mountains of Cervin, and flew south, closer to the Great Inland Sea. The sun broke over the land and scattered its light in countless fragments upon the freshwater sea, drops of gold and red and pink. On the farthest shore, its stone fortifications set aglow by the morning warmth, was Eugene's castle. We circled it once, very high, then set down about a kilometer away, so as not to alarm his guards.

I thanked Bakkeglossides again, bargained briefly to provide future services, then made my way toward the shore.

Eugene's lands were not as well cared for as the De Marcos'. Patches of earth lay barren, stripped of soil, where nothing grew, and the wind blew continuously. What did I expect on an earth sorcerer's land if not wind and stone?

Along the seashore were windmills painted white, yellow, and green. Under their great spinning blades, nestled five or six dozen smaller cottages with well-weathered shingled roofs. Every dwelling had a flag rippling over it. They seemed like struggling butterflies, beating their cloth wings in the wind. The road forked at that point, and I took the branch that led away from the village, to the castle by the sea.

It was a purely utilitarian structure of heavy geometric lines, unlike the artistic architecture of the Golden Age. Short dense towers, built for defense, squatted on each corner. The outer walls were four meters thick and had a slight outward slant to them.

To keep my presence secret until this evening, I entered through the servant's entrance on the shaded side of the fortress. There, I met the seneschal, who gave me a quick tour before showing me to my quarters.

Constructed of smooth granite with no mortar, the castle only rarely had a rug or an animal skin to adorn the floor. Paintings, however, were in every corridor and every chamber to enliven the otherwise gloomy atmosphere. Landscapes of vast deserts, the high glass walls of Sartesh full of light, luminous blue mountains that glowed in the twilight, an Irish stag who gave mounted hunters and their hounds a merry chase through thick forests, and a watercolor of the Fields of Fire with clouds of rust and sun-colored pollen drifting over them, I observed as I explored the breezy halls. But most of these masterpieces were portraits of family members. Beneath noble stares, or perfect smiles, were tiny silver plates naming the individuals and giving the dates of their birth and demise. I counted forty-two different clans. Names like Kalmenoff, Dunn, Vanderhouse, Black Hawk, Mauriac, and Alexander, all captured by the brush strokes of artists. I failed to find a single picture of Clay or Judith, and thought that slightly odd.

And only five families left now . . . Eugene got them all to come somehow. He was certain there would be conflict, and ultimately, violence between the royal clans tonight. He was probably right, but I had planned for that too, if reason failed to motivate them. No more dreamers could be killed. The realm couldn't stand to lose any more.

While I awaited the De Marcos, I washed the grime and sweat from a week's worth of travel off my bruised body. Tailors came to fit me with more appropriate garb, a linen shirt with lace cuffs, a shamrock green cloak lined with dense fur, and a pair of durable trousers. While I ate lunch, the server informed me that Smoking Bear and Aesop were here and requested my presence.

With the cloak pulled over my head, I went to them, trusting I wasn't seen by any who might relay the information to the Bishops. I entered their room without knocking.

"About time you got here," Smoking Bear said, quickly embraced me, then asked, "did you get Morgan's automatic?"

"Yes." I handed it to Aesop. To him I whispered, "It's good to see you, my friend. I wish there was more I could have done in the desert. It is my fault for dragging you into my personal conflict."

This was his first day without sleep. His tattoos were smeared and bleached of their vivid colors; his eyes were dull with circles under them. "If Sabrina truly has as much power as you claim," he replied, "then she is every clan's worry, not only yours." He checked the gun, loaded a round into the firing chamber, and added, "We all die eventually, Roland. I am glad I was fighting when it happened to me."

Smoking Bear saved me from an emotional display by changing the subject. "What room is Eugene throwing us together in?"

"The trophy chamber."

"Good, at least it has a nice warm rug and a fireplace." She rubbed her arms. "How do the Rhodes stand the cold here?"

"Ice water in their veins," Aesop answered. "Remember?"

We waited for the families to gather.

Smoking Bear paced for a few hours, ate a light meal, sharpened her sword twice, and eventually napped. Aesop and I played three games of chess (he won twice), and he drank two pots of strong coffee. I wondered how many days it took a dreamer to go mad from lack of sleep? I didn't ask.

Servants sent by Eugene informed us when the clans arrived. First to show were the Chandlers. They came by sailing ship just before sunset. Aesop told me they were ancient enemies with the Bishops, so their relationship with the Rhodes, was at best neutral. We could not count on them automatically to side with us either, since they were fiercely independent. "Opportunistic" was the word Aesop used to describe them. Smoking Bear had a less elegant description.

The Bishops showed shortly after dark. I kicked myself for telling Sabrina how to halt the flow of forces and observe magic. Did she possess sufficient dualities now to leave her body as I could? I maintained a slight gradient of power in case she decided to scout around and make trouble.

Xuraldium, the last to show, came when the moon was at its zenith. I hadn't thought to invite him, but when I asked Eugene to invite all clan leaders, he must have assumed I meant Xuraldium too. How had he been persuaded to leave his sunny palace and come to this windy castle?

I was told there was one last family member, the dragon that lived in the Aetna Mountain, but it probably wouldn't come. The men who volunteered to carry that invitation never returned. I would take that as a *no* and count my blessings.

When it was time for us to go, butterflies came to visit my stomach. Could I really go through with this? I glanced at Smoking Bear. She had no doubts or worries etched on her face. She had nearly died once for me, lost her grandson, and was ready to put herself at risk again—all for me. I took heart from her courage and led the way.

The trophy room had many decorations, symbols of conquest, and stuffed mythical beasts . . . more than appropriate for what I wanted to do. Dozens of mounted heads gazed back at me from the walls, along with curved horns, claws, and even what appeared to be a massive pair of shark jaws. A fire crackled in the wide hearth, and as Smoking Bear had said, a wool rug, hand-knotted patterns of vermilion and gold, covered the frigid stone floor. A tapestry of mounted knights outside this very castle hung across the west wall, while the north was all glass with French doors that opened onto a balcony and a priceless view of the choppy, moonlit sea.

My cousin Violet, the leader of the Chandlers, entered after we did on the arm of her son, James. She possessed a cool beauty, hard, scrutinizing eyes the color of her namesake, and black hair combed straight down her back. James loosened his sword when he saw Smoking Bear, nodded at Aesop, and greeted me with polite distance. Violet merely smiled at the De Marcos and me without a word of greeting. She retreated silently to the far corner, close to the door.

Xuraldium entered after them, muttering about the icy climate and holding his tail off the floor. He ignored all of us and marched straight to the fireplace, then practically stood in the flames to warm himself. Turning his back to us, he examined eight curved swords, set in a circular pattern, mounted above the mantel. I got the impression he wasn't in the mood for small talk.

Next to assemble were the Bishops—a moment I was not looking forward to. Morgan marched in, followed by Sabrina. She was especially ravishing, and I found my mind wandering from the complex politics. Her hair had been done up so loose curls framed her perfect face; she looked to me like an angel would, exquisite and innocent.

Morgan left his manners at the door and went to Eugene's liquor cabinet. He poured himself a shot of something brown, downed it, drank another, then started on his third.

Sabrina's eyes widened when she saw me, and widened farther when she noticed Aesop, then, smooth as glass, she glided over and gave me a kiss on the lips.

Her mouth was warm, moist, and the contact lasted just long enough to let me know it was more than a friendly hello.

She whispered into my ear, "I have heard untrue things of your demise. We have much to discuss later, alone." She left me puzzled and went to the side of her uncle.

Her soft words stirred up doubts about my plan. Was it true she schemed against me? Was it necessary to expose her? I poured myself a glass of water and drank it, hoping to steady my nerves. Smoking Bear shot me a dirty look and impatiently drummed her fingers on the head of a stuffed saber-toothed tiger (mounted mid-pounce, with its claws extended). Yes, if I didn't go through with my plan, she certainly would, and with more violence than I desired.

Daring to view the room magically, I first noticed that my own life pulse was out of rhythm. Had it been altered by Sabrina's magic, her single kiss? I quickly amended the situation and regained my composure.

All manners of sorcery were present. Xuraldium surrounded himself with vast fields of energy, opening like the petals of a lotus, delicate, more layers than I could easily count, and possessing a cold fire of power at its center. Smoking Bear's magic, I perceived as tiny globes of amber and black in slow motion about her. Morgan had nothing I could see, other than a small amount of death collecting in his liver, but I didn't trust him. Sabrina emanated fine silvery threads of magic, covered in diamond dust, that reached out to touch everyone, probing, testing, and waiting. It was the same sorcery I had seen in the desert, the magic that controlled Lloyd, and the fear that paralyzed me. Pure power coalesced within her and grew stronger as I watched, beating in resonance to the pulse of the children she carried. I could even see their tiny life forces, twins as I suspected. They were feeding and being fed upon, a complex pattern of magics interacting with one another. I had severely underestimated her, and their, potential powers.

Eugene arrived last with Lloyd. He closed the door

behind them and threw the bolt shut. Lloyd, dressed in a silk doublet, fine hose, and a slim rapier, welcomed me to their castle. There was a brief glimmer of recognition in his eyes, then confusion. He did not greet the De Marcos. How much did he really recall of our battle?

"Now that we are all here," hissed Xuraldium, "what merits such an assembly?"

All eyes turned to Eugene.

"While I have summoned you here, some under protest, I only acted on the behalf of our newest family member. Allow me to introduce Roland Pritchard, son of Clay Pritchard, grandson of Horace, the last surviving member of his clan. In less than a week, he has aided in the recovery of the De Marcos' heirloom and has spoken with the Oracle at the Abbey of Glossimere."

Violet whispered to her son at the mention of the heirloom, and Morgan stopped drinking when he heard I had been to the Oracle and was still alive to tell about it. He gave me a narrow calculating look, then set his glass down, still full.

I stomped on the butterflies in my gut one more time, cleared my throat, then said, "Family members, thank you for coming. I assure you this is not a fanciful meeting or simply for the sake of introduction. I have two matters of import to discuss with you. First, as Eugene stated, I have been to the Oracle, where I learned of the imminent destruction of Meredin."

"Come on," Morgan interrupted. "You brought us here to scare us with tales of doom? I've been hearing that yarn since I was a kid."

"Then you should have paid closer attention, for the destruction of the dream realm is nearly complete." I paused and noticed there *was* indeed magic about Morgan's throat. It was nothing I could pin down, but whatever it was, it was gathering force. I quickly continued. "Before I realized that I was part of the royal families, I served as an acolyte at the Abbey of Glossimere and I studied the history of Meredin. When I journeyed forth, I observed the realm to be very different than the past I knew. I saw a diminished and demoralized population, and a culture in ruins. Attribute this to whatever reasons you wish, famine, warring, treachery, but it *is* happening.''

Xuraldium nodded as I spoke, and picked contemplatively under one of his scales with a razor claw.

''Why do you tell us this young man?'' Violet asked, slightly annoyed. ''*We* know all this.''

''The Oracle,'' I answered, ''in addition to foretelling the end, has also revealed to me a way to restore Meredin to a second Golden Age. All the warring between the clans must cease, and all families must formally align with one another.''

''And how will you manage this peace?'' Eugene inquired, crossing his arms and appearing very unconvinced.

Morgan laughed. ''An alliance between *all* the families? Doesn't that defeat the purpose of a formal alliance, to protect one family from the others?''

''Are you proposing to lead us?'' Xuraldium asked.

''No,'' I told him. ''The Oracle specifically suggested a confederacy, ruled by the heads of the represented families. Those who oppose the will of this ruling body, will, in turn, oppose all its member families.''

Silence.

No one stopped me, so I went on. ''Our enemy is more subtle than any one clan. It is the destruction of our lands, the loss of irreplaceable ancient knowledge, and the perpetuation of senseless blood feuds. This confederation will bring order and prosperity to our kingdoms.''

''It seems to me,'' Morgan said with a smirk, ''that the one who's going to benefit most from this deal is you, Roland. You'd have as much power as any one of us, and you're only the leader of a one-man family. Nice try, kid, an *A* for effort, but I don't buy it.''

''I'm glad you opened your mouth, Morgan,'' I snapped back, ''because that brings me to the next topic I wanted to discuss, the punishment of the Bishop clan for the murder of Aesop.''

''What?'' Morgan thundered. ''You're calling some

sort of Ruah-vindicare over a man you're not even allied with? And he's still alive!''

"Not a Ruah-vindicare," I replied, "and not with you." I turned to face Sabrina. "Aesop died on Earth, and you killed him." She smiled, giving me the slightest shake of her head as a warning, but I ignored it. "She controlled Lloyd's mind with her sorcery, and in an attempt to murder me, she slew Aesop."

"Why," she asked with a short laugh, "would I want to do such a thing?"

"Because you are pregnant with my children. Because you, for nine months, will wield more power than any of us, and because I was the only one who knew. You should not have taken lot 54," I told her. "That's what tipped me off. There had to be two parties at work there. First, Lloyd you made steal the least valuable items to provoke me. Then you took the most valuable items for yourself. If you weren't so greedy, I'd have never guessed there was another person involved, someone influencing him."

"What precisely are you speaking of?" Lloyd politely inquired. He honestly looked bewildered.

"Poor Roland," Sabrina cooed with the innocence of a child. "The exertion of your heroic efforts has strained your mind past endurance. I carry no children, and I certainly never coerced any family member. Perhaps you should rest until your thinking is again clear."

"We shall see how clear it is when Aesop tells his version of the story and Xuraldium divines the truth for us," I said.

"Truly," the reptile mused, flicking his tongue out to test the air. A third eye, barely visible to my mystic vision, opened in his forehead, centered above his golden slitted stare. A gentle light diffused across the room from this orb, touched Sabrina, and came to rest on her abdomen. "Indeed," he whispered, "it does appear that she has . . .''

Sabrina raised her arms.

Xuraldium's light washed away, and the sagely lizard exploded backward into the fireplace. Embers and flaming logs rolled out, and the priceless wool rug was set ablaze.

There was a split second pause as my cousins assessed what happened, who their enemies were, who their friends were, and what their chances of escaping were . . . then things happened very fast.

Death and life gathered in my hands, and the room filled with rainbows of magic, lights, sounds, the vibrations of sorcery. It was more magic than I had ever seen in one place before.

Smoking Bear's sabers flashed from their sheath, and a dozen spinning globes of emerald and crimson circled both the blades and her in a wide figure eight. Eugene stared into space with pure concentration; beneath him, crystalline patterns of force aligned; the floor bulged and pulsed with a life all its own. Morgan backed into the corner, behind the liquor cabinet, and from his shirt pulled an amulet of tarnished silver shaped like a fanged open mouth. This mouth sucked up the seven pairs of delicate veils, the good and evil drifting about him, and blended their subtle shades into a uniform gray, a vortex of sin and virtue. Violet took three steps toward the fireplace, then turned to face the rest of the room with her hands laced together. Particles of cold azure and sparks from the burning logs danced about her, and fingers of frost traced abstract patterns upon her skin.

But Sabrina . . . she was a flare that cast shadows upon everything else in the room. Her silvery cords of emotions sizzled pure white. They whipped forward, snakelike, and struck everyone's mind . . . including mine.

I braced myself for the same kind of terror I experienced in the desert, but was pleasantly surprised. This was pure rapture. How could anything possibly be amiss when my skin tingled with this ecstasy? Certainly it had been a mistake to confront her; I realized that now. Perhaps it would be best to forget her pregnancy.

We all stood smiling, all dumbfounded. Xuraldium lay inert, smoldering in the fireplace; the Chandlers stared blankly; Eugene and Lloyd giggled between themselves; and even Smoking Bear, next to me, wore a stupid grin. Morgan, I noted, had none of the pleasing magic attached to him (poor guy, he was really missing something). And Aesop, had only the smallest thread of magic whispering into his ear.

Slowly, with a shaking hand, Aesop withdrew the gun from his tunic. His mouth was twisted into a forced frown. Why did he resist the sensation? We talked about taking action should Sabrina try anything. But whatever she was doing, it was no threat. Everything was going to work out fine.

I strolled over to stop him. Couldn't he see it had all been a mistake? Aesop, however, did not wait for me to discuss this rationally with him. With both hands he steadied the gun, aimed, and fired.

The air exploded.

Sabrina was thrown against the tapestry; her mercury lines of sorcery ruptured, and her shoulder blossomed with blood. She fell, leaving a large stain and hole in the tapestry behind her.

My thoughts were again my own. But my summoned power was gone . . . perhaps my life magics canceled her emotional sorcery. The others were still enthralled and a film of the magic coated their minds.

Morgan was busy. In both hands, he cupped the amulet and called forth a single name. It was a complex sound, full of consonants that were never meant to be pronounced together; it was a demon's name: Nebtuchmadnezzar. The open mouth of silver expelled what it had previously consumed, the powers of good and evil. This colorless sorcery stretched, thinned, then faded from my perception.

"Get Morgan," I shouted to Smoking Bear.

She shook the stupor off, glanced about, found Morgan in the corner and sprang toward him.

"Rhodes!!" Morgan urged as soon as he saw her break the spell. "We have been betrayed! Attack her!"

Eugene squinted painfully, brought his hand up to massage his temple and tried to overcome the effects of Sabrina's sorcery. Lloyd, however, unleashed his sorcery against Smoking Bear. A wave rolled from him, a ripple in the floor. It caught her and snapped her back as quickly as an ocean wave captures a piece of driftwood in its wake. She flipped, twisted, landed on her feet, then continued her forward dash.

Eugene, confused and not knowing who his enemies were, curled his right hand into a fist and raised it. From the granite beneath him came a sound of stone grinding over stone, then a hand, proportioned like his but three meters tall, ripped through the wool carpet. Its fingers were outstretched and it grabbed for Smoking Bear.

Smoking Bear threw her weight into the rock palm and a word of power thundered from her. The disembodied hand cracked and shattered into wriggling fragments. "A fine time to take the moral high ground and uphold your stupid alliance," she yelled to Eugene. "Snap out of it!"

I reorganized my power, crossed the room without my body, and dissolved the haze of magic that clung about Eugene's head with my life force. With the death within me, I cooled his overstimulated pleasure centers. He blinked twice, looked to Morgan, then turned to his son and shook him by the shoulder.

I moved back to Sabrina and saw the tapestry undulate as if in a breeze, but there was none in the room. These were waves of magic, ripples upon the surface of reality. A shining figure dashed across the field of the cloth. Mounted knights in the woven art scattered before it. The flash of a blade and one of the valiant warriors within the picture was cut down. What was this thing?

It ran straight for the center, then broke through into our world!

A boy leapt from the tapestry and landed by Morgan's side. His skin was pure polished copper, and his metallic face was of perfect form—one that Michelangelo might have sculpted. He wore a golden breastplate with intricate flowers enameled upon it, and in his hand, he held a battle ax of copper, its edges gleaming with certain sharpness. The warm metal was mirrorlike, and flames appeared to dance upon him, reflections from the fireplace. But his eyes were the most striking—pure empty black, save the faint glittering of stars beyond.

The young boy of copper turned to Morgan and asked, "What is your wish, O Master of the benign and the malicious?"

Xuraldium recovered from Sabrina's offense and stood steaming, but apparently unblistered by the fire. "Morgan," he demanded, "what is the meaning of this?"

My cousin James placed himself, sword drawn, between Violet and the demon.

"Get 'em," was Morgan's answer.

I *knew* Morgan could have summoned help faster when we fought together in the desert. He must have delayed then, hoping one of the De Marcos would be killed. He probably didn't attack me then because he still thought there was a chance he'd get the Matrix. Good thing I told him I had found it.

Smoking Bear carefully circled to the copper boy's flank, but the child ignored her, spun his ax joyfully in the air once, then swung it at Lloyd with surprising speed.

Lloyd wasn't caught off guard. He held his hands before him and a torrent of wind erupted. The pressure fell in the room, and my ears popped. The beautiful glass French doors leading to the balcony shattered. The miniature tornado swept the flat of the boy's ax up and away, off target.

Smoking Bear lunged, but the copper boy snapped his weapon back and parried—then riposted with an impossible swiftness. She parried and took a step back. The boy spun a web of copper razor about himself. Smoking Bear had to keep parrying his attacks, and twice her orbiting globes absorbed a set of skillful blows to her abdomen. James stepped forward to add his own blade to the battle and to ease the pressure on her. He parried four strikes, then his arm was slashed to the bone by the boy's ax. Without pause, he switched to his left hand and continued.

The boy of copper was better and faster than both of them together. He was an extremely efficient guard for

Morgan, who hid behind him, back in the corner. Aesop moved to get a decent shot at him, but Smoking Bear and James were in the way.

I went to Sabrina while they fought. Perhaps I could use her wound to siphon off this demon's life. A quick check revealed that she was shot in the same area where Smoking Bear had been injured. This time, however, the bullet angled up and out her arm rather than down into the abdominal cavity. She had lost a good deal of blood and was in shock—exactly what I needed.

Concentrating, I looked to the boy, his blade whistling through the air, alien magics of his own flicking on the surface of his polished body, then inside, to search for his life force. There was none. Within him was all hot oil, gears worming together, and springs. A massive mechanical heart pumped the fluid about, coating his working parts. Deeper still was a boiler that shot steam into his limbs, making him move with lightning velocity. Morgan picked a perfect opponent for me, one with no life, a machine.

Of course, Morgan . . . I went to him for his life. There was plenty there, and if I drained him to death, perhaps this demon would leave, having no master to command him.

Morgan sensed my approach somehow and yelled, "The Pritchard brat, get him too. He's slipping by you."

The copper boy swung at my ethereal form.

Now, I don't know why I ducked then. I shouldn't have, since the ax couldn't touch me—just instinct I guess. The blade bit into my arm, not deep, but it drew blood from my body across the room! This thing could kill me even without touching my body. I backed away.

Xuraldium opened a petal of the magical lotus that surrounded him. A star of light drifted from it, landed on the floor at the demon's feet, then another star followed, and another, until there were five. Lines sprang betwixt the points, a pentagon, then more lines scribed on the interior, a pentagram within the pentagon.

The copper boy, while slashing at Smoking Bear and

James, struck at this and shattered the reptile sorcerer's enchantment.

Xuraldium regrouped his magic and tried again, and again the demon's ax broke the magical construct . . . only this time the stone floor was soft. His weapon sank up to its shaft, then the floor strained and groaned, solidifying. The demon pulled, pulled with both hands, but his weapon was frozen in solid rock.

Lloyd shouted in triumph from across the room.

Violet was still concentrating, weaving an enchantment. What pairs of opposites was she manipulating? And why was she taking so long? Was she waiting to see who won this battle, so she could join the victorious side at the last moment?

"Hold it," Morgan shouted. Then to the copper boy he whispered, "Cool it a second, Neb."

My cousins backed off. Smoking Bear and James were exhausted, panting from the brief, but fierce, combat. The demon crouched before them, ready to continue if ordered.

"Look," Morgan said, "there's been a mistake here. I thought you were attacking me. Sabrina must have done something to my mind."

"You are a liar," I said. "I saw the magic, and you were the only one *not* affected. You and Sabrina must have been in on this together. I'm willing to bet that was the real reason you approached Eugene, not for the Matrix, or my heirloom, but to find me for her."

Eugene stepped forward to confront him. The copper boy watched him with wary, star-filled eyes. "You knew about her plan from the beginning? You convinced me to find Roland just so you could increase your clan's power in this repulsive manner?"

"So what if I did?" he spat back. "You'd have done the same if you thought of it. The Matrix was a longshot; I thought it was destroyed. But this was a sure thing. Don't be a fool, Eugene, you can still join us."

"Morgan," he replied, "I am sorely disappointed in you. To participate in such a plot . . . not that I am free of all scheming either. I once thought more of you, my friend.'' He shook his head, then, ''I hereby formally dissolve the alliance between our families.'' Eugene turned to me and announced, ''Roland, I shall join this confederacy of yours and the De Marcos. I grow weary of these continual wars. If this''—he gestured to Morgan cringing in the corner—''is what the future holds for the independent families, then I have no desire to be a part of it.''

Aesop aimed the gun at Morgan. ''Now, Bishop,'' he said calmly, ''please dismiss your associate, or I shall be forced to kill you.''

''Hey, that's *my* gun! How in the hell did it get here?'' Understanding then crossed his face, and he gave me a sly look. ''So you figured out your dad's watch, huh? Clever boy. Too clever if you ask me.''

''Yes, it is your gun,'' I told him, ''the same gun you used to kill my friend at the Gas n' Mart. I would think it poetic justice if you gave Aesop a reason to shoot you with it.''

''The demon . . .'' Aesop warned, and his finger tightened about the trigger.

''OK, OK,'' Morgan muttered with his hands raised. ''There's no need for any more violence.'' He then yelled to the demon: ''Neb, seize him!''

The copper boy was a blur; before anyone reacted, it grabbed Eugene by the neck and twisted him into a headlock. Eugene, muscular as he was, only struggled in the mechanical boy's arms.

''Hold him and kill him if I'm hurt,'' Morgan said. He then laughed. ''What idiots! You should have shot me before I opened my mouth.''

''Let him go, Morgan,'' Smoking Bear demanded and took a step forward.

The boy tightened his hold on Eugene's neck.

''I wouldn't do that if I were you, Ms. Bear. I've got all the good cards for once.''

Aesop pointed the gun at Sabrina. ''Release him.''

''Or what? You'll kill her? Go ahead, she's useless to me now that everyone knows her little secret.''

''What do you want then?'' Lloyd asked timidly.

"I'm going to leave our family reunion unscathed—
that's what I want. But don't worry, I'll be back. This
confederacy won't last long, and when it falls apart, I'll
be here to pick up the pieces."

He dropped his amulet on the floor and muttered two
words. The mouth stretched open and expanded to a
meter in diameter. I saw a whirling force, similar to Xuraldium's tunnel of light, only this was a tunnel of
shadow that led straight down. Morgan sat on the edge
of the gaping mouth and dangled his feet into whatever
lay beyond. Turning one final time to face me, he said,
"Roland, I'll be making special plans for you, rest assured." He braced himself, then pushed off, and disappeared down the hole of sorcery. From the mouth came
his echoing voice, "Kill him, Neb."

The copper boy twisted Eugene. There was a crack I
heard all too well, then his body went limp.

Violet, yet to release her magics, did so now, a bolt
of sorcery that flashed across the room and struck the
demon's forehead. Green and blue designs erupted
across his perfect face. A disease? No, the copper was
oxidizing! The corrupting magic spread over him, down
his neck, and into his shoulders like fire through a field.
He dropped Eugene and ran toward the rapidly shrinking
amulet.

"Not so fast," Smoking Bear growled, and tackled
the demon from behind, held him as Violet's verdigris
worked its way into its joints and froze them. Yet even
with all this to secure it, the boy-demon crawled halfway
into his master's portal before it closed. When it did, it
severed the demon. Only his legs remained behind.

Lloyd knelt by his father's side and held the dead man
in his arms.

Aesop whispered to me, "If there is a way to bring
him back, Roland, I would volunteer my own life."

"No, not you my friend. Lloyd, hurry, bring your father to me. There may be a way yet to bring him back."

"What do you mean?" he asked.

"I can heal him, but we must hurry before his brain
is deprived of oxygen for too long."

"Yes, of course." James and he dragged Eugene to me, by Sabrina's unconscious body.

Eugene's face was frozen in agony; his head wrenched into an unnatural angle, and bruises ringing his neck. There were two extra lives within her, lives that I could use to save him. I focused on the unborn twins and the damage within Eugene, then let the outer world slip away.

I gazed at her and discovered that the attraction I originally felt was still there, even though she had almost murdered me, destroyed Aesop, and tried to control us all. Was her magical charm over me permanent? Or did I have genuine feelings for her? No, I refused to indulge myself now. The question I had to ask myself was: had I a right to do this? They were only children after all, my children for that matter, innocent in all this. I didn't want to kill them, yet if Sabrina carried the twins, the families would eliminate her, and they would be slain anyway. She possessed too much power for the clans to be comfortable with. If I went through with it, then she would not be a threat, and perhaps I might persuade them to let her to live.

Yes. It was the only solution.

I saw them, a double collection of cells, my children, less than a week old within her. Their lives were already strong, pulsing with a number of dualities and a number of magics, life and death, light and shadow, and the complex emotional sorceries of their mother, sparkling silver.

I drained them, begging their forgiveness as I did so, and transferred the power into the cold death in Eugene. I mentally pushed his vertebrae into the proper shape, using those undamaged as models, then knit the delicate spinal tissues together. With a final surge of power, I forced the impulse of life up through the new cord, up into his brain. He inhaled sharply, alive again, and the awful deed was done.

Eugene sat up and rubbed his neck. "There was a crack," he whispered, "then a flash. Did it . . .?"

"Yes," I replied, "you were dead. I used the life of the twins to restore you, so Sabrina is no longer a threat to us—no more than normal."

Violet came to me and placed a hand on my shoulder. "Roland, please accept my condolences for your children. You did the only honorable thing." She paused, considering her next words carefully, then said, "While the Chandler family usually exlude themselves from the dealings of the other families, I have seen evidence this evening that this has been an unwise policy. Perhaps we should work together. I am willing to participate in this confederacy." She motioned to James and he scooped Sabrina up and took her away from me. Then she whispered, "I shall see to her injuries. You have done enough."

More than enough.

Eugene rose, flexed his fingers, and stomped his feet to make certain everything still worked. "Roland, how can I begin to thank you?"

"Don't worry about it. We are all on the same side now."

"Yes, so it would seem." Then to everyone, he said, "Please, my new allies, let us retire to the ballroom and have a proper feast. We have many plans to discuss . . . and the fate of Sabrina to deliberate upon."

"I'll need a few seconds to collect my thoughts," I told him.

"Certainly, Roland, take as long as you need." He and Lloyd then left with the Chandlers and Xuraldium.

Would this work? Peace among *four* families? Or would they revert to their traditional murderous ways tomorrow? Maybe it was as Eugene said, that they were tired of the fighting, the backstabbing, and the scheming. Maybe they wanted to change, but never had the chance to let their guards down.

Moving to the corner of the room, I found Morgan's amulet under the demon's legs, covered in machine oil. The mouth was tightly closed now, and there was no magic I could detect. I'd find a nice safe place for it, maybe the Oracle's pool, and make certain it was a *one-way* trip for the master of good and evil.

Aesop and Smoking Bear were on the balcony. The moon was golden and sinking beyond the mountains, leaving a trail of liquid light shimmering on the dark mirror of the Inland Sea.

I went to them.

Smoking Bear had a bottle. She popped the cork and poured herself, Aesop, and me a glass. I lifted it to my nose, a dry champagne.

"What will you do now?" I asked my half-dead friend.

Aesop stared intently at the bubbles rising in his glass. "There is the matter of who shall take Starchaser's place to animate his statue. I think I am a likely candidate. I would like my death to mean something . . . And perhaps you shall find a way in the future to revive me. There is always a spark of hope."

"Tell me," Smoking Bear whispered after a quick glance over her shoulder, "what did the Oracle *really* say? Xuraldium thought you were going to lead us, not form a confederacy. He's never wrong about things like that."

I sipped my wine, then told her, "The Oracle suggested I take control of the families as king. It told me the rivalry between the clans would destroy the dream realm."

"Why didn't you try?" she asked with her eyes wide. "We would have backed you."

I shook my head. "The Oracle was imprisoned in that tower by our forefathers. How could I trust it? It may still want revenge." I added with a smirk, "It may even be a cousin of ours, who knows?"

"So you came up with your own solution," Aesop remarked.

I raised my glass to catch the last of the moonlight and declared, "I shall no longer be a pawn in this game. I am a player now."

"A toast then," Smoking Bear said, and clinked hers

against mine. "To Meredin, long may it prosper."

Aesop joined his glass to ours to make three.

I drank deeply, then added, "Let's go rebuild some dreams."